About the Author

Andrea Laurence is an award-winning contemporary author who has been a lover of books and writing stories since she learned to read. A dedicated West Coast girl transplanted into the Deep South, she's constantly trying to develop a taste for sweet tea and grits while caring for her husband and two spoiled golden retrievers. You can contact Andrea at her website: andrealaurence.com

Cat Schield lives in Minnesota with her daughter, their opiniated Burmese cats and a silly Doberman puppy. Winner of the Romance Writers of America 2010 Golden Heart® for series contemporary romance, when she's not writing sexy, romantic stories for Mills & Boon Desire, she can be found sailing with friends on the St Croix River or in more exotic locales like the Caribbean and Europe. You can find out more about her books at catschield.net

Scarlet Wilson wrote her first story aged eight and has never stopped. She's worked in the health service for twenty years, trained as a nurse and a health visitor. Scarlet now works in public health and lives on the West Coast of Scotland with her fiancé and their two sons. Writing medical romances and contemporary romances is a dream come true for her.

The Crown

Falling for the Crown

ANDREA LAURENCE

CAT SCHIELD

SCARLET WILSON

MILLS & BOON

First Published in Great Britain 2023
by Mills & Boon, an imprint of HarperCollins*Publishers* Ltd,
1 London Bridge Street, London, SE1 9GF

www.harpercollins.co.uk

HarperCollins*Publishers*
Macken House, 39/40 Mayor Street Upper,
Dublin 1, D01 C9W8, Ireland

Falling for the Crown © 2023 Harlequin Enterprises ULC.

Seduced by the Spare Heir © 2015 Harlequin Enterprises ULC.
A Royal Baby Surprise © 2015 Catherine Schield
A Royal Baby for Christmas © 2016 Harlequin Enterprises ULC.

Special thanks and acknowledgement are given to Andrea Laurence for her contribution to the *Dynasties: The Montoros* series.

Special thanks and acknowledgement are given to Scarlet Wilson for her contribution to the *Christmas Miracles in Maternity* series.

ISBN: 978-0-263-31974-3

SEDUCED BY THE SPARE HEIR

ANDREA LAURENCE

To my fellow authors in the Montoros series –

Janice, Katherine, Kat, Jules and Charlene.

It was a joy working with all of you. Thanks for tolerating my eighty million questions on the loop.

And to our editor, Charles –

You're awesome, as always. I look forward to working with you again.

One

This party was lame. And it was *his* party. How could his own party be lame?

Normally parties were Gabriel Montoro's thing. Much to the chagrin of his family, he'd earned quite the reputation as "Good Time Gabriel." Music, alcohol, dim lighting, superficial conversation… He was the king of the party domain. But now that Gabriel had been tapped as the new king of Alma, everything had changed.

Gabriel gripped his flute of champagne and looked around the ballroom at his family's Coral Gables estate. Their tropical retreat seemed incredibly stuffy tonight. There wasn't a single flip-flop in the room, much less one of the feral parrots that lived on their property and flew in the occasional open door. His family had always had money, but they hadn't been pretentious.

But things had changed for the Montoro family since the tiny European island nation of Alma decided to restore their monarchy. Suddenly he was Prince Gabriel, third in line to the throne. And before he could adjust to the idea of that, his father and his older brother were taken out of the running. His parents had divorced without an annulment, making his father ineligible. Then, his ever-responsible brother abdicated and ran off with a bartender. Suddenly he was on the verge of being King Gabriel, and everyone expected him to change with the title.

This suffocating soiree was just the beginning and he knew it. Next, he'd have to trade in his South Beach penthouse for a foreign palace and his one-night stands for a queen with a pedigree. Everything from his clothes to his speech would be up for public critique by "his people." People he'd never seen, living on an island he'd only visited once. But his coronation was only a month or two away. He left for Alma in a week.

That was why they were having this party, if you could even call it that. The music was classical, the drinks were elegant and the women were wearing far too much clothing. He got a sinking feeling in his stomach when he realized this was how it was going to be from now on. Boring parties with boring people he didn't even know kissing his ass.

There were two hundred people in the room, but there were more strangers than anything else. He found that terribly ironic. People had come out of the woodwork since his brother, Rafe, abdicated and Gabriel was thrust into the spotlight. Suddenly he wasn't just the vice president of South American Operations, cast into the Southern Hemisphere where he couldn't embarrass the family; he was the hot ticket in town.

Him! Gabriel—the middle child whom no one paid any attention to, the one dismissed by his family's society friends as the bad boy, the spare heir and nothing more. Now that he was about to be king, he had strangers at every turn fighting to be his new best friends.

He hated to break it to them, but Gabriel didn't have friends. Not real ones. That required a level of trust in other people that he just didn't have. He'd learned far too young that you can't trust anyone. Even family could let you down when you need them the most.

Speak of the devil.

From across the room, his cousin Juan Carlos spied him and started in his direction. He was frowning. Nothing new there. Ever serious, Juan Carlos never seemed to have any fun. He was always having business discussions, working, being responsible. He was the kind of man who should be the king of Alma—not Gabriel. After hundreds of years, why hadn't people figured out that bloodlines were not the best indicator of leadership potential?

"You're not talking to anyone," Juan Carlos noted with a disapproving scowl as he loomed over his cousin. At several inches over six feet, he had a bad habit of hovering over people. Gabriel was never quite sure if his cousin deliberately tried to intimidate with his size or if he was unaware how much it bothered people when he did that.

Gabriel wasn't about to let his cousin's posture or his frown get to him. He tended not to worry too much about what his cousin thought, or what anyone thought, really. When it came down to it, Juan Carlos was serious enough for them both. "No one is talking to me," he corrected.

"That's because you're hiding in the corner sulking."

Gabriel scoffed at his blunt observation. "I am not sulking."

His cousin sighed and crossed his arms over his chest. "Then what would you call it?"

"Surveying my domain. That sounds kingly, right?"

Juan Carlos groaned and rolled his eyes. "Quit it. Don't even pretend you care about any of this, because I know you don't. You and I both know you'd much rather be in South Beach tonight chasing tail. Pretending otherwise is insulting to your family and insulting to your country."

Gabriel would be lying if he said the neon lights weren't beckoning him. There was nothing like the surge of alcohol through his veins and the thumping bass of music as he pressed against a woman on the dance floor. It was the only thing that could help him forget what a mess he was in, but after the drama with Rafe, he'd been on a short leash. The family couldn't take another scandal.

That didn't mean he felt like apologizing for who he was. He wasn't raised to be king. The Alman dictatorship had held strong for nearly seventy years. Who would've thought that when democracy was restored, they'd want their old royal family back? They hadn't anticipated this summons and he certainly hadn't anticipated his brother, the rightful king, would run off with a Key West bartender and send Gabriel's life into a tailspin. "I'm sorry if that offends your sensibilities, J.C., but I didn't ask to be king."

"I know you didn't ask to be king. It is plainly obvious to every person in this room that you don't want the honor. But guess what? The crown has landed in your lap and you've got to step up and grow up." Juan Carlos sipped his wine and glared at Gabriel over the rim. "And what have I told you about calling me that?" he added.

That made Gabriel smile. Annoying his cousin was one of his favorite pastimes since childhood. The smile was short-lived, though.

It wasn't the first time he'd been told to grow up. What his family failed to realize was that Gabriel had grown up a long time ago. They all liked to pretend it didn't happen, but in a dark room with thick rope cutting into his wrists, he'd left his childhood and innocence behind with his captors. If his family had wanted him to act responsibly, they should've done more to rescue him. He'd survived because of his own quick thinking and his first choice as an adult was to live the life he wanted and not care what anyone else thought about it.

Grow up, indeed. Gabriel took a large swallow of his champagne and sighed. The days of living his life as he chose were numbered. He could feel it. Soon it wouldn't just be his father and cousin trying to tell him what to do.

"Always good talking with you, cuz. Don't you have someone to schmooze?"

Juan Carlos didn't respond. Instead he turned on his heel and walked over to the dessert table. Within seconds, he was chatting with someone influential, whose name Gabriel had forgotten, over silver platters of chocolate truffles and cream puffs.

Gabriel turned away, noticing the side door that led

out to the patio and garden pavilion. Hopefully he could make it out there before someone noticed.

Glancing around quickly, he spied his father with his back to him. His sister was chatting with a group of ladies in the corner. This was his chance. He moved toward the door and surged through it as fast as he could.

Gabriel was immediately rewarded with the oppressive wave of heat that July in Miami was known for. The humid blast hit him like a tsunami after the air-conditioned comfort of the ballroom, but he didn't care. He moved away from the door and out into the dark recesses of the patio.

There were some tables and chairs set up outside in case guests wanted to come out. They were draped with linens and topped with centerpieces of candles and roses. All the seats were empty. Gabriel was certain none of the ladies were interested in getting overheated in their fancy clothes with their meticulously styled hair and makeup.

Glancing over at the far end of the semicircular patio, he spied someone looking out into the gardens. The figure was tall, but slender, with the moonlight casting a silver silhouette that highlighted the bare shoulders and silk-hugging curves. She turned her head to watch a bird fly through the trees and he was rewarded with a glimpse of the cheekbones that had made her famous.

Serafia.

The realization sent a hot spike of need down his spine and the blood sped through his veins as his heart beat double-time. Serafia Espina was his childhood crush and the fantasy woman of every red-blooded man who had ever achieved puberty. Eight years ago,

Serafia had been one of the biggest supermodels in the industry. Like all the greats, she'd been known by only her first name, strutting down catwalks in Paris, New York and Milan wearing all the finest designers' clothes.

And she'd looked damn good in them, too.

Gabriel didn't know much about what had happened, but for health reasons, Serafia had suddenly given up modeling and started her own business of some kind. But judging by the way that red dress clung to her curves, the years hadn't dulled her appeal. She could walk the catwalk right now and not miss a beat.

He hadn't spoken to Serafia in years. When his family was overthrown by the Tantaberras, they had fled to the United States and the Espinas moved to Switzerland. In the 1980s, they'd moved to Spain and their families renewed their friendship. When Gabriel and Serafia were children, their families vacationed together on the Spanish Riviera. Back then, he'd been a shy, quiet little boy of ten or eleven and she was the beautiful, unobtainable older woman. She was sixteen and he was invisible.

This was a fortunate encounter. They weren't children anymore and as the future king of their home country, he was anything but invisible. As Mel Brooks famously said, "It's good to be the king."

Serafia felt the familiar, niggling sensation of someone's eyes on her. It was something she'd become keenly attuned to working in the modeling business. Like a sixth sense, she could feel a gaze like a touch raking over her skin. Judging. Critiquing.

She turned to look behind her and found the man

of the evening standing a few feet away. Gabriel had certainly grown up a lot since she saw him last. He was looking at her the way most men did—with unmasked desire. She supposed she should be flattered to catch the eye of the future king, but he was in his twenties, just a baby. He didn't need to get involved with an older, has-been model with enough baggage to pack for a long vacation.

"Your Majesty," she replied with a polite bow of her head.

Gabriel narrowed his gaze at her. "Are you being sarcastic?" he asked.

Serafia's mouth dropped open with surprise, her response momentarily stolen. That wasn't what she was expecting him to say. "Not at all. Did it come out that way? If it did, I sincerely apologize."

Gabriel shook his head dismissively and walked toward her. He didn't look like any king she'd ever seen before. He exuded a combination of beauty and danger, like a great white shark, gliding gracefully across the stone patio in a tailored black suit and dress shirt. His tie was bloodred and his gaze was fixed on her as if she were prey.

She felt her chest tighten as he came closer and she breathed in the scent of his cologne mingling with the warm smell of the garden's exotic flowers. Her fight-or-flight instincts were at the ready, even as she felt herself get drawn closer to him.

He didn't pounce. Instead he leaned down, rested his elbows on the concrete railing and looked out into the dark recesses of the tropical foliage. "It's not you, it's me," he said. "I still haven't quite adjusted to the idea of all this royalty nonsense."

Royalty nonsense. Wow. Serafia's libido was doused with cold water at his thoughtless words. That wasn't exactly what the people of Alma wanted to hear from their new king. After the collapse of the dictatorship, restoring the monarchy seemed like the best way to stabilize the country. The wealthy Alma elite would get a little more than they bargained for with Gabriel Montoro wearing the crown. He didn't really seem to care about Alma or the monarchy. He hadn't grown up there, but neither had she. Her parents had raised her to value her heritage and her homeland, regardless.

Perhaps it was just his youth. Serafia knew how hard it was to have the spotlight on you at such a young age. She'd been discovered by a modeling agency when she was only sixteen. Whisked away from her family, she was making six figures a year when most teenagers were just getting their driver's licenses. By the time she was old enough to drink, she was a household name. The pressure was suffocating, pushing her to her personal limits and very nearly destroying her. She couldn't even imagine what it would be like to be the ruler of a country and have over a million people depending on her.

"I think you'll get used to it pretty quickly," she said, leaning her hip against the stone railing. She picked up her glass of wine and took a sip. "All that power will go to your head in no time."

Gabriel's bitter laugh was unexpected. "I doubt that. While I may be king, my family will ensure that I'm not an embarrassment to them."

"I thought a king can do what he likes."

"If that was true, my father or my brother would still be in line for the crown. In the end, even a king has a mama to answer to." Gabriel looked at her with a charming smile, running his fingers through his too-long light brown hair.

It was shaggy and unkempt, a style popular with men his age, but decidedly unkingly. The moonlight highlighted the streaks of blond that he'd probably earned on the beach. She couldn't tell here in the dark, but from the pictures she'd seen of him in the papers and online, he had the tanned skin to match. Even in his immaculate and well-tailored suit, he looked more like a famous soccer player than a king.

"And I know your mama," she noted. Señora Adela was a beautiful and fierce woman who lived and loved with passion. She'd also been one to give the lecture of a lifetime while she pulled you down the hallway by your ear. "I'd behave if I were you."

"I'll try. So, how have you been?" he asked, shifting the conversation away from his situation. "I haven't seen you since you became a famous supermodel and forgot about all of us little people."

Serafia smiled, looking for the right answer. She knew people didn't really want to know how she was doing; they were just being polite. "I've been well. I started my own consulting business since I left modeling and the work has kept me fairly busy."

"What kind of consulting?"

"Image and etiquette, mostly. I traveled so extensively as a model that I found I could help companies branch out into unfamiliar foreign markets by teaching them the customs and societal norms of the new country. Other times I help wealthy families groom their daughters into elegant ladies."

Although families mostly paid her to teach etiquette

and poise and give makeovers, she also spent a lot of time trying to teach those same girls that being pretty wasn't all they had to offer the world. It was an uphill battle and one that had earned her the label "hypocrite" more than a time or two. Sure, it was easy for a supermodel to say that beauty wasn't everything.

"Do me a favor and don't mention your consulting business around my father or Juan Carlos," Gabriel said.

Serafia's dark eyebrows knit together in confusion. "Why is that? Do they have daughters in need of a makeover?" Bella certainly didn't need any help from her. The youngest Montoro was looking lovely tonight in a beaded blue gown with her golden hair in elegantly twisted curls.

Serafia had heard rumors that the Montoro heirs had been allowed to run wild in America, but from what she had seen, they were no different from the youths of any other royal family. They wanted to have fun, find love and shirk their responsibilities every now and then. Until those desires interfered with the crown, as Rafe's abdication had, there was no harm done.

Gabriel shook his head and took a large sip of his champagne. "No daughters. They've just got *me*. I wouldn't be surprised if they'd jump at the chance to have you make me over. I don't really blame them. I'm about to be the most unsuitable king ever to sit upon the throne of Alma. The bad boy...the backup plan... the worst possible choice..."

Her eyes widened with every unpleasant description. "Is that their opinion or just your own?"

He shrugged. "I think it's everyone's opinion, including mine."

"I think you're exaggerating a little bit. I'm not sure

about what your family thinks behind closed doors, but I haven't heard anything about you being unsuitable. Everyone is surprised about Rafe abdicating, of course, but I just came from Alma and the people are very excited to have you come home and serve as their monarch."

She hadn't originally planned on visiting Alma, but she'd gotten a call from a potential client there. She was already coming to Florida to consult with a company in Orlando, so she made a stop in Alma on the way. She was glad she had. It was inspiring to see an entire country buzzing with hope for the future. She wished she saw some of that same excitement in Gabriel.

He narrowed his gaze, seemingly searching her expression for the truth in her words, but he didn't appear to find it. "That won't last long. I wouldn't be surprised if they'd start begging for the dictatorship to come back within a year of my reign beginning."

And Serafia had thought she was the only one around here with miserably low self-esteem. "The people of Alma fought long and hard to be free of the Tantaberras. You would have to be a wicked, bloodthirsty tyrant for them to wish his return. Is that what you have planned? A reign of terror for your people?"

"No. I guess that changes things," he said with a bright smile that seemed fake. "I didn't realize they had such low expectations for their king. As long as I don't decapitate all my enemies and force my subjects to cower in fear, I'll be a success! Thanks for letting me know that. I feel a lot better about the whole thing now."

Gabriel was leaving for Alma in a week, and that attitude was going to be a problem. Before she could curb her tongue, Serafia leaned in to him and plucked the champagne glass from his hand. "The citizens of Alma have been through a lot over the last seventy years. While the wealthy upper class could afford to flee, most of the people were trapped there to suffer at the hands of Tantaberra and his sons. They're finally free, some of them having waited their whole lives to wake up in the morning without the oppressive hand of a despot controlling them. These people have chosen to restore your family to the throne to help them rebuild Alma. They can probably do without your sarcasm and self-pity."

Gabriel looked at her with surprise lighting his eyes. He might not be comfortable with the authority and responsibility of being king, but he seemed shocked that she would take that tone of voice with him. She didn't care. She had lived in Spain her whole life. She wasn't one of his subjects and she wasn't about to grovel at his feet when he was being like this.

She waited for him to speak, watching as the surprise faded to heat. At first she thought it was anger building up inside him, but when his gaze flicked over her skin, she could feel her cheeks start to burn with the flush of sexual awareness. She might have been too bold and said too much, but he seemed to like it for some reason.

At last, he took a deep breath and nodded. "You're absolutely right."

That was not what she'd expected to hear at all. She had braced herself for an argument or maybe even a come-on line to change the subject, but she certainly didn't think he would agree with her. Perhaps he wasn't doomed to failure if he could see reason in her words.

She returned his glass of champagne and looked out into the garden to avoid his intense stare and hide her blush. "I apologize for being so blunt, but it needed to be said."

"No, please. Thank you. I have spent the days since my brother's announcement worried about how it will impact me and my life. I've never given full consideration to the lives of all the people in Alma and how they feel. They have suffered, miserably, for so long. They deserve a king they can be proud of. I'm just afraid I'm not that man."

"You can be," Serafia said, and as she spoke the words, she believed them. She had no real reason to be so certain about the success of the Montoro Bad Boy. She hadn't spoken to him in years and he was just a boy then. Now there were only the rumors she'd heard floating across the Atlantic—stories of womanizing, fast cars and dangerous living. But she felt the truth deep in her heart.

"It might take time and practice, but you can get there. A lesser man wouldn't give a second thought to whether he was the right person for the job. You're genuinely concerned and I think that bodes well for your future in Alma."

Gabriel looked at her and for the first time, she noticed the signs of strain lining his eyes. They didn't entirely mesh with the image that had been painted of the rebellious heir to the throne. He seemed adept at covering his worry with humor and charming smiles, but in that moment it all fell away to reveal a man genuinely concerned that he was going to fail his country. "Do you really believe that?"

Serafia reached out and covered his hand with her

own. She felt a warm prickle dance across her palm as her skin touched his. The heat of it traveled up her arm, causing goose bumps to rise across her flesh despite the oppressive Miami summer heat. His gaze remained pinned on her own, an intensity there that made her wonder if he was feeling the same thing. She was startled by her reaction, losing the words of comfort she'd intended to say, but she couldn't pull away from him.

"Yes," she finally managed to say in a hoarse whisper.

He nodded, his jaw flexing as he seemed to consider her response. After a moment, he slipped his hand out from beneath hers. Instead of pulling away, he scooped up her hand in his, lifting it as though he was going to kiss her knuckles. Her breath caught in her throat, her tongue snaking out across her suddenly dry lips.

"Serafia, can I ask you something?"

She nodded, worried that she was about to agree to something she shouldn't, but powerless to stop herself in that moment. The candlelight flickering in his eyes was intoxicating. She could barely think, barely breathe when he touched her like that.

"Will you…" He hesitated. "…help me become the kind of king Alma deserves?"

Two

Gabriel watched as Serafia's expression collapsed for a moment in disappointment before she pulled herself back together. He couldn't understand why he saw those emotions in her dark eyes. He thought she would be excited that he wanted to step up and be a better person for the job. Wasn't that what she'd just lectured him about?

Then he looked down at her hand clutched in his own, here in the candlelight, on the dark, secluded patio, and realized he had a pretty solid seduction in progress without even trying. That might be the problem. He'd been too distracted by their conversation to realize it.

He had to admit he was pleased to know she responded to him. In the back of his mind, he'd considered Serafia unobtainable, a childhood fantasy. The moment she'd turned to look at him tonight, he felt his heart stutter in his chest as if he'd been shocked by a defibrillator. Her stunning red silk gown, rubies and diamonds dangling at her throat and ears, crimson lipstick against the flawless gold of her skin…it was as though she'd walked out of a magazine spread and onto his patio.

She was poised, elegant and untouchable. And bold. With a razor-sharp tongue, she'd cut him down to size, sending a surprising surge of desire through him instead of anger. She didn't care that he was the crown prince; she was going to tell it the way it was. With everything ahead of him, he was beginning to think he needed a woman like that in his life. Gabriel was already surrounded by too many yes-men or needling family members.

Serafia was a firecracker—beautiful, alluring and capable of burning him. A woman like that didn't exist in real life, and if she did, she wouldn't want anything to do with a man like Gabriel. Or so he'd always thought. The disappointment in her dark eyes led him to believe that perhaps he was wrong about that.

He wasn't entirely sure that a haircut and a new suit would make him a better king, but he was willing to give it a try. It certainly couldn't hurt. Working with a professional image consultant would get his father and Juan Carlos off his back. And if nothing else, it would keep this beautiful, sexy woman from disappearing from his life for at least two more weeks. It sounded like a win-win for Gabriel.

"A makeover?" she said after the initial shock seemed to fade from her face. She pulled her fingers from his grasp and rubbed her hands together for a moment as if to erase his touch. Serafia didn't seem to think his plan was the perfect solution he'd envisioned. "For you?"

"Why not? That's what you do, right?"

Her nose wrinkled and her brow furrowed. "I teach teenage girls how to walk in high heels and behave themselves in various social situations."

"How is what I'm proposing any different? Obviously I don't need the lesson on heels, but I'm about to face a lot of new social situations. With the way my family has been nagging at me, there seem to be a lot of land mines ahead of me. I could use help on how I should dress and what I should say. And I think you're the right person for the job."

Serafia's dark eyes widened and she sputtered for a moment as she struggled for words to argue with him. "I thought you didn't want a makeover," she said at last.

Gabriel crossed his arms over his chest. "I didn't want my family to force me into one. There's a difference. But you've convinced me that it's needed if I'm going to be the kind of king Alma needs."

"I don't know, Gabriel." She turned back to the gardens, avoiding his gaze. She seemed very hesitant to agree to it and he wasn't sure why. She'd pretty much dressed him down and chastised him for being a self-centered brat. Her words were bold and passionate. But then, when he asked for her help, she didn't want to be the one to change him. He didn't get it. Was he a lost cause?

"Come on, Serafia. It's perfect. I need a makeover, but I don't want everyone to know it. You're a friend of the family, so no one will think twice of you traveling with me or being seen with me. No one outside of the family even needs to know why you're here. We can come up with some cover story. I've got a week to prepare before I leave for Alma and another week of welcome activities once I arrive before things start to settle down. I'm not sure I can get through all that without help. Without *your* help."

"I can't just drop everything and run to your side, Gabriel."

"I'll pay you double."

She turned back to him, a crimson frown lining her face. Even that didn't make her classic features unattractive. "I don't need the money. I have plenty of that. I don't even have to work, but I was tired of sitting around with my own thoughts."

He wasn't sure what kind of thoughts would haunt a young, successful woman like Serafia, but he didn't feel that he should ask. "Donate it all to charity, then. I don't care. It's good for your business."

"How? I'd be doing this in secret. That won't earn me any exposure for my company."

"Not directly, but having you by my side in all the pictures will get your name in the papers. After you're seen with royalty, maybe your services will be more in demand because you have connections."

Serafia sighed. She was losing this battle and she knew it.

Gabriel looked at her, suppressing a smile as he prepared to turn her own argument against her and end the fight. "If for no other reason, do it for the people of Alma. You yourself just said how much these people have suffered. Do your part and help me be the best king I can possibly be."

She tensed up and started biting her lower lip. Picking up her wineglass, she took a sip and looked out at the moon hovering over the tree line. At last, her head dropped in defeat. The long, graceful line of her neck was exposed by the one-shoulder cut of her gown and the style of her hair. The dark, thick strands were twisted up into an elegant chignon, leaving her flawless, honey-colored skin exposed.

He wanted to press a kiss to the back of her neck and wrap his arms around her waist to comfort her. His lips tingled as he imagined doing just that, but he knew that would be pushing his luck. If she agreed to work with him over the next few weeks, there might be time for kisses and caresses later. It couldn't take every hour of the day to make him suitable. But if she left now, he'd never have the chance.

Taking a deep breath, she let it out and nodded. "Okay. We start tomorrow morning. I will be here at nine for breakfast and we'll begin with table manners."

"Nine?" He winced. Most Saturday mornings, he didn't crawl out of bed until closer to noon. Of course, he wouldn't be closing down the bars tonight. If he left the family compound, they'd likely release the hounds to track him down.

"Yes," she replied, her voice taking the same tone as the nuns had used when he was in Catholic school. Serafia didn't look a thing like Sister Mary Katherine, but she had the same focused expression on her face as she looked him over. The former supermodel had faded away and he was left in the presence of his new image consultant.

"Modern kings do not stay up until the wee hours of the morning and sleep until noon. They have a country to lead, meetings to attend and servants that need a reliable schedule to properly run the household. After breakfast, you're getting a haircut." She reached out for his hand, examining his fingernails in the dim lights. "And a manicure. I'll have someone come in to do it. If we went to a salon, people would start talking."

Getting up early, plus a haircut? Gabriel self-consciously ran his fingers through the long strands of his hair. He liked it long. When it was short, he looked too much like his toe-the-line brother, CEO extraordinaire Rafe. That wasn't him. He was VP of their South American division for a reason. Since the news of Alma's return to monarchy, he'd spent most of his time in Miami, but he preferred his time spent south of the equator. Life down there was more colorful, less regimented. He didn't even mind the constant threat of danger edging into his daily routine there. Once you'd been kidnapped, beaten and held for ransom, there wasn't much else to fear.

All that would end now. A new VP would take over South American Operations and Gabriel would take a jet to Alma. He'd be ruling over a country with a million citizens and dealing with all the demands that went with it.

What had he signed himself up for?

"I wish I had my tablet with me, but I'll just have to make all my notes when I get back to my hotel. Sunday, we're going through your wardrobe and determining what you can take with you to Alma. Monday morning, I'll arrange for a private shopper to come to the house and we'll fill in the gaps."

"Now, wait a minute," he complained, holding up his hands to halt her long list of tasks. He knew he could use some polishing, but it sounded as if Serafia was preparing to gut him and build him up from scratch. "What is wrong with my clothes? This is an expensive suit."

"I'm sure it is. And if you were the owner of an exclusive nightclub in South Beach, it would be perfect, but you are Prince Gabriel, soon to be King Gabriel."

He sighed. He certainly didn't feel like royalty. He felt like a little boy being scolded for doing everything wrong. But he'd brought this pain upon himself. Spending time with his fantasy woman hadn't exactly gone to plan. It had only been minutes since he made that decision and he was already starting to regret it.

"Are you dating anyone?"

Gabriel perked up. "Why? Are you interested?" he said with the brightest, most charming smile he could conjure.

Serafia wrinkled her nose at him and shook her head. "No. I was just wondering if I needed to work with you on dealing with any sticky romantic entanglements before you leave."

That was disappointing. "I'm not big on relationships," he explained. "There are plenty of women I've seen on and off, but there shouldn't be any heartbroken women trying to follow me to Alma."

"How about pregnant bartenders?" she asked pointedly.

Gabriel chuckled. His brother's relationship drama had everyone in the family on edge. If he didn't work out, the crown would be dumped on Bella and she was only twenty-three, barely out of college. "No pregnant bartenders that I am aware of," he answered. "Or dancers or cocktail waitresses or coeds. I'm extremely careful about that kind of thing."

"You always use protection? Every time?"

Gabriel stiffened. "Do we really have to talk about my sex life?"

Serafia sighed and shook her head. "You have no real idea what you've gotten yourself into, do you? From now on, your sex life is the business of a whole country. Who you're seeing and who might be your future queen will be one of the first issues you'll tackle as king. After that, fathering heirs and continuing the Montoro bloodline will be the chief concern of each of your subjects. Every woman you're seen with is a candidate for queen. Every time your wife turns down a glass of wine or puts on a few pounds, there will be pregnancy rumors. Privacy has gone out the window for you, Gabriel."

"There's not going to be someone in the room while I *father* these heirs, is there?"

At that, Serafia smiled. "No. They have to draw the line somewhere."

That offered little comfort to Gabriel in the moment. Each step he took toward being king, the more concerned he became. He wanted to be a good leader, but the level of scrutiny in every aspect of his life was suffocating. His hair, his clothes, his sex life... He could feel the pressure crushing against his chest like a pile of stones.

Serafia pointed to a pair of chairs nearby. "Why don't we sit down for a minute. You look like you're about to pass out and these shoes are starting to pinch."

Gabriel pulled out a chair for her and took the one beside her. "I guess I just never thought about all this before. A few weeks ago, I was just a VP in my family company, someone with far-off ties to a country and a history most of us have forgotten all about. Then, boom, I'm a prince. And before I can adjust to that, I find out that I'm going to be king of the place. My life has taken a strange turn."

She nodded sympathetically. "I hate to be the one to tell you this, but it's just going to get worse. Once you're in the spotlight, your life is no longer your own. But from someone who's lived through it, know that the sooner you adjust to the idea of it, the better off you'll be."

Serafia hated to see Gabriel like this. He seemed like such a vibrant, fun-loving man, and the weight of his future was slowly crushing him like a bug. She was pushing him. Maybe more than she had to, at least at first, but he needed to know how things were going to be now. He would adjust to the crown much more easily if he understood the consequences of it.

"Is that what it was like for you? Is that why you gave up modeling?"

Serafia couldn't help the pained expression she felt crossing her face. It happened every time her old career came up. She smiled and shook her head. "That was just a part of it."

"Do you miss modeling?" he asked.

"Not at all," she said a touch too quickly, although she meant it. It wasn't the glamorous business everyone thought it was. It was harsh, and despite how many millions she made doing it and how famous she became, there were still days where she was treated like little more than a walking coat hanger. And a fat one at that. "I'm not really interested in being in the spotlight anymore. It is both a wonderful and terrifying place to live."

Gabriel nodded thoughtfully. "The runways and magazine covers suffer for your absence. I understand why you stopped after what happened to you on the runway, though. I can imagine it's scary to come that close to death without any kind of warning. I mean, to go all that time without knowing you had…what was it, exactly?"

"A congenital heart defect," she replied, the lie slipping effortlessly off her tongue after all these years.

"Yeah, that's terrifying to think your own body is just waiting to rebel against you."

Serafia stiffened and tried to nod in agreement. That would be frightening, although she really wouldn't know. Her parents had done an excellent job spreading misinformation about her very public heart attack. Why else would a perfectly healthy twenty-four-year-old woman go into cardiac failure on the runway and drop to the floor with a thousand witnesses standing by in horror?

She could think of a lot of reasons, and for her, all of them were self-inflicted. Serafia had fallen victim to an industry-endorsed eating disorder, which had spiraled out of control leading up to that day. Anorexia was a serious illness, an issue that needed more visibility in the cutthroat modeling industry, but her family wanted to keep the truth out of the papers for her own protection. At the time, she had been in no condition to argue with them on that point.

Instead the word was that she'd retired from the modeling business to get treatment for her "heart condition" and no one ever questioned it. Instead of surgeries, her actual treatment had included nearly a year of intensive rehabilitation. She had to slowly put on thirty pounds so she didn't strain her heart. Then she learned to eat properly, how to exercise correctly and most important how to recognize the signs in herself that she was slipping into bad habits again.

"Are you better now?" he asked.

That was debatable. With an eating disorder, every day was a challenge. It wasn't like being an alcoholic or a drug user, where you could avoid the substance of choice. She had to eat. Every day. She needed to exercise. Just not too much. She had to maintain her weight and not swing wildly one way or another, or she'd put too much strain on her damaged heart. But she was managing. One day at a time, she reminded herself. "Yes," she said instead. "The doctors got me all fixed up. But you're right, I couldn't face the catwalk again after that. After nearly dying, I realized I wanted to do something else with my life. I'm much happier with what I'm doing now."

"Gabriel Alejandro Montoro!" a sharp voice shouted through the doorway to the patio. It was followed by several loud steps across the stone and a moment later, the figure of his younger sister, Bella, appeared.

"There you are. Everyone has been looking for you."

Gabriel shrugged, unaffected by his sister's exasperation. "I've been right here the whole time. And since when do you get to call me by my full name? Only Mama gets to do that."

"And if Mama were here, she'd haul you back into the house by your ear."

Serafia chuckled. Her memories of Adela were spot-on. "I'm sorry to monopolize Gabriel's time," she said, hoping to draw down some of his sister's ire. "We were discussing the plans for his royal transformation."

Bella eyed Serafia suspiciously, then turned to look at Gabriel. "Good luck with that. Either way, Father wants you inside, and now. He's wanting to do some kind of toast and then he wants to see you out on the dance floor. The press wants a shot of you dancing."

Gabriel stood with a reluctant sigh, reaching out his hand to help Serafia up. "And so it begins. Would you care to join me inside?"

"Absolutely." Serafia slipped her arm through his and they walked back into the house together.

There were even more people in the room now than there were when she'd decided it was too crowded and gone outside. Nothing she could do about it, though. She stayed by his side as they cut through the crowd in search of his father. They found him standing by the bar with Gabriel's cousin, Juan Carlos.

Serafia had never had much contact with the Salazar branch of the Montoro family, but she had heard good things about Juan Carlos. He had a good head on his shoulders. He was responsible and thoughtful. To hear some people talk, he was Gabriel's polar opposite and a better choice for king. She would never tell Gabriel that, though; he had enough worries. Perhaps Juan Carlos would accept a post as the king's counsel. He would make an excellent adviser for Gabriel or royal liaison to Alma's prime minister.

"There you are," Rafael said once he spied them. "Where have you..." He paused when his gaze flicked over Serafia. "Ah. Never mind. Now I know what has occupied your time," he said with a smile.

"It's good to see you again," she said, returning his grin and leaning in to hug her father's oldest friend.

"Too long!" Rafael exclaimed. "But now that some

of us will be back in Alma, that will not be the case. Your father tells me he's considering moving back if the monarchy is stable."

"He told me that, as well." Her dad had mentioned it, but the Espina family was a little gun-shy when it came to their home country. Their quick departure from Alma in the 1940s had been a messy one. There were rumors and accusations thrown at anyone who fled before Tantaberra rose to power, and her family was not immune. Serafia knew they would move slowly on that front and some might never return. Spain was all she had ever known and she had fallen in love with Barcelona. It would take a lot to lure her away from her hacienda with beachfront views of the Mediterranean.

Rafael clapped his son on the back. "Now that you're here, I want to make a small speech, do a toast, and then maybe you can take a spin around the dance floor and encourage others to join you. The party is getting dull."

Gabriel nodded and Juan Carlos went over to silence the band and bring Rafael the microphone. The music stopped as Rafael stepped onto the riser with the band and raised his hand to get the crowd's attention. He had such a commanding presence; the whole room went deathly silent in a moment. He would've made a good king, too. Alma's archaic succession laws needed to be changed.

"Ladies and gentlemen," Rafael began. "I want to thank all of you for coming here tonight. Our family has waited seventy years for a night like this, when we could finally see the monarchy restored to Alma. With it, we hope to see peace, prosperity and hope restored for the people of Alma, as well. I'm thrilled to be able to stand up here and join all of you in wishing my son and future king, Prince Gabriel, all the success in the world as he returns to our homeland."

Several of the people in the crowd cheered and applauded Rafael's statement. Gabriel stood stiff at Serafia's side, his jaw tight and his muscles tense. He didn't seem to be as excited as everyone else. After their discussion outside, she understood his hesitation. Still clinging to his arm, she squeezed it reassuringly and smiled at him.

"I ask everyone here to raise their glass to the future king of Alma, Gabriel the First! Long live the king!"

"Long live the king!" everyone shouted as they held up their glasses and took a sip. Serafia raised her glass as well, drinking the last of her wine.

"Now I would like to ask Gabriel to step out onto the dance floor and show us a few moves. Everyone, please, join us."

"Looks like I have to ask a lady to join me on the dance floor." Gabriel leaned in closer to her, a sly smile curling his full lips. "Have your doctors cleared you for vigorous physical activity?"

Serafia smiled at Gabriel and nodded. "Oh yes, I've got a clean bill of health. I could go all night on the dance floor if you can keep up with me."

Gabriel took her hand and led her out into the center of the room. As the band started playing an upbeat salsa tune, his hand went to her waist and tugged her body tight against his. "Is that a challenge?" he asked.

The contact of his hard body against hers sent a shock wave through her system that she had little time to recover from. He was no longer the mop-topped little boy she remembered running up and down the beach with his kite. Now his green eyes glittered with attraction and a flash of danger. And he *was* dangerous. She might not have finished high school, but she read enough history to know that getting involved with a king never ended well.

Before she could answer him they started moving in time with the music. It had been a long time since she'd danced, but the movement came easily with his strong lead. She almost seemed to float across the wooden floors, the rhythm of the music pulsing through their bodies. The crowds and the cameras around them faded away as they moved as one.

Soon other couples joined them on the dance floor and she didn't feel so exposed. The people around her made her feel better about the prying eyes, but being in Gabriel's arms was still a precarious place to be. The way he held her, the way he looked at her... The next two weeks were going to be a challenge to her patience and her self-control. Gabriel wanted more from her than just a makeover, and when he held her, she felt the same way. She never should've accepted the job, and she knew that now.

This was no teenage girl or Spanish businessman she was dealing with here. Gabriel Montoro was a sexy, rebellious handful and if she wasn't careful, she was going to get in way over her head.

Three

"You're late. Again."

That wasn't anything Gabriel didn't already know. After the last few days he'd had, he wasn't really in the mood to hear it. He'd signed himself up for this nightmare, but he was almost to the point where he'd pay Serafia more to leave him alone than to stay. He was used to the constant criticism of his family, but for whatever reason, Serafia's critical comments grated on him. He just didn't want a woman like her pointing out his faults. He wanted her nibbling on his ear. Unfortunately critiquing him was her job.

"Thanks for the information," he snapped. "When I'm king, I will have you named the official court time-keeper."

He expected her to respond with a smart comment, but instead she turned on her heel and walked across the room. She returned a moment later with a velvet-covered tray in her hands. Laid across it were four different styles of watches.

"One of these, actually, will be the official court timekeeper. I had them brought over from a local jeweler for you to choose the one you like."

His cell phone chimed and he looked down at the screen to avoid the display of watches in front of him. It was a text from a woman he'd gone out with a few weeks ago: a brunette named Carla. He opted to ignore it. He'd been getting a lot of those texts lately and he couldn't do anything about them now that he was on house arrest. What would he say, anyway? "Sorry, love, I've got to fly to a country you've never heard of and be king"?

Slipping the phone back into his pocket, he sighed when he realized the tray of watches was still there, waiting on him. *Watches*. Gabriel hated watches. He didn't wear one, ever. And why did he need to with the clock on his cell phone? "I don't need a watch."

Her resolve didn't waver. "You say that, and yet I've noticed punctuality seems to be a problem for you."

Was she an image consultant or a drill sergeant? "It's not a problem for me. I'm fine. It seems to be more of a problem for you."

Serafia's pink lips tightened as she seemed to fight a frown. "Please choose one."

"I told you, I'm not going to wear a watch." Gabriel couldn't stand the feel of something on his wrists. He'd worn watches all through high school and college, but after his abduction, he gave them all away. Even the nicest watches reminded him of the restraints he'd worn for too long. In an instant, he was back in that cold, dark basement and he never ever wanted to go back to that place.

"There's a Ferragamo, a Patek Philippe and two Rolexes. How can you turn your nose up at a Rolex?" Serafia reached down and plucked one off the tray. "Try this on. It's steel and yellow gold, so it will coordinate nicely with whatever you might be wearing. The faceplate is surrounded by pave diamonds and there are diamonds on the hours. I think it will really look elegant—"

Gabriel didn't move fast enough and before he knew what she had planned, he felt the cold steel of the metal at his wrist. His whole body tensed in an instant. On reflex, he hissed and jerked away from her. He was instantly transported back to Venezuela and the dark, claustrophobic room he was held in for almost a week. He could smell the mildew and filth, the air stale and thick with humidity.

"I said no!" he shouted without intending to. His eyes flew open, taking in the open, airy bedroom. He drew in a deep breath of air scented with hibiscus flowers and felt the tension fade from his shoulders. Looking at Serafia, he immediately regretted his reaction. There was fear as real as his own reflected in her dark eyes. "I'm sorry to yell," he said, but it was too late. The damage was done.

She shied away from him, turning her back and carrying the hundred thousand dollars' worth of watches back to the desk. She didn't speak again until she returned, more composed. It was amazing how she always seemed so put together. He could rattle her for a moment, but she always seemed to snap right back.

That was one skill he could use, but she hadn't taught him that yet.

She crossed her arms over her chest and looked at him. "What was all that about?"

Gabriel didn't like talking about his abduction. And his family had done a good job keeping the story out of the media. "I…I just don't like to wear a watch. I don't like the feel of anything around my wrists." He didn't want to elaborate. She already looked at him as if he was flawed. She had no idea how truly flawed he was. He was broken.

Serafia sighed, searching his face for answers he wasn't going to give her. "Okay, fine. No watch." She picked up her tablet and tapped through a few screens. "Your first public event in Alma will be a party hosted by Patrick Rowling. We need to get you fitted for your formal attire."

Patrick Rowling. Gabriel had heard his father and brother talking about the man, but he hadn't paid any attention. "Who is Patrick Rowling?"

"He's one of the richest men in Alma. He's British, actually, but when oil was discovered in Alma, his drilling company led the charge. He owns and operates almost all the oil platforms and refineries in the country. He's a very powerful and influential man. This party will be your first introduction to Alman society. Forging a solid relationship with the Rowlings will help secure a strong foothold for the monarchy."

Gabriel would be king, but somehow he got the feeling that he would be the one kissing Patrick's ring and not the other way around. He was already dreading this party and he didn't know anything about it.

"Now, this is a formal event, so custom dictates that you should wear ceremonial dress."

Serafia swung open the door of the armoire and pulled out a navy military uniform that looked like something out of an old oil painting in a museum. It looked stiff and itchy and he had absolutely no interest in wearing it.

"All right, now," he complained. "I've been a really good sport about most of this makeover stuff, but this is going too far." Gabriel frowned at Serafia as she held up the ridiculous-looking suit. "I let you cut my hair, give me a facial, a manicure, a pedicure and all other kinds of cures. You've given half my wardrobe to charity and spent thousands of dollars of my own money on suits no man under sixty would want to wear. I've tried to keep my mouth shut and go with it. But that… that outfit is ridiculous."

Serafia's eyes grew wider the longer he complained. "It's the ceremonial dress of the king!" she argued.

Of course it was. "It's got ropes and tassels and a damn baby-blue sash. I'm going to look like Prince Charming at the ball."

Serafia frowned. "That's the point, Gabriel. You are going to be *Su Majestad el Rey Don Gabriel I.* That's what kings wear."

"Maybe in the 1940s when my great-grandfather was the king. It's old-fashioned. Outdated."

"It's not for every day. It's for events like coronations, weddings and formal events like this party at the Rowling Estate. The rest of the time you'll wear normal clothes."

"Normal clothes you picked out," he noted. Not much better in his estimation.

Serafia sighed and returned the suit to the armoire. When she shut the door, she slumped against it in a posture of defeat. Closing her eyes, she pinched the bridge of her nose between her fingers. "We leave for Alma in two days and we have so much to cover. At this rate, we're never going to get it all done. You hired me, Gabriel. Why are you fighting me on every little thing?"

He didn't think he was fighting her on everything. The watch issue was nonnegotiable, but they'd gotten that unpleasantness out of the way. The clothing was just a hard pill for him to swallow. "I'm not intentionally trying to make your job more difficult. It just seems to be a gift I have."

Serafia rolled her eyes. "So it seems. Admittedly, you appear to enjoy getting me all spun up. I've seen you smile through my irritation."

Gabriel had to admit that was true. There was something about the flush of irritation that made Serafia even that much more beautiful, if it was possible. In his mind, he imagined the same would hold true when she was screaming out in passion, clawing at the sheets. The woman who had sashayed down the runway all those years ago had nothing on the vision in his mind as he thought of her at night.

And he had. Since the night on the patio, he'd lain alone in bed every night thinking about her. He hadn't intended to. Serafia was a fantasy from his younger years; the image of her in a bikini was the background of his first computer. It had been a long time since he'd had a crush on Serafia, and yet those desires had rushed back at the first sight of her.

It was probably his family-imposed curfew. The day his brother abdicated, he was practically dragged from his penthouse to the family compound. He'd gone weeks with no clubs, no bars, no socializing with friends at parties. His every move was watched and that meant he was on the verge of his longest dry spell since he broke the seal on his manhood.

It didn't really matter, though, at least where Serafia was concerned. He could've bedded a woman this morning and he would still want her the way he always had wanted her.

"Yes," he admitted at last. "I get pleasure from watching you spin."

"Why? Are you a sadist?"

Gabriel smiled wide and took a few steps closer to her. "Not at all. It might be cliché to say it, but, Serafia, you are even more beautiful when you're angry."

Serafia rejected the flicker of disbelief in the back of her mind and silenced the denial on her lips. As her therapist had trained her, she identified the negative thoughts and reframed them. She was a healthy, attractive woman. Gabriel found her eye-catching and it wasn't her place to question his opinion of her. "Thank you," she said. "But please don't spend the rest of our time together trying to annoy me. You might find I'm more attractive, but it's emotionally exhausting."

Gabriel took another step toward her, closing in on her personal space. With her back pressed against the oak armoire, she had no place to go or escape. A part of her didn't really want to escape, anyway. Not when he looked at her like that.

His dark green eyes pinned her in place, and her breath froze in her lungs. He wasn't just trying to flatter her with his words. He did want her. It was very obvious. But it wasn't going to happen for an abundance of reasons that started with his being the future king and ended with his being a notorious playboy. Even dismissing everything in between, it was a bad idea. Serafia had no interest in kings or playboys.

"Well, I'll do my best, but I do so enjoy the flush of rose across your cheeks and the sparkle of emotion in your dark eyes. My gaze is drawn to the tension along the line of your graceful neck and the rise and fall of your breasts as you breathe harder." He took another step closer. Now he could touch her if he chose. "If you don't want me to make you angry anymore, I could think of another way to get the same reaction that would be more...*pleasurable* for us both."

Serafia couldn't help the soft gasp that escaped her lips at his bold words. For a moment, she wanted to reach out for him and pull him hard against her. Every nerve in her body was buzzing from his closeness to her. She could feel the heat of his body radiating through the thin silk of her blouse. Her skin flushed and tightened in response.

One palm reached out and made contact with the polished oak at her back. He leaned in and his cologne— one of the few things she hadn't changed—teased at her nose with sandalwood and leather. The combination was intoxicating and dangerous. She could feel herself slipping into an abyss she had no business in. She needed to stop this before it went too far. Serafia was first and foremost a professional.

"I'm not sleeping with you," she blurted out.

Gabriel's mouth dropped open in mock outrage. "Miss Espina, I'm shocked."

Serafia chuckled softly, the laughter her only release

for everything building up inside her. She arched one eyebrow at him. "Shocked that I would be so blunt or shocked that I'm turning you down?"

At that, he smiled and she felt her knees start to soften beneath her. Much more of that and she'd be a puddle in her Manolos.

"Shocked that you would think that was all I wanted from you."

Serafia crossed her arms over her chest. She barely had room for the movement with Gabriel so close. She needed the barrier. She didn't believe a word he said. "What exactly were you suggesting, then?"

His jewel-green gaze dropped down to the cleavage her movement had enhanced. She was clutching herself so tightly that she was on the verge of spilling out of her top. She relaxed, removing some, if not all of the distraction.

"I'm feeling a little caged up. I was going to suggest a jog around the compound followed by a dip in the swimming pool," he said.

"Sure you were," she replied with a disbelieving tone. "You look like a man who's hard up for a good run."

He smiled and she felt a part deep inside her clench with need. Desire had not been very high on Serafia's priority list for a very long time. She was frustrated at how easily Gabriel could push her body's needs to the top of the list.

"The king's health and well-being should be at the forefront of the minds of the Alman people. Long live the king, right?"

"Long live the king," she responded, albeit unenthusiastically.

"So, how about that run?"

The way he looked at her, the way he leaned into her, it felt as if he was asking for more than just a run. But she answered the question at hand and tried to ignore her body's response to his query. "First, you need your ceremonial dress tailored. It will take a couple days to get it back and we need it before we leave. Then you can run if you like."

"And what about you? Don't you need a little rush of endorphins? A little...release?"

"I exercised when I got up this morning," she replied. And she had. Every morning when she woke up, she did exactly forty-five minutes on her elliptical machine. No more, no less, doctor's orders. Her treadmill at home was gathering dust, since running was out of the question unless her life was in danger.

His gaze raked over her, making every inch of her body aware of his heavy appraisal before he made a sucking sound with his tongue and shook his head. "Pity."

He dropped his arm and took a step back, allowing her lungs to fill with fresh oxygen that wasn't tainted with his scent. It helped clear her head of the fog that had settled in when he was so close.

The persistent chirp of his cell phone drew his attention away and for that, Serafia was grateful. Apparently Gabriel's harem of women were lonely without him. Since they'd begun this process four days ago, he averaged a text or two an hour. Most of the time he didn't respond, but that didn't stop the messages from coming in. She didn't care about what he'd been involved in, but she couldn't help noticing all the different names on the screen.

Carla, Francesca, Kimi, Ronnie, Anita, Lisa, Tammy, Jessica, Emily, Sara…it was as if his phone was spinning through a massive Rolodex of names. His little digital black book would be ungainly if it were in print.

"I'm going to go see if the tailor has arrived," she said as he put the phone away again. "Do you think you can fight off all your lovers long enough to get this jacket fitted properly?"

Gabriel narrowed his eyes at her and slipped his phone into his pocket. "You sound jealous."

Maybe a little. But that was none of his concern. She would deal with it accordingly. "Not jealous," she corrected. "I'm concerned."

He frowned at her then. "You sound like my father. Why would you be concerned with my love life?"

"It's like I told you that first night, Gabriel. Your life is no longer your own. Not your relationships or your free time or even your body. You can't drive your sports cars around like a Formula One driver and put the king's health at risk. You can't party every night with a different woman and put the future of your country in the hands of a bastard you father with some girl you barely remember. You can't waste the realm's money on the hedonistic pleasures you've built your whole life on."

"From what I learned in school, that's what most kings do, actually."

"Maybe four hundred years ago, but not anymore. If King Henry the Eighth had to deal with the modern press, things would've ended very differently for him and all his poor wives."

"So you're saying it's all about appearances? I have

to be squeaky clean on the outside to keep the press and the people happy?"

"It's bigger than that. Your recklessness is indicative of an emotional disconnect. That's what worries me. You need to prepare yourself for the marriage that is just around the corner for you. You may not even have met the woman yet, but I guarantee you'll be married before the first year of your reign comes to an end. That means no more skirt chasing. You have to take this seriously. You have to really connect with someone, and I don't see that coming easily to you."

"You don't think I can connect with someone?" He seemed insulted by her insinuation.

"Relationships—*real relationships*—are hard. Love and trust and honesty are difficult to maintain. I've only been around here for a few days, but I haven't seen you interact with a single person on a sincere level. You have no real relationships, not even with your family."

"I have real relationships," he argued, but even as he spoke the words, she sensed a question in his voice.

"Name one. If something huge happened in your life, who would you run to with the news? If you had a secret, who would you confide in?"

There was an extended silence as he thought about the answer to her question. There would be a quicker response for almost anyone else she asked this question of. A mother, a brother, a best friend, a buddy from college… Gabriel had no answer. It was both sad and disconcerting. Why did he keep everyone at arm's length?

"I have plenty of friends and family. Since I've been announced as the future king, they've been coming out of the woodwork. I don't know what you're talking about."

"I'm talking about having a person in your life who you can tell anything, good or bad. Someone to confide in. I don't think Jessica or Tammy is the right answer. But I also don't think Rafe or Bella are, either. Everyone needs a person like that in their lives. I feel like there are people who would be there for you, but you won't let them in. I feel a resistance, a buffer there, even with your own family, and I don't know what it's about. What I do know is that you need to learn to let those walls down or this week will be nothing compared to the next year."

"I figured the opposite would be true," he replied at last. "When you're the king, everyone wants something from you. You can't trust anyone. Your marriage is arranged, your closest advisers jockeying for their own pet projects. I would've thought that keeping my distance would be an asset in that kind of environment."

"Maybe you're right," she admitted with a sad shrug. "I certainly would've been more prepared for the world of modeling if I'd gone in believing that everyone wanted something from me and that I couldn't trust them. But I think everyone, even a king, needs someone."

"Believe me, it's easier this way," he said. "If you don't trust anyone, they can't betray you and you'll never be disappointed."

There was an honesty in his words that she hadn't heard in anything else he'd said when they were together. That worried her. Someone, at some point, had damaged Gabriel. She knew it shouldn't be her concern, but she couldn't help wondering what had happened and how she could help.

The people of Alma—Serafia included—wanted

more from their king than Gabriel was willing to give them. He hadn't even been crowned king yet and she worried this was going to be a mistake. No amount of haircuts or fancy clothes could fix the break deep inside of him.

He had to do that himself.

Four

Two days later, Gabriel stepped onto a private jet and left the life he knew behind him. They flew overnight, his father, Rafael, sleeping in the bedroom of the plane as he and Serafia slept in fully reclining leather chairs. It was a quiet flight without a lot of conversation once they finished their dinners and dimmed the cabin lights.

Gabriel slept soundly, and when he awoke, they were thirty minutes out from landing in his new country. He'd only been there once before with Rafe on a whirlwind tour, but when he got off the plane this time, he was supposed to be their leader.

"You need to get dressed," Serafia said beside him. "Your suit is hanging up in the bathroom."

He hadn't heard her get up, but she had changed her clothes, refreshed her makeup and styled her thick,

dark hair into a bun. For the next week, she was publically filling the role of his social secretary while privately coaching him through all the events. She was
dressed for the part in a ladies' taupe suit. The blazer
was well tailored and didn't look boxy, and the sheath
dress beneath it was fitted and came down just to her
knee, showcasing her long and shapely calves.

It was elegant, but Gabriel found himself longing
for the clingy red silk gown from their first night together. In this outfit, she completely faded into the
background. He supposed that was the idea, but he
didn't like it. Serafia might not care for the spotlight,
but she was born to be in it.

He went to the bathroom, getting ready and changing into the navy suit she'd hung out for him. She'd
paired it with a lighter blue shirt and a plain blue tie.
It was a sophisticated look, she'd argued, but it seemed
boring to him. It made him want to wear crazy socks,
but he wouldn't. She'd already laid out a pair of navy
socks for him.

By the time he came back out, his father had emerged
from the bedroom and the pilot was announcing their
descent into Del Sol, the capital of Alma.

"The press will be waiting for you when we arrive.
They've arranged for a carpet to be laid out and your
royal guards will be there for crowd control. They've
already secured the area and screened all the attendees.
Your press secretary, Señor Vega, briefed everyone on
appropriate questions, so things should go smoothly.
I will exit the plane first and make sure everything is
okay," Serafia explained. "Then Señor Montoro, and
then you're last. Wait until the carpet is clear. Take your
time so everyone can get their photos."

Gabriel nodded, taking in her constant stream of instructions as he had done all week. She was a font of information.

"Don't forget to smile. Wave. It should just be the press, so no need to greet anyone in the crowd. No speeches, no interviews. Just smile and wave."

The wheels of the jet touched down and suddenly everything became very real. Gabriel looked out the window. Beyond the airport, he could see the great rock hills that rose on the horizon, their gray stone peppered with evergreens. Closer to Del Sol was a smaller hill topped with some kind of ancient fortress. Climbing up the incline were whitewashed buildings clustered together with clay tile roofs.

Ahead, clear blue skies with palm trees led the way toward the beach. His last trip here with his brother had been all business, so he had no idea what kinds of beaches they had in Alma, but he prayed they were at least halfway as nice as the ones in Miami. He was already feeling pangs of homesickness.

The plane stopped and the engines turned off. The small crew unlocked and extended the staircase. Serafia gathered up her bag and her tablet. "Smile and wave," she said one last time before disappearing down the stairs.

His father followed her a moment later and then it was Gabriel's turn. His heart started pounding in his rib cage. His lungs could barely take in enough air, his chest was so tight. Once he stepped out of this plane, he was a coronation away from being *Su Majestad el Rey Don Gabriel I.* It was a terrifying prospect, but he pushed himself up out of his seat anyway.

Taking a deep breath, he stepped into the doorway.

He was momentarily blinded by the sun. He paused for a moment to adjust, a smile on his face and his arm raised in greeting. He slowly made his way down the stairs, careful not to fall and make the worst possible impression. By the time he reached the bottom, he could look out into the crowd of photographers. There were about fifty of them gathered with cameras and video crews.

To the left and right of the stairs were two large gentlemen in military suits similar to the one Serafia had recently had tailored for him. In addition to their shiny brass buttons and collections of metals, they wore earpieces with cords that disappeared under their collars. He hadn't really given the idea of his personal security much thought until now.

The men bowed, and after he nodded to them both, they walked two paces behind Gabriel as he made his way down the carpet. At the end of the path, he could see his father and Serafia waiting for him with a man he presumed was his press secretary. Serafia had an exaggerated smile like a stage mom, reminding him to smile and wave.

He was almost to the end when a man with a video crew charged to the edge of the barricade and shouted to him. "Gabriel! How do you feel about your brother's abdication? Did you know he had a child on the way?"

The bold question startled him.

"Rafe made his choice. I don't blame him for his decision." Serafia had told him he wasn't to answer questions, but he was thrown off guard with a film crew pointing the camera right in his face.

"What about the child?" the man pressed.

He felt a protectiveness build up inside him, his fists

curling tight at his side. "I was unaware of the seriousness of his relationship with Ms. Fielding, but the matter of their child is their business, and I must insist that
you respect their privacy."

"Have you chosen a queen yet?" Another reporter
shouted before he could take another step. From there,
it was a rapid fire he couldn't escape.

"Will she be a citizen of Alma or a member of a European royal family to strengthen trade agreements?"

"Did you leave a lover behind in America?"

Gabriel felt his throat close. He didn't know how
to even begin addressing these questions, but he was
certain his required smile had faded.

"Please!" Serafia shouted, stepping in front of him
and holding her hands up to the camera. "He's been in
Del Sol for five minutes. Let's allow Don Gabriel to get
settled in and perhaps coroneted before we start worrying about the line of succession, shall we?"

She took his arm and with a forceful tug, led him
down the rug and inside the terminal. From there, security ushered them quickly out a side door to a black
SUV with Alma's flag flying on each corner of the
hood.

The door had barely shut before the convoy was on
the road. The inside of the vehicle was quiet. He was
stunned by the turn of events. Serafia was stiff beside him.

"What the hell was that?" his father finally asked.

"I didn't realize—" Gabriel began to defend himself
to his father, but he realized he was looking at Serafia
with eye daggers.

"You said there were to be no questions," Rafael
snapped. "Why wasn't the press properly briefed?"

"They were," she argued, her spine lengthening in defiance. "Hector assured me that they were told Gabriel wasn't answering questions, but to tell them they can't ask is suppression of free press. No matter what they're told, reporters will ask questions in the hopes they can catch someone off guard and get an answer that will provide a juicy headline."

"Unacceptable."

Serafia sighed angrily. "I can assure you that I will work with Hector to have the offending reporters identified and will see to it that their press privileges are suspended."

"Gabriel should've been briefed. If you knew the press might push him for questions, he should've been better prepared. That's your job."

"I'm an image consultant, not his press secretary. What kind of briefing does he need to walk down a rug and wave? I suggest that when we arrive at the palace, we arrange to meet with Hector immediately. He'll need to be able to handle those sorts of things better in the future. There are more public appearances this week. We can't risk that happening again. I'm sorry that—"

"Stop," Gabriel said. He'd grown angrier with every apologetic word out of her mouth. There was no reason for her to ask for forgiveness. "You've done nothing wrong, Serafia. I apologize for my father's harsh, inappropriate tone. I should've anticipated they would ask questions like that. I will be more prepared next time. End of discussion. For now, let's just focus on getting settled in and prepared for our next event."

His father's sharp gaze raked over him as he spoke, the older man's tan Mediterranean complexion mottled with red. He was clearly angry his son had shut him down, but that was too bad. The balance of power had shifted in the family. The moment Gabriel stepped off that plane, he was in charge. They weren't in Miami anymore where his father ruled over the family with an iron fist.

They were in Alma now and Gabriel was going to be the king. His father had ruined his chance to be the boss when he divorced Gabriel's mother without an annulment, so he'd better get used to the way things were going to be now. Gabriel was no longer the useless middle son who could be berated or ignored.

Gabriel was going to be king.

"It's beautiful," Serafia said as they entered the main room of the palace.

El Castillo del Arena was the official royal residence in Del Sol. Looking like a giant sandcastle, hence its name, it sat on a fortified wall overlooking the bay. The early Arabian influences on the architecture were evident everywhere you looked, from the arches to the intricate mosaic tile work. The inner courtyards had gardens that made a cool escape from the sun with lush trees, fountains and blooming flowers in every direction.

Clearly it wasn't as grand a palace as it had once been: the Persian rugs had threadbare corners and the upholstery on the furniture was worn and dirty. Seventy years in the hands of a dictatorship had made their mark, but it still had the grand design and details of its former glory. It wouldn't take long to restore the palace.

Few people had been allowed in under the Tantaberras. It was a pity. The grand rooms with the arched ceilings were begging for a royal event with all the elite of Alma in attendance.

From the expression on his face, Gabriel wasn't as impressed. Since the heated discussion in the car, he'd been quiet. She thought that when Señor Montoro skipped the tour and asked to be shown to his rooms so he could nap Gabriel would perk up, but he didn't. Now he silently took it all in as they followed his personal steward, Ernesto, on a tour through the palace.

"These are the king's private chambers," Ernesto said as he opened the double doors to reveal the expansive room.

There was a king-size bed in the center of the room with a massive four-poster frame. It was draped in red fabric with a dozen red and gold pillows scattered across the bed. Large tapestries hung on the walls, and a Moroccan rug covered the stone floors.

"Your bath and closet are through those doors," Ernesto continued.

She watched as Gabriel looked around, a slightly pained expression on his face. "It's awfully dark in here," he complained. "It's like a cave or an underground cellar. Are there only those two windows?"

Ernesto looked at the two arched windows crafted of stained glass and nodded. "Yes, Your Majesty."

She watched Gabriel tense at the use of the formal title. "I'm not king yet, Ernesto. You can just call me Gabriel."

The man's eyes grew wide. "I would rather not, Your Grace. You're still the crown prince."

"I suppose." Gabriel sighed and fixed his gaze on a set of double doors on the other side of the room. "Where do those doors go to?"

Ernesto, lean and dark-complexioned, moved quickly to the doors and opened them. "Through here are the queen's rooms. And beyond it are chambers for her ladies-in-waiting, although the rooms may be better suited in these times as an office or a nursery. The rooms haven't really been used since your great-grandmother, Queen Anna Maria, fled Alma."

Gabriel frowned. "The queen doesn't share a room with the king?"

"She may. Traditionally, having her own space allowed her to pursue more feminine activities with her ladies such as sewing or reading without interfering with the running of the state."

"It's like I've gone back in time," Gabriel grumbled, and ran his fingers through his hair in exasperation.

"The staff is still working on restoring and modernizing the palace. Perhaps Your Majesty would prefer to spend some time prior to the coronation at Playa del Onda. It's a more modern estate, built for the royal family to vacation at the beach in the summers. It's lovely, with floor-to-ceiling windows that overlook the sea and bright, open rooms."

For the first time since they'd arrived, Serafia noticed Gabriel perk up. "How far is it from here?"

"It's about an hour's drive along the coastal highway, but you won't mind a minute of it. The views are exquisite. I can call ahead to the staff there and let them know you'll be coming if you'd like."

Gabriel considered his options for a moment and finally turned to look at Serafia. "I know we'll be coming back to Del Sol for a lot of activities this week, but I think I'd like to stay out there while I can. Care to continue our work at the beach?" he asked.

She nodded. The location wasn't important to her, but she could tell it mattered to him. He seemed to have a tense, almost claustrophobic reaction to his own quarters, despite the room being massive in scale with tall, arched ceilings. If he could relax, he would absorb more information. She could accommodate the extended drive times in their schedule.

"Then let's do that. My father will be staying here, but Señorita Espina and I will be going to Playa del Onda. We'll be staying there for the next week. I'll return as we start preparing for the coronation."

"Very good. I'll arrange for your transportation."

"Ernesto?"

The steward paused. "Yes, Your Majesty?"

"See if you can arrange for a convertible with a GPS. I'd like to drive myself to the compound and enjoy the sun and sea air on the way."

"Drive yourself?" Ernesto seemed stumped for a moment, but then immediately shook off his concerns. It wasn't his place to question the king's requests. "Yes, Your Grace." He turned and disappeared down the hallway.

"They're not going to know what to do with a king like you," Serafia said.

"Me, neither," Gabriel noted dryly. "But maybe if we spend a couple days at the beach, we can all be better prepared for my official return to the palace."

They walked out of the king's chambers and down the winding staircase to the main hall. Within minutes, they were greeted by the royal guard, who reported that they already had a car waiting for him outside. They would be following in the black SUV that brought him there.

Gabriel didn't argue. Instead they walked out into the courtyard. A cherry-red Peugeot convertible was parked there. "Whose car is this?" he asked as an attendant opened the door for Serafia to get in.

"It is Señor Ernesto's car, Your Majesty."

"What will he drive while I have it?"

"One of the royal fleet." The attendant pointed to an area with several vehicles parked there. "He is happy to let you borrow it. The address of the beach compound is already entered in the system, Your Majesty."

Gabriel took the keys, slipped out of his suit coat and got in beside her. He waited until the guard had assembled in the SUV behind them; then he started the car and they headed toward the gates.

Once they slipped beyond the fortress walls, Serafia noticed Gabriel's posture relax. It was as if a weight had been lifted from his shoulders. She couldn't help feeling the same way. Ernesto had been right: the view was amazing. Once they escaped Del Sol and started climbing up the mountain, everything changed. The winding coastal road showcased wide vistas with bright blue skies, turquoise waters and ships along the shoreline.

With the sun warming her skin and the ocean air whipping the strands of her hair around her face, she felt herself relax for the first time since she'd left Barcelona. Although the Atlantic islands were different from her Mediterranean hacienda, it felt as if she were back there, the place where she felt the most at home, and safe.

"Are you hungry?" he asked.

"Yes." They'd had croissants and juice on the plane, but it was past lunchtime now and she was starving.

Gabriel nodded. A mile up the road, he slowed and

pulled off at a small, hole-in-the-wall restaurant overlooking the sea. A moment later, the royal guard pulled up beside them and lowered a window.

"Is there a problem, Your Majesty?" the one with the slicked-back brown hair who was driving the SUV asked.

"I'm hungry. Have you two had lunch?"

The two guards looked at each other in confusion and the driver turned back to him. "No, we haven't."

"Is this place any good?" he asked.

"I have eaten here many times, but in my opinion, it isn't fit for the king."

Gabriel looked at her and smiled widely. "Perfect. I'm starving. Let's all grab something to eat."

The two of them waited outside with the younger blond guard as the other went inside to make sure the restaurant was secure. It wasn't big enough to house much more than a tiny kitchen and a few tables on the veranda.

When they got the all-clear, a small, slow-moving old woman greeted them as they came in and gave them their choice of tables outside. As Gabriel had insisted they eat as well, the guards took a table near the door to watch anyone coming in or out, allowing him and Serafia privacy while they dined.

The menu was limited, but the royal guard with the dark hair named Jorge recommended the *caldereta de langosta*. It was a seasonal lobster stew with tomatoes, onions, garlic and peppers, served with thin slices of bread.

They all ordered the caldereta and Serafia was not disappointed. Normally she gave great care and thought into every bite she put in her mouth, but the stew was too amazing to worry about it. The lobster was soft and buttery in texture, while spicy in flavor thanks to the peppers. The bread soaked up the broth perfectly and helped carry the large pieces of lobster to her mouth without her wearing most of it on her pale taupe suit.

"This is wonderful," she said, when she was more than halfway finished with her stew. "Thank you for stopping."

"I was getting cranky," Gabriel said. He glanced over the railing at the sparking blue sea below them. "If I can be cranky looking at a view like this, I've got to be hungry."

"I would've thought the incident this morning had more to do with it than hunger."

"This morning was nothing and my father wanted to make it into something. I have enough to worry about without him making you uncomfortable. You've gone out of your way to help me through this. You've tolerated my bad moods and my childish behavior. I think I will be a better king for what you've done, so I should be thanking you, not criticizing you."

Serafia was stunned by his thoughtful words. He seemed to be almost a different person since they'd arrived in Alma. Or at least since the moment he'd stood up to his father. He had seemed to grow taller in that moment, physically stronger even, as he sat in the vehicle. Perhaps he truly was gaining the confidence he needed to rule Alma.

"Thank you," she said. "I appreciate that. And I appreciate you standing up for me this morning. The look on your father's face when you put an end to the discussion was priceless, really."

Gabriel looked at her with a wry grin. "It was good,

wasn't it? It's the first time I've stood up to him in my whole life and I'm glad I did."

"Is he always like that?"

Gabriel sipped his sparkling water and nodded. "Nothing was ever good enough for my father, but especially me. I could never understand it growing up. I did everything right, everything he wanted me to do. I went to school where he wanted me to go, took the position at the company he wanted me to have. I let him banish me to South American Operations. After everything that happened there, I almost got the feeling he was disappointed I came back. I've never understood why."

"After everything that happened there?" Gabriel seemed to be alluding to some incident she was unaware of. "What happened?"

With a sigh, he popped the last of his bread in his mouth and shook his head. "It doesn't matter. What matters is that I learned some valuable lessons. First, that you have to be careful who you can trust. And second, that I'm a grown man who can live and do however I please. These last few years my behavior has just been written off by my family as reckless and selfish, but it's been good for me. If my father doesn't approve of me either way, I should do whatever I want to, right?"

Serafia suppressed her frown. How had she not seen how wounded he was before now? The cracks in his facade were starting to show and they made her wonder what had turned the obedient middle son into the rebellious, distant one. He didn't want to talk about it and she understood. She had dark secrets of her own, but she couldn't help wondering if his past and its effect on him might hinder his leadership in Alma.

"I never wanted to be king, but now that I'm here, I think this might work out. My father may still disagree with what I do and how, but now I don't have to listen to it any longer." Abruptly standing, he pulled some euros from his wallet and threw them down on the table to cover everyone's lunch tab. Serafia got up as well, placing her napkin on the table.

"Let's get back on the road."

Five

"You look very handsome tonight."

Serafia stood at Gabriel's side and looked over the railing at the crowd below. There was a sea of people there, all dressed in their finest tuxedos and gowns. A string quartet was in the corner, filling the large space with a soothing background melody. It was a glittering display of marble floors, towering flower arrangements and twinkling crystal chandeliers. Patrick Rowling spared no expense when it came to his home or the parties he hosted there.

They had arrived at the Rowling mansion via a side door and were escorted upstairs to wait in Patrick's library so Gabriel could make a grand entrance. To their right was an elaborate marble staircase that twisted its way into the center of the ballroom. It just begged for a king to stroll down with a regal air.

Regal was not the vibe she was getting from Gabriel. Her compliment seemed to unnerve him. He shifted uncomfortably under her scrutiny, although there was no reason for him to be nervous. The ceremonial dress had been tailored beautifully and despite his complaints, he looked noble, powerful and very appropriate for a party like this. He had come a long way in the last week and she'd felt a swell of pride in her chest when he stepped out of his bedroom in full regalia earlier.

"I still feel like Prince Charming at the ball. And from the look of the crowd here tonight, all the eligible young maidens have come to land a king for a husband."

"I did notice that," she admitted. There were a lot of young women at the party, all painted and coiffed to the max. Decked out in an array of eye-catching jewel-tone silks and satins, they were like parading peacocks among the dark tuxedos. If Serafia had to guess, she'd say that millions of dollars had been laid out tonight in the hopes that they might catch the future king's eye.

She had gone the opposite route. Her gown was a very soft pink, almost a blush color. The organza ruching wrapped around her body, dotted with tiny crystals and beads. While sedate in color, it still had a few scandalous details like a plunging V-cut neckline and a slit on the side that almost reached the top of her thigh. She wanted to look as if she belonged, but she didn't want to stand out. She wasn't here to enjoy a party; she was here to help Gabriel get through his first real event in Alma.

"It certainly looks like you have your pick of ladies here tonight."

"Do I?"

Serafia turned to look at him and was surprised to see the serious way he was looking at her. He had the same heated intensity in his eyes he'd had the day he pinned her against the armoire. What exactly did he mean by that? She couldn't possibly be his pick when there were so many younger, more attractive women in the room tonight. "I...uh..." She hesitated. "I...think you've got a lot to choose from and a long night ahead of you. Don't make a decision too quickly. Keep your options open."

Gabriel sighed and turned away to look at the crowd. "I'll try."

A man in a tuxedo approached them on the landing and bowed to Gabriel. "If Your Majesty is ready, I'll cue the musicians to announce your arrival."

"Yes, I suppose it's time."

"May I escort you downstairs, Señorita Espina?"

"Yes, thank you." She took the man's arm and turned back to Gabriel. "I'll see you downstairs after the guests have all been presented."

"You're not going down with me?"

Serafia chuckled. "This is like the arrival at the airport, but without the pushy reporters. You need to have your moment. Alone." She wouldn't make many new girlfriends tonight if she showed up on the king's arm and beat them all to the punch.

"Good luck," she said, giving him a wink before carefully descending the staircase and joining the crowd. She parted with her escort, finding a spot at the edge of the room near one of the royal guards to watch Gabriel's entrance.

The orchestra started playing Alma's national anthem. The bustling crowd immediately grew silent and everyone turned their gaze to the flag hanging from the second-floor railing. When the last note died out, Gabriel appeared at the top of the stairs looking as much like a king as a man raised to have the position.

"His Royal Highness, El Príncipe Gabriel, the future El Rey Don Gabriel the First of Alma."

The crowd applauded as he came down the stairs. The air in the room was electric with excitement. Gabriel didn't fully appreciate how important this was for the people of Alma. They were free, and his arrival was the living, breathing evidence of that freedom. People bowed and curtseyed as he passed.

"Oh my God, he's so handsome. I didn't think it was possible, but he's even more attractive than Rafe."

Serafia turned to see a young woman and her mother standing nearby. The woman was maybe twenty-three and she was in a sapphire-blue gown that looked amazing with her golden skin and flaxen hair. Her mother was an older carbon copy in a more sedate silver gown. They were both dripping with diamonds, but the twinkle in their eyes sparkled even brighter as they looked at Gabriel.

"Oh, Dita," the mother gushed. "He's perfect for you. This is your big chance tonight. You look absolutely flawless, better than any of the other girls here." She looked around the room, scanning the competition again. Her gaze lit on Serafia for only a moment, then moved on as though she were an insignificant presence. Apparently the woman didn't read *Vogue*, or she would realize she was standing beside a former supermodel.

Serafia recognized *her*, however. At the mention of her daughter's name, she realized the mother was Felicia Gomez. The Gomez family was one of the richest in Alma, although unlike the Rowlings, they were natives like the Espinas. Many of the wealthier families had fled Alma when Tantaberra came to power, but the Gomez family had stayed.

Serafia had never met them, but she had heard her mother talk about them from time to time. It was rarely flattering. She got the impression that they were fair-weather friend types who worked hard to ingratiate themselves with whoever was in power. She didn't know what they had to do to maintain their money and lands under the dictatorship, but she was certain it was a price the Espinas wouldn't have paid.

It would not surprise her mother at all to know they were here on the hunt for a rich husband. With the dictatorship dissolved, they had to put themselves in a good position with the new royal family, and what better way than to marry into it? Serafia took a step closer to listen in as Felicia continued her instructions to Dita.

"When we're introduced to the king, remember everything I've told you. You've got to make a good impression on him. Be coquettish, but not too aggressive. Make eye contact, but don't hold it for too long. Make him come to you and then you'll have him like putty in your hands. It worked on your father. It will work on him. You deserve to be queen, always remember that."

Serafia tried not to chuckle. She was certain a similar conversation was taking place all over the room. There were easily thirty bright-eyed girls here with their parents. All were after the same prize. Serafia might be the only single woman in the room who wasn't on the hunt. She had no interest in competing with a bunch of little girls for Gabriel's attention.

When Gabriel reached the bottom of the stairs, he

was greeted by his father and Patrick Rowling. They escorted him over to a raised dais on the far side of the room. They took their seats there and the crowd gathered for a receiving line. Everyone was excited for their chance to be introduced to the new king.

Serafia took advantage of the distraction to go to the empty bar. She got glasses of wine for them both, hugging the edge of the room to deliver the drink to Gabriel. As she got close, Patrick was introducing his sons, William and James, to Gabriel and his father. Will was Patrick's heir apparent to the oil and real estate empire they'd built. James, like Gabriel, was the second son, the spare heir, even though he was born only minutes after his twin brother.

Neither of the men looked particularly happy to be here tonight. Even then, they seemed more comfortable than Gabriel. He kept cycling between a stiff regal pose, a slightly slumped-over bored stance and a fidgety anxious carriage that made it obvious to Serafia that he was very uncomfortable. Perhaps a glass of wine would be enough to relax him without loosening his tongue too much.

Out of the corner of her eye, Serafia spied one of the party's many servers. The petite girl with chin-length black hair was lurking along the edge of the room, her gaze focused fully on the Rowling brothers as they greeted the king.

It took a moment, but Serafia was finally able to wave her over. As a model, she was used to towering over people, but the server was probably close to five feet tall, a little pixie of a thing with sparkling dark eyes that immediately caught Serafia's attention. On her immaculately pressed black shirt, she wore a small brass nametag that read *Catalina*.

"Yes, ma'am?"

"Would you please take this wine to Prince Gabriel?" Serafia placed the wine on her tray.

Catalina took a deep breath and nodded. "Of course," she said, immediately departing. Well trained, she waited until Will and James were escorted away, slipping over quietly to deliver the drink, then disappearing so quickly that some people might not have even seen her.

Gabriel took a heavy sip of the wine, searching Serafia out in the crowd. When his gaze lit on her, Serafia felt a chill run down her spine. Goose bumps rose across her bare arms, making her rub them self-consciously. He winked at her, and before she could prompt him to smile, he broke out his practiced grin and turned to the next family being presented.

Serafia had to admit she was pleased with the results of her work. In only a week, they had managed to smooth over his rough edges and mold him into a man fit to be royalty. As she watched him interact with the Gomez family and the young and beautiful Dita, she couldn't help the pang of jealousy inside her.

Perhaps she had done too good a job. She had polished away all the reasons she needed to stay far, far away from Gabriel Montoro.

Gabriel was exhausted. All he'd done for the last hour was get introduced to people, but he was done. He was tired of smiling, tired of greeting people. It wasn't as if he was going to be able to remember a single name once each person turned away and the next was presented.

Unfortunately there were hours left in the night. Now started the dancing and the mingling. With the formalities out of the way, people would seek him out for more casual discussions. The ladies would expect him to solicit a dance or two.

He did none of those things. Instead he sought out another glass a wine and a few bites from the buffet of canapés and fresh fruits. He was hoping to find Serafia, who had disappeared at some point, but instead his father cornered him at the baked brie.

"What do you think of William?"

William? Gabriel went through the two hundred names he'd just heard and drew a blank.

"William Rowling, Patrick's oldest son," Rafael clarified, seemingly irritated with Gabriel for dismissing the Rowlings so easily.

"Oh," Gabriel said, taking a sip of wine. He refrained from mentioning to his father that he couldn't tell the two brothers apart. That would just agitate him. "He seemed very nice. Why? Are you trying to fix me up with him? He's really not my type, Dad."

"Gabriel," Rafael said in a warning tone. "I was thinking about him and Bella."

Gabriel tried not to frown at his father. All this royalty nonsense was going to his father's head if he thought he could start arranging marriages and no one would question it. "I think Bella would have a great deal more to say on the subject than I would."

"Rowling is the most powerful businessman in Alma. Combining our families would strengthen our position here, both financially and socially. If he had a daughter I'd be shoving her under your nose, too."

"Dad, it's a marriage, not a business merger."

"Same difference. I had a similar arrangement with your mother and now our company is in the Fortune 500."

"*And* you're divorced," Gabriel added. Their mother was living happily on another continent and had been since Bella turned eighteen and she had fulfilled her obligation to Rafael and the children. That was just what Bella would want for her own marriage, Gabriel was sure. Turning from his father, he scanned the crowd again.

"Who are you looking for?" Rafael pressed.

"Serafia."

Rafael popped a shrimp into his mouth and chewed it with a sour expression. "Don't get too dependent on her, Gabriel. She's just here through the end of the week. You've got to learn to stand on your own without her."

Gabriel was taken aback by his father's words. What did he care as long as Gabriel parroted all the right words and did all the right things? "I'm not dependent on her. I simply enjoy her company and I'm finding this party tedious without her."

"Yes, well, don't get too involved on that front, either. If you're bored, I suggest you focus on the ladies here tonight. Take Dita Gomez or Mariella Sanchez for a spin around the dance floor and see if you feel differently."

"And what if I want to take Serafia for a spin around the dance floor, Father? Stop treating her like she's just an employee. The Espinas are just as important a noble family in Alma as any of these others."

His father stiffened and the red blotchiness Gabriel had seen so often lately started climbing up his neck.

"Now is not the time to discuss things like this," he hissed in a low voice. "Now is the time to mingle with your new countrymen and start your search for a suitable queen. We will talk about the Espina family later. Now go mingle!" he demanded.

Gabriel didn't bother arguing with him. If mingling meant he could get away from his father for a while, he'd do it gladly. Perhaps he'd find where Serafia was hiding in the process. With a nod, he set aside his plate and ventured out into the crowd. Every few feet he was stopped by someone and engaged in polite banter. How did he like Alma so far? Did the weather suit him? Had he had the opportunity to enjoy the beaches or any of the local culture?

He was halfway through one of these discussions when he spied Serafia over the man's shoulder. She was standing across the room chatting with a gentleman whose name he had immediately forgotten when they were introduced in the receiving line.

Gabriel had seen a lot of beautiful women tonight, but he just couldn't understand how his father could think that any of them could hold a candle to Serafia. She was breathtaking, catwalk perfection. Sure, she wasn't as rail-thin as she had been in her modeling days, but the pounds had just softened the angles and filled out the curves that her gown clung to. The pale pink of her dress was like soft rose petals scattered across her olive complexion. It was a delicate, romantic color, unlike all the bold look-at-me dresses the other women were wearing.

Serafia didn't need that for men to look at her, at least for Gabriel to look at her. He had a hard time looking anywhere else. Her silky black hair was loose tonight in shiny curls that fell over her shoulders and down her back. She wore very little jewelry—just a pair of pink sapphire studs at her ears—but between the beads of her dress and the glitter of her delicate pink lipstick, she seemed to sparkle from head to toe.

He felt his mouth go dry as he imagined her leaving a trail of glittering pink lipstick down his bare stomach. He wanted to pull her body hard against his and bury his fingers in the inky black silk of her hair. For all he cared, this party and these people could disappear. He wanted to be alone with Serafia and not for etiquette lessons or strategy discussions.

He hadn't given much thought to the man she was speaking to, but when he laid a hand on Serafia's upper arm, Gabriel felt his blood pressure spike with jealousy. Quickly excusing himself from the conversation he'd been ignoring, he moved through the room, arriving at her side in an instant.

Serafia's eyes widened at his sudden arrival. She took a step back, introducing him to the man she was speaking to. "Your Majesty, may I reintroduce you to Tomás Padillo? He owns Padillo Vineyards, where we'll be taking a tour tomorrow afternoon. I was just telling him how much you've enjoyed the Manto Negro from his winery since you arrived."

"Ah yes," Gabriel replied with a nod of recognition. He held up his glass. "Is this a vintage of yours, as well?"

"Yes, Your Majesty, that's my award-winning Chardonnay. I'm honored to have you drink it and looking forward to hosting your visit with us tomorrow."

The man seemed harmless enough; then again, Gabriel didn't see a ring on the man's hand. He didn't intend to leave Serafia alone with him.

"I'm looking forward to it, as well. May I steal away Miss Espina?" he asked.

"Of course, Your Majesty."

Gabriel nodded and scooped up Serafia's arm into his own. He led her away into a quiet corner behind the staircase where they could talk.

"Is everything going all right?" she asked.

Gabriel nodded. "I think so. My dad is pressuring me to mingle with the ladies, but I haven't gotten that far yet."

Serafia sighed and patted his forearm. "You've done your fair share of wooing ladies, Gabriel. This shouldn't be very difficult for you."

"That was different," he argued. "Picking up a woman at a nightclub for a little fun is nothing like shopping for a wife. It feels more like a hunt anyway, except I'm the fox. I'm surprised one of the hounds hasn't ferretted me out from our hiding place by now. Would you stay with me for a while?"

"Not while you dance!"

"Of course not. But go around with me while I mingle for a while. I think I'll be more comfortable that way. You might remember people's names."

"Gabriel, you need to be able to—"

"Please…" he said, looking into her eyes with his most pathetic expression.

"Okay, but you have to promise me you will ask no fewer than two ladies to dance tonight. No moms or grandmothers, either. Eligible, single women of marrying age. And not me, either," she seemed to add for good measure.

"If I dance with two women who meet your criteria, would you be willing to dance with me just for fun?"

Serafia gave him a stern look, but the smile that teased at the corners of her full lips gave her away. "Maybe. But you've got to put in a good effort out there. You're looking for a queen, remember. If you don't find a good one, your father will do it for you, like poor Bella."

"You've heard about that?" Gabriel asked.

"Yes. I overheard Patrick discussing the idea of it with Will."

"How'd he take it?"

"About as well as Bella would, I expect. But my point is that you need to get out there and make that decision yourself."

"Fair enough." Offering her his arm, he led them back into the main area of the room. As they slipped through the crowd, he leaned down to whisper in her ear, "Who would you choose for me? Where should I start?"

Serafia looked thoughtfully around the room, her gaze falling on a buxom, almost chubby redhead whose fiery hair was in direct contrast to her personality. She was a shy wallflower of a girl who had barely met his gaze when they were introduced.

"Start with Helena Ruiz. Her family is in the seafood business and they provide almost all the fresh fish and shellfish to the area and to parts of Spain and Portugal, as well. And," she added, "unlike the others, she seems to be *reluctantly* hunting for a husband. She reminds me very much of a lot of the girls I work with in my business. Choosing her first might be good for her social standing and her self-esteem."

Gabriel was pleased with Serafia's choice and her reasoning behind it. It was one of the things about her that really stuck with him. She wasn't just concerned about making over his outside, but his inside, as well. In their training sessions, they'd discussed charities he'd like to support and causes he wanted to rally behind as king. Parliament and the prime minister would draft and enforce the laws of Alma, but as king, he would have a major influence over the hearts and minds of the people. He had a platform, so he needed to be prepared to have a cause.

In such a short time, Serafia had not just made over his wardrobe. She had made over his soul. He felt like a better person, a person more deserving of a woman like her. He'd never felt that way before in his entire life. He'd always been second to Rafe, not good enough in his father's eyes. His mother had recognized the value in him, but even she couldn't sway his father's opinion.

Since he returned home from Venezuela after the kidnapping, he'd been a different man. He'd stopped seeking everyone's approval, especially his father's. With his mother traveling the world and unable to call him on it, he'd settled happily into his devil-may-care lifestyle. It had suited him well and no one had questioned the change in him. But Serafia had. She had the ability to see through all his crap, and it made him think that perhaps he could open up to her, really trust her, unlike so many others in his life.

As he left her side and approached the doe-eyed Helena, he knew Serafia had made the right choice. The bright, genuine smile on the girl's face and the pinched, jealous expressions of some of the other girls proved that much. He led her out onto the dance floor for the first official dance of the evening. Helena was nearly trembling in his arms, but he reassured her with a smile and a wink.

Serafia made him want to be a better man. She helped him become a better man. He could think of no other woman who should be at his side but her. And he would tell her that.

Tonight.

Six

"Okay," a voice announced over Serafia's shoulder. "I have met your requirements."

She turned to find Gabriel standing behind her. She'd been expecting his arrival. It had been nearly two hours since she sent him out onto the dance floor with Helena Ruiz. He had danced with her and at least five other ladies Serafina had chosen for him. Her inner spiteful streak had led her not to choose Dita as one of the dance partners. She wasn't entirely sure if it was because she knew the Gomezes were disingenuous, or if it was because the idea of him dancing and potentially falling for the statuesque beauty made her blood boil.

"You have," she said with a pleased smile. "You've more than met them. You've exceeded them. Well done, Your Majesty. Any pique your interest?"

Gabriel arched an eyebrow at her and held out his hand. "Join me on the dance floor and I'll tell you."

There were quite a few pairs dancing now, so the two of them would not stand out as much as they would have earlier. Deciding there was no harm in it—and she had promised—she took his hand and followed him out into the center of the dance floor.

Gabriel slipped his arm around her waist and cupped her hand with his own. For the first twenty seconds or so of the dance, she found she could hardly breathe. Her bare skin sizzled where they touched, and her heart was racing in her chest. Fortunately Gabriel was a strong lead and she didn't have to think too much about her feet. She simply followed him across the floor and focused internally on suppressing the physical reaction she had to his touch.

"So, find any chemistry out on the dance floor?" she asked, desperate for a distraction.

"Not until now," he said, his green gaze burrowing into her own.

"Gabriel," she scolded, but he shook his head as though he wasn't having any of that.

"Don't start. I've had enough of the reasons why I can't have what I want. I don't really care. All I know is that I want you."

The power of his words struck her like a wave and she struggled to argue against it. "No, you don't."

"Are you honestly going to stand there and tell me you know my feelings better than I do?"

She shook her head, focusing her gaze on the golden ropes at his shoulder instead of the intensity in his eyes. "You might want me for tonight, for one of your one-night flings, but not for your queen."

"Do we have to decide what it will be tonight?"

If she had to decide in the moment, she would say

no. She was wrapped up in the sensation of being so close to him. Her body was rebelling against her, desiring him desperately even as she argued against the very idea of it. "You aren't in Miami anymore, Gabriel. Every eye in the room is on you tonight. This feeling for me will pass and then you can focus on making a smart decision about your future. A future without me."

"Serafia, you are beautiful. You're the most stunning woman I've ever seen in real life or on a magazine cover. You're graceful, elegant, thoughtful, smart and incredibly insightful. I don't know why you find it so hard to believe that I could want you so desperately."

Desperately? Her gaze met his, her lips parting softly in surprise. His words were said with such sincerity, but she simply didn't believe a single one. She was too aware of her own faults to do that. She'd spent too many years having every aspect of her appearance ripped apart by modeling experts, their voices far louder than any of her fans' praises. And even if he could see past all her imperfections, he didn't know how broken she was. The truth of her past would send any man running. "You don't want me, Gabriel. You want your teenage fantasy from ten years ago. That person doesn't exist anymore."

She pulled away from his grasp as the music ended and made her way through the crowd of people coming on and off the dance floor. Spying a set of French doors, she opened them and slipped outside into the large courtyard of the Rowling mansion. She kept going, following a path into the gardens. It was landscaped like the formal English gardens of Patrick's homeland, so she continued on a gravel path along a long line of neatly trimmed shrubs until she came upon a clearing and a circular fountain.

She collapsed onto the stone ledge of the fountain and took a deep breath. She felt much calmer out here, away from the crush of people in the ballroom, but the sense of relief didn't last long. Not a minute later, she heard the sound of footsteps on the gravel and spied Gabriel coming toward her on the garden path.

He approached silently and sat on the edge of the fountain beside her. She expected him to immediately give her the third degree for running out on him. It was incredibly rude, after all, and she kept forgetting he was the king. People were probably inside talking about her hasty departure.

But Gabriel didn't seem to be in a hurry. He seemed to enjoy the garden as well, taking a deep breath and gazing up at the blanket of stars overhead. She did the same, relaxing as she tried to identify different constellations. Looking at the stars always made her problems seem less important, less significant. The universe was a big place.

When he finally got around to speaking, Serafia was ready to answer his questions. She was tired of hiding her illness, anyway. She might as well put it all out there, warts and all. It would likely put an end to their pointless flirtation and she could stop torturing herself with possibilities that didn't really exist.

"What was that all about in there? Really? Why is it so impossible that I would want you as you are, right now?"

"It's impossible for me to believe it because I know how seriously messed up I am, Gabriel. The truth is that I don't have a congenital heart defect and I didn't spend a year having surgeries to correct it."

Gabriel frowned at her. "Well, then, what really happened to you?"

Serafia sighed and shook her head. "No one knows the truth but my family and my doctors. My parents thought it would be easier for me if we told everyone the cover story, but that was all a lie. I had a heart attack on that runway because I had slowly and systematically tried to kill myself to be beautiful. The modeling industry is so high pressure and I couldn't stand up to it. I swallowed the lies they told me along with the prescription diet pills. I barely ate. I exercised six to eight hours a day. I abused cocaine, laxatives…anything that I thought would give me an edge and help me drop those last few pounds. My quest to be thinner, to be prettier, almost made me a very attractive corpse."

She was terrified to say the words aloud, but at the same time, it felt as if a weight was lifted from her chest. "The day I collapsed on the runway, I was five foot nine and ninety-three pounds. I was nothing but a walking skeleton and I received more compliments that morning than I ever had before. After I collapsed, I knew I had to leave the modeling industry because the environment was just too toxic. I had to spend a year in rehab and inpatient therapy for anorexia. I had to be completely reprogrammed, like I'd left some kind of cult."

Gabriel didn't recoil or react to her words. He just listened until she got it all out. "Are you better now?" he asked.

That was a difficult question to answer. Like an alcoholic, the danger of falling off the wagon was always there. "I've learned to manage. I've put so much strain on my heart that my day-to-day life is a very delicate balancing act. But for the most part, yes, the worst of it is behind me."

He sat studying her face for a few minutes. "I can't believe anyone had the audacity to tell you that you were anything but flawless. I mean, you're *Serafia*—supermodel extraordinaire, catwalk goddess and record holder for most *Vogue Italia* covers."

Once again, she started to squirm under his praise. "When you say things like that, Gabriel, it's really difficult for me to listen and even harder for me to accept. I was told for so long that I was fat and ugly and would never make it in the business. Even when I made it to the top, there's always someone there to try and knock you down. The modeling industry can be so venomous. You're never thin enough, pretty enough, talented enough, and both your competition and your customers feed you those criticisms every day. You believe something after you hear it enough times. Even all these years later, after all the therapy, there's a part of me that still believes that and thinks everything you're saying is just insincere flattery."

Gabriel reached out and covered her hand with his own. It was comforting and she was thankful for it, even as it surprised her. She expected him to finally see her flaws and run, but he didn't.

"It might be flattery, Serafia, but it's true. Every word. If I have to say it each day until you finally believe it, I will. I know how hard it can be to trust someone once that faith is abused. Once it's lost, it's almost impossible to get back, but I want to help you try."

There was a pain in his expression as he spoke. The lines deepened in his forehead with his frown. She knew something had happened to him in South

America. Perhaps now, perhaps here, after she'd told her story, he might finally tell her his. "How do you know? What happened to you, Gabriel?"

With a sigh, he sat back and looked up at the sliver of a moon overhead. "I was fresh from college and my father named me VP of South American Operations. As part of my job, I had to travel to our various shipping and trade ports in Brazil, Argentina, Venezuela and Chile. Dealing with Venezuela was controversial, but my father had decided that the country had oil and needed it shipped. Why shouldn't we profit from it instead of someone else?

"I saved Caracas for my last stop and things had gone so well in the other locations that I wasn't wary any longer by the time I arrived in Venezuela. I went down there and spent a few days getting acclimated and met with the team there. One evening, my guide and translator, Raoul, offered to take me out for an authentic Venezuelan dinner. The moment we stepped outside, a van pulled up by the curb. Raoul hit me on the back of the head with something and I blacked out. The next thing I knew, I was lying on a stinky, lumpy mattress in a cold, dark room with no windows. My wrists and ankles were tied with thick rope."

Serafia could barely believe what she was being told. How had she never heard about this before? She wanted to ask, but she didn't dare interrupt.

"When my captor finally showed up a few hours later, he told me that I was being held for ransom and as soon as my family paid them, I'd be released."

"Did they pay them?" she asked.

He avoided her gaze, swallowing hard before he spoke. "No. I was in that underground room in virtual darkness for over a week. Every day the guy would come down and bring me a jug of water and some food, but that was it. After about the sixth day alone with my thoughts, and with constant taunts from my captor that my family hadn't paid the ransom yet and must not care if I lived or died, I came to the conclusion that if I wanted out of this place, I'd have to save myself. And I decided that when I did, I was going to live the life I wanted from that moment on."

"You escaped?" Serafia asked, near breathless with suspense.

"My rusty metal bed frame was my savior. I used it to slowly cut through my bindings. It took almost all day to do it. When my captor opened the door to bring my evening meal, I was waiting for him. I leaped on him, beating his head against the concrete floor until he stopped fighting me. Once I was sure he was unconscious, I took his gun and keys, locking him in the room. It turned out he was my only guard, so I literally went up the stairs and walked out onto the busy streets of Caracas. I made my way to the US embassy, told them what had happened and I was back in Miami by sunrise."

Serafia was nearly speechless. "Did they ever catch the people responsible?"

"Raoul was arrested for his part in the conspiracy, but he was just a facilitator paid a flat fee for delivering me at a special place and time. They found my captor still locked in the room where they kept me. Anyone else who was involved got away with it. But really, in the end, I wasn't angry with them. I was angry with my family. They knew what could happen if they sent me down there."

"What did they say when you showed up at home?"

Gabriel stiffened beside her and shrugged. "They welcomed me home and then tried to pretend it never happened. But I could never forget."

It was a horrible story to hear, but suddenly so much of Gabriel's personality suddenly made sense to her. He never got close to anyone and got a lot of grief from his family for being superficial. Even Serafia had been guilty of judging him, thinking he cared more about partying than worrying about anything serious. She'd accused him of being reckless, but when they were both faced with death, they reacted differently. She became supercautious, nearly afraid to live life for fear of losing it for good. He had done the opposite: living every moment to the fullest in case it was his last. Who was she to judge him?

Serafia reached out and took his hand. She felt a surge of emotion when they touched. When she looked at him, for the first time she was able to see the sadness in his green eyes, the wariness behind the bright smile. The bad boy facade kept people away and she had fallen for it. She didn't want to keep him at arm's length any longer.

Gabriel gripped her hand in his, letting his thumb brush across her skin. It sent a shiver of awareness down her spine, urging her to lean in closer to him.

"I know that's a lot of information to process," he said. "I didn't tell it to you so you'd feel bad for me. I told you because I wanted you to understand that we're coming from a similar place. No one is perfect. We're all messed up somehow. But it's how we deal with it that matters. I'm an expert at pushing people away. You're the first woman I've ever met who had made me want to try to trust someone again. Stop thinking that you don't measure up somehow, because you're wrong."

Serafia gasped at his bold words. She couldn't hold back any longer. She lunged forward, pressing her lips against his own before she lost her nerve. It had been a long time since she had trusted herself in all the various areas of her life, and romance had fallen to the bottom of the stack. What good was she to a man in the state she was in? Especially a prince? Still, she couldn't help herself. And neither could Gabriel.

He met her kiss with equal enthusiasm. He held her face in his hands, drawing her closer and drinking her in. He groaned against her lips and then let his tongue slip along hers. His touch made her insides turn molten with need and wore away the last of her self-control.

At last, Gabriel pulled away, their rapid breaths hovering between them in the night air. "Is it too early to make our exit?" he asked.

Serafia shook her head and looked into his eyes. "I think the prince can leave whenever he wants to."

It wasn't as simple to leave as Gabriel had hoped. He'd had to make the rounds, thank Patrick for his hospitality and avoid the cutting glares of his father, but within half an hour, he and Serafia were in the back of the royal limousine on their way home to Playa del Onda.

When they climbed inside, Gabriel couldn't look away from the high slit in her pink gown and how it climbed nearly to her hip as she sat. He wanted to run his hands over that bare skin. His palms tingled with the need to reach for her, but there was a forty-five-minute drive home from the Rowling Estate.

Eyeballing the limousine's tinted partition, Gabriel called out to his driver, "We're going to need a little privacy back here, please."

"Of course, Your Majesty." In an instant, the heavily tinted glass slid up, blocking them from their driver's view and making for a more private drive home.

"What are you doing?" Serafia asked.

Gabriel turned to her, placing his hand on her knee. "I want you. Right now. I can't wait until we get back."

"We're in a car, Gabriel. The driver is right there. The royal guard are in the SUV right behind us."

"They can't see us." His hand glided higher up her leg, brushing at the sensitive skin of her inner thigh. "Whether or not the driver *hears* us is up to you."

"I don't know about this," Serafia said, biting her full bottom lip.

Gabriel brushed his fingertips along the lacy barrier of her panties, making her gasp. "You may have reformed me, but there's still a little bad boy inside me." He stroked harder, making her stiffen and close her eyes. He leaned into her, placing a searing kiss against her neck before he whispered, "Let's both be bad tonight."

He gripped one strap of her gown, easing it down her shoulder, and then dipped his head to taste her flesh, nibbling on the column of her throat, the hollow behind her ear and the round of her shoulder. He slipped one hand behind her, finding the zipper of her gown and tugging it down enough to allow her gown to slip farther and expose the round globes of her large breasts.

They were more glorious than he'd ever imagined after seeing her in bikinis and skimpy gowns on magazine covers. "So beautiful," he murmured as his gaze devoured her. They were full and heavy, tipped with tight mocha nipples that he immediately covered with his hands and then his mouth.

Serafia bit her lip hard to keep from crying out as his tongue flicked across her skin. He teased her flesh, and then sucked hard at her breast. The hand he'd kept beneath her gown continued to stroke her, finally slipping under the lacy edge of her panties to feel the moist heat of her desire hiding beneath it.

"Gabriel!" she exclaimed in a hoarse whisper.

"Just lie back and enjoy it," he replied, turning with her as she leaned back across the seat to rest on her elbows. When she shifted her hips, he was better able to slide her gown out of the way and part her thighs. He stopped touching her only long enough to slip off her panties.

When he returned, he leaned down, parted her flesh and stroked her with his tongue. Serafia squirmed and writhed against him, but he didn't let up. He wrapped his arms around her thighs to hold her steady as he teased at her sensitive flesh again and again. Gabriel waited until he had her hovering on the edge; then he slipped one finger inside her. It sent her tumbling over, gasping and whimpering as quietly as she could manage while her release rocked through her.

When at last her body stilled except for her rapid breaths, Gabriel pulled away. While she recovered, he unbuttoned his suit pants and tugged them down. Reaching into his back pocket, he pulled a condom from his wallet and slipped it over the length of him. When he turned back to Serafia, she was watching him with a twinkle of deviousness in her dark eyes.

He reached for her and tugged her into his lap, her thighs straddling him as the limousine raced down the highway. Gabriel gripped her waist as she eased down and pushed him inside her. He gritted his teeth and pressed desperate fingertips into her flesh as he fought for control. She felt amazing. When he was buried fully inside her, he held her still for a moment, then reached for her face. He pulled her forward and captured her lips with his own.

As his tongue slipped inside her mouth and stroked her, he started moving slowly beneath her. Pushing the pink organza of her gown out of the way, he gripped the curve of her rear to guide her hips. At first, their movements were deliciously slow, and he savored every pang of pleasure. As the intensity built, they moved more frantically. Serafia grasped his shoulders and threw her head back, a silent cry in her throat.

"Let go for me," Gabriel pressed. "I want to watch it happen. You're so beautiful when you come undone."

She found her release again. This time, he held her close, not just watching, but feeling the pleasurable tremors running through her body and experiencing them with her. Her inner muscles tightened around him, coaxing his own release. As she collapsed against him, he wrapped his arms around her waist and thrust into her one last time. He buried his face in her neck, growling his climax against her flushed skin.

They sat together, not moving for several minutes.

In the stillness, Gabriel was finally able to mentally catch up with everything that had happened in the last few hours.

The moment he had stepped out into the garden after her, he knew things would be different. He wasn't going to let her keep pulling away from him, and if opening up to her about his own past was what it took, he was willing to do it. She…inspired him in a way no other woman had. It wasn't just an attraction; it was more. She didn't want anything from him. Unlike the sharks circling around the Rowling ballroom, Serafia didn't need his money and she certainly didn't want to share his spotlight. He felt that she was someone he could trust, especially after she shared her own story with him. Her past was different from his but he could tell that it had scarred her in a similar way. The difference was that he didn't trust others and she didn't trust herself. But she should. And he wanted to help her with that.

It made her ever more attractive to him, if that was possible. She wasn't just the supermodel from his teenage fantasies. She was so much more. He just had to convince her of that.

"The car is slowing down," Serafia noted. She climbed from his lap and quickly started pulling herself back together.

Gabriel turned and looked out the window. They were approaching the gate to the compound. "We're home. Time to get dressed so we can go inside and I can take it all off you again."

Serafia tugged the top of her dress back up over her shoulders and looked at him. "Really?"

How silly she was to doubt him on that point. "Oh yes," Gabriel said in a tone as serious as he was capable of. "That was just to hold me over until we got home."

Seven

Serafia woke up the next morning with a small smile on her lips. Opening her eyes, she spied Gabriel's broad shoulders as he slept beside her. She rolled onto her back with a yawn and reached for her phone to check the time. It was eight-thirty, practically midday for her. She wasn't surprised, considering that Gabriel hadn't let her sleep until after three.

Flinging back the sheets, she gently slipped out of the bed so she wouldn't wake Gabriel. She snatched up a blanket off the foot of the bed, wrapped it around her naked body and walked toward the wall of French doors that led from the master bedroom onto a secluded patio that overlooked the sea.

She stepped out onto the balcony, pulling the door shut behind her. The sun was bright, warming her skin as she took in the remarkable view.

Playa del Onda was built on a sheer cliff overlooking the sea. It was perched at the apex of a crescent-shaped bay lined with sailboats and beaches that would hopefully draw tourists now that the Tantaberras had fallen. The water was an enchanting mix of blues and greens that begged you to dip a toe into it. It reminded her of her hacienda in Barcelona. Her view overlooked the Mediterranean, but the feelings it inspired in her were the same. Peacefulness. The ability to breathe. Relaxation.

She wanted to take a mug of coffee and sit out here the rest of the morning, but that just wasn't possible. The house was crawling with guards and servants. She couldn't stroll into the kitchen wearing a blanket and slip back into the prince's suite without someone noticing. Not that it was necessarily a secret to those who'd traveled back to the beach house with them last night, but she thought it was inappropriate to flaunt it.

As it was, she needed to get down the hall to her own room. Going back inside, she checked to see that Gabriel was still asleep. She had worked wonders with his transformation, but bless him, he was still a night owl.

She retrieved her gown from the floor and slipped it back on, and then slowly opened the door of his bedroom, glancing both ways down the hall to see if anyone was there. The coast was clear. She slipped out, pulling the door closed. She had taken about three steps toward her room when she heard something behind her.

"Good morning, Señorita Espina."

She turned to find the houseman, Luca, standing behind her. "Good morning, Luca," she said, self-consciously smoothing her hand over her tousled hair and trying to downplay how overdressed she was for the early morning hours.

His dark gaze traveled over her quickly, a twinkle of amusement in his eyes, but he didn't mention her appearance. "Is His Majesty still sleeping?" he asked.

"Yes, he is. But he should be getting up soon. Please wake him by ten if he hasn't roused by then."

"As you wish."

Serafia started to turn back toward her room, and then she stopped. "Please don't mention this to anyone," she said.

Luca shook his head. "Of course not, señorita. The affairs of the prince are no one's concern but the prince's. But..." He hesitated. "You should know your involvement with the prince is no secret."

Serafia looked up at him with eyes wide with panic. "What does that mean?"

He unfolded the Alma newspaper he'd been clutching in his hand and held it up for her to read. On the front page, just below the article about Gabriel's big introduction at the Rowling party, was a headline that read *"The Future Queen?"* Another article followed, speculating about a romance brewing between her and Gabriel. A grainy black-and-white photo of them kissing by the fountain accompanied the story.

With a sigh, she closed her eyes. She felt foolish for thinking she could have one moment of privacy. "Thank you for showing me this, Luca. May I take it to my room and read it?"

He folded the paper and handed it to her. "Of course."

Serafia tucked it under her arm. "Please don't mention it to the prince until I have a chance to read the article. I'll discuss it with him at breakfast."

"As you wish. I'll have Marta start preparing it."

Luca disappeared down the hallway, leaving Serafia with the newspaper clutched against her. Before anyone else saw her, she dashed down the hallway to her own room.

Throwing the paper onto the bed, she headed straight for the shower. As the steaming hot water pounded her sore muscles and washed away Gabriel's scent from her skin, her mind started to race with the implications of the article. From what little she'd read, the tone didn't seem negative. The prince and his quest for a bride would be front page news no matter who he was seen with. But that didn't do much to calm her anxiety.

She should've known better than to think that someone hadn't noticed their departure from the ballroom and followed them outside. She hadn't noticed anyone there, but with the walls of hedges and arborvitae columns, there were plenty of places to hide and spy on their painfully private moments together.

Hopefully whoever took their picture hadn't been able to hear their conversation over the sound of the nearby fountain. The photo was one thing, but she didn't want the revelations about her departure from modeling to taint Gabriel somehow.

Stepping from the shower, Serafia wrapped herself in a fluffy white towel and started combing through the thick and easily tangled strands of her hair. She rushed through the rest of her morning routine. Trying to maintain a bit of professionalism, she put her hair up in a tight bun and dressed in a dark plum pantsuit. They had another official event to attend this afternoon, so she might as well get ready and put her consultant hat back on.

After she slipped on her shoes, she reached for the paper and read through both articles on Gabriel. The first, about his introduction at the Rowling party, was extremely positive. The consensus was that he was well received and those in attendance were pleased to have such a fine man to be their future king.

The second article, about her, wasn't really bad, either. It discussed the various ladies he had danced with that night, highlighting Helena Ruiz as his first choice and Serafia as his last. Of course, there was the photo of them kissing, and then a lot of speculation about whether or not she was really his social secretary, or if it was a cover for their relationship. If they were dating, was it serious? Might she be their new queen? The few people they interviewed for the article seemed to think she'd make a good candidate for queen of Alma and would make a charming match for Gabriel.

It wasn't a horrible write-up, but she really wished she could have avoided the papers. How could he turn around and select one of the other women in Alma after this? No one wanted to be second choice and really, she wasn't in the running to be queen, despite what they might think.

Or was she?

Gabriel seemed as serious about her as he had been about anything they'd discussed so far. He'd swept her off her feet and for once, she'd gone with it and had an amazing night. She hadn't entertained second thoughts about it, but now anxiety started pooling in her stomach. She wasn't opposed to being his lover, but queen? She wasn't sure she could handle that. The only people more famous in Europe than models were the royal families. The United Kingdom's Princess Kate couldn't wear an unflattering dress or have a bad hair day without it being in the papers and commented on. Every time Prince Harry was seen with a woman, the rumors would fly.

Serafia knew what it was like. In her modeling days, it wasn't enough for everyone to critique her appearance, and they did. Her whole life was public. The cameras showed up on dates, on vacations, while she was trying to spend a day with her family. If she was dating anyone famous, the magnifying glass tripled along with the coverage. It was incredibly difficult to maintain a relationship under the microscope, much less a shred of self-esteem.

It had nearly killed her to do it, but Serafia had escaped the spotlight. Gabriel's queen would be subject to the same kind of scrutiny. The private would become painfully public, with every aspect of her life exposed. She had no intention of ever going back in front of the cameras.

Even for Gabriel. Even for the chance to be queen. She would be much happier in Barcelona, living a quiet, unexciting life. Passionless, yes, but private.

With a sigh, she folded up the paper and headed out to breakfast. By the time she reached the dining hall, Gabriel was dressed and waiting for her there. Without her standing by the closet, laying out his clothes, he'd opted for a pair of jeans and a clingy green T-shirt that matched his eyes. His hair was still wet and slicked back, his cheeks still slightly pink from his shave. He was sipping a cup of coffee and thumbing through emails on his smart phone.

"Good morning," she said as she entered the room.

She had her tablet in one hand and the newspaper in the other.

Gabriel smiled wide when he looked up at her. There was a wicked light in his eyes. "Good morning."

Serafia took a seat at the table across from him, holding off their discussion as Marta poured her a cup of coffee and returned to the kitchen to bring out their breakfast. They were three bites into their *tortilla de patatas* before she spoke about it.

"Apparently," she began, "we were not the only people out in the garden last night. Our kiss made the front page of the newspaper." She laid the paper out on the table for Gabriel to look at it.

He picked it up, reading over the article as he chewed his eggs, a thoughtful expression on his face. "I'm not surprised," he said at last, dropping the paper on the table and returning to his breakfast. He didn't seem remotely concerned.

"It doesn't bother you?" she asked.

"This isn't my first romance documented in a gossip column. Nor is it yours, I'd wager. There's nothing inflammatory about it, so why should I care? You're not a dark secret I'm trying to hide."

"The press scrutiny will be higher now. They'll question every moment we're together. We'll need to meet with your press secretary, Hector, to discuss how to handle it."

"I know how we'll handle it," he said, sipping his orange juice. "The palace will not comment on the personal life of the prince. Period. If and when I select a queen, I will announce it through the proper channels, not through some gossip column. They can speculate all they like. It doesn't concern me."

Serafia sat back in her chair. She was near speech-less. That was the most tactful and diplomatic thing he could've said on the subject. Maybe her lessons were finally sinking in. "That is an excellent answer. I'll make sure Hector knows that's the official position of the palace."

After a few minutes of silent eating, Gabriel put down his fork and looked at her. "What do you think about the article? You seemed to be more concerned about it than I am. Am I missing something?"

"No, it's not the content of the article itself, so much as being in it. I've lived happily out of the spotlight for years," she explained. "Finding myself back in the papers was…unnerving to say the least."

"Do you regret last night?" he asked.

Serafia's gaze lifted to meet his. "No. But I regret not being smarter about it."

Gabriel nodded and speared a bite of tortilla with his fork. "Good. Then we can do it again."

Lord, but Gabriel was hot. He would've been much more comfortable in the jeans and T-shirt he'd started the day in, but Serafia had made him change before they left Playa del Onda. Did Serafia give no thought when she selected his wardrobe that he would be tour-ing the countryside of Alma in July? The vineyards were beautiful, and he really was interested in every-thing Tomás was telling him, but it was hard to focus when he could feel his back sweating under his suit coat.

As they walked through the arbors, he turned to look at Serafia. She had her hair up in a bun off her neck. She was wearing a wide-brimmed hat and a linen shift dress in a light green that looked infinitely cooler than his own suit.

"I'm dying here," he whispered, leaning into Serafia's ear. "I'm no good to anyone if I melt into a puddle."

"We're going inside in a minute."

Gabriel sighed. "We better be or I'm going to look terrible if the press take any more photos." There was a small group invited to the vineyard today. They'd taken some shots as he arrived and as they toured the fields and sampled grapes from the vines, but they had given him some space after that. They were probably hot, too, and waiting for the group to return to the air-conditioned comfort of the building.

"Such a warm day!" Tomás declared. "Let's head inside. I'll give you a tour of the wine cave, and then we'll get to the good part and sample my wares."

Gabriel's ears perked up at the mention of a wine cellar. He was happy to go inside, but that didn't sound like a place he was interested in visiting. "Did he say 'cave'?" he asked as they trekked back up the hill to the villa.

Serafia frowned at him. "Yes. Why?"

"I don't like going underground."

"I'm sure it will be fine. Just relax," she insisted. "We really need a nice, uneventful visit today."

Gabriel snorted. She was optimistic to a fault. "Do you actually think that's ever going to happen with me as the king?"

She tipped her head up to look at him from under the wide brim of her white-and-green hat. Her nose wrinkled delicately as she said, "Probably not, but I'll keep striving for it. Before long, I'll be turning you over to your staff and going home. I hope they're prepared."

They finally reached the top of the hill and stepped through the large doors of the warehouse. Inside, they were greeted by a servant with a tray of sparkling water and a bowl with cool towels.

"Please, take a minute to cool off," Tomás said. "Have you enjoyed the tour so far?"

"It's been lovely, Tomás. There's no doubt that this is the finest vineyard in Alma," Serafia said, sipping her water.

She must not have trusted Gabriel to say the right thing. "It's a beautiful property," he chimed in. "How many acres do you have here?"

"About two hundred. It's been in my family for ten generations."

"You withstood all the political upheaval?"

Gabriel felt Serafia tense beside him. He supposed it was impolite to ask the residents of Alma how they managed to cope with the dictatorship, but he was curious. Some fled, but most made the best of it somehow.

"My great-grandfather refused to abandon his family's home. It was that simple. To survive, we supplied our finest wines to the Tantaberras and were forced to pay their heavy commercial taxes, but we survived better than others. We had a commodity he wanted."

Lucky. Gabriel sipped the last of his water and after dabbing his neck and forehead, returned the cloth to the bowl. "And now?"

Tomás smiled brightly. "Much better, Your Grace. Now we are finally able to export our wines to Europe and America. Before, we were restricted by heavy trade embargos that punished us more than the dictatorship. The free trade of the last few months has had a huge impact on our sales and profits. We were able to hire more staff and plant more grapes this year than ever before. We are prospering."

Gabriel smiled. He had nothing to do with the changes, but he was happy to see them. Serafia had impressed upon him how hard it had been on his people since the Montoros left. He was glad to see the course reverse so quickly with the Tantaberras gone.

"Are we ready to continue?"

Gabriel was not, but he followed behind Tomás, anyway. A few of the journalists joined them as they walked through the warehouse to a heavy oak door. Tomás went down first with a few others, leaving Gabriel standing at the top of the stairs with a sense of dread pooling in his stomach. His hands clutched the railing, but his feet refused to take another step.

"Go!" Serafia urged him from behind.

He could see Tomás standing at the bottom of the stairs waiting for him with a few reporters. The light was dim and the air cool. Their host had an expectant look on his face as he stood there waiting for Gabriel to follow.

Serafia nudged him in the back with her knee and he took a few steps down without really wanting to. It was only two more steps to the bottom, so he forced himself to go the rest of the way down. At the very least he needed to keep going so that the ladder would be clear for his escape. Right now Serafia, a vineyard assistant and a few other reporters were behind him.

Gabriel took a labored breath and looked around him. The room was bigger than he'd expected. The long corridor with its arched ceiling stretched on for quite a distance. Dim gold lights were spaced out down the hall, providing enough light to see the hundreds of barrels stored there.

The air was also fresher than he'd anticipated. He looked up, spying air vents that led to some type of ventilation system. At least the room didn't smell of stale bread and mildew. But it didn't need to. Gabriel's brain easily conjured those smells. Dank, musty air filled his lungs, tainted with the stench of his own waste and leftover food that was rotting in the corner of his prison.

"This is my pride and joy," Tomás said, taking a few steps down the rows of barrels. "This is a natural cave my family found on the property. It was perfect for storing our wine barrels, so we didn't have to build a separate cellar. My great-grandfather added the electrical lighting and ventilation system so we can maintain the perfect temperature and humidity for the wine."

He continued to talk, but Gabriel couldn't hear him. All he could hear was his own heartbeat pounding in his ears. There were no windows, no natural light. He hated that. He couldn't even stand his room at the palace with the dim light and cavelike conditions.

It was all too much. He could feel the walls start to close in on him. He could feel the rope chafing his ankles. Beads of perspiration that had nothing to do with heat formed on his brow and on his palms. He rubbed his hands absently against the fabric of his light gray suit, but it didn't help. They were starting to tremble.

"We have nearly five hundred barrels—"

"I have to go!" Gabriel announced, interrupting Tomás and pushing through the crowd to reach the staircase. He ignored the commotion around him, taking the steps two at a time until he reached the ground floor.

There, he could finally take a breath. Bending over, he clasped his knees and closed his eyes. He breathed slowly, willing his heart rate to drop and his muscles to unwind. He stood upright and turned when he heard the stampede of footsteps coming up the steps behind him.

"Your Majesty, are you well?" Tomás approached him, placing a cautious hand on his shoulder.

Gabriel raised his arm to dismiss his concerns. "I'm fine. I'm sorry about that. I don't do well in closed in spaces."

"I wish I had known. I would never have taken you down there. Señorita Espina didn't mention it."

"She didn't know." Not really. He'd explained about his kidnapping the night before, but he hadn't expressed how much things like small spaces or wrist watches bothered him as a result. He didn't like talking about it. To him, it felt like a weakness. Kings weren't supposed to have panic attacks. He didn't mind being flawed, but he hated for anyone, and especially Serafia, to think of him as weak.

"Gabriel, are you okay?" Serafia asked, coming to his side with concern pinching her brow.

"I just needed some air. Sorry, everyone, the heat must've gotten to me," he said more loudly to the crowd that followed him.

"I think what you need is a seat on the veranda with some wine and food to reinforce you," Tomás suggested.

They followed the crowd into the villa, but before they entered, Serafia tugged at his jacket and held him back. "What was all that about?" she asked once they were alone.

As much as he hated to tell her, he needed to. He couldn't have another incident like this. "I've developed a sort of claustrophobia since my kidnapping. I can't take small or dark spaces, especially underground ones like the room where I was kept. I have panic attacks. It's the same with watches. I can't bear the feel of things against my wrists."

Serafia sighed and brought her hand to his cheek. "Why didn't you tell me?"

Gabriel covered her hand with his own and pulled it down to his chest. When he looked into her dark brown eyes, he felt overcome with the urge to tell her whatever she wanted. He wanted to be honest with someone for the first time since he came home from Venezuela. Serafia was the one person he could trust with his secrets.

"Because I've never told anyone."

Eight

Serafia got up early the next morning, slipping from Gabriel's bed to get ready. An hour later she returned and started sifting through his clothes for the perfect outfit.

"It's seven-thirty," he groaned as he sat up in bed. His hair was tousled and as the sheets pooled around his waist, Serafia couldn't help stealing a glance at the hard muscles she'd become accustomed to touching each night. "Why are you up so early clinking wooden hangers together?"

With a sigh, she turned back to the closet. "I'm trying to figure out what you should wear today for the parade."

"I'm going to be in a parade?"

It was becoming clear to her that in the early days of working together, Gabriel had paid very little attention to what she'd said. The prime minister's office had arranged for a full week of activities and Gabriel had been briefed on them in detail while they were still in Miami. And yet each day was like a surprise for him.

After the incident at the vineyard, Serafia was afraid to know if Gabriel had a problem with parades, too. She didn't dare ask. "Yes. As we discussed in Miami," she emphasized, "they're holding a welcome parade for you this morning that will go through the capital of Del Sol."

"Are there going to be marching bands and floats or something?"

"No, it's not really that kind of parade." She pulled out a gray pin-striped suit coat. It would be too hot for his ceremonial attire and that was better saved for the coronation parade, anyway. A nice suit would be just right, she thought. Eyeing the ties, she pondered which would look best. She knew Gabriel would be more inclined to skip the tie, but that wouldn't look right. She frowned at the closet. The more she got to know Gabriel, the more she realized she was trying to force him into a box he didn't really fit in, but he was still royalty and needed to dress appropriately.

"People are just going to stand out on the sidewalk and wait for me to come by and wave? Like the pope?"

Serafia looked at him with exasperation and planted her hands on her hips. "You're going to be the king! Yes. People want to see you, even if it's just for a moment as you drive by and wave. It won't be as big as your formal coronation parade, but it gives everyone in Alma the chance to come and see you, not just the press or the rich people at Patrick Rowling's party."

"For their sake, I hope there are at least vendors out

there selling some good street food," he muttered as he climbed out of bed.

"Get in the shower," Serafia said, laying the suit out across the bed.

Gabriel came up behind her and pulled her into his arms, crushing her back against his bare body. "Wanna get in there with me?" his low voice grumbled into her ear.

Serafia felt a thrill rush through her body, but she fought the reaction. They didn't have time for this now, as much as she'd like to indulge. There were thousands of people already lining the streets in the hopes of getting a good spot to see Gabriel. She turned in his arms and kissed him, then quickly pulled away. "Sorry, but you're going it alone today," she said. "We leave in less than an hour."

She was amazed they were able to keep to their schedule, but everything went to plan. They rendezvoused with the rest of the motorcade a few miles away from the advertised route. Gabriel was transferred to a convertible where he could sit on the top of the backseats and wave to the crowd. Royal guards and Del Sol police would be driving ahead of his car and behind, with guards running alongside them.

"Remember," Serafia said as he got settled in the back of the car. "Smile, wave, be sure to turn to look at both sides of the street. People are excited to see you. Be excited to see them, too, and you'll win the hearts of your people. I'll see you at the end of the route."

"I thought you might ride with me."

Serafia shook her head. "You're Prince Gabriel, soon to be King Gabriel. As far as anyone else knows, I'm your social secretary. Social secretaries wouldn't ride along on something like this. We don't need to give the newspapers any more material to put into their gossip columns. So no, I'm not going with you. You'll do fine."

Ignoring nearly everything she'd just said, he leaned in and gave her a kiss in front of fifty witnesses. Hopefully none of them had cameras. "See you on the flip side," he said.

Serafia shook her head and climbed into another car that was driving ahead to ensure that the route was clear and to secure the end rendezvous location.

Looking out the window, she was impressed by how many people were lining the streets. Thousands of people from all over, young and old alike, had come to the capital to see Gabriel. Some held signs of welcome; others had white carnations, the official flower of Alma, to throw into the street in front of Gabriel's car. Their faces lit up with excitement and anticipation as they saw Serafia's official palace vehicle drive down the road, indicating that the new king would soon follow.

They needed a reason to smile. The Tantaberras had ruled over these people with an iron fist for too long. They deserved freedom and hope, and she sincerely believed that Gabriel could be the one to bring it to them. He wasn't the most traditional choice for a king, but he was a good man. He was caring and thoughtful. There might be a rocky start, but she could tell these people were desperate for the excitement of a new king, a new queen and the kind of royal baby countdown that the British had recently enjoyed.

Serafia spied a different sign as they neared the end of the route. A little girl was holding up a board with Gabriel's picture and her own. Across the top and bottom in blue glitter it read "We need a fairy tale romance! King Gabriel & Queen Serafia forever!"

A few feet down, another declared "We have our king, please choose Serafia as our queen!" This one was held by an older woman. A third declared "Unite the Montoros & the Espinas at last!"

Serafia sat back in her seat in surprise. Although she preferred to avoid the press in general, the tone of the earlier article about her and Gabriel had been positive. The crowd here today seemed to corroborate that. They had their king and now they wanted their fairy tale. But her? Serafia didn't need to be anyone's queen. She was done with the spotlight.

The only hitch was her growing feelings for Gabriel. She'd never planned them. If she was honest, she hadn't wanted to have feelings for him at all. And yet, over the last two weeks, he had charmed his way into her heart. She wasn't in love, but she was closer than she'd been in a very long time. Her time with Gabriel was coming to an end. Soon he would be on his own, transitioning into his role as king. Serafia planned to return to Barcelona when it was over.

But as the time ticked away, she felt herself dreading that day. What was her alternative? To stay? To let her relationship with Gabriel grow into something real? That would give the people of Alma what they wanted, but it came at too high a price. Serafia didn't want to be queen. She was done with the criticism and the magnifying glass examining her every decision and action.

The car stopped at a park and she got out, waiting with a small crew of guards and Hector Vega, who was speaking to some journalists. She found a spot in the shade where she could lean against one of the vehicles and wait for the royal motorcade. It wasn't in sight yet, so she glanced down to pull out her tablet to make some notes.

"Serafia?"

She looked up at the sound of a woman's voice and noticed Felicia Gomez and her daughter crossing the street to speak with her. The older woman had traded her ball gown for a more casual blouse and slacks, but she was wearing almost as many diamonds. She was smiling as much as her Botox would allow, but there wasn't much sincerity in the look. Dita was wearing a sundress and a fresh-faced look guaranteed to turn Gabriel's head.

Serafia swallowed her negative observations and tried to smile with more warmth than she had. "Señora Gomez, Dita. Good morning. How are you?"

"I'm well," Felicia replied, coming to stand beside her. "We came down in the hopes we'd get a chance to speak with the prince after the parade. We didn't get a lot of time at the Rowling party."

Felicia's tone was pointed, as though Serafia were the one responsible for that fact. In a way she was, she supposed. Serafia didn't want the crown, but she really didn't want the spoiled Dita to have it, either.

Instead of responding, Serafia just smiled and turned to look down the street. She could see the motorcycle cops leading the motorcade. "Here's your opportunity," she said.

Within a few minutes, all the vehicles had pulled into the park. Gabriel leaped out of the back of the convertible with athletic grace. He shook the hands of his driver and the guards who were running along with him, and then made his way over to Serafia. He was smiling as he looked at her, barely paying any attention to the Gomez women standing beside her.

"I'm starving," he said. "All that waving and smiling has worked up a hellacious appetite. I caught a whiff of something delicious on the parade route. I think it was coming from this little tapas place. I tried to remember the landmarks and I'm determined to track it down for lunch."

"That's fine, we're almost done here."

"What else do I have to do?" he asked.

Serafia shifted her gaze toward the two expectant women beside her without turning her head. Gabriel followed the movement and put on his practiced smile when he noticed who it was. She'd taught him well, it seemed. "Señora and Señorita Gomez have been waiting for you."

"Your Grace," Felicia said as both she and Dita gave a brief curtsey. "We'd hoped to have a moment of your time after the parade. The party had simply too many people for us to have a proper conversation."

That translated to: *You didn't spend enough time with my daughter and if she's going to be queen, she needs time to work her charms on you.*

"Are you hungry?" he asked.

Felicia seemed a little taken aback. "Hungry, Your Grace?"

"I was just telling Señorita Espina that I spied the most delicious-smelling tapas restaurant. It looks like a hole in the wall, but I'm anxious to try it. Would you care to join us?"

Serafia could see the conflict in Felicia's eyes. The Gomez family wasn't one to be seen at a run-down tapas restaurant. Serafia fought to hold in a twitter of laughter as she watched the older woman choose between two unpleasant fates—dining with commoners and being turned away by the prince once again. There was a pained expression on her face as she finally responded.

"That is very kind of Your Grace. We have already eaten, unfortunately. But perhaps you would give us the honor of hosting you at our home for dinner sometime soon."

"That's a very kind offer. I'll see when I can take you up on it. It was good to see you both again. Señora Gomez. Señorita Gomez," he said, tipping his head to each in turn. "Have a lovely afternoon."

At that, he smiled and put his arm around Serafia's shoulder. Together, they made their way from the disgruntled Gomez women over to his private car to track down some tasty tapas.

Serafia waited until the car door was shut and the tinted windows blocked them from sight, and then burst out laughing. "Did you see the look on her face when you invited her to go get some lunch? I nearly dislocated a rib trying not to laugh."

"Did I handle it okay?"

"You did very well. It isn't your fault she won't stoop to the level of an average person. She isn't going to give up, though. She wants you to marry Dita and she'll keep trying until you do."

Gabriel looked at her in a way that made her bones turn to melted butter. "She can *try*," he said. "But I'll be the one with the crown on my head. I make the decisions when it comes to who I date and who I'll marry."

Serafia felt her heart stutter in her chest as he spoke the words, looking intently at her. She knew in that moment that she needed to be very, very careful if she didn't want the crown of Alma on her head, as well.

The following morning, Gabriel decided he wanted to take his breakfast out on the patio overlooking the sea. The weather was beautiful, the skies were blue and the fresh sea air reminded him of home.

Sitting in the shade of the veranda, he sipped the coffee Luca brought him and watched a sailboat slip across the bay. How long had it been since he'd gone sailing? Too long. Once this coronation business was over and he could settle into being king, he intended to remedy that.

He could just picture Serafia standing on the deck, clutching the railing and watching the water as they cut through the waves. He imagined her wearing nothing but a pair of linen shorts hugging the curve of her rear and a bikini top tied around her neck. Her golden skin would darken in the sun, her long dark hair blowing in the sea breeze.

That sounded like heaven. It made him wonder if there was already a boat in the possession of the royal family. If there was, he'd ensure that they took it out for a spin as soon as possible.

As he took another sip, Luca appeared in the doorway. "Luca, do you know if we have a boat?"

"A boat, Your Grace?"

"Yes. We have a beach house. Do we have a boat?"

"Yes, there is a sailboat at the marina. The youngest Tantaberra was an avid sailor."

At the marina. Perhaps they could go out sooner than later. When he looked back at Luca, he realized he had the Alma newspaper in his hand. "Is that today's paper?" he asked.

Judging by the concerned expression on Luca's face, the latest royal coverage was not as positive as he'd hoped. He imagined the press had had a field day ragging on him about that panic attack at the vineyard. It wasn't the most kingly thing he'd done this week. He'd thought the parade went alright, though.

Gabriel frowned as he looked at Luca. "That good, eh? Should I go ahead and call Hector?"

"Señor Vega already knows, Your Grace. Ernesto called a moment ago to let me know that Señor Vega was already on his way here to speak with you."

Great. Gabriel would much rather use his spare time to get acquainted with every square inch of Serafia's body, but instead he would be discussing damage-control strategies with his high-strung press secretary. He had only met Hector a few times, and that was enough. The man consumed entirely too much caffeine. At least, Gabriel hoped he did. If the man was naturally that spun-up, he felt bad for the mother who'd had to chase him around as a toddler.

Hector made him anxious. Serafia made him calm. He knew exactly who he preferred to work with. He had to convince her to stay beyond the end of the week, be it as a paid employee or as his girlfriend.

"Let me see the damage before he gets here," Gabriel said, reaching out for the paper. "It must be bad if Hector immediately hopped in his car."

Gabriel glanced at the headlines, expecting the story to be about him, but instead he found a scathing story about the Espina family. He looked up at Luca. "Have you told Miss Espina about this, yet?"

"No, sir, but she should be down for breakfast momentarily. Would you like me to warn her?"

"No, I'll tell her."

Maybe they could have a game plan before Hector arrived and started spinning.

Turning back to the article, he started reading it in depth. Apparently, back when the coup took place in the 1940s, there were rumors about the loyalty of the Espina family. He hadn't heard that before. Surely if there had been any legitimacy to that claim, their families wouldn't have vacationed together and his father wouldn't have allowed Serafia to work with him these past few weeks.

Of course, his father had been quite curt where Serafia was concerned. He'd alluded to her family being unsuitable somehow, but Gabriel hadn't had a moment alone with his father to press him on that point. He was sure it was nothing to do with Serafia herself. Gabriel had chalked up his father's bad mood to jealousy. That was the most likely reason for his behavior since they arrived in Alma.

"Good morning." Serafia slipped out onto the patio in a pair of black capris and a sleeveless top. Her dark hair was swept up into a ponytail and she was wearing bejeweled sandals instead of dress pumps. They didn't have any official events on the calendar today, so she had apparently dressed for a more casual afternoon by the sea.

"Hector is on his way," he replied, not mincing words.

Serafia's smile faded and she slipped down into the other chair. "What happened?"

"Apparently the newspaper headlines have gone from speculating about your role as future queen to speculating about your family's role in the overthrow of the Montoros."

Serafia's eyebrows drew together in concern as she reached for the paper. "What are they talking about?" Her gaze flicked over the paper. "This is ridiculous. Our families aren't enemies and we most certainly didn't have anything do with the coup. Have they forgotten that the Espinas were driven from Alma, too? They lived in Switzerland for years until the dictatorship fell in Spain. I was born in Madrid just a few years after they left Switzerland."

Gabriel shrugged. "I am deficient in Alman history. We should probably fix that. I didn't even have a clue our families had been rivals for the throne at one point."

"That was over a hundred years ago. How is that even relevant to what's going on now?"

"It has everything to do with what's happening now," Hector Vega said, appearing in the doorway and butting into their conversation. He, too, had the newspaper under his arm. "Your family had the crown stolen away from them two hundred years ago. The Espinas and Montoros fought for years to seize control of these islands. The Montoros ended up winning and eventually the families did reconcile. They even planned to marry and combine the bloodlines.

"But," he continued ominously, "Rafael the First broke off his engagement with Rosa Espina to marry Anna Maria. There were more than a few hurt feelings about that and plenty of rumors went around during the time of the coup about the Espinas' involvement. Your whole family vanished from Alma right before everything fell apart. Some see that as suspicious."

"And now?" Serafia pressed. "I think my family has gotten over the embarrassment of a broken engagement during the last seventy years. There is no reason to suspect us of anything."

"Isn't there? With the Tantaberras gone and the Montoros returning to Alma, your family is closer to reclaiming their throne than ever before," Hector explained.

"How?" Gabriel asked. "By marrying me? That plan only works if I'm on board with it."

Hector shrugged. "That's one way to do it." He moved out onto the veranda with them, but instead of taking a chair, he started pacing back and forth across the terra-cotta tiles of the patio. "Another way is to remove the Montoros entirely. If the Montoros and the Salazars were scandalized or discredited, Senorita Espina's family would be the next in line."

Gabriel had no idea that was the case, and judging by the surprised drop of Serafia's jaw, she didn't know it, either. "But there are several of us in line. They'd have to discredit us all, not just me."

"There are fewer of you than you think. Your father and brother have already been put aside. That just leaves you, Bella and Juan Carlos. Don't think it can't be done."

"There is no way that Juan Carlos can be discredited by scandal," Gabriel insisted. "He's annoyingly perfect."

"It doesn't matter," Hector said. "That article insinuates that Serafia was deliberately planted within the royal family to undermine you from the inside."

"She's here to help me!" Gabriel shouted. He was

irritated that this stupidity had ruined a perfectly beautiful morning.

"Is she?" Hector stopped moving just long enough to look over Serafia with suspicion.

"Of course I am. How dare you suggest otherwise?" Serafia flushed bright red beneath her tanned glow.

Hector raised his hands in defeat. "Fine. Fine. But the accusations are out there. We have to figure out how we're going to address them."

"They're ridiculous," Gabriel said. "I don't even want to address the rumors. At least not yet. It could all blow over if we treat it like the unfounded gossip it is."

Hector nodded and stopped pacing long enough to take notes in the small notebook he had tucked into his breast pocket.

"I just don't understand," Serafia said. "The press was so positive toward our relationship just a day ago. What changed so quickly?"

Hector put his notebook away and turned to look out at the sea, his fingers tapping anxiously on the railing. "My guess would be that someone leaked the story to discredit Serafia."

"Why?" Gabriel asked. "What could she have done to anger someone so quickly?"

Hector's gaze ran over Serafia with his lips pressed together tightly. "She didn't do anything. My guess is that it was your doing. You rejected the daughters of all the wealthiest families at the Rowling party."

Gabriel rolled his eyes. "Even if I hadn't left that night with Serafia—which really means nothing, since she's staying here with me for work—only one woman can be chosen as queen. There were easily twenty or thirty girls there that night. How could I possibly choose without offending *someone*?"

"It bet it was Felicia Gomez," Serafia said, speaking up. "Yesterday's incident just compounded their irritation over the party. The Gomez family doesn't like to lose and as I recall, you didn't even dance with Dita that night. I imagine Felicia would see that as a major snub. Combine that with yesterday after the parade... I'm sure they ran right to the press after we left. She can't take it out on you, as king, so she focused her ire on their main competition—me."

Gabriel muffled a snort and shook his head. "They wouldn't go to this much trouble if they knew the truth."

"What's the truth?" Serafia asked.

Gabriel looked into her dark eyes with a serious expression. "They're hardly your competition."

Nine

"How, exactly, did you come up with a boat?" Serafia asked as she turned to Gabriel.

Gabriel looked up from the wheel of the yacht and grinned. After a morning of unpleasantness with Hector, he'd had Luca arrange for the boat to go out. He needed to escape, to think, and there was nothing better than the sea for that.

Marta had packed them a picnic basket so they could dine on the water. The sea was calm and the breeze was just strong enough to fill the sails and keep them from getting too hot. "Turns out it's mine," he said. "Or at least it is now. I thought it was a good day to be out on the water."

"To escape the press?" she asked.

He chuckled and shook his head. "That's just a bonus. Mainly I wanted to see you in a bikini."

Serafia smiled and held out her arms to display her mostly bare curves. She was wearing a bright blue-and-pink paisley bikini top with a pair of tiny denim shorts that made her legs look as if they went on for miles. He ached to touch them, but he needed to steer the boat.

"You got your wish," she declared.

"Indeed I did." The reality standing in front of him was even better than he'd imagined this morning.

"If they know we're out here, the paparazzi will follow us, you know."

"Then they'll get an eyeful and the pictures will leave no doubts that their seedy story made no impact on my opinion of you."

He focused on steering the boat out of the sheltered bay and into open water as she laid a beach towel down on the polished wooden deck. She slipped out of the tiny shorts and went about rubbing sunblock all over her golden skin.

Thank goodness there weren't many ships out on the water today. His eyes were so glued to her that he could've run aground or rammed another boat. He couldn't wait to find a good place to stop so he could join her on the deck.

Serafia glanced up at him and smiled. She looked beautiful and carefree for once; she'd even left her tablet behind today. Not at all like someone scheming her way into his life, he thought, as the events from the morning intruded on his admiration of her. The whole thing was just absurd. Their families might have had animosity a hundred years ago, but that wasn't the case now. The people involved in that were long dead. It didn't have a thing to do with him or Serafia.

The idea that she had been "planted" in his inner

circle to undermine him made his hands curl into fists at his side. Serafia hadn't been *planted* anywhere. He had hired her. She hadn't even suggested the idea; in fact, she'd been very reluctant to take the job. If she was here to lure him into bed, she'd certainly made it difficult. He'd worked harder on her seduction than he had in a long time.

As much as he wanted to just laugh off the story, he couldn't. It made him too angry. He wouldn't tolerate such ugly speculation, especially about Serafia or her family. He'd quietly tasked Hector with tracking down the author of the article and seeing if the source could be identified. If the Gomez family really was behind this story, they'd regret it. If they thought his snubbing Dita at the dance was a huge deal, they'd better be prepared to be shut out of his court entirely. Gabriel was able to carry grudges for a very long time. He wouldn't quickly forget about the people who tried to undermine his faith in the one person he trusted.

Everyone had seen that article. Not long after Hector left, Gabriel's father had called from Del Sol. Rafael was agitated about the whole thing, repeating what he'd said at the Rowling party about the Espinas. Since this time they weren't in public where they could be overheard, Gabriel had pushed his father for more information. Arturo Espina was one of his father's best friends. How could he turn around and be suspicious of the family?

Rafael insisted it wasn't the truth that was the problem. It was seventy years of rumors that would taint his relationship with her. If he were to go as far as to make Serafia his queen, they would forever be dogged by those same ugly stories. Everyone had seen this article and it was just the beginning. Rafael insisted he was just trying to help Gabriel avoid all that. Being king was hard enough, he reasoned, without adding unnecessary complications.

If staying away from Serafia was the only way to save his reign from rumors, innuendo and scandal, too bad. He wasn't going to let something like this drive a wedge between them.

"It's so beautiful out here," Serafia declared, pulling him from his dark thoughts.

It was beautiful. The water was an amazing mix of blues and greens; the sky was perfectly clear. Looking back to the shore, you could see the coastline dotted with marinas and tiny homes hanging on the side of the cliffs. He couldn't imagine a more amazing place to rule over.

Before too long, he would be king of this beautiful country.

From the moment he found out, he had fought the news. He'd made a bold decision to take control of his own life after his abduction, and yet somehow fate had taken away his free will once again. Most people would probably jump at the chance to be in his shoes, but all Gabriel had been able to see were all the reasons why he was a bad choice.

But now that he was here with Serafia at his side, it seemed as though things might work out. The people were welcoming and friendly. The land was beautiful and full of natural resources that would help the country bounce back from oppression. Prime Minister Rivera was a smart man and a good leader, taking the reins on the important decisions for the management of the country. The press were the press, but once he chose a queen and married, hopefully they would settle down.

Gabriel was told that he would soon sit down with his council of advisers, a group of staffers that included Hector and others. He was certain they would have lots of opinions about whom he should choose for his queen. There were geopolitical implications that even he didn't fully understand. Marrying a Spanish or Portuguese princess would be smart. Securing trade by marrying a Danish princess wouldn't hurt, either. Then there were the local wealthy citizens whose support was so important to the success of the new monarchy.

But factoring in all those things would mean he was following his head, not his heart. Gabriel wasn't exactly known for making the smart choices where women were concerned. When it came to Serafia, none of those other things mattered. The minute he saw her out on the patio in Miami, he'd wanted her. And the more he'd had of her, the more he'd wanted. He wasn't just flattering her when he told her the other women in Alma were no competition. It was the truth.

Serafia was smart, beautiful, honest, caring…everything a good queen should be. She was from an important Alman family—one with blood ties to the throne if that article could be believed. He saw more than one sign at the parade declaring the people's support for her as queen. She was a good choice on paper and a great choice in his heart.

He wasn't in love with Serafia. Not yet. But he could see the potential there. In any other scenario, he would've anticipated months or years together before they discussed love and marriage, but as king, he saw this as an entirely different animal. He was expected to make a choice and move forward. With Serafia, he had no fears that their marriage would be a stiff, arranged situation with an awkward honeymoon night. It could be the best of both worlds if they played their cards right.

He just had to get her to stay past the end of the week. If he could do that, then maybe, just maybe, she would agree to be his queen someday soon.

"This looks like a good spot. Drop the stupid anchor and get over here. I'm lonely."

Gabriel checked the depth sounder for a good location. They seemed to be in an area with a fairly level depth. He lowered and secured the two sails, slowing the boat. It took a few minutes to get the anchor lowered and set, but the boat finally came to a full stop.

He turned off any unnecessary equipment and made his way over to where Serafia was lying out. She was on her back, her inky black hair spilling across the sandy blond wood of the deck. She had her wide, dark sunglasses on, but the smile curling her lips indicated she was watching him as he admired her.

Gabriel dropped down onto the deck beside her. He slipped out of his shoes and pulled his polo shirt over his head, leaving on his swimming trunks.

Serafia sat up, grabbing her bottle of sunscreen and applying some to his back. He closed his eyes and enjoyed the feel of her hands gliding across his bare skin. After she finished his back and arms, she placed a playful dab on his nose and cheeks. "There you go."

He rubbed the last of the sunscreen into his face. "Thanks. Are you hungry?"

"Yes," she said. "After everything this morning, I couldn't stomach any breakfast."

Gabriel reached for the picnic basket and set it closer to them on the blanket. Opening it, they uncovered a container filled with assorted slices of aged Manchego and Cabrales cheeses, and cured meats like *jamón ibérico* and *cecina de León*. Smaller containers revealed olives, grapes and cherry tomatoes dressed in olive oil and sherry vinegar. A jar of quince jam, a couple fresh, sliced baguettes and a bottle of Spanish Cava rounded out the meal. His stomach started growling at the sight of it.

Serafia started unpacking the cartons, laying out the plates and utensils Marta had also included. "Ooh," she said, lifting out a package wrapped in foil. "This smells like cinnamon and sugar." She unwrapped a corner to peer inside. "Looks like fruit empanadas for dessert."

"Perfect," Gabriel said.

They scooped various items onto their plates and dug into their meals. They took their time enjoying every bite in the slow European fashion he was becoming accustomed to. In America, eating was like a pit stop in a race—to quickly refuel and get back on the track. Now, he took the time to savor the food, to really taste it while enjoying his company. He sliced bread while Serafia slathered it with jam. She fed him olives and kissed the olive oil from his lips. By the time the jars were nearly empty, they were both full and happy, lying on the deck together and gazing up at the brilliant blue sky.

Gabriel reached out beside him and felt for Serafia's hand. He wrapped his fingers through hers and felt a sense of calm and peace come over him. He didn't know what he would've done without her these last few days. In that short time, she had become such a necessary fixture in his life. He couldn't imagine her going back to Barcelona. He wanted her here by his side, holding his hand just as she was now.

"Serafia?" he asked, his voice quiet and serious.

"Yes?"

"Would you...consider staying here in Alma? With me?"

She turned to him and studied his face with her dark eyes. "You're going to be fine, Gabriel. You've improved so much. You're not going to need my help any longer."

Gabriel rolled onto his side. "I don't want you here for your help. I'm not interested in you being my employee, I want you to be my girlfriend."

Her eyes grew wide as he spoke, her teeth drawing in her bottom lip while she considered his offer. Not exactly the enthusiastic response he was hoping for.

"You don't want to stay," he noted.

Serafia sat up, pulling her hand away from his to wrap her arms around her knees. "I do and I don't. I have a life in Barcelona, Gabriel. A quiet, easy life that I love. Giving that up to come here and be with you is a big decision. Being the king's girlfriend is no quiet, easy life. I don't know if I'm ready."

Gabriel sat up beside her and put a comforting hand on her shoulder. He knew he was asking a lot of her, but he couldn't bear the idea of living in Alma without her. "You don't have to decide right now. Just think on it."

She looked at him with relief in her eyes. "Okay, I will."

* * *

After a day at sea, they'd returned to the house and taken naps. They decided to dine al fresco on the patio outside his bedroom. It was just sunset as they reconvened with glasses of wine to watch the sun sink into the sea. The sky was an amazing mix of purples, oranges and reds, all overtaken by inky blackness as the night finally fell upon Alma.

It was beautifully peaceful, but Serafia felt anything but. Despite the surroundings, the wine and the company, she couldn't get Gabriel's offer out of her mind. To stay in Alma, to be his girlfriend publically...that would change her entire life. She wasn't sure she was ready for that, even though her feelings for him grew every day.

The king didn't have a girlfriend. At least not for long. Unless something went wrong pretty quickly, being his girlfriend would mean soon being his fiancée, and then his queen. That meant she would never return home to her quiet life in Barcelona.

But was that life becoming too quiet? Had she been hiding there instead of living?

The questions still plagued her as they finished the last of the roasted chicken Marta had made for dinner. She felt pleasantly full as she eased back in her chair, a sensation she wasn't used to. She might be comfortable hiding from the world in her hacienda, but she wasn't living her life and she wasn't really getting better. She was managing her disease, controlling it almost to the point that she'd once let it control her. But in Alma, with Gabriel, the dark thoughts hadn't once crept into her mind. He was good for her. And she was good for him.

Maybe coming here was the right choice. Her heart certainly wanted to stay.

She didn't have to decide now, she reflected, and the thought soothed her nerves. To distract herself, she decided now was the right time to give Gabriel his gift. "I got you something."

Gabriel looked at her in surprise and set down his glass of wine. "Really? You didn't have to do that."

"I know. But I did it, anyway." Serafia got up and went to her room, returning a moment later with a small black box.

Gabriel accepted it and flipped open the hinged lid. She watched his face light up as he saw what was inside. "Wow!" He scooped the gift out of the box, setting it aside so he could admire his gift with both hands. "A pocket watch! That's great. Thank you."

Gabriel leaned in to give her a thank-you kiss before returning to admiring his gift. The pocket watch was a Patek Philippe, crafted with eighteen-karat yellow gold. It cost more than a nice BMW, but Serafia didn't care. She wanted to buy him something nice that she knew he didn't have. "I told you in Miami that I would find a way to get around your watch issue."

"And you've done a splendid job. It's beautiful."

"It comes with a chain so you can attach it inside your suit coat."

He nodded, running his fingertip along the shiny curve of the glass. Closing the box, he put it on the table and stood up. He approached her slowly, wrapping his arms around her waist and tugging her tight against him. "Thank you. That was an amazingly thoughtful gift."

Serafia smiled, pleased that he liked it. When she

bought it, she wasn't sure if he would see it as a further criticism of his time-management issues or if he would feel it was too old-fashioned for him. She'd known it was perfect the moment she saw it, and she was pleased to finally know that he agreed.

"I feel like I need to get you something now," he said.

"Not at all," she insisted. "After our discussions about watches earlier and realizing why you disliked them so much, I knew this was something I wanted to do for you. There's no need to reciprocate."

He stared at her lips as she spoke, but shook his head ever so slightly when she was finished. "I'll do what I like," he insisted. "If that means buying you something beautiful and sparkly, I will. If that means taking you into that bedroom and making love to you until you're hoarse, I will."

"Sounds like a challenge," she said.

When his lips met hers, the worries in her mind faded away. Serafia wrapped her arms around his neck and melted into him. The roar of the waves below was the only sound except for the pounding of her heart.

After a moment, he started backing them into the bedroom. Their lips were still pressed together as they moved across the tile to the king-size bed against the far wall. Serafia clung to him, losing herself in touching and tasting Gabriel. No matter what happened each day, she knew it was okay because she knew he would help her forget all her worries each night.

When her calves met with the bed, they stopped. Serafia tugged at his shirt, pulling it up and over his head. She ran her fingertips across his bare chest and scattered soft kisses along his collarbone. His skin was warm from a day in the sun and scented with the hand-made soaps they kept in the bathrooms here.

She felt Gabriel's fingertips on her outer thighs, slowly gathering up the fabric of her dress. Before he could pull it any higher, she turned them around so that his back was to the bed. Then she shoved, thrusting him onto the mattress, where he sprawled out and bounced.

"Are we playing rough tonight?" he asked with a laugh.

Serafia shook her head and took a few steps backward. "I just wanted you to sit back and enjoy the view."

Pushing aside her self-consciousness, she let the straps of her sundress fall from her shoulders, the soft cotton dress pooling at her feet. She coyly turned her back to him, unfastening her bra and letting it drop to the floor. With a sly glance over her shoulder at him, she slipped her thumbs beneath her cheeky lace panties and slid them down her legs. Completely nude, she turned back to face him.

Gabriel watched from the bed with a glint of appreciation in his eyes. He really, truly thought she was beautiful, and knowing this made her feel beautiful. She lifted her arms to brush the cascading waves of her hair over her shoulders, displaying her breasts and narrow waist. He swallowed hard as he watched her, his jaw tightening.

"Come here," he said.

Serafia took her time, despite his royal command. She sauntered over to the bed, crawling across the coverlet on all fours until she was hovering between his thighs. She reached for the fly of his jeans, but the moment she was within Gabriel's reach, he lunged for her.

Before she knew quite what had happened, she was on her back and the weight of Gabriel's body was pressing her into the soft mattress.

He kissed her, his mouth hard and demanding against her own. His fingertips pressed into her, just as hard. She gasped for air when he pulled away to taste her throat. His teeth grazed her delicate skin, almost as though he wanted to mark her, claim her as his own.

She wanted to be his. His alone. At least for tonight. She could feel his desire against her bare thigh, the rough denim keeping them apart. She reached between them, slipping her hand beneath his waistband to grip the length of him. He growled against her throat, leaning into her for a moment, and then reluctantly pulling away before she wore out the last of his self-control.

Slipping off the edge of the bed, he removed the last of his clothes, sheathed himself in latex and returned to his home between her thighs. Without saying a word, he drove into her, stretching her body to its limit. She cried out and clung to his back, her fingernails pressing crescents into his skin.

Their lovemaking was more frantic tonight, more passionate and intense. She wasn't sure if it was the end of their relationship looming that pushed them to a frenzy, but she happily went along for the ride. Nothing else mattered as he drove into her again and again. All she could do was give in to the pleasure, live in the moment and not let the future intrude on their night together. It wasn't hard. Within minutes he had her gasping and on the verge of unraveling.

That was when he stopped moving entirely.

Her eyes flew open, her breath ragged. "Is something wrong?" she asked.

"Stay with me," he demanded.

She wanted to. She wanted to give him her body, her heart and her soul. In that moment, she knew she already had. Despite her hesitation, despite her worries, she had fallen in love with Gabriel Montoro, future king of Alma. But was she good for him? Would she be the queen the country needed?

Those critical articles were just the first of many she was sure would surface. Rumors about her family wouldn't disappear overnight. She didn't want to bring scandal to the new monarchy. It was too new, too fragile. She couldn't risk that, even for love.

She also couldn't risk herself. Would she slip back into her old habits with the eyes of an entire country on her? It was a dangerous prospect.

But when he looked at her like that, his green eyes pleading with her, how could she say no? She wanted to stay. She wanted to be with him, to help him on his new journey. If that meant she might someday be queen and take on all the pressures and joys that entailed…so be it.

"Yes," she whispered into the darkness before she could change her mind.

Gabriel thrust hard into her and she was lost. The waves of emotions and pleasure collided inside her, making her cry out desperately. She repeated her answer again and again, encouraging him and confirming to herself that she truly meant it. She loved him and she was going to stay.

His release came quickly after hers. He groaned loud against her throat, surging into her one last time as he came undone. Serafia held him, cradling his hips between her thighs until it was over.

the hook for a while until the coronation. Today, we'll be flying over with Prime Minister Rivera. He asked to join us on the tour."

"What about Hector?"

"Apparently he doesn't do helicopters, but he's briefed everyone and he'll be meeting with you afterward to go over how it went with Rivera."

"That's fine. I've only had one short meeting with the prime minister, so it's probably a good idea to have some more face time. I don't think we'll get much talking done in the helicopter, though. Aren't they loud?"

Serafia had never been in one, but she'd heard they were. "Yes. I'm pretty sure you won't be conducting any business in the helicopter."

He nodded and relaxed back into the seat. "Good. I'm not sure I'm ready for any hard-core discussions. Is the helicopter large enough for the royal guard, as well? That's quite a few of us to fit into one."

Serafia shook her head. "They've already got a crew of guards there at the rig. They cleared the platform this morning and are standing by for your arrival. All the details have been taken care of," she assured him. Turning to glance out the window, she realized they were at their destination. "And here we are."

They climbed from the car at the heliport and their way over to the helicopter waiting prime minister was already there. Gabriel's hand. Then as a gr helicopter and headed out to

Serafia was glad Gabriel ters. She wasn't exactly thrille was good that at least one of them When the engine started, she pu

When he'd finally stilled, she heard him whisper almost undetectably in her ear, "Thank you."

He was grateful that she'd agreed to stay. She just hoped that would still be the case in the upcoming weeks.

Ten

Serafia should've woken up on cloud nine. She was in love, she'd agreed to stay in Alma with Gabriel and everything was perfect. And yet there was a cloud hanging over her head. It was as though she couldn't let herself breathe, couldn't let herself believe that this was really going to work between them, until after today.

Today was the last hurdle before the coronation. After today's public appearance, Gabriel would have met all the initial requirements and could settle quietly into his life at Alma while the preparation for the coronation took place. She didn't anticipate any problems today. All they had to do was make it through the tour of one of Patrick Rowling's oil platforms off the coast, but for some reason, she woke up anxious.

They got on the road after breakfast, driving the hour back into Del Sol, where they would take a heli-copter out to sea. Helicopters. Better safe than she decided to get his opinion on it during their to the capital.

"Are you okay with helicopters?" Serafia asked

Gabriel straightened his tie and nodded. "Helicopters are fine. The weather seems pretty calm today, s it shouldn't be a bumpy ride."

"Good." She sighed with relief. That was one less worry. "The only other option to get out there is to take a boat and get lifted by crane onto the platform while you cling to a rope and metal cage called a Billy Pugh. I wasn't looking forward to that at all."

Gabriel smiled. "That actually sounds pretty cool."

"You're the rebellious one," she said. "I'm interested in staying alive."

"Fair enough. How far out is the oil platform?"

Serafia looked down at her tablet as their car approached the heliport. "The one we're going to is about twelve kilometers off the coast. It's the newest one they've constructed and Patrick is very eager to show off his new toy."

Gabriel frowned. "I'm sure he is."

"What's that face about?"

"I'm not sure how I feel about the Rowlings yet. least Patrick. He seems a little showy, a little too co for my taste. His sons seem nice enough, althou can't wait to see the look on Bella's face when troduced to the guy Dad wants her to marry. If 't instant fireworks between them, she just r father in his sleep. We might need her each house when she gets here."

ldn't worry too much about Patrick ure the trip will be fine and yo

tion and closed her eyes. The liftoff sent her stomach into her throat, but after a few minutes the movement was steady. Thankfully it wouldn't take long to get out there, so she took some deep breaths and tried not to think about where she was.

A thump startled her, and she opened her eyes in panic only to realize they'd already landed on the oil platform. Thank goodness. Everyone climbed out and Patrick came to greet them. With him, he had the lead rig operator, his son William and a few members of Patrick's management team who always seemed to be following him around. This, in addition to a large contingent of press, as always. They'd come out earlier on the boat. Once everyone was fitted with hard hats, the tour began.

With all the cameras so near today, Serafia decided to take a step back from Gabriel. There was no need to stir any more rumors or give any of them a reason to write another scathing article about her family or their romance. He didn't seem to notice she was gone. With everything going on, he surged ahead, carried by the crowd with Rivera and Patrick Rowling at his side.

Serafia trailed the group as they walked around the open decks of the platform, admiring the massive drill and other equipment. She couldn't hear what Patrick and the others were saying, but she didn't mind. She wasn't really that interested.

After that, they went inside to tour the employee quarters and cafeteria, the offices and the control room. It was a tight fit for the men who lived on the rig up to two weeks at a stretch.

The day was going fairly well, so far. She'd begun to think she'd been anxious for no reason.

It wasn't until they went back outside and started climbing down a set of metal stairs that went below the platform that Serafia started to feel the niggling of worry in the back of her mind. The only thing below the platform were the emergency evacuation boats, some maintenance equipment and the underwater exploration pod they used for maintenance.

Oh God. Her heart very nearly leaped out of her chest and into her throat when she realized what was about to happen.

The submarine.

She'd forgotten all about it. It had always been a part of the plan. They were to tour the oil rig, and then their exploration pod, which was essentially a small, four-man submarine, would take Gabriel under the surface to see the rig at work. It was a harmless photo op, and when she was given the original itinerary, she hadn't thought a thing about it. Gabriel certainly hadn't mentioned having a problem with it when they discussed the agenda back in Miami.

Since then, she'd learned about Gabriel's issues with small, dark spaces, but so much had happened that the submarine had slipped her mind.

That had to be where they were going. Unfortunately there were twenty people between Gabriel and her on the narrow deck and staircase. He was below the platform and she was stuck above it at the very back of the pack. She was unable to get close enough to warn him before it was too late.

She rushed to the metal railing, peering over the side at the party below. They were still walking around while Patrick pointed out one thing or another, but she

copter out to sea. Helicopters. Better safe than sorry, she decided to get his opinion on it during their drive to the capital.

"Are you okay with helicopters?" Serafia asked.

Gabriel straightened his tie and nodded. "Helicopters are fine. The weather seems pretty calm today, so it shouldn't be a bumpy ride."

"Good." She sighed with relief. That was one less worry. "The only other option to get out there is to take a boat and get lifted by crane onto the platform while you cling to a rope and metal cage called a Billy Pugh. I wasn't looking forward to that at all."

Gabriel smiled. "That actually sounds pretty cool."

"You're the rebellious one," she said. "I'm interested in staying alive."

"Fair enough. How far out is the oil platform?"

Serafia looked down at her tablet as their car approached the heliport. "The one we're going to is about twelve kilometers off the coast. It's the newest one they've constructed and Patrick is very eager to show off his new toy."

Gabriel frowned. "I'm sure he is."

"What's that face about?"

"I'm not sure how I feel about the Rowlings yet. At least Patrick. He seems a little showy, a little too cocky for my taste. His sons seem nice enough, although I can't wait to see the look on Bella's face when she's introduced to the guy Dad wants her to marry. If there aren't instant fireworks between them, she just might kill our father in his sleep. We might need her to stay at the beach house when she gets here."

"I wouldn't worry too much about Patrick or Bella today. I'm sure the trip will be fine and you'll be off the hook for a while until the coronation. Today, we'll be flying over with Prime Minister Rivera. He asked to join us on the tour."

"What about Hector?"

"Apparently he doesn't do helicopters, but he's briefed everyone and he'll be meeting with you afterward to go over how it went with Rivera."

"That's fine. I've only had one short meeting with the prime minister, so it's probably a good idea to have some more face time. I don't think we'll get much talking done in the helicopter, though. Aren't they loud?"

Serafia had never been in one, but she'd heard they were. "Yes. I'm pretty sure you won't be conducting any business in the helicopter."

He nodded and relaxed back into the seat. "Good. I'm not sure I'm ready for any hard-core discussions. Is the helicopter large enough for the royal guard, as well? That's quite a few of us to fit into one."

Serafia shook her head. "They've already got a crew of guards there at the rig. They cleared the platform this morning and are standing by for your arrival. All the details have been taken care of," she assured him. Turning to glance out the window, she realized they were at their destination. "And here we are."

They climbed from the car at the heliport and made their way over to the helicopter waiting for them. The prime minister was already there, rushing over to shake Gabriel's hand. Then as a group, they climbed into the helicopter and headed out to sea.

Serafia was glad Gabriel was okay with helicopters. She wasn't exactly thrilled with the idea, so it was good that at least one of them wasn't freaking out. When the engine started, she put on the ear protec-

When he'd finally stilled, she heard him whisper almost undetectably in her ear, "Thank you."

He was grateful that she'd agreed to stay. She just hoped that would still be the case in the upcoming weeks.

Ten

Serafia should've woken up on cloud nine. She was in love, she'd agreed to stay in Alma with Gabriel and everything was perfect. And yet there was a cloud hanging over her head. It was as though she couldn't let herself breathe, couldn't let herself believe that this was really going to work between them, until after today.

Today was the last hurdle before the coronation. After today's public appearance, Gabriel would have met all the initial requirements and could settle quietly into his life at Alma while the preparation for the coronation took place. She didn't anticipate any problems today. All they had to do was make it through the tour of one of Patrick Rowling's oil platforms off the coast, but for some reason, she woke up anxious.

They got on the road after breakfast, driving the hour back into Del Sol, where they would take a heli-

could see the open hatch of the exploration pod a few yards in front of them.

"Gabriel!" she shouted, but no one but a few of the reporters and crew members turned to look at her. The sounds of the ocean and the operating rig easily drowned out everything. Everything but the expression on his face.

Serafia knew the instant that he realized where they were going. He stiffened, his jaw tightening. His hands curled into fists at his side. Everyone around him continued to talk and laugh, but he wasn't participating in the discussion. He was loosening his tie, looking around for another option to escape, short of leaping into the ocean and swimming back to the mainland.

Patrick Rowling and the prime minister were the first to crawl inside the exploration pod. Gabriel stood there at the entrance for several moments, looking into the small space. He was white as a sheet and he gripped the railing with white-knuckled intensity. She could tell the others were trying to encourage him, but he likely couldn't hear anything they said if he was having a full-blown panic attack.

Then he shook his head. Backing up, he nearly ran into someone else, then turned and pushed his way through the crowd back to the stairs. Serafia could barely make out the sounds of shouts and words of concern. Patrick climbed back out of the submarine, calling toward Gabriel, but he didn't stop. He leaped up the stairs, finally colliding with Serafia as he reached the top.

He looked at her, but his eyes were wild with panic. It seemed almost as if he didn't really see her at all.

"I'm so sorry, Gabriel. I forgot all about the submarine. I would've warned you if I remembered."

He looked at her, his expression hardening. There was venom in his gaze, a place where she'd only ever seen attraction and humor. She reached out for his arm, but he shoved it aside and took a step back.

"It's not a big deal," she reassured him. "They can go on ahead without you. I'm sure you're not the only person who doesn't fancy the idea of a ride in that thing."

The look on his face made it clear that he didn't agree. It was a big deal, at least to him. Without saying a word, he turned and took off down the metal-grated walkway toward the helipad.

"Gabriel, stop! Wait!" she shouted as she pursued him, but he kept on going. She finally gave up just as she was overtaken by the press. They pushed her aside as they chased Gabriel, but before they could reach him, she spied the helicopter rising over the top of the rig.

With nothing else she could do, Serafia stood and watched the helicopter disappear into the horizon. Once it was gone, all she could see, all she could think of, was the look of utter betrayal on his face. He blamed her for this. And maybe he should. She'd made a very big error today.

"What happened?" The prime minister stopped beside her, his brow pinched in confusion. "Is the prince okay? He looked quite ill."

"I don't know," Serafia said. She wasn't going to be the one to tell him, and any of the surrounding reporters, that Gabriel was claustrophobic. That would make it seem as if she was deliberately trying to undermine him. He should've been the one to say it. All it would've taken was a polite pass and he could've avoided it. Instead, he'd run like he'd been ambushed.

A sinking feeling settled into Serafia's stomach at the thought. Was that what Gabriel believed she was doing? This was just one oversight, but when added to the string of other problems they'd had over the last week, did it add up to the appearance of sabotage? He couldn't possibly believe she'd do that to him. He hadn't given that newspaper article a second thought.

Or had he?

Serafia feared he'd begun to suspect her. That look had said everything. Serafia had ruined it. She hadn't meant to, but she'd ruined her relationship with Gabriel before it ever started.

Even though Gabriel had his driver take him back to Playa del Onda right away, he was discouraged to find Hector already waiting for him there. Judging by his press secretary's dour expression, the news of the incident on the oil rig had beaten Gabriel home. He just wanted to take off his tie, pour a glass of scotch and relax, but Hector was the hitch in that plan.

"Where's Serafia?" he asked as Gabriel blew past him.

"I don't know. I left her at the oil platform."

Hector made a thoughtful noise and followed him into the den. Gabriel poured a drink and ripped off his tie before collapsing onto the couch. "Why?"

"Well, I wanted to speak to you privately about those rumors. I'm concerned that the Espinas may be trying to undermine your coronation."

Gabriel was tired of hearing about this. "We've discussed this already."

"Yes, but that was before the prime minister called and briefed me about what happened today. He was concerned about you. He'd heard about the incident at the winery, as well."

Great. Now they were talking about him and his issues behind his back. "I don't do well in small spaces," Gabriel explained. "When I start having a panic attack, I have a very aggressive flight response. I overreact, I'm aware of that, but in the moment, I just have to get away from the situation. All the pressure I'm under to be poised and perfect every moment is just making it that much worse because I try to fight my way through it and it doesn't work. Then I feel like a fool."

Hector listened carefully. "I'll make certain we don't have these issues in the future. In exchange, I ask that you speak up when you're uncomfortable so we don't make a bigger scene out of it. Does Serafia know about your claustrophobia?"

"Yes." She didn't know until after the winery incident, but she knew today.

"I see. Your Majesty, my concern is about why these situations keep popping up. Rivera said he asked Patrick Rowling about the submarine and said that it had been Serafia's idea. I understand that you two are… whatever you are. But you really need to put your feelings for her aside and consider the possibility that all these unfortunate incidents are actually carefully orchestrated by the Espina family."

Gabriel dropped his face into his hand. He'd had a horrible day and he didn't really want to face this right now. "I'll take care of it," he said.

"Your Majesty, I—"

"I said, I'll take care of it!" Gabriel shouted. Suddenly his overwhelming apprehension had morphed into anger. He knew he shouldn't direct it at Hector, but he didn't care. He would kill the messenger because he didn't know what else to do.

"Very good, Your Grace. Thank you for your time." Hector gave a curt bow and left the room.

Gabriel watched Hector leave, the questions and anxiety spinning in his mind. Unable to sit still, he headed out to the veranda to await Serafia's return to the compound. The longer he waited, the more his blood began to heat in his veins. He had been upset at the oil platform, but after his discussion with Hector, every minute that ticked by tipped his emotions over into pure anger.

If he was right, this was the ultimate betrayal. Serafia would've known exactly what she was doing. She knew he couldn't stand small, confined spaces. How could she schedule him for what amounted to a miniature submarine ride under an oil platform? Even people who hadn't been through the kind of experience he'd had would balk at that. And yet, he felt this pressure as the future king to do it. He had to be strong; he couldn't show weakness. His father expected it. His country expected it. And all it did was backfire on him and make him look like more of a coward when he fled.

The situation had snuck up on him. They were walking around the lower level and the next thing he knew, he was confronted with his personal nightmare. As he'd looked down into the small round hatch at the metal ladder that would take him into a space too cramped for more than four full-grown men, he felt himself launch into a full-blown panic attack.

This wasn't like the incident at the vineyard. There, the room was dark and underground, but he could escape any time he chose, and did. The minute Gabriel climbed down that ladder, and the hatch was sealed, he would be trapped. His lungs had seized up as if a vise was crushing his rib cage. His heart had been racing so quickly he could barely tell the rhythm of one beat from the next. He'd been sweating, wheezing and damn near on the verge of crying while Patrick Rowling and the prime minister tried to coax him on board.

No way. He didn't care if he offended the richest man in Alma. He wasn't about to have that image on him on television, blasted around the internet and on the front page of every paper. New King of Alma Cries Like a Baby When Forced Into a Submarine! They might as well send a stamped invitation for the Tantaberra family to come back and take over again. It was better to leave before it got worse.

It was bad enough everyone had witnessed his behavior. The Rowlings, the press and even the prime minister were all standing by as he'd completely flipped out, shoved people aside to escape and run across the platform to the helicopter pad as if he were on fire. It must have been a sight to see…his guards chasing after him, people shouting at him to come back, the press recording every moment of it… *The Runaway King*. Now, there was a nickname for his upcoming illustrious reign.

He hadn't registered much in the moment. Gabriel had only been motivated by a driving need to get away from that submarine, off the platform and onto dry land with sunshine on his face as soon as possible. But he could hear Serafia as she'd tried to comfort him. He'd registered the panic and worry on her face as she rushed toward him, but he wasn't slowing down for her or anyone else. Besides, it had been too late. The damage was already done.

Of course, that might have been part of her plan, right? The article had insinuated that the Espina family was determined to gain the throne back one way or another. If not through seduction, perhaps through scandal and humiliation. Serafia had been throwing grenades at him since he arrived. The watch, the debacle at the airport, the vineyard and now the oil platform... Even the supposedly successful party at Rowling's house had proven controversial when he snubbed the Gomez girl at Serafia's suggestion.

He'd paid her to help this week go smoothly, to prepare him for any eventuality as king, and it had started to seem more as if she was deliberately setting him up to fail.

He heard the sound of his bedroom door open. After taking a large sip of his scotch, he set the mostly empty glass down. The amber liquid burned in his stomach, just as his anger shot hot through his veins.

Finally Serafia stepped through the open doorway, looking as worn and ragged as if she'd jogged all the way back from the oil platform. Her shirt was untucked and wrinkled. There was a run in her stocking, and her heels were scuffed. Her hair had been up in a bun, but now it was half up, half down in a silky black mess. She was flushed, with bloodshot eyes and dried tear tracks down her cheeks. It made him wonder how long it had taken her to put together this look and assume the role of the innocent in all this. Maybe that was why it took forever for her to get here.

"I'm so sorry, Gabriel. I didn't—"

"Just stop!" he shouted more forcefully than he intended. The anger that had simmered inside him was approaching a full boil now that he was face-to-face with her again. "Don't tell me you didn't know about this, because I know that's a lie." He gestured to the white sheet of paper on the table in front of him. "I found the schedule you gave me back in Miami for this week. This event was on there. Patrick Rowling said you actually suggested it. You knew all this time what we were building up to."

Serafia crossed her arms over her chest in a defensive posture. "In Miami, I didn't know anything about your abduction. Yes, it was my suggestion because I thought it would be an interesting activity for you. When we reviewed your schedule for the visit, I mentioned it and you said nothing. You just tuned me out half the time. I'm surprised you even had the schedule anymore."

"And after you knew about what happened to me in Venezuela? After the incident at the vineyard? Did it not occur to you then that these plans for the visit to the oil platform might be a bad idea?"

"I'd forgotten," she said, tears forming in her eyes again. "With everything that has happened over the past week, I forgot all about the submarine. It slipped my mind and by the time I remembered, it was too late. We were separated by the crowd and I couldn't warn you without making a scene. I was trying to warn you before they got to that part of the tour."

Gabriel stood up, his dark gaze searching her face

for signs of the treachery he knew was there. Hector had helped him cast her under a shadow of suspicion he couldn't shake. She'd been hiding her secret agenda beneath a disguise of coy smiles and stiff, respectable suits, but it was there nonetheless. And he'd fallen for it.

"And you showed up to warn me at the perfect time," he replied with bitterness in his voice. "Late enough for me to embarrass myself and undermine my future as king, but not so late as to convince me that it was deliberate just in case the ploy didn't work and you might still end up queen."

A strange combination of emotions danced across Serafia's face, ending in a look of exasperation. "I don't want to be queen. I never have and you know why!"

If she really didn't want to be queen, that only left one option. "Just wanting to stay close enough to ruin me and my family, then?"

Serafia threw her arms up, spinning in a circle before facing him with her index finger held up. "One incident. *One*. And suddenly those newspaper accusations you dismissed are gospel? Do you have no faith in me at all?"

"I did. For some stupid reason, I pushed aside all my suspicions and allowed myself to trust you more than I've trusted anyone in years. Even when that article came out, I dismissed it as nasty gossip or old news from another time and place. I couldn't believe that you could be using me to get to the throne."

"Because I'm not," she insisted.

Gabriel just shook his head sadly. "You're just as bad as the Gomez family. You know what? You're even worse. At least they're transparent about their ambitions. You and your family just sidle up to us like friends, then pervert the entire relationship to suit your own purposes."

"Gabriel, you said yourself that that story was nonsense. I didn't get planted with you. You hired me."

That was the detail that had bothered him, but the longer he sat on the patio, the more he'd begun to wonder if that was really true. "What *were* you doing in Miami, Serafia? I hadn't seen you in years, and then all of a sudden, you fly all the way to Miami from Barcelona for my going-away party? You could've just waited to see me in Alma if you were that interested in congratulating me, and saved yourself a fortune in time and money."

Serafia stiffened, her eyebrows drawing together into a frown. "I was in the States for another project and my father asked me to attend on behalf of the family."

"What project?" he pressed. "Who were you working for?"

Serafia started to stutter over her words, as though she was failing to come up with an adequate lie when she was put on the spot. "I—it w-was for a confidential client. I can't tell you who it was."

"A confidential client? Of course it was." Gabriel tried not to take it personally that she thought he was so stupid. "You may not have been a plant, but you were a tempting little worm dangling on a hook right in front of me. I snatched you up just as surely as you'd weaseled your way into my inner circle on your own. You pretended to help me be a better king, building up my confidence in and out of bed, while slowly undermining every inch of progress I've made along the way."

Serafia looked at him with hurt reflecting in her

dark eyes. "Is that all you think of the two of us? Of what we have together?"

"I didn't at first, but now I see how wrong I was. I can see it must have been really difficult for you."

She narrowed her gaze at him, her tears fading. "What must be?"

Gabriel swallowed hard and spat out the words he'd been holding in all day. "Trying to screw me in two different ways at once."

Serafia gasped and raised her hand to cover her mouth. She stumbled back on her heels until her back collided with the doorframe. "You're a bastard, Gabriel."

"Maybe," he said thoughtfully. "But it's people like you who made me this way."

"I quit!" she shouted, disappearing into the house.

"Fine. Quit!" he yelled back at her. "I was just going to fire you, anyway."

He heard her bedroom door slam shut down the hallway. With her gone, the anger that had boiled over suddenly drained out of him. He slumped back into his chair and dropped his head into his hands.

It didn't matter whether she quit or he fired her. In the end, the damage was done and she would soon be gone.

Eleven

Harder. Faster. Keep pushing.

It didn't matter if Serafia's lungs were burning or that her leg muscles felt as if they could rip from her bones at any second. She had to keep going.

Just when she hit the point where she couldn't take any more, she reached out for the console and dropped the speed on the treadmill by half a mile. Giving herself only a minute or two to recover, she then increased it by a whole mile. Her sneakers pounded hard against the rotating belt, which was reaching speeds she could barely maintain in the past.

But she had to now. She had to keep running or everything would catch up with her. It wasn't until she could feel her heart pounding like Thor's hammer against her breast that she realized she'd taken this too far. She reached out and pounded the emergency stop button, slamming into the console and draping her broken body over it. The air rushing from her lungs blazed like fire, her heart feeling as if it was about to burst. She'd run for miles today. Hours. Longer and harder than her doctor-appointed forty-five-minute daily limit.

And yet the moment she looked up, the world around her was just the same. The same heartache. The same confusion. The same anger at herself and at Gabriel. All she'd managed to do was pull a hamstring and sweat through her clothes.

She gripped her bottle of water and stepped down onto the tile floor with gelatinous, quivering legs. Unable to go much farther, she opened the door to her garden courtyard. The cold water and ocean breeze weren't enough to soothe her overheated body, so she set down her bottle and approached her swimming pool. Without stopping to take off her shoes, she stepped off the edge, plunging herself into the cool turquoise depths.

Rising to the surface, she pushed her hair out of her face and took a deep breath. She felt a million times better. Her heart slowed and her body temperature was jerked back from the point of disaster.

And yet she was still at a loss over what to do with herself. She had returned home to Barcelona in disgrace. Her last-minute flight had delivered her home late in the night; she hadn't even told her family or staff that she was returning. All she knew was that she had to get out of Alma that instant. She would work the rest out later.

Once she'd escaped…she didn't know what to do. She had no jobs lined up for several weeks. She'd cleared her calendar when she took the Montoro job because she wasn't sure how long it would truly take. The first few days in Miami had been excruciating and she'd wondered if two weeks would be enough.

Two weeks were more than enough, at least for her. And while she was relieved to be home, returned to the sanctuary she'd built for herself here, something felt off. She'd wandered through the empty halls, sat on the balcony overlooking the sea, lay in bed staring at the ceiling…the thought of Gabriel crept into everything she did.

Serafia swam to the edge of the pool and crossed her arms along the stone, lifting her torso up out of the water. She dropped her head onto her forearms and fought the tears that had taunted her the last few days. As hard as she'd resisted falling for the rebellious prince, it had happened, anyway. Even with the threat of returning to the spotlight, the potential for becoming queen and all the responsibilities that held, she couldn't help herself.

And then he turned on her. How could he think she would do something like that on purpose? The minute she realized where they were headed, the panic had been nearly overwhelming. And then when he'd looked at her with the betrayal reflecting in his eyes, she felt her heart break. He was so used to people using and abusing his trust that he refused to see that wasn't what she was doing.

Perhaps she should have stayed in Alma and fought to clear her name. Running away made her look guilty, but she just couldn't stay there. Her family might have been from Alma decades ago, but she was born and raised in Spain and that was where she needed to be.

She just needed to get her life back on track. The

dramas of Alma would fade, Gabriel would choose his queen and she would go on with her life, such as it was.

At least that was what she told herself.

The French doors to the courtyard opened behind her, and Serafia's housekeeper stepped out with a tray. "I have your lunch ready, señorita."

Serafia swam back to the shallow end of the pool to greet her. She wasn't remotely interested in food with the way she felt, but it would hurt her housekeeper's feelings if she didn't pretend otherwise. "Thank you, Esperanza. Please leave it on the patio table."

Esperanza did as she asked, hesitating a moment by the edge of the pool with a towel in her hands. She seemed worried, her wrinkled face pinched into an expression of concern. "Are you going to eat it?"

Serafia frowned and climbed up the steps. "What do you mean?"

"You barely touched your breakfast, just picking at the fruit. I found most of last night's dinner plate scraped into the trash so I wouldn't see it. I have all your favorite snacks and drinks in the house since your return and I haven't had to restock a single thing."

Serafia snatched the towel from the housekeeper's hands, the past anxiety of being caught in the act rushing back to her. "That's none of your business. I pay you to cook my meals, not monitor them like my mother."

The hurt expression on the older woman's face made her feel instantly guilty for snapping at her. Esperanza was the sweetest woman she knew and she didn't deserve that kind of treatment. "I'm sorry. I shouldn't have said that. Forgive me." Serafia slipped down into the patio chair and buried her face in her towel.

"It's nothing. When I don't eat, I get grumpy, too," Esperanza offered with a small smile. She was a plump older woman with a perpetually pleasant disposition. Probably because she got to eat and wasn't eternally stressing out about how she looked. "But I worry about you, señorita, and so do your parents."

Serafia's head snapped up. "They've called?"

"*Sí*, but you were out walking on the beach. They asked me not to tell you. They seemed very interested in your eating habits, which is why I noticed the change. They said if you started visibly losing weight, I should call them straightaway."

Great. Her parents were having her own employee spy on her. They must really be concerned. Serafia sighed and sat back in her chair. They probably were right to be. In the last few days since returning from Alma, she'd already lost five pounds that she shouldn't have. She was at the low end of the range her doctors had provided her. If she got back into the red zone, she risked another round of inpatient treatment, and she didn't want to do that.

Damn it.

"Thank you for caring about me, Esperanza." Serafia eyed the tray of food she brought her. There was a large green salad with diced chicken, a platter with a hard-boiled egg, slices of cheese and bread and a carafe of vinaigrette. Ever hopeful, Esperanza had even included two of her famous cinnamon-sugar cookies. All in all, it was a healthy, balanced lunch with plenty of vegetables, proteins and whole grains. The kind Serafia asked her to make most days.

And yet she had a hard time stopping her brain from mentally obsessing over how many calories were sitting there. If she only ate the greens and the chicken with no dressing, it wouldn't be too bad. Maybe one piece of cheese, but definitely no bread. They were the same compulsive thoughts that she'd once allowed to take over her life. She'd battled this demon for a long time. A part of her had hoped that she'd beaten it for good, but one emotional blow had sent her spiraling back into her old bad habits.

Habits that had almost killed her.

"It looks wonderful," she said. "I promise to eat every bite. Are there any more cookies?"

"There are!" Esperanza said, her face brightening.

"I'll take some of those this afternoon after my siesta."

"Muy bien!" Esperanza shuffled back into the house, leaving Serafia alone on the patio.

She knew she should change out of her wet workout clothes, but she didn't care. She knew that she needed to eat. Now. Voices in her head be damned.

She started with one of the cookies for good measure. It dropped into her empty stomach like lead, reminding her to take it slow. Her doctors had warned her about starving herself, then binging. That was another, all new, dangerous path she was determined not to take.

Nibbling on the cheese and bread, she started to feel better. She knew that her body paid a high toll for her anorexia. As she was driven to exercise and ignore all the food she could, it made her feel terrible. Even this small amount of food made the difference. Picking up her fork and pouring some of the vinaigrette over the salad, she speared a bite and chewed it thoughtfully.

All this was in marked contrast to the way she'd felt in Alma. For some reason, her past worries had slipped away as she focused on preparing Gabriel to be king. Perhaps it was because he thought she was so beautiful, even with the extra pounds she resented. He worshipped every inch of her body in bed, never once stopping to criticize or comment on her flaws. That made her feel beautiful. When they ate together, it was a fun, enjoyable experience. She was too distracted by the good food and even better company to worry about the calories. There were a few days in Alma where she'd even forgotten to exercise. Before that, she hadn't missed a day of exercise in years. When she was with Gabriel, she'd been able to stop fighting with her disease and simply *live*.

She had been doing so well, and the minute it was yanked away from her, the negative thoughts came rushing back in. She couldn't do this. If there was one thing she'd learned in the years since her heart attack, it was that she loved herself too much to keep hurting herself.

Reaching for a slice of bread with cheese, she took a large bite, then another, and another, until her lunch was very nearly gone.

She couldn't allow loving Gabriel to undo all the progress she'd made.

The report on Gabriel's lap told him what he already knew in his heart, but somehow, seeing the words in black-and-white made him feel that much more like the ass he was.

Hector had done as he'd asked. His people in the press office had reached out to the author of the scathing article on the Espinas. It hadn't taken much pressure for him to reveal that he'd been approached by Felicia Gomez. He admitted that while the historical portions of the article were researched and fact-checked, the insinuations of Serafia's nefarious intentions were purely speculation based on Felicia's suggestions. It didn't mean that her family didn't help overthrow the Montoros, but in the end, that really didn't matter anymore. All that mattered was that Serafia was innocent of all those charges.

He knew it. He knew it when he'd read the article the first time and he knew it when he'd thrown accusations at Serafia and watched her heart break right before his eyes. He'd been humiliated. Angry. He'd lashed out at her because he'd allowed his own fears to rule his life and publically embarrass him. It was easier to blame her in the moment than face the fact that he'd done this to himself.

Gabriel felt awful about the whole thing. Serafia had been the only person in his life he thought he could trust, and yet he'd turned around and abused her trust of him at the first provocation. It made him feel sick.

He needed to do something to fix this. Right now.

Looking up from his report, he spied Luca walking down the hallway past his office. "Luca, can you find out if the Montoro jet is still in Alma?"

Luca nodded and disappeared down the hallway.

Gabriel took a deep breath and resolved himself to his sudden decision. He didn't entirely have his plan together, but he knew he needed to get out of Alma to make this happen. That meant getting on a plane. Serafia had returned to Barcelona. He was certain she wouldn't answer his calls if he tried, and anyway, he knew in his heart that they needed to have a conversation in person. The only catch would be whether or not the jet was here. His father had sent for Bella to come to Alma. Gabriel wasn't sure what day that was happening, but if the jet was with her in Miami, he'd have to find another way to get to Serafia. Could a prince fly coach?

He didn't care if he was crammed in a middle seat at the back of the plane, he had to get to her. Saying he was sorry wasn't enough. He needed to follow that up with how he felt about her. It had taken losing her for him to get in touch with how he truly felt. There was nothing quite like waking up and realizing he was in love and he'd just ruined everything.

But maybe, just maybe, apologizing and confessing his love for her would be enough for Serafia to forgive his snap judgments.

Luca appeared in the doorway, an odd expression on his face.

"Where's the jet?" Gabriel asked.

"It's still at the airport in Del Sol, Your Grace."

He breathed a sigh of relief. "Good. Tell them I want to go to Barcelona as soon as possible. I need a car to meet me at the airport and I need someone to track down Serafia's home address. I have no idea where she lives."

"Yes, Your Grace. I will see to all that. But first, you have…a visitor."

Gabriel could feel his own face taking on Luca's pinched, confused expression. "A visitor?" Could people just stroll up to the royal beach compound and knock on the door to join him for tea?

"Yes. It's an old woman from Del Sol. She told the guards at the gate that she took a taxi out here to speak with you. She said it's very important."

Gabriel was certain that everything people wanted to say to the king was very important, but he was at a loss. He wanted to pack his bag and be in Barcelona before dinnertime. Certainly this could wait…

"She says it's about Serafia."

Gabriel stiffened. That changed everything. "Have her escorted into the parlor. Tell Marta to bring some tea and those almond cookies if we have any left. That will give us some time to make the arrangements before I leave."

Luca nodded and went off to fulfill his wishes. Gabriel returned to his closet to pick a suit coat. He'd been dressing himself for the last few days and if he was honest with himself, he wasn't doing a very good job. He knew that Serafia would want him to wear a jacket to greet a guest, especially an elderly one with more conservative ideas about the monarchy. He selected a black suit coat that went with the gray shirt he was already wearing. He knew he should add a tie, but he just couldn't do it. He was in his own home; certainly he could get away with being a little more casual there.

By the time he reached the parlor, all his instructions had been executed beautifully. Marta had placed a tray of lovely treats on the coffee table and was pouring two cups of tea. Seated on the couch was a tiny woman. Perhaps the smallest he'd ever seen, withered and hunched over with age. She was at least eighty, the life shriveling out of her just as the sun had seemed to tan her skin to near leather. Her hair was silver and pulled back into a neat bun. She looked like everyone's *abuela*.

"Presenting His Majesty, Prince Gabriel!" one of

the guards lining the wall announced as he entered the room.

The old woman reached for her cane to stand and curtsey properly, but Gabriel couldn't bear for her to go to that much trouble just for him. "Please, stay seated," he insisted.

The woman relaxed back into her seat with a look of relief on her face. "*Gracias*, Don Gabriel."

He sat down opposite her, offering the woman sugar or cream for her tea. "What can I do for you, señora?"

She took a sip of tea, and then set it down on the china dish with a shaky hand. "Thank you for taking the time to see me today. I know you are very busy. My name is Conchita Ortega. In 1946 when the coup happened, I was just fifteen years old and working as a servant in the Espina household. I have seen what was published in the papers over the last week or so, and now I have heard that Señorita Espina has left Alma."

"Señorita Espina was only working for me for a few weeks. She was always supposed to return home."

The older woman narrowed her gaze at him. "I understand, Your Grace, but I also understand and know *amor* when I see it. I know in my heart you were a couple in love and those vicious lies have ruined it. I had to speak up so you would know the truth."

Gabriel listened carefully, his interest in what the woman had to say growing with each additional word she spoke. Even though he didn't hold the past of her family against Serafia, it would help to know the truth of what really had happened back then. This woman might be one of the only people left alive who knew the whole story. "Please," he replied. "I'd love for you to tell me what you know."

She nodded and relaxed back in her seat with a cookie in her hand. She took a bite and chewed slowly, torturing Gabriel by delaying her story. "By the time everything fell apart," she began, "the hurt feelings about the broken engagement between Rafael the First and Rosa Espina were nearly a decade in the past. Rafael had married Anna Maria, Rosa had married another fine gentleman and the young Prince Rafael the Second, your grandfather, was seven years old. All had turned out for the best. The Espina family would not, and did not, conspire against the Montoros during the coup. In fact, they were your family's closest confidantes."

"How do you know?"

"At fifteen, I was like a little mouse, moving quiet and unseen through the house. I was privy to many discussions with no one giving any thought to my presence. I was serving tea when Queen Anna Maria came to the Espina Estate in secret. She'd come to ask your family to help them. Alma had weathered the Second World War, but they feared the worst was yet to come for them. Tantaberra was growing in power, staging large demonstrations and causing unrest all over Alma. The royal family was worried that they were losing hold of the country.

"The queen asked the Espinas to help them protect Alma's historical treasures by smuggling them out of the country before things got worse. The Montoros had to stay as long as they could to appear strong against their opposition, but they feared that when they did leave, they'd have to leave everything behind. The queen couldn't bear for such important things to be lost, so they arranged for the Espinas to move to Swit-

zerland and take the country's most important historical artifacts with them."

Serafia had mentioned that her family lived in Switzerland before moving to Spain. The article had said
the family fled before the coup, which was interpreted
as suspicious at the time. "What kind of things?" he
asked.

"The royal jewels and stores of gold, an oil portrait
of the first king of Alma, handwritten historical re-
cords of the royal family...everything that would be
considered irreplaceable."

"Were they successful in smuggling everything out?"
he asked.

"Yes. I helped load the ship myself. They sailed
from Alma with all of their things and a secret cargo of
Alman treasure. They traveled down the Rhine River
to Switzerland, arriving just weeks before everything
fell apart. Your family was not so lucky. They fled to
America with nothing, leaving everything else behind
for Tantaberra to claim as his own."

"What about you?"

"I had the option to go with the Espinas, but I
couldn't leave my family behind. I stayed. But I'm
glad I did so I could be here to tell you the truth. The
Espinas are not traitors. They're heroes, but no one
knows the truth."

"Why doesn't anyone know about this? Not even
my father has mentioned it."

"It is likely he does not know. The queen orchestrated everything and may not have told anyone in
the family so they could not be tortured for the information. It was a closely guarded secret and everyone
was instructed not to speak of it while the Tantaber-

ras were still in power. At the time, they had ties with Franco in Spain and they feared that if anyone knew the truth, their network would seek out the Espinas and retaliate. They were instructed not to breathe a word to anyone until the royal family was restored officially to the throne again."

"Do you think the family still has the treasures after all these years?"

"I have no doubt of it. I ask you to reach out to Señor Espina in Madrid. He can tell you the truth. After all these years, I'm sure he will be happy to return the royal treasure to where it belongs after the coronation."

Gabriel was stunned by the entire conversation. Apparently this information had not been passed down through the generations the way it should've been. But as they finished their tea, a plan started to form in his mind. He arranged for a car to take Señora Ortega home and finalized the preparations for his flight. Instead of going to Barcelona, he decided a visit to Madrid to see Serafia's father was in order. If her family had his country's treasures, they needed to be restored to the people. Once he knew for certain the story was true, he intended for the whole country to know the truth about the Espinas. They deserved a parade in their honor, and all the vicious rumors to be put to bed once and for all.

And while he was there…he wanted to ask Señor Espina for his daughter's hand in marriage.

Twelve

It was a quick flight to Madrid, but still too long in Gabriel's eyes. The car that picked him up at the airport rushed him through the streets of the city to the Espina residence. Now all he had to do was face Serafia's father and accept his punishment for hurting her.

Arturo Espina opened the front door and glared at Gabriel. He had been expecting a less than warm reception. Serafia had no doubt told her family how horribly he'd treated her. He was on a journey to make amends not only with Serafia, but also with her parents. If what Señora Ortega said was true, things needed to be made right with the Espinas. By keeping Queen Anna Maria's secret so diligently, they'd lived in the shadow of suspicion and rumors for too long. And Gabriel had a long path to redemption where Serafia was concerned. The pain would start here, now, but it had to start somewhere.

"Señor Espina," he said, hoping his smile didn't give away how nervous he was. "Hello."

The older man glanced over Gabriel's shoulder at the royal guard hovering nearby. The irritation suddenly faded and was replaced with a respectful bow. "Prince Gabriel. To what do we owe the honor of your presence?"

"Please," Gabriel said. "You bandaged my skinned knee once. Let's drop the formalities. I'm not here as prince. I'm here about Serafia."

Arturo nodded and took a step back to allow him inside. The guard remained outside the door at Gabriel's request. Arturo led him through the large mansion to an inner courtyard landscaped with trees and a sparkling tile fountain. "Please, have a seat," he said. "May I offer you a drink? Something to eat?"

Gabriel shook his head. "No, thank you."

"I'm surprised to see you here, Gabriel. Serafia hasn't mentioned what happened in Alma, but considering how she rushed home, I'm assuming things did not end well. What I've read in the Alma newspapers has been disheartening, to say the least."

"I know, and what I'm really here to do is apologize. And maybe, if my apology is accepted, I'd like some information only you can give me."

Arturo sat down across from him and waited for the questions to come.

"First, I want to apologize for the way I've handled all this. Regardless of the truth, I behaved poorly, lashing out at Serafia, and I'm ashamed of that. Your family, and specifically your daughter, never gave me any reason to doubt your loyalty."

"You are not the first to be suspicious of our family over the years."

"I had never heard any of those stories before," Gabriel explained. "The papers have had some terrible things to say about your family. I grew up in America in a household that very rarely, if ever, discussed Alma and what happened. Our families have always been friends, so I was blindsided by those stories. I feel like a fool, but I allowed those articles to taint my feelings for your family and for your daughter. I shouldn't have let that happen, but I was upset with myself and took it out on her."

"I read about what happened at the oil rig. Am I wrong in thinking that was related to your abduction?"

Gabriel looked Arturo in the eye. "It was. I wasn't sure how many people knew about it. My father wanted to keep it all pretty quiet."

"He called me while it was happening and asked for advice. Rafael was torn up about the whole thing and how it was taking so long to bring you home. Rafael was so frustrated—he felt helpless for the first time in his life. When you showed back up in Miami, I think he was embarrassed about how it was all handled and never wanted to talk about it again. He thought you would blame him for everything, so he wanted to forget about it all."

"I didn't blame him," Gabriel said. "But I've always felt like I was a disappointment to him, somehow. I tried to hide my claustrophobia because I thought he'd see it as another weakness."

"No one—your father included—would hold something like that against you. You went through a terrible experience. He probably thought that putting it behind you would help. We did that with Serafia and I've never been certain it was the right course. But as parents, you do what you can to protect your children."

Gabriel sighed. He'd come here for answers about the Espina family and ended up with more than he'd expected. "Thank you for telling me that. I've never really been able to get past what happened. I don't do well in small spaces since my kidnapping, and I blamed Serafia for not warning me ahead of time about what was in store on the oil rig. It wasn't her fault. I ruined everything with her, and then I find out that all those rumors that poisoned my mind weren't even true."

"Do you mean the rumors about the Espinas helping Tantaberra depose your family?" Arturo asked. His tone was flat, as though he'd had to hear these slanderous charges his whole life.

"Yes. An old woman who worked for your family back then came to the house today and explained the truth about how the Espinas safeguarded the royal treasure. At least, I hope it's the truth."

Arturo nodded. "We've had to keep quiet about our family's role in all this for decades, ignoring the rumors so we didn't risk anyone finding out the truth. I don't think any of them believed the dictatorship would last as long as it has. We feared that the Tantaberras would come after us if they knew what we were hiding, or worse, come after your family if they had any knowledge of it. Even after all this time, we had to deliberately keep it from you and others in your family."

"I can't imagine that burden."

"I think it was worth it. I heard that Tantaberra was furious when he took the palace and all the gold and jewels he'd coveted were gone."

Gabriel had never given much thought to his great-grandmother, Anna Maria, but in that moment, he admired her fire. He wished he could've seen the dictator's face when he realized that the Montoros had outsmarted him. "That means your family still has it?"

Arturo stood. "Wait here. I'll be right back." He disappeared down a hallway and returned a few minutes later with something in his hand. When he sat down again, he placed two small items on the table. One, a gold coin, and the other, a diamond and ruby ring. "This is just a small part of what my family has protected for seventy years."

Gabriel reached out and picked up the coin. It was a coin minted in Alma in the 1800s. "You keep it here?"

"No. I've always kept a few tiny items in my safe for a moment like this, but the rest is in a vault in Switzerland. We were to keep it until the coronation took place, to ensure it was official, and then it can all be restored to the palace. I've always hoped to see this day happen. It's been a weight on my shoulders since my father told me the truth."

Returning the coin, Gabriel examined the ruby ring and felt a touch of sadness come over him. It was so beautiful, with a dark red oval ruby that had to be nearly four carats. It was surrounded by a ring of tiny diamonds and flanked on each side by a pear-shaped diamond. The setting was a mix of platinum and gold filigree. It was more beautiful than any ring had a right to be. He was incredibly grateful the Espinas had hidden it away from the Tantaberras, yet sad that no one had enjoyed the ring for all these years. This ring was meant to be on the hand of a queen—a woman like Serafia.

"I've betrayed the family that I should've trusted above all others. I'm so sorry. I can't apologize enough. I want to see to it that the truth gets out. When the treasure is restored, I want it put on display in Alma's national museum so that everyone will know how the Espinas safeguarded it all these years, and put an end to the rumors once and for all."

"That would be wonderful," Arturo said. "I would like to move back to Alma one day. My father was born there. I grew up in Switzerland, but I've always dreamed of going back to where my people belonged."

Looking down at the ring, Gabriel was reminded of the other reason he'd come here today. The truth was nice, but even if the old woman's story was just a fabrication, his first priority was getting Serafia to forgive—and marry—him. He put the ring back on the table and looked at Arturo.

"I also came here today because I want Serafia in my life," he said. "I…I love her. I want her to be my queen. Do you think she'll ever be able to forgive me for the way I've treated her?"

Arturo sat back in his seat and looked at him with a serious expression. "I don't know. She's taken this very hard. Her mother and I have been worried about her."

Gabriel's gaze met his. "Worried?"

"Did she tell you about her illness?" Arturo asked.

"The anorexia? Yes, but she said that was behind her."

"We'd hoped so," Arturo explained, "but her doctors had warned us that patients are never fully cured of this disease. Stress, especially emotional upheaval, can send her spiraling back into her bad habits. Her house-keeper has told us that she is hardly eating. That she does nothing but exercise and sleep since she returned to Barcelona. There have been a few times where she's fallen into this slump before, but she's righted herself before it went too far. I'm hoping that you can help pull her out of it."

Gabriel sensed the worry and fear in Arturo's voice and felt even more miserable than he had before. He knew how much Serafia struggled with her image and how hard she'd worked to overcome her illness. She'd done so well when they were together that he never would've known about the anorexia if she hadn't told him the truth. If he'd sent her into such an emotional state that she fell prey to it again—if she got hurt because of it—he'd never forgive himself.

"I'm flying directly to Barcelona from here. I'll do everything I can to make things right, I promise. Even if she doesn't want me, even if she won't forgive me, I won't leave until I'm certain she's safe."

Arturo watched him as he spoke, and then nodded. "You said earlier that you wanted my daughter to be your queen. You're serious about this?"

Gabriel swallowed hard. "Yes, sir. With your permission, I'd like to ask Serafia to be my wife. I know that under the circumstances, the public role will not be an easy one for her, but I love her too much to let her out of my life. I don't think I could choose a better woman to help me make Alma that great country it once was."

Arturo nodded. "You are good for her, I know it. I've watched you two on the news together. She looks happier with you than she has been in years. You make sure she stays that way and you have my blessing."

"Yes. Of course. I only want Serafia to be happy. Thank you, Señor Espina."

Serafia's father finally smiled for the first time since Gabriel had arrived, and he felt a weight lifted from his chest.

"Do you have a ring for her?" the older man asked.

Gabriel was embarrassed to admit that he didn't. "I rushed here to see you without thinking all of it through. I don't have anything for her yet."

Arturo reached out and picked up the ruby ring from the table. "This is the wedding ring of Rafael the First's mother, Queen Josefina. If you truly love my daughter and want her to be queen, this is the ring you should give her."

Gabriel took the ring from the man who might soon be his father-in-law and shook his hand. "Thank you, sir. It's perfect."

"Good job," Esperanza said as she took away Serafia's mostly empty dinner plate.

Serafia chuckled. "Does this mean I get the tiramisu you promised me?"

"Of course."

Esperanza disappeared inside, leaving her alone on her patio, watching the sun set. It seemed like only yesterday that she was doing the same with Gabriel, only overlooking the Atlantic instead of the Mediterranean. The moment had been romantic and full of promise.

And now here she was, alone. What a difference a few days could make.

But she wasn't going to dwell on it. She'd had her moment to mope, and now it was time for her to figure out what she wanted to do with her life. Being with Gabriel had helped her realize that she was hiding here in Barcelona. She got out, she worked, but she hadn't really allowed herself to have the full life she deserved. That was over. She was determined that from this point forward, she was going to live her life to the fullest.

"Señorita?" Esperanza was at the door again.

"Yes?" Serafia said as she turned and froze in place. Standing tall behind her tiny housekeeper was Gabriel. He was looking incredibly handsome in a gray shirt and a black suit coat. Without a tie, of course.

She felt her heart skip a beat in her chest when she saw him. Every nerve awakened as her body realized he was so close. She tightened her hands around the arms of her chair to fight her unwanted reaction to him. He was a bastard. He said terrible things to her. She absolutely should not react to him like this. And yet she couldn't help it. He might be a bastard, but she still loved him. She still hadn't managed to convince her heart differently.

Taking a deep breath, she wished away her attraction and tried to focus on more important things, like what had brought him all the way to her doorstep.

Esperanza looked a little stunned. Serafia imagined that opening the door and finding a prince standing there was not exactly what the older woman had anticipated when the bell rang. "Prince Gabriel is here to see you. He would not wait outside."

"I didn't want to give you the chance to turn me away," he said, with a sheepish smile that seemed to acknowledge he was the guilty party.

"Smart move," Serafia noted in a sharp tone. He *was* the guilty party and she wanted to make sure he got his punishment. "Esperanza, could you please bring out a bottle of merlot and two glasses, please?" She wasn't sure how this conversation was going to go, but drinking certainly wouldn't hurt matters. At the very least it would help her relax. She was drawn tight as a drum.

Esperanza disappeared into the house and Gabriel joined Serafia outside. He took a seat in the chair beside her and looked out at the sea as she had been doing earlier.

"You have a beautiful home," he said.

"Thank you."

He turned back to look at her, his concerned gaze taking in every inch of her, but not in the hungry way she was used to. He seemed to be cataloguing her somehow. "How are you?" he asked.

Not once in the weeks they'd spent together had he asked her that question. Now she knew it was probably her parents' doing. They'd started calling each day, never directly asking if she was eating, but hinting around the subject, not knowing Esperanza had already ratted them out. She frowned at him. "Did my family send you down here to check on me?"

"What?" He looked startled. "No. I came here on my own, but I made a stop in Madrid on the way. Your father mentioned they were concerned about you."

"They usually are," she said. "That's why I opted to move to Barcelona and give myself some breathing room. They're very overprotective of me."

"They just want to make sure you're happy and healthy. As do I."

"Is that why you've come?" she snapped. "To make sure you didn't break my heart too badly?"

"No," he said with a grave seriousness in his voice. "I came to apologize."

"It's not necessary," she said.

"Yes, it is. I lashed out at you and it wasn't your fault. I let my own fears get the best of me, then used the most convenient excuse I could find to push you away. It was the dumbest thing I've ever done, and that's saying a lot after the antics I've gotten into the last few years. I've relived that moment in my head over and over, wishing I'd handled everything differently. I was a fool and it cost me the woman I love."

Serafia gasped at his words, but before she could respond, Esperanza returned with the wine. The interruption allowed Serafia a minute to think about his words and consider what her response should be. He loved her. She wanted to tell him that she loved him, too, but she was wary of giving away too much. He'd hurt her, abused her trust. She wasn't just going to take him back because he decided he was in love and that made everything better.

When Esperanza went back into the house, he picked up where he'd left off. "I never believed those stories about your family, and now that I know the truth, I'm going to see to it that those rumors are put to bed for good. The Espinas are heroes and I want everyone to know it."

"Heroes?" Serafia frowned. What was he talking about?

"Your family protected the royal treasure from the Tantaberras. That's why they left before the coup. Your father and I are going to work to have the treasure restored and put on display after the coronation. Without your family's help, the Tantaberras would've used up and destroyed our country's history."

Serafia had never heard any of this before, but she didn't doubt the truth of it. Her father had made more than a few mysterious trips to Switzerland over the years. At the same time, the truth didn't make everything okay, either. "So now that you know I don't come from a line of traitors, you've decided you can love me?"

"No. Stop jumping to these horrible conclusions. I'm happy I found out the truth, but no, that's got nothing to do with why I'm here. I had one foot out the door to come see you when all this fell into my lap. But in the end, none of it has to do with us. That's all in the past. What I'm interested in is you and me and the future."

Serafia's breath caught in her throat. She reached a shaky hand out for her wine, hoping it would steady her, but all she could do was hold the glass as he continued to speak.

"I love you, Serafia, with all my heart and all my soul. I am a fool and I don't deserve your love in return, but if someday I could earn it back, I would be the happiest man in the world." Gabriel reached out and took her hand and she was too stunned to pull away.

"I don't just love you. I don't just want you to come back to Alma. I went to Madrid because I wanted to ask your father for his blessing to marry you. I want you to be my queen."

Gabriel slipped out of his chair and onto one knee. Serafia sat stunned as she watched him reach into his inner breast pocket. She saw a momentary flash of gold and realized he was wearing the pocket watch she gave him, but then he pulled out a small ring box and her thoughts completely disintegrated into incoherence.

"I don't know if I'm the right man to be king. But fate has put the crown in my hands and because of you, I feel like I'm closer than I could ever be to the kind of man my people deserve. With you by my side as queen, all my doubts are gone. We can restore Alma to its former glory together. I don't think Alma could ask for a better queen and I couldn't ask for a smarter, more beautiful, graceful and caring bride. Would you do me the honor of being my wife?"

Gabriel opened the box and stunned her with an amazing bloodred ruby with diamonds. It was unlike any ring she'd ever seen before. It was the kind of ring that was fit for royalty.

"This ring belonged to my great-great-grandmother, Queen Josefina. It was her wedding ring and part of the treasure entrusted to your family to protect. Your father returned it to me today. He told me that it belonged on your finger and I quite agree."

Serafia let him slip the ring onto her finger. She couldn't take her eyes off it and couldn't stop thinking about everything it represented. He loved her. He wanted to marry her. He wanted her to be his queen. In that moment, all her doubts and hesitations about being in the spotlight disappeared. Before, she had been there alone. If Gabriel was by her side, it would okay. She couldn't believe how quickly everything in her life had changed.

"Serafia?"

She tore her gaze away from the ring to look at Gabriel. He looked a little confused and a little anxious as he watched her. "Yes?"

"I, uh, asked you a question. Would you like to answer it so I can stop freaking out?"

Serafia smiled, feeling quite silly for missing the critical step in the proposal process. "Yes, Gabriel, I will marry you."

He grinned wide, opening his arms to catch her just as she propelled herself at him. Her lips met his with an enthusiasm she couldn't contain. Just an hour ago, she thought she might never be in his arms again. And here she was...his fiancée. There was a sudden lightness in her heart and she felt as though she had to cling to Gabriel so she wouldn't float away.

"I love you, Serafia," he whispered against her lips.

"I love you, too, Gabriel," she answered, happy to finally say those words out loud.

Gabriel stood up, pulling her up with him. "The coronation is over a month away. I don't want to wait that long to marry you."

She knew exactly how he felt. She would happily elope if she thought they would get away with it. Unfortunately the people of Alma would want their royal wedding. As would her mother. There was no avoiding that. "How quickly do you think we can pull off a wedding?"

"Well," Gabriel said thoughtfully, "my brother's wedding is already in the works. He abdicated, but he's still prince, so father insisted he and Emily have their ceremony in Alma. That's only a few weeks away. What would you say to a double wedding?"

"A double wedding?"

"Why not? They've already got the plans in place. All the same people will be coming. Why can't we have one giant celebration and both marry at the same time?"

Serafia looked at her handsome fiancé thoughtfully. He was not a woman. He didn't understand what kinds of expectations went into a wedding. Serafia might not mind a double wedding, but Emily certainly might.

"How about this...?" she proposed. "You talk to Rafe and Emily about it. If they are both fine with it, then I'm okay with it, too."

Gabriel grinned wide. "I'm sure they will be, but I'll check. And then you'll be Mrs. Gabriel Montoro, soon to be *Su Majestad la Reina Serafia de Alma.* Are you ready for that?"

Serafia wrapped her arms around his neck and nodded. "I think so, although I'm sure that being queen will be the easy part."

Gabriel arched one brow curiously at her. "What's going to be the hard part?"

She climbed to her bare toes and planted a kiss on his full lips. "Keeping the king out of trouble."

* * * * *

A ROYAL BABY SURPRISE

CAT SCHIELD

To the 2008 Ionian Islands Crew: Erik, Sonia, Charie, Renee, Jean and Val

"You never talked about your family. Why is that?"

"There's not much to say."

"Here's where we disagree."

She stepped closer. Vanilla and honey enveloped him, overpowering the scent of cypress and the odor of brine carried on the light morning breeze. With her finger she eased his dark sunglasses down his nose and captured his gaze. Her delicate brows pulled together in a frown.

He braced himself against the pitch and roll of emotions as her green-gray eyes scoured his face. He should tell her to go away, but he was so damned glad to see her that the words wouldn't come. Instead, he growled like a cranky dog that wasn't sure whether to bite or beg to be petted.

"You look like hell."

"I'm fine." Disgusted by his suddenly hoarse voice, he knocked her hand aside and slid his sunglasses back into place.

She, on the other hand, looked gorgeous. Rambunctious red hair, streaked with dark honey, framed her oval face and cascaded over her shoulders. Her pale, unblemished skin, arresting dimples and gently curving cheekbones made for the sort of loveliness any man could lose his head over. A wayward curl tickled his skin as she leaned over him. Shifting his gaze, he took the strand between two fingers and toyed with it.

"What have you been doing all alone in your fancy villa?" she asked.

"If you must know, I'm working."

"On your tan maybe." She sniffed him and wrinkled her slender nose. "Or a hangover. Your eyes are bloodshot."

"I've been working late."

"Riiight." She drew the word out doubtfully. "I'll make some coffee. It looks like you could use some."

Safe behind his dark glasses, he watched her go, captivated by the gentle sway of her denim-clad rear and her long legs. Satin smooth skin stretched over lean muscles, honed by yoga and running. His pulse purred as he recalled those strong, shapely legs wrapped around his hips.

Despite the cool morning air, his body heated. An hour ago, he'd opened his eyes, feeling as he had most of the past few mornings: queasy, depressed and distraught over the accident that had occurred during a test firing of their prototype rocket ship.

Brooke's arrival on this sleepy, Greek island was like being awakened from a drugged sleep by an air horn.

"Someone must be taking care of you," she said a short time later, bringing the smell of bitter black coffee with her when she returned. "The coffeepot was filled with grounds and water. All I had to do was turn it on."

Nic's nostrils flared eagerly as he inhaled the robust aroma. The scent alone was enough to bring him back to life.

She sat down on the lounge beside his and cradled her mug between both hands. She took a tentative sip and made a face. "Ugh. I forgot how strong you like it."

He grunted and willed the liquid to cool a little more so he could drain his cup and start on a second. It crossed his mind that coping with Brooke while a strong jolt of stimulant rushed through his veins was foolhardy at best. She riled him up admirably all by herself, making the mix of caffeine and being alone with her a lethal combination.

"So, am I interrupting a romantic weekend?"

Luckily he hadn't taken another sip, or the stuff might have come straight out his nose. His fingers clenched around the mug. When they began to cramp, he ground his teeth and relaxed his grip.

"Probably not," she continued when he didn't answer. "Or you'd be working harder to get rid of me."

Damn her for showing up while his guard was down. Temptation rode him like a demon every time she was near.

But he couldn't have her. She mustn't know how much he wanted her. He'd barely summoned the strength to break things off a month ago. But now that he was alone with her on this island, her big misty-green eyes watching his every mood, would his willpower hold out?

Silence stretched between them. He heard the creak of wood as she settled back on the lounge. He set the empty cup on his chest and closed his eyes once more. Having her here brought him a sense of peace he had no right to feel. He wanted to reach out and lace his fingers with hers but didn't dare to.

"I can see why you and your brothers bought this place. I could sit here for days and stare at the view."

Nic snorted softly. Brooke had never been one to sit anywhere and stare at anything. She was a whirling dervish of energy and enthusiasm.

"I can't believe how blue the water is. And the town is so quaint. I can't wait to go exploring."

Exploring? Nic needed to figure out how to get her on a plane back to America as soon as possible before he gave in to temptation. Given her knack for leading with her emotions, reasoning with her wouldn't work. Threats wouldn't work, either. The best technique for dealing with Brooke was to let her have her way and that absolutely couldn't happen this time. Or ever again, for that matter.

When she broke the silence, the waver in her voice betrayed worry. "When are you coming back?"

"I'm not."

"You can't mean that." She paused, offering him the opportunity to take back what he'd said. When he didn't, her face took on a troubled expression. "You do mean that. What about *Griffin*? What about the team? You can't just give it all up."

"Someone died because of a flaw in a system I designed—"

She gripped his forearm. "Glen was the one pushing for the test. He didn't listen when you told him it wasn't ready. He's the one to blame."

"Walter died." He enunciated the words, letting her hear his grief. "It was my fault."

"So that's it? You are giving up because something went wrong? You expect me to accept that you're throwing away your life's work? To do what?"

He had no answer. What the hell was he going to do in Sherdana besides get married and produce an heir? He had no interest in helping run the country. That was Gabriel's job. And his other brother Christian had his businesses and investments to occupy him. All Nic wanted to do, all he'd ever wanted to do, was build rockets that would someday carry people into space. With that possibility extinguished, his life stretched before him, empty and filled with regret.

"There's something else going on." She tightened her grip on his arm. "Don't insult my intelligence by denying it."

Nic patted her hand. "I would never do that, Dr. Davis." A less intelligent woman wouldn't have captivated him so completely, no matter how beautiful. Brooke's combination of sex appeal and brains had delivered a fatal one-two punch. "How many doctorates do you have now, anyway?"

"Only two." She jerked her hand from beneath his, reacting to his placating tone. "And don't change the subject." Despite her annoyance, a huge yawn practically dislocated her jaw as she glared at him.

"You're tired." Showing concern for her welfare might encourage her, but he couldn't help it.

"I've been on planes since yesterday sometime. Do you know how long it takes to get here?" She closed her eyes. "About twenty hours. And I couldn't sleep on the flight over."

"Why?"

A deep breath pushed her small, pert breasts tight against her sleeveless white cotton blouse.

"Because I was worried about you, that's why."

The admission was a cop-out. It was fourth on her list of reasons why she'd flown six thousand miles to talk to him in person rather than breaking her news over the phone.

But she wasn't prepared to blurt out that she was eight weeks pregnant within the first ten minutes of arriving.

She had a lot of questions about why he'd broken off their relationship four weeks earlier. Questions she hadn't asked at first because she'd been too hurt to wonder why he'd dropped her when things between them had been so perfect. Then the fatal accident had happened with *Griffin*. Nic had left California and she'd never received closure.

"I don't need your concern," he said.

"Of course you don't." She crammed all the skepticism she could muster into her tone to keep from revealing how much his rebuff stung. "That's why you look like week-old roadkill."

Although his expression didn't change, his voice reflected amusement. "Nice image."

She surveyed his disheveled state, thought about the circles she'd seen beneath his eyes, their utter lack of vitality. The thick black stubble on his cheeks made her wonder how long it had been since he'd shaved. No matter how hard he worked, she'd never seen his golden-brown eyes so flat and lifeless. He really did look like death warmed over.

"Brooke, why did you really come here?"

Her ready excuse died on her lips. He'd believe that she'd come here to convince him to return to the project. It would be safe to argue on behalf of her brother. But where Nic was concerned, she hadn't played it safe for five years. He deserved the truth. So, she selected item number three on her list of why she'd chased after him.

"You disappeared without saying goodbye." Once she better understood what had spooked him, Brooke would confess the number one reason she'd followed him to Ithaca. "When you didn't answer any of my phone calls or respond to my emails, I decided to come find you." She gathered a fortifying breath before plunging into deep water. "I want to know the real reason why things ended between us."

Nic tunneled his fingers into his shaggy black hair, a sure sign he was disturbed. "I told you—"

"That I was too distracting." She glared at him. Nic was her polar opposite. Always so serious, he never let go like other people. He held himself apart from the fun. She'd treated his solemnity as a challenge. And after years of escalating flirtation, she'd discovered he wasn't as in control as he appeared. "You weren't getting enough work done."

She exhaled in exasperation. For five months he'd stopped working on the weekends she'd visited and spent that entire time focused on her. All that attention had been heady and addictive. Brooke hadn't anticipated that he might wake up one morning and go back to his workaholic ways. "I don't get it. We were fantastic together. You were happy."

Nic's mouth tightened into a grim line. "It was fun. But you were all in and I wasn't."

Brooke bit her lip and considered what he said for an awkward, silent minute. "You broke up with me because I told you I loved you?" At the time she hadn't worried about confessing her feelings. After all, she was pretty sure he suspected she'd been falling for him for five years. "Did you ever intend to give us a chance?"

"I thought it was better to end it rather than to let things drag out. I was wrong to let things get so involved between us."

"Why didn't you tell me this in the first place?"

"I thought it would be easier on you if you believed I'd chosen work over you."

"Instead of being truthful and admitting I wasn't the one."

This wasn't how she'd expected this conversation to go. Deep in her heart she'd believed Nic was comfortable with how fast their relationship had progressed. She'd been friends with him long enough to know he didn't squander his time away from the *Griffin* project. This led her to believe she mattered to him. How could she have been so wrong?

Conflicting evidence tugged her thoughts this way and that. Usually she considered less and acted more, but being pregnant meant her actions impacted more than just her. She needed a little time to figure out how to approach Nic about her situation.

"I guess my optimistic nature got the better of me again." She lightened her tone to hide the deep ache centered in her chest.

"Brooke—"

"Don't." She held up both hands to forestall whatever he'd planned to say. "Why don't we not talk about this anymore while you give me a tour of your palatial estate."

"It's not palatial." His thick black eyebrows drew together in a grim frown.

"It is to a girl who grew up in a three-bedroom, fifteen-hundred-square-foot house."

Nic's only reply was a grunt. He got to his feet and gestured for her to precede him. Before entering the house, Brooke kicked off her sandals. The cool limestone tile soothed her tired feet as she slipped past him. Little brush fires ignited along her bare arm where it came into contact with his hair-roughened skin.

"This is the combination living-dining room and

kitchen," he said, adopting the tour guide persona he used when escorting potential *Griffin* investors.

She took in the enormous abstract paintings of red, yellow, blue and green that occupied the wall behind the white slip-covered couches. To her left, in the L-shaped kitchen, there was a large glass table with eight black chairs, offering a contrast among the white cabinets and stainless appliances. The space had an informal feel that invited relaxation.

"The white furniture and walls are a little stark for my taste," she said. "But it works with the paintings. They're wonderful. Who did them?"

"My sister."

He had a sister, too? "I'd like to meet her." Even as Brooke spoke the words, she knew that would never happen. Nic had made it perfectly clear he didn't want her in his life. She had a decision to make in the next day or so. It was why she'd come here. She needed his help to determine how the rest of her life would play out. "Did Glen know about your family?"

"Yes."

That hurt. The two men had always been as tight as brothers, but she never expected that Glen would keep secrets from her.

"Tell me about your brothers." She didn't know what to make of all these revelations.

"We're triplets. I'm the middle one."

"Two brothers and a sister," she murmured.

Who was Nic Alessandro? At the moment he looked nothing like the overworked rocket scientist she'd known for years. Although a bit wrinkled and worse for wear, his khaki shorts and white short-sleeved shirt had turned him into an ad for Armani's summer collection. In fact, his expensive sunglasses and elegant clothes transformed him from an absentminded scientist into your basic, run-of-the-mill European playboy. The makeover shifted him further out of reach.

"Is there anyone else I should know about?" Despite her best efforts to keep her tone neutral, her voice had an edge. "Like a wife?"

"No wife."

Brooke almost smiled at his dark tone. Once upon a time she'd taken great delight in teasing him, and it should have been easy to fall back into that kind of interaction. Unfortunately, the first time he'd kissed her, she'd crossed into a deeply serious place where his rejection had the power to bruise and batter her heart.

"Who takes care of all this when you're not here?" Keeping the conversation casual was the only way to keep sadness from overwhelming her.

"We have a caretaker who lives in town. She comes in once a week to clean when we're not in residence, more often when we are. She also cooks for us, and her husband maintains the gardens and the boat, and fixes whatever needs repairing in the house."

Brooke looked over her shoulder at the outdoor terrace with its informal wood dining table and canvas chairs. A set of three steps led down to another terrace with more lounge chairs. Potted herbs lined the three-foot-high walls, softening all the concrete.

"What's upstairs?"

Nic stood in the middle of the living room, his arms crossed, a large, immovable object. "Bedrooms."

"One I can use?" she asked in a small voice.

A muscle twitched in his jaw. "There are a number of delightful hotels in town."

"You'd turn me out?" Something flared in his eyes that brought her hope back to life. Maybe she hadn't yet heard the complete explanation for why he'd broken off their relationship. She faked a sniffle. "You can't really be so mean as to send me in search of a hotel when you have so much room here."

Nic growled. "I'll show you where you can shower and grab some sleep before you head home."

Although it stung that he was so eager to get rid of her, she'd departed California suspecting he wouldn't welcome her intrusion.

"Then, I can stay?"

"For the moment."

Mutely, she followed him back out through the open French doors and onto the terrace. He made a beeline toward the duffel bag she'd dropped beside the stairs that lead up from the beach.

"I can't get over how beautiful it is here."

"Most people are probably more familiar with the islands in the Aegean," he said, picking up her bag. "Mykonos, Santorini, Rhodes."

"I imagine there's a lot more tourists there."

"Quite a few. Kioni attracts a number of sailors during the summer as well as some people wanting to hike and enjoy a quieter island experience, but we're not overrun. Come on, the guesthouse is over there." He led the way along the terrace to a separate building.

"You should take me sightseeing."

"No. You are going to rest and then we're going to find you a flight home."

Brooke rolled her eyes at Nic's words and decided to take the fact that he kept trying to be rid of her as a challenge. "My return ticket is for a flight a week from now."

"Don't you have a lot to do to prepare for your students at Berkeley?"

"I don't have the job yet." Though Brooke held a position at UC Santa Cruz, teaching Italian studies at Berkeley had been a dream of hers since her sophomore year in college. And then she and Nic had begun a relationship. Soon the distance from San Francisco to the Mojave Desert had become an impediment to what she wanted: a life with Nic.

He shot her a sharp look.

She shrugged. "The interview got postponed again."

"To when?"

"Not for a few weeks yet."

In truth she wasn't sure when it was. There'd been some scheduling conflicts with the head of the department. He'd already canceled two meetings with her in the past month. Not knowing how many people were up for the position she wanted gnawed at her confidence. Few shared her research credentials, but a great many had more experience in the classroom than she did.

And before Nic had abruptly dumped her, she'd begun thinking she wanted to be closer to where he lived and worked. Seeing him only on the weekends wasn't enough. So she'd interviewed for a position at UCLA and been offered a teaching job starting in the fall. The weekend Nic had come up to San Francisco to break up with her, she'd been preparing for a very different conversation. One where she told him she was moving to LA. Only he'd beaten her to the punch and she'd decided to put the Berkeley job back on the table.

"Are you sure?" Nic questioned. "It's July. I can't believe they want to put off their decision too much longer."

She frowned at him, butterflies hatching in her stomach as she realized the risk she'd taken by flying here when she should be waiting by the phone in California. "Yes, I'm sure."

"Because I couldn't live with myself if you lost your dream job because you stayed here imagining I'm going to change my mind about us."

Had she been wrong about his initial reaction to her arrival? Had she so badly wanted him to be glad to see her that she'd imagined the delight in his gaze? It wouldn't be the first time she'd jumped to the wrong conclusion where a man's behavior was concerned. And Nic was a master at keeping his thoughts and emotions hidden.

"Don't worry about my dream job," she countered. "It will still be there when I get back."

She hoped.

When they arrived at the small guesthouse, Nic pushed open the door and set her luggage inside. "There's a private bathroom and a great view of Kioni. You should be comfortable here." Neither his impassive expression nor his neutral tone gave anything away. "Relax. Sleep. I'm sure you're exhausted from your travels. Breakfast will be waiting when you're ready."

"I'm not really hungry." Between morning sickness and anxiety, her appetite had fled. "And no matter how tired I am, you know I can't sleep when the sun is up. Why don't we go into town and you can show me around."

"You should rest."

His tone warned her not to argue. The wall he'd erected between them upset her. She wanted to tear it down with kisses and tears and impassioned pleas for him to change his mind about breaking up. But a big emotional scene would only cause him to retreat. She needed to appeal to that big logical brain of his.

"I've come a long way to find you. And talk."

"Later." He scowled at her to forestall any further discussion.

The determined set of his mouth told her she would get nowhere until he was ready to listen. She nodded, reluctant to provoke Nic into further impatience. She wanted him in a calm, agreeable state of mind when she imparted her dramatic news.

Left alone, Brooke took a quick shower in the white, marble bathroom and dressed in a tribal-print maxi dress of cool cotton. There was enough of a breeze blowing in through the open windows to dry her hair, but she didn't want to give Nic too much time to plan his strategy for getting her to leave. She decided to braid the damp strands rather than leave them loose. The last time they'd made love a little over a month ago, he'd shown a great appreciation for the disarray of her long, curly tresses, but now it seemed better to approach him logically and for that she needed to be restrained, not flirty.

Unfortunately, the mirror over the dresser reflected a woman in love, with wide eyes and a slightly unfocused gaze. Her mouth had a rosy fullness and her cheeks were pink. She doubted that this would go over well with Nic.

And after what he'd told her about his reasons for breaking up, Brooke was certain her pregnancy news would be unwelcome, too.

She hadn't given much thought to what came after she told Nic the news. Maybe she was afraid to face more rejection. What if he wanted nothing further to do with her? He'd said he wasn't returning to California. Would the news that he was going to be a father change his plans?

Brooke slid her feet into sandals, but paused before leaving the room. Talking with Nic about her Berkeley interview reminded her she hadn't checked her messages since leaving San Francisco. She dug her cell phone out of the side pocket of her duffel bag and tried to turn it on, but the battery had died. Time ticked away as she dug out her charger and searched for the adapter she'd borrowed. Then there were the minutes it took for the phone to charge enough to come back to life. By the time the display lit up and showed she'd missed a dozen calls, Brooke crackled with impatience.

Her heart sank as she listened to the messages. Her Berkeley interview had been rescheduled for 10:00 a.m. three days from now. This considerably shortened the amount of time Brooke had to tell Nic she was pregnant and figure out what form her future relationship with him would take. A quick check of flight schedules revealed that it would be daunting, but doable.

Brooke tossed the phone onto the middle of the bed and took several deep breaths until the tightness in her throat eased. After a few more deep breaths, the urge to throw herself onto the mattress and scream into a pillow subsided, too. Everything would work out just fine. Somehow it always did.

Applying a bright smile to her face, she strolled along the terrace. But as she stepped into the living room of the main house, the absolute quiet told her something was awry. A quick check confirmed her suspicions, but what clinched it was the car missing from the driveway.

Nic had vanished.

Two

Nic had switched from Greek coffee to beer by the time Brooke showed up in Kioni, the village rising from the harbor to cling to the side of Ithaca's rocky hills. From the shade beneath the taverna's white awning, he squinted against the bright sunlight sparkling off the cerulean water and watched his thirty-four-foot cruiser pull alongside the quay. Three Greek men, each wearing broad smiles, converged to issue instructions and help Brooke settle the boat. Although the distance prevented Nic from hearing their conversation, from Brooke's animated gestures and the men's cheerful faces, he guessed she was chattering away and doing what she did best: charming men.

"You're not drinking them as fast today."

Nic switched his attention to the voluptuous, dark-haired, dark-eyed waitress standing at his side. Natasa had waited on him all but one of the past ten days he'd been on the island. She picked up his half-full bottle, which he'd been nursing for the past hour.

"I'm not as thirsty."

Since arriving on Ithaca, Nic had been keeping himself anesthetized with boredom and beer. The combination was barely enough to keep his demons at bay. Before Brooke's arrival he'd given himself a week or so before he had to make peace with his failures and accept his fate. Now it was all coming to a head faster than he could handle.

Natasa gave him a smoky look and set her hand on her hip. "Perhaps you need some company."

Nic hadn't seen her flirt with any of the other men that came to the taverna, only him. He figured she knew who he was and suspected that had prompted her offer. Acid churned in his gut. Being treated like a personality rather than a person was something he hadn't had to endure in America. He hadn't had to be on his guard and question everyone's motives.

"I get off in two hours," she continued. "I would be happy to join you then."

Natasa had made him a similar proposition last night at closing time. Nic had been moderately drunk, but not enough to wish to share the bed with this woman, no matter how attractive she was. His carefree bachelor days had ended a month ago with Gabriel's marriage. Soon every woman he glanced at twice would become fodder for news stories.

It was worse for him being in Europe than living in America. In California he was an anonymous scientist trying to build a rocket ship. On this side of the Atlantic, he was known as Prince Nicolas, second in line to the throne of Sherdana. Avoiding reporters and paparazzi and being wary of helpful strangers had become a routine part of his life. That's why he and his brothers had chosen Ithaca as a retreat. Homer had described the island as "good for goats" but it gave the Alessandro brothers an escape from their hectic world.

Not that Nic was a fool. He knew his "anonymity" on this sleepy island was tenuous at best. But he and his brothers maintained a low profile, and the locals generously pretended the Sherdanian royals were like any other part-time inhabitants.

"I'm afraid I'm already due for some company," Nic said, nodding toward the harbor.

When the boat was snugly tied, three tanned hands extended to help Brooke onto the quay. She seemed to hesitate before accepting the hands of the two men nearest to her and offering the third man an engaging smile.

Natasa shielded her eyes as she gazed in the same direction Nic was looking. "Isn't that your boat?" Her keen black eyes narrowed as she glanced at him for confirmation.

"Yes."

"And the girl?"

"She's staying with me for a few days." Until the words left his lips he hadn't realized he'd changed his mind about putting her on a plane home as soon as humanly possible. Keeping her around was a mistake, but he was feeling battered and raw. Her company was the balm his psyche needed. He just needed to keep her at arm's length.

Natasa sniffed and tossed her head. Then, without another word, she turned to go. Nic gave a mental shrug. He'd retreated to Ithaca to come to grips with his future, not to tumble into some local's bed. He liked his own company. In fact, most days, he preferred it. Why didn't people understand that and leave him alone?

Reality smacked Nic right between the eyes. Soon enough he'd never be left alone again. Returning to Sherdana meant not only a return to duty, but also a complete loss of privacy and peace. Long, solitary hours in his workshop would be a thing of the past. His father and brothers would ensure that his calendar was packed with meetings, speeches and public appearances. He'd been absent for ten years, five years of studying and another five working with Glen on the *Griffin* project.

Now that he was returning home for good, his family would expect him to get up to speed on a variety of political, economic and environmental issues affecting the country. He would be surrounded by advisers, besieged by demands for decisions and sought after for his opinions.

Balls and state dinners with visiting foreign dignitaries would replace basketball tournaments and pig roasts with the team of specialists that he'd assembled to help build the *Griffin* rocket ship. Then there would be the selection of his bride. Once his mother finished narrowing the field of marriage prospects—women his brother had already rejected—Nic would have to choose whom he would spend the rest of his life with. And he wouldn't be allowed to dawdle over his decision because the succession needed to be secured by the birth of a royal heir.

The burden of what lay ahead of him sat on Nic's shoulders like a sack of cement. Was it any wonder he'd kept Brooke in the dark about his true identity all these years? He would have liked to continue pretending that he was just an ordinary man instead of a royal prince in serious trouble of doing the wrong thing with the right woman. But she'd never agree to back off unless she knew his whole story.

In disgruntled admiration, Nic followed Brooke's progress as she made her way around the horseshoe-shaped harbor. Since he'd left the house, she'd changed into an earth-toned sundress and accessorized with chunky bracelets and a peace sign necklace. Her red hair lay in a braided rope across her left shoulder. The breeze that frolicked through the streets teased the strands around her face that weren't long enough to be restricted by the braid.

Gulls jeered as they swooped past her. She appeared

oblivious to their taunts, focused as she was on scanning the quay. The hem of the sundress brushed her calves as she walked. The thin spaghetti straps were too narrow to hide a bra so he knew she was at least partially bare beneath the dress. Speculating on just how bare renewed the pounding in his head despite the aspirin he'd taken earlier.

She neared the taverna. Nic wasn't sure she'd spotted him yet. Eight restaurants edged the water. This particular taverna was Nic's favorite. He'd sampled enough of the menu in the years since they'd bought the villa to be able to make recommendations. The waitstaff always kept the cold beer coming while he took in the view of the vivid blue harbor, a welcome change from the beige and russet California desert where he'd spent the past several years.

For entertainment he liked to watch the comings and goings of the sailboats chartered by vacationers. The captains often wrestled with the difficulties presented by Mediterranean mooring, the docking technique where the anchor was dropped forty feet into the harbor and then the boat was backed up against the cement quay. Only an hour ago he'd been witness to what could go wrong when you had twenty boats snugged in side by side. One departing boat had lifted its anchor, catching its neighbor's as it went, only to at last drop that anchor across the lines belonging to the boat on the other side, hopelessly tangling the two boats. To Nic's amusement, much shouting and gesturing had accompanied the maneuver.

His earlier question about whether Brooke had spotted him was answered as she wove through the tables, aiming straight for him.

"Where did you get the keys to the boat?" he quizzed as she plopped a big canvas purse on the table and sat down with a whoosh of breath.

"Elena showed up shortly after you left. She fed me breakfast and told me where to find them. She's very nice.

And had flattering things to say about you. I think you're her favorite triplet."

Nic wondered what else Elena had said. Had the housekeeper divulged the rest of his secret?

"I doubt that very much. She's always been partial to Christian. He's the youngest. And the one all the ladies love."

"Why is that?"

"He's not as serious as Gabriel or me."

"What does he do?"

"He buys companies and takes them apart so he can sell off the pieces."

"And Gabriel?"

"He runs the family business." Not the truth, but not exactly a lie.

"And your sister paints."

"Ariana."

"And you build rocket ships. Sounds like you're all successful."

Not all of them. With the failure of his life's work, he certainly wasn't feeling particularly successful at the moment.

"I hope you don't mind, but I used your computer to print out some forms I needed to sign."

Even while on vacation the Alessandro triplets were often working on a project or a deal and having a state-of-the-art computer as well as a combination printer and scanner often came in handy.

"You figured out how to turn it on?"

As brilliant as she was when it came to learning languages or analyzing Italian literature, Brooke was technically challenged. She'd handwritten most of her first thesis until Nic had taken her to buy a laptop. He'd then lost an entire weekend to teaching her the ins and outs of the word-processing software as well as an app that enabled her to organize her research for easy reference.

"Ha-ha. I'm not as inept as you think I am."

"That's not saying much."

She pulled a face at him. "You had about forty unopened emails from the team. Why haven't you answered any of their questions?"

Nic shifted his gaze to the harbor and watched an inbound sailboat. "As I explained to you earlier, I'm done."

"How can you walk away from your team and all the hard work they've put in on the project?"

Why didn't she understand? Even if it wasn't his duty to return to Sherdana, Nic couldn't let go of the fact that his faulty design had destroyed the rocket and resulted in a man's death. Besides, Glen was the heart of the project. He would carry on in Nic's absence.

"Glen will find a new engineer," Nic said. "Work will continue."

The rocket's destruction had hastened the inevitable. Nic had known he couldn't stay in California forever. It was only a matter of time before responsibility to his country would have forced him to return home.

"But you were the brains behind the new fuel delivery system."

And his life's work had resulted in a complete disaster. "They have my notes."

"But—"

"Leave it alone." He kept his voice low, but the sharp snap of the words silenced her. An uneasy tension descended between them. "Are you hungry? If you like eggplant, the moussaka is very good."

She pressed her lips together, but Nic could see she wanted to argue with him further. Instead, she asked, "So, what are you going to do?"

"My family is going through a hard time right now. I'm going home."

"For how long?"

"For good."

"Wow."

The shaky breath she released was a punch to his gut. A week ago he'd left California as soon as the initial investigation of the accident concluded. He hadn't spoken to her before getting on a plane. His emotions were too raw. And he'd had no idea how to say goodbye.

"I wish I could make you understand, but I can't."

"You're afraid."

Nic eyed Brooke. Her perceptiveness where he was concerned had always made him wary of letting her get too close. Maybe telling her the truth would be a mistake. Giving her access to his life would increase his connection to her, and keeping his distance would become that much harder.

"Of hurting more people, yes."

She would assume he meant another scientist like Walter Parry, the man who'd died. But Nic was thinking about his family and her brother. And most of all her. When Gabriel's engagement had been announced, Nic had felt a loosening of the ties that bound him to Sherdana. Gabriel and Olivia would get married and go on to produce the future monarchs of Sherdana, raising them with Gabriel's twin two-year-old daughters, Bethany and Karina, who'd come to live with Gabriel after their fashion model mother had died a month earlier. They were illegitimate and the only children Gabriel would ever have.

Lady Olivia's infertility—and Gabriel's decision to make her his wife—meant Nic and Christian were no longer free to marry whomever they wished. Or, in Christian's case, to continue enjoying his playboy lifestyle and never marry at all.

Nic cursed the circumstances that had turned his life upside down and sucked him back into a world that couldn't include Brooke. If he'd been a simple scientist, he wouldn't have to resist the invitation in her eyes. Nic shoved away the traitorous thought. It was pointless to dwell on what could never be.

"I can't believe you're really going to give it all up," she said. "You and my brother were excited about the future. The pair of you would get so caught up in a new discovery you wouldn't have noticed if a tornado swept the lab away. You love being a scientist."

"I do, but…" In the three weeks since the rocket had blown up, he'd lost confidence in his abilities. Yet his passion continued to burn. The opposing forces were slowly tearing him apart.

"What are you going to do when you go home?"

"My brothers are interested in luring technology-based companies into the country. They want me to be their technical consultant."

He tried to inject some enthusiasm into his voice and failed. While he agreed with Gabriel that Sherdana's economy would benefit from an influx of such businesses, he wasn't excited about his role in the process. His whole life he'd been actively engaged in creating technologies that would shape the future. The idea of promoting someone else's vision depressed him.

"Sooo," she dragged the word out, "you're never coming back to California?"

"No."

"If this is about the rocket…"

"It's not."

"I don't understand what's going on with you." She looked more than puzzled. She looked worried. "It's not like you to give up."

Nic knew she deserved a full explanation, but once she

found out he'd been keeping a huge secret from her all these years she was going to be furious. "There's a little something about me you don't know."

"Oh, I think there's more than a little something."

He ignored her sarcasm. "It's complicated."

"It's okay. As you pointed out earlier, I have two doctorates. I can understand complicated."

"Very well. I'm not an ordinary scientist." He lowered his voice, wishing he'd had this conversation with her at the villa. "I'm Prince Nicolas Alessandro, second in line to the throne of Sherdana."

"A prince? Like a real prince?" Her misty-green eyes blurred and she shook her head as if to rid her brain of his admission. "I don't get it. You sound as American as I do."

"I went to college in Boston. In order to fit in, I eliminated my accent." Nic leaned forward, glad that there was a table between them. He longed to pull her into his arms and kiss away her unhappiness. That was something he could never again do. "My country is Sherdana. It's a small kingdom tucked between France and Italy."

"How small?"

"A little less than two thousand square kilometers with a population of just over four hundred thousand. We're mostly known for our—"

"Wines." She slapped her palm on the table. His beer rattled against the hard surface. "Now I remember why the name is so familiar. Glen had bottles of Sherdanian wine at one of his recent parties."

Nic remembered that evening without pleasure. "It was his way of sending me a message. He wanted me to tell you the truth."

She stared at Nic with dawning horror. "You jerk. I've known you for five years. And you've kept this huge thing from me the whole time? What did you think I was going to do with the information? Sell you out to the press? Torment you with Disney references? Well, that I would have done, but you're a prince—you could have handled that."

Nic waited for her rant to wind down, but she was on a roll and wasn't going to be stopped until she had her say.

"I thought we were friends." Below the irritation in her voice, she sounded as if her heart was breaking. "Why didn't you tell me any of this?"

"I've concealed my identity for a lot of years. It's a hard habit to break."

"Concealed it from strangers, coworkers, acquaintances." The breath she needed to take wasn't available. "How long has my brother known? Probably since you met. You two are as close as brothers." She shut her eyes. "Imagine how I feel, Nic. You've been lying to me as long as I've known you."

"Glen said—"

"Glen?" She pinned him with a look of such fury that a lesser man would have thrown himself at her feet to grovel for forgiveness. "My brother did not tell you to lie to me."

No. Nic had decided to do that all on his own. "He told me you'd never leave it alone if you knew."

"Are you kidding me?" Her eyes widened in dismay. "You were worried that I'd come on even stronger if I knew you were a prince? Is that how low your opinion is of me?"

"No. That's not what I meant—"

"I came here looking for scientist Nic," she reminded him. "That's the man I thought I knew. Who I've—"

"Brooke, stop." Nic badly needed to cut off her declaration.

"—fallen in love with."

Pain, hot and bright, sliced into his chest. "Damn it. I never wanted that." Which was his greatest lie to date.

"Was that how you felt before or after we became intimate?"

"Both." Hoping to distract her, he said, "Do you have any idea how irresistible you are?"

"Is that supposed to make me feel better?"

"It's supposed to explain why I started a relationship with you six months ago after I'd successfully withstood the attraction between us for the last five years."

"Why did you fight it?" She frowned "What happened between us was amazing and real."

His breath exploded from his lungs in a curse. "A month ago we had this conversation. I thought you understood."

"A month ago you claimed your work was the most important thing in your life. Now I find out you never had deep feelings for me and didn't mean to mislead me about where our relationship was heading. But I've always been of the opinion that a woman should react to how a man behaves, not what he says, and you acted like a very happy man when we were together."

"I was happy. But I was wrong to give you the impression I could offer you any kind of future."

"Because you don't care about me?"

"Because I have to go home."

Her brows drew together. "You didn't think I would go with you?"

"You have a life in California. Family. Friends. A career."

"So instead of asking me what I wanted, you made the decision for me."

"Except I can't ask." His frustration was no less acute than hers. "A month ago my older brother made a decision that affects not only my life, but the future of Sherdana."

"What sort of decision?"

"He married a woman who can never have children."

Brooke stared at him in mystified silence for a long moment before saying, "That's very sad, but what does it have to do with you?"

"It's now up to me to get married and make sure the Alessandro royal blood line is continued."

"You're going to marry?" She sat back, her hands falling from the table onto her lap.

"So that I can produce an heir. I'm second in line to the throne. It's my duty."

Her expression flattened into blank shock for several seconds as she absorbed his declaration. He'd never seen her dumbfounded. Usually she had a snappy retort for everything. Her quick mind processed at speeds that constantly amazed him.

"Your younger brother can't do it?"

The grim smile he offered her conveyed every bit of his displeasure. "I'm quite certain mother intends to see that we are both married before the year is out."

"It is a truth universally acknowledged," she quoted, "that a single man in possession of a good fortune, must be in want of a wife." She stared at the taverna's logo printed in blue on the white place mat as if the answers to the universe were written there in code. "And I'm not the one you want."

"It isn't that simple." He gripped his beer in both hands to keep from reaching out and offering her comfort. "In order for my child to be eligible to ascend Sherdana's throne someday, the constitution requires that his mother has to be either a Sherdana citizen or a member of Europe's aristocracy."

"And I'm just an ordinary girl from California with two doctorates." The corners of her mouth quivered in a weak attempt at a smile. "I get it."

Three

Beneath the grapevines woven through the taverna's roof beams, the afternoon heat pressed in on Brooke. Light-headed and slightly ill, she didn't realize how much she'd set her hopes on Nic's returning to California and giving their relationship another try until he crushed her dreams with his confession. Her fingers fanned over her still-flat abdomen and the child that grew there. Not once since she'd learned she was pregnant had she considered raising this child utterly on her own. Nic had always been there for her. First as her brother's friend. Then her friend. And finally as her lover.

When she'd strayed from her topic during the writing of her second thesis he'd spent hours on the phone talking her through her research and her arguments. He'd gone with her to buy both her cars. He always shared his dessert with her when they went out to dinner even though she knew it drove him crazy that she never ordered her own. And in a dozen little ways, he stayed present in her life even though physically they lived miles apart.

For an instant she recalled the last time she and Nic had made love. She'd gazed deep into his eyes and glimpsed her future. During their time together, their lovemaking had been in turn fast, hot, slow and achingly sweet. But on their last night in particular, they'd both been swept away by urgent intensity. Yet there'd been a single look suspended between one breath and the next that held her transfixed. In that instant, an important connection had been made between them and she'd been forever changed.

But now...

A prince.

The conversion from distracted, overworked scientist to intense, sexy aristocrat had been apparent when she'd arrived this morning. At first she'd ascribed the change to his European-style clothing, but now she understood he'd been transformed in a far more elemental manner.

A month ago he'd given her a speech about how he needed to refocus on *Griffin*, and that meant he had to stop seeing her. She'd been frustrated by the setback, but figured it was only a matter of time until he figured out they were meant to be together. When he'd left California in the wake of the accident, the bond had stretched and thinned, but it had held. Awareness of Nic had hummed across that psychic filament. Although compelled to track him down and investigate if her instincts were correct, she'd decided to give him some space to process the accident before she followed him. Her pregnancy had made finding him much more urgent.

But what good was the bond between them when the reality was he was a prince who needed to find a wife so he could father children that would one day rule his country?

And what about her own child? This was no longer a simple matter of being pregnant with Nic's baby. She was carrying the illegitimate child of a prince. For a moment the taverna spun sickeningly around her. Telling Nic he was going to be a father had become that much more complicated.

Somehow she found the strength of will to summon a wry smile. "Besides, you and I both know I'm not princess material."

"You'd hate it," Nic told her in somber tones. To her relief he'd taken her self-deprecating humor at face value. "All the restrictions on how you dressed and behaved."

"Being polite to people instead of setting them straight." He was right. She'd hate it. "The endless parties to attend where I had to smile until my face hurt. I'm so not the type."

The litany leached away her optimism. With hope reaching dangerously low levels, she cursed the expansive hollowness inside her. Nothing had felt the same since she'd stepped onto this island. It wasn't just Nic's fancy clothes, expensive villa and the whole prince thing. He was different. And more unreachable than ever.

How am I supposed to live without you?

The question lodged in her throat. She concentrated on breathing evenly to keep the tears at bay.

"Are you okay?"

Her pulse spiked at his concerned frown. In moments like these he surprised her by being attuned to her mood. And keeping track of how she was feeling was no small task. Her family often teased her about being a drama girl. She enjoyed life to the fullest, reveling in each success and taking disappointments as world-ending. As she'd gotten older, she'd learned to temper her big emotions and act on impulse less frequently.

Except where Nic was concerned. Common sense told her if she'd behave more sensibly, Nic might be more receptive to her. But everything about him aroused her passion and sent her into sensory overload.

"Brooke?"

Unable to verbalize the emotions raging through her, she avoided looking at Nic and found the perfect distraction in a waitress's hard stare. The woman had been watching from the kitchen doorway ever since Brooke had sat down. "I don't think that waitress likes me," Brooke commented, indicating the curvaceous brunette. "Did I interrupt something between you two?"

"Natasa? Don't be ridiculous."

His impatient dismissal raised Brooke's spirits slightly. She already knew Nic wasn't the sort to engage in casual encounters. Her five-year pursuit of him had demonstrated that he wasn't ruled by his body's urges.

"She's awfully pretty and hasn't taken her eye off you since I sat down."

"Do you want something to eat?" Nic signaled Natasa and she came over.

"Another beer for me," he told the waitress. "What are you drinking?" He looked to Brooke.

"Water."

"And an order of *taramosalata*."

"What is that?" Brooke quizzed, her gaze following the generous sway of Natasa's hips as she wound her way back toward the kitchen.

"A spread made from fish roe. You'll like it."

You'll like it.

Did he realize the impact those words had on her nerve endings?

It was what he'd said to her their first night together. To her amazement, once he'd stopped resisting her flirtatious banter and taken the lead, she'd been overcome by his authoritative manner and had surrendered to his every whim. Her skin tingled, remembering the sweep of his fingers across the sensitized planes of her body. He'd made love to her with a thoroughness she'd never known. Not one inch of her body had gone unclaimed by him and she'd let it all happen. Her smile had blazed undiminished for five months until he'd driven up to San Francisco for *the talk*.

Natasa returned with their drinks. She gave Brooke a quick once-over, plunked two bottles on the table and shot Nic a hard look he didn't notice. Brooke grinned as Nic reached for her bottled water and broke the seal without being asked. He didn't know it, but this was just one of the things that had become a ritual with them. During the past five years, Brooke had repeatedly asked him to do her small favors and Nic had obliged, grumbling all the while about her inability to do the simplest tasks. He'd never figured out that each time he helped her, he became a little more invested in their relationship.

Six months ago all her subtle efforts had brought results. After a successful test firing of the *Griffin*'s ignition system, the team had been celebrating in Glen's backyard. Nic had been animated, electrified. She'd been a moth to his flame, basking in his warm smiles and affectionate touches. At the end of the evening he'd meshed their fingers together and drawn her to the privacy of the front porch where he'd kissed her silly.

Lying sleepless in her bed that night she'd relived the mind-blowing kiss over and over and wondered what she'd done to finally break through Nic's resistance. She hadn't been able to pinpoint anything, nor did she think that day's success had been the trigger. The team had enjoyed several triumphs in the previous few months. In the end Brooke had decided her years of flirting had finally begun to reach him.

After that night, she'd noticed a subtle difference in the way Nic behaved toward her and began to hope that he might have finally figured out she was the one for him.

Brooke increased the frequency of her weekend visits to the Mojave Air and Space Port, where the *Griffin* team had their offices. Despite the increased urgency to finish the rocket and get it ready for a test launch, Nic had made time for quiet dinners. Afterward, they'd often talked late into the night. After two months, he'd taken things to the next level. He'd shared not just his body with her, but his dreams and desires, as well. At the time, she'd thought she was getting to know the real Nic. Now she realized how much he'd kept from her.

With fresh eyes, Brooke regarded her brother's best friend and saw only a stranger. In his stylish clothes and expensive shades he looked every inch a rich European. She contemplated the arrogant tilt of his head, the utter command of his presence as he watched her. Why had she never picked up on it earlier?

Because his English was flawlessly Americanized. Because he went to work every day in ordinary jeans and T-shirts. Granted, he filled out his commonplace clothes in an extraordinary manner, but nothing about his impressive pecs and washboard abs screamed aristocracy. She'd always assumed he rarely let off steam with his fellow scientists because he was preoccupied with work.

Now she realized he'd been brought up with different expectations placed upon him than people in her orbit. A picture formed in her mind. Nic, tall and proud, his broad shoulders filling out a formfitting tuxedo, a red sash across his chest from shoulder to hip. He looked regal. Larger than life. Completely out of reach.

Brooke had always believed that people didn't regret the things they did, only the things they didn't. She liked to believe she was richer for every experience she'd had, good or bad. Would she have given her heart to Nic if she'd known who he was from the beginning? Yes. Brief as it had been, she cherished every moment of their time together.

While logic enabled her to rationalize why she couldn't marry him, her heart prevented her from walking away without a backward glance. And she suspected he wasn't thrilled to be sacrificing himself so that his family could continue to reign. As devastating as it was to think she'd have to give up on a future with Nic, wanting to be with him was a yearning she couldn't shake off.

"I'm going to ask you a question," she announced abruptly, her gaze drilling through his bland expression. "And I expect the truth this time."

Nic's beer bottle hung between the table and his lips. "I suppose I owe you that."

"You're darned right you do." She ignored the brief flare of amusement in his eyes. "I want to know the real reason you broke up with me."

"I've already explained the reason. We have no future. I have to go home and I have to marry." He stared at the harbor behind her, his expression chiseled in granite.

She'd obviously phrased her question wrong. "And if your brother hadn't married someone who couldn't have children? Would you have broken things off?"

What she really wanted to know was if he loved her, but she wasn't sure he'd pondered how deep his feelings for her ran. Also, a month ago he'd apparently accepted that he had to marry someone else and it wasn't his nature to dwell on impossibilities.

"It's a simple question," she prompted as the silence stretched. He surely hated being put on the spot like this, but she couldn't move on until she knew.

His chest rose and fell on a huge sigh as he met her gaze with heavy-lidded eyes. Something flickered within those bronze-colored depths. Something that made her stomach contract and her spirits soar.

She'd journeyed to Ithaca to tell him about the baby, but also because she couldn't bear to let him go. Now she understood that she had to. But not yet. She had two days before she had to return to the States. Two days to say goodbye. All she needed was a sign from Nic that he hadn't wanted to give her up.

"No." He spoke the word like a curse. "We'd still be together."

The instant the words left his lips, Nic wished he'd maintained the lies. Brooke's eyes kindled with satisfaction and her body relaxed. She resembled a contented cat. He'd seen the look many times and knew it meant trouble.

"I think we should spend the time between now and when you leave *together*." She gave the last word a specific emphasis that he couldn't misinterpret.

Nic shook his head, vigorously rejecting her suggestion. "That's not fair to you." *Duty. Honor. Integrity.* He repeated the words like a prayer. "I won't take advantage of you that way."

Brooke leaned forward, her gaze sharpening. "Has it ever occurred to you that I like it when you take advantage of me?"

The world beyond their table blurred until it was only him and her and the intense emotional connection that had clicked into place the first time they'd made love, a connection that couldn't be severed.

"I never noticed." His attempt to banter with her so that she'd adopt a less serious mood fell flat.

Her determination gained momentum. "Tell me you don't want to spend your last days of freedom with me."

Every molecule that made up his body screamed at him to agree. "It's not that I don't want to. I shouldn't." He spoke quickly to prevent her from arguing with him. "Ever since finding out I had to return home and get married, I promised myself I wouldn't touch you again."

"That's just silly." She gave him a wicked smile. "You like touching me."

In the time he'd known her, he'd learned just how powerful that smile could be. It had whittled away at his willpower until he'd done the one thing he knew he shouldn't. He'd fallen hard.

Duty. Honor. Integrity. The lament filled his mind. If only Brooke didn't make it so damned hard to do the right thing.

She got up from her chair and stepped into his space.

He tipped his head back and assessed her determined expression. His heart shuddered as she put her palms flat on his shoulders and settled herself on his lap. Even though Nic had braced himself for the arousing pressure of her firm rear on his thighs, it took every bit of concentration he possessed to put his hands behind his back, safely out of range of her tempting curves. What sort of hell had he let himself fall into?

"What do you think you're doing?"

"Are you all right?" she asked, tracing her fingertips across his furrowed brow.

God, she was a tempting lapful.

"I'm fine."

"You don't look fine."

"I'm great, and you didn't answer my question." He pulled her spicy scent into his lungs and held it there. He longed to bury his face in her neck and imprint her upon his senses. "What are you doing on my lap?"

"Demonstrating that you want me as much as I want you."

He hated himself for hoping she'd continue the demonstration until he couldn't catch his breath. Making love to her was amazing. He'd never been with anyone who matched him the way she did. Anticipation gnawed on him like a puppy with a stolen shoe.

"I assure you I want you a great deal more." How he kept his voice so clinical, Nic would never know.

"Then you'll let me stay on the island for the next few days?"

She knew him better than anyone and once she'd discovered his weakness where she was concerned, she'd pressed her advantage at every opportunity. Before they'd made love, she'd slipped past his defenses like a ninja. Now they'd been intimate and he didn't doubt that she would exploit his passion to get her way.

"I left California without saying goodbye because leaving you was so damned hard." When he'd broken off things a month ago, he'd been lucky to escape before her shock at his announcement wore off. Ending their relationship was one of the hardest things he'd ever done. If she'd begged him to stay, he wasn't sure if he could have done the right thing by Sherdana. "Nothing good will come of putting off the inevitable."

"The way you disappeared left me feeling anxious and out of sorts. I understood that we'd broken up, but what I didn't get was how you could take off without saying anything. You should have explained your circumstances. I could have processed the situation and gotten closure. That's what I need now. A few days to say goodbye properly."

"And by properly you mean…?"

Her serious expression dissolved into one of unabashed mischief. "A few days of incredible sex and unbridled passion should do it."

How could any man resist such an offer? Visions of her flat on her back with his hands skimming along her soft, delectable curves rose to torture him. A smile and a frown played tug-of-war on his face. But this was not the time to stop listening to the voice inside his head that reminded him he had to give her up. The smartest thing would be to avoid making more memories that would haunt him the rest of his life.

"Don't you think it would be better if we didn't let ourselves indulge in something that has no future?"

"I'm not going to pretend we have a future. I'm going to cherish every moment of our time together with the knowledge that in the end we'll say goodbye forever." She slid her fingers into his hair. Her thumbs traced the outline of his ears. "I can see you need more convincing, so I'm going to kiss you."

He drank in the scent of honey and vanilla rising off her skin, knowing she tasted as good as she smelled. Her generous lips, rosy and bare of lipstick, parted in anticipation of the promised kiss. Nothing would make him happier than to spend the rest of his life enjoying the curve and texture of her lips. The way she sighed as he kissed her. The soft hitch in her breath as he grazed her lower lip with his teeth.

A tremor transmitted her agitation to him. He longed to inspire more such trembling. To revisit her most ticklish spots, the erogenous zones that made her moan. With erotic impulses twisting his nerves into knots, Nic snagged her gaze. Silver flecks ringed her irises, growing brighter as she stared at his mouth. His pulse thundered in his ears as the moment stretched without a kiss coming anywhere near his lips.

"Damn it, Brooke."

He would not scoop the wayward strand of hair behind her tiny ear and let his knuckles linger against her flushed cheek. He refused to tug on her braid and coax her lips close enough to drift over his.

"What's the matter, Nic?" Her fingers explored his eyebrows and tested his lashes.

Duty. Honor. Integrity. The litany was starting to lose its potency.

"In less than a week I'll never see you again." He locked his hands together behind his back. Tremors began in his arm muscles.

"I know." She switched her attention to his mouth. Her long, red lashes cast delicate shadows on her cheeks.

Heat surged into his face. Hell, heat filled every nook and cranny of his body. Especially where her heart-shaped rear end rested. How could she help but notice his aroused state?

"We'd only be prolonging the inevitable," he reminded her, unsure why he was holding out when he wanted so badly to agree to her mad scheme.

"I need this. I need you." She stroked her thumb against his lower lip. "An hour. A day. A week. I'll take whatever I can get."

Nic counted his heartbeats to avoid focusing on the emotions raging through him. The need to crush her in his arms would overwhelm him any second. Denying himself her compassion and understanding in the days following the accident hadn't been easy, but at the time he'd known that he had to return to Sherdana. Just because Brooke now knew what was going on didn't give him permission to stop acting honorably.

He wasn't prepared for the air she blew in his ear. His body jerked in surprise, and he sucked in a sharp breath. "Stop that."

"You didn't like it?" Laughter gave her voice a husky quality.

"You know perfectly well I did," he murmured hoarsely. "Our food is going to be here any second. Perhaps you should return to your own seat."

"I'm here for a kiss and a kiss is what I'm going to get." She was enjoying this far too much. And, damn it, so was he.

With a fatalistic sigh, Nic accepted that he'd let himself

be drawn too far into her game to turn back. As much as he wanted to savor the expressions flitting across her face, he stared at the fishing boats bobbing near the cement seawall. Alert to her slightest movement, he felt the tingle on his cheek an instant before her lips grazed his skin.

"Let's stop all the foreplay, shall we," he finally said.

"Oh, all right. Spoilsport. I was enjoying having you at my mercy. But if you insist."

Lightning danced in her eyes. She secured his face between her hands and grazed her lips across his.

"Again." His voice was half demand, half plea. He hardened his will and inserted steel into his tone. "And this time put a little effort into it."

"Whatever you say."

He let his lashes drop as her mouth drifted over his again. This time she applied more pressure, a little more technique. As kisses went, it was pretty chaste, but her little hum of pleasure tipped his world on its axis. And when she nibbled on his lip, murmuring in Italian, desire incinerated his resistance.

"Benedette le voci tante ch'io chiamando il nome de mia donna ò sparte, e i sospiri, et le lagrime, e 'l desio."

How was he supposed to resist a woman with a PhD in Italian literature? Although he knew what she'd said, he wanted to hear her speak the words again.

"Translation?"

"And blessed be all of the poetry I scattered, calling out my lady's name, and all the sighs, and tears, and the passion."

"Italian love poetry?" he groused, amused in spite of the lust raking him with claws dipped in the sweetest aphrodisiac.

"It seemed appropriate." Her fingers splaying over his rapidly beating heart, she swooped in for one last kiss before getting to her feet. "I think I made my point." With a satisfied smirk, she returned to her chair.

"What point?"

"That we both could use closure."

Over the course of the kiss he'd grasped what she wanted to do, but he'd worked diligently over the past month to come to grips with living without her and couldn't imagine reopening himself to the loss all over again. And she'd just demonstrated he'd never survive a few days let alone a week in her company. He'd be lucky if he made it past the next hours. No. She had to go. And go soon. Because if she didn't, he'd give in and make love to her. And that would be disastrous.

"I got my closure a month ago when I broke things off," he lied. "But I understand that I've sprung a lot of information on you today that you'll want to assimilate. Stay for a couple days."

"As friends?" She sounded defeated.

"It's for the best."

Four

The discussion before lunch dampened Brooke's spirits and left her in a thoughtful mood as she ate her way through a plate of moussaka, and followed that up with yogurt and honey for dessert. Nic, never one for small talk, seemed content with the silence, but he watched her through half-lidded eyes.

Telling him she was pregnant had just become a lot more complicated. As had her decision regarding the teaching position at Berkeley. Before Nic had broken it off with her a month ago she'd been confident that he was her future and she'd chosen him over her ideal job. When he left she should have returned to her original career path, but finding out that she was pregnant had created a whole new group of variables.

Gone was her fantasy that once Nic heard he was going to be a father, he would return to California and they would live happily ever after as a family. Since that wasn't going to happen, the Berkeley job was back on the table. Brooke wished she could summon up the enthusiasm she'd once felt at the possibility of teaching there.

And then there were the challenges that came with being a single mom. If she moved back to LA she would be close to her parents and they would be thrilled to help.

Thanks to Nic's revelations she was a bundle of indecisiveness. They returned to Nic's car for the ride back to the villa. He told her he would have Elena's husband, Thasos, return the boat later. As the car swept along the narrow road circling Kioni's tranquil bay, Brooke felt her anxiety rise and fall with each curve.

From this vantage point, halfway up the side of the scrubby hills that made up the island's landscape, she could see beyond the harbor to the azure water of the Ionian Sea. Glen had described Ithaca as a pile of rocks with scrubby brush growing here and there, but he'd done the picturesque landscape a disservice.

"We'll be to my house in ten minutes." Nic pointed toward a spot on the hill where a bit of white was visible among the green hillside.

In the short time she'd been here, Brooke had fallen in love with Nic's villa. It made her curious about the rest of his family and the life they lived in Sherdana. Did they live in a palace? She tried to picture Nic growing up in a fussy, formal place with hundreds of rooms and dozens of servants.

As the villa disappeared from view around another bend, Brooke glanced over her shoulder and estimated the distance back to the village. Two or three miles. The car turned off the main road and rolled down a long driveway that angled toward the edge of the cliff. When first the extensive gardens and then the house came into view, she caught her breath.

"This is beautiful," she murmured, certain her compliment wasn't effusive enough. "I didn't see this side of the house earlier."

"Gabriel found the place. We bought it for our eighteenth birthday. I'm afraid I haven't used it much."

Built on a hillside overlooking the bay, the home was actually a couple buildings connected together by terraces and paths. Surrounded by cypress and olive trees, the stucco buildings with the terra-cotta tile roofs sprawled on the hillside, their gardens spread around them like skirts.

The nearby hills had been planted with cosmos, heather and other native flowering plants to maintain a natural look. A cluster of small terra-cotta pots, containing bright pink and lavender flowers greeted visitors at the door. A large clay urn had been tipped on its side in the center of the grouping to give the display some height and contrast.

Nic stopped the car. Shutting off the engine, he turned to face her, one hand resting on the seat behind her head. The light breeze blew a strand of hair across her face. Before Brooke could deal with it, Nic's fingers drifted along her cheek and pushed it behind her ear. She half shut her eyes against the delight that surged in her. Her stomach turned a cartwheel as she spied the thoughtful half smile curving his lips. Nic's smile was like drinking brandy. It warmed her insides and stimulated her senses.

"Maybe tomorrow I can show you the windmills," he said, his gaze drifting over her face. The fondness in his eyes made her chest tighten.

"Sure." Her voice had developed a disconcerting croak. She cleared her throat. "I'd like that."

She let out an enormous yawn while Nic was unlocking the front door. He raised his eyebrows and she clapped her hand over her mouth.

"I see you didn't take my advice earlier about getting some sleep."

"I was too wound up. Now I'm having trouble keeping my eyes open. Feel like joining me for a nap?"

Only a minute widening of his eyes betrayed Nic's reaction to her offer. "From what you've told me I have a bunch of emails to answer. I'll catch up with you before dinner."

All too familiar with Nic's substantial willpower, Brooke retreated to the terrace where she'd first found him. In the harbor a hundred feet below, the water was an incredible cerulean blue, the color accentuated by the tile roofs of the houses that lined the wharf and scaled the steep verdant green hills cupping the horseshoe-shaped harbor.

She rested her hands on the stone wall and pondered the nature of fate. Before she'd met Nic, she'd been pursued by any number of men who were ready to do what it took to win her affection. But instead of falling for one of them, she'd chosen a man who was far more interested in his rocket ship than her. All the while, she'd hoped that maybe his enthusiasm for his work could somehow translate into passion for her.

The explosive chemistry between her and Nic had seemed like a foundation they could build a relationship on. The way he'd dropped his guard and given her a glimpse of his emotions had left her breathless with hope that maybe his big-brother act had been his way of protecting his heart. Thanks to all her previous romantic escapades that Glen was only too happy to bring up over and over, Nic had regarded her as a bit of a loose cannon when it came to love.

Brooke turned her back on the view. She had a lot to think about. Following Nic to this island had proved way more interesting and enlightening than she'd expected.

While she'd only been his best friend's little sister, it hurt that neither man trusted her with the truth. She didn't blame Glen for keeping Nic's confidences. Her brother wouldn't have been the amazing man he'd been without his honorable side. But she could, and did, blame Nic for keeping her in the dark.

For five years he'd kept some enormous secrets from her. That knowledge stung. But now she had a secret of her own. Given what she now knew about Nic, what was her best course of action?

Despite her exhaustion after being awake for twenty-four hours, she paced, the sound of her sandals slapping against the stone of the terrace breaking the tranquil silence. Seeing Nic, kissing him and finding out that he was not the hardworking scientist she'd always known but a prince of some country she'd only heard of in passing, had her thoughts in a frenetic whirl.

And then there was the big question of the day. The one she'd been avoiding for the past hour. Was she going to tell Nic about her pregnancy?

In the wake of all she'd learned, was it fair to tell him he was going to be a father? He couldn't marry her even if he'd wanted to. Nor would they be living on the same continent. Being the prince of a small European country meant he would be under the keenest scrutiny. Would he even want to acknowledge an illegitimate child? Yet was it fair to deny him the opportunity to make that decision?

Her best friend, Theresa, would help her answer some of these questions. She was the most sensible and grounded person in Brooke's life. Brooke went down to the guesthouse, retrieved her phone from the bed where she'd left it and dialed Theresa's number.

"Well, it's about time you called me back," Theresa started, sounding more like Brooke's mother than her best friend. "I've left you, like, four messages."

Brooke tried to shrug away the tension in her shoulders, but that was hard when she was braced against an onslaught of lecturing. "Five, actually. I'm sorry I didn't call sooner—"

"You know I'm just worried about you. The last time we talked, you were going to get your brother to tell you where Nic had gone."

"I did that."

"So where is he?"

"About two miles down the road from the most gorgeous Greek town you've ever seen."

"And you know this Greek town is so gorgeous because...?" Theresa's voice held a hint of alarm.

"I've seen it."

"Brooke, no."

"Yep."

A long pause followed. Brooke almost wished she was there to watch her best friend's expression fluctuate from annoyed to incredulous and back again.

"What about the Berkeley interview?"

"It's in three days."

"Are you going to make it back in time?"

In truth she wasn't sure she wanted to. The idea of raising a baby by herself scared her. She wanted to be close to family and that meant living in LA. "That's my intention."

"What was Nic's reaction when you showed up?"

"He was pretty surprised to see me."

"And when you told him about the baby?"

Panic and longing surged through her in confusing, conflicting waves. Twenty-four hours earlier, coming to find him had felt necessary instead of reckless or impulsive. And in hindsight, it had been foolishly optimistic. She'd been convinced Nic would return to California with her once he knew he was going to be a father.

"I haven't yet."

"What are you waiting for?"

Brooke fell back on the bed and stared at the ceiling. "Things got a little complicated after I got here."

"Did you sleep with him again?"

"No." She paused to smile. "Not yet."

"Brooke, you are my best friend and I want nothing but the best for you," Theresa began in overly patient tones. "But you need to realize if he wanted to be with you he would."

"It's not as simple as that." Or was it? Hadn't Nic chosen duty to his country over her? Once again Brooke pictured Nic in formal attire, standing between two other men who looked just like him. Beside them were two thrones where an older couple wearing crowns sat in regal splendor. "But he cares about me. It's just that he's in a complicated situation. And I couldn't tell him over the phone that I'm pregnant."

"Okay. I'll give you that." Theresa was making an effort to be positive and supportive, but clearly she didn't believe that Brooke's actions were wise. "But you chased him all the way to Greece. And now you haven't told him. So what's wrong?"

"What makes you think anything is wrong?"

"Gee, I don't know. We've been best friends since third grade. I think I can tell when something's bothering you. What's going on?" Theresa's voice softened. "Is he doing okay?"

As long as the two girls had known each other, Theresa never understood Brooke's restless longing for the drama of romance. The thrill of flirting. The heart-pounding excitement of falling in love. Married to a man she'd dated since college, Theresa was completely and happily settled. Safe with a reliable husband. And although Theresa would never say it out loud, Brooke always felt as if her friend judged her because she wanted more.

"Physically yes, unless you count hungover. He looked terrible when I showed up this morning."

"So, he's really taking the accident hard."

"Of course he is. He and Glen have been obsessed with

this dream of theirs for five long years. And as you said, he blames himself for what happened." Brooke's breath came out in a ragged sigh as her reaction to what she'd learned finally caught up with her. "He's not coming back."

"Sure he is. If anyone can convince him to not give up it's you."

"I can't. There's a bunch of other things going on."

"What kind of other things?"

"Turns out there are problems at home and he has to go back and marry someone."

"What?" Theresa screeched. "He's engaged?"

"Not yet, but he will be soon."

"Soon? How soon? Does he have a girlfriend he's going to propose to? Is that why he broke your heart?"

"No." Brooke knew she wasn't being clear, but was having a hard time explaining what she still struggled to grasp. "Nothing so simple. Theresa, he's a prince."

Silence. "I'm sorry, a what?"

"A prince." Her reaction was beginning to settle in. Brooke swiped away a sudden rush of tears as her ears picked up nothing but the hiss of air through the phone's speaker. "Are you still there?"

"Yes, I'm here, but this damned international call has gone wonky. Can you repeat what you said."

"Nic is a prince. He's second in line to the throne of a small European country called Sherdana."

Her breath evened out as she waited out her best friend's stupefaction. It wouldn't last long. Theresa was one of the most pragmatic people she knew. It was part of what kept them friends for so long. Opposites attract. Theresa needed Brooke's particular variety of crazy to shake up her life, and Brooke relied on Theresa's common sense to keep her grounded.

"You're kidding me, right? This whole phone call is some sort of setup for one of those wacky reality shows where people get punked or filmed doing stupid things." She paused and waited for Brooke to fill in an affirmative. When Brooke remained silent Theresa sighed and said, "Okay, you'd better give it to me from the top."

Nic sat in the small den off the living room, his laptop on the love seat beside him, his thoughts lingering on Brooke and her crazy notion that they should say goodbye and gain closure by spending the next few days in bed together. Had he done a good enough job convincing her that wasn't going to happen when he desperately wanted to make love to her again? During their five months together, she'd learned all she had to do was crook a finger and he was happy to abandon his work in favor of spending hours in her arms. Nic growled as he pondered his susceptibility to her abundant charms. He was fighting a battle with himself and with her. In a few hours she would return, refreshed and ready for the next skirmish and he'd better have his defenses reinforced.

With a snort of disgust, Nic turned on the computer in the den and cued up his email. She'd claimed there were dozens of unanswered emails, but the inbox was empty. It took him fifteen minutes to find them among the folders where he shunted the messages he didn't wish to delete and restore the settings to the way he liked them. Brooke was a disaster when it came to anything involving technology. Glen had found his sister's deficiency funny and endearing. Nic just found it exasperating. Like so many other things about her.

She was always late. In fact, her sense of time was so skewed that if he needed her to be somewhere, he usually built in a cushion of thirty minutes. Then there was her inability to say no to anyone. This usually led to her getting involved in something she needed to be bailed out of. Like at *Griffin*'s annual team picnic when she'd agreed to take all the kids for a nature hike and then got lost. It had taken Nic and Glen, plus a half dozen concerned parents, to find them. Of course, the kids all thought it was the best adventure they'd ever been on. Brooke had kept them calm and focused, never letting them know how much trouble they were in. Later, when he'd scolded her for worrying everyone, she'd simply shrugged her shoulders and pointed out that nothing bad had happened. She just didn't think about the consequences of her actions. And that drove him crazy.

As crazy as the way she leveraged her lean, toned body to incite his baser instincts. Whenever she took a weekend break from school and came to visit, he found it impossible to concentrate on the *Griffin* project. She hung out in his office, alternating between cajoling and pouting until he paid attention to her. Most days he held out because eventually she'd grow tired of the game and let him get back to work. Unfortunately before that happened, he had to endure her flirtatious hugs and seemingly innocent body brushes. Usually by the time she headed back to San Francisco on Sunday afternoon, he was aroused, off schedule and in a savage mood.

His phone rang. Gabriel. The first in line to the throne sounded relaxed and a touch smug as he passed along the message Nic had been dreading.

"Mother is sending the jet to pick you up the day after tomorrow and wants to know what time you can be at the airport."

"What's so urgent? I thought I had over a week until your wedding."

"She has a series of parties and events leading up to the big day that you and Christian will be expected to attend. From what I understand she has compiled quite a list of potential brides for you two to fight over."

And so it began. Nic's thoughts turned toward the woman napping in the guesthouse. His heart wrenched at the thought of being parted from her so soon after reconnecting. She would be disappointed to find out their time would be cut short, but he had warned her.

"Are any of these women...?" What was he trying to ask? Without meeting any of them, he'd already decided they were unacceptable. None of them were Brooke.

"Beautiful? Smart? Wealthy? What?"

"Am I going to *like* any of them?" As soon as the question was out Nic felt foolish.

"I'm sure you're going to like all of them. You just have to figure out which one you can see yourself spending the rest of your life with." Gabriel's words and tone were matter-of-fact.

"Is that how you felt when you first started poring over the candidates?"

Gabriel paused before answering. "Not exactly. I had Olivia in mind from the first."

"But you spent a year considering and meeting possible matches. Why do that if you already knew who you wanted?"

"Two reasons. Because Mother would not have accepted that I had already met the perfect girl and at the time only my subconscious realized Olivia was the one."

Nic wished he was having this conversation face-to-face because his brother's expression would provide clues mere words lacked. "You've lost me."

"As I worked my way through the list, I realized I compared each woman I met to Olivia."

"She was your ideal."

"She was the one I wanted."

The conviction throbbing in Gabriel's low voice spurred Nic to envy his brother for the first time since they were kids. Before Nic had discovered his passion for science and engineering, he'd wondered what contribution he could make to the country. Gabriel would rule. All Christian cared about was having fun and shirking responsibility. Nic had wanted to have a positive effect on the world. A lofty ambition for an eight-year-old.

Gabriel continued speaking, "Only I resented my duty to marry and didn't know how perfect Olivia was for me. Even when I proposed to her I was blind to my heart's true desire. Thank goodness my instincts weren't hampered by my hardheadedness."

"At what point did you figure out you'd selected the perfect woman?"

"The night my girls came to stay at the palace. Olivia took them under her wing and zealously guarded them from anyone she believed might upset them. Me included." He chuckled. "And she never wavered in her love for them, not even when she thought I was still in love with their mother."

"And speaking of Karina and Bethany, how are your girls?"

"Growing more beautiful and more terrifying by the week. Thank goodness they adore Olivia or they'd be terrorizing the palace staff a lot more than they do. Somehow she guides their energy into positive channels and makes the whole process look effortless. No one else can manage them without being ready to pull their hair out."

"Not even Mother?"

"At first, but now they realize she is too fond of them to scold. Father indulges their appetite for sweets and Ariana has shown them every good hiding place the palace has to offer."

"It's not called the terrible twos for nothing."

"You'll see soon enough. I'll have the plane pick you up tomorrow around noon."

"Fine." That should give him time to make sure Brooke was safely on a plane heading for home.

"See that you're there on time."

"Where else would I be? I have nowhere to go but home."

Nic ended the call with a weary sigh and mulled what Gabriel had said about his search for a wife. That his brother had settled on the perfect woman before his quest had even begun didn't lessen Nic's unease over what was to come. Already his mind and body had chosen the woman for him. She was currently stretched out on the bed in the guesthouse. If he was anything like Gabriel, he was going to have an impossible time finding anyone who could match her perfect imperfection.

Several hours later, he was opening a bottle of Sherdana's best Pinot Negro to let it breathe when Brooke sailed into the living room. She'd changed clothes again. The tail of her pastel tied-dyed kimono fluttered behind her as she walked, exposing a mint-green crocheted tank and the ruffled hem of her leg-baring floral shorts.

A light breeze swept in from the terrace and plucked at her dark copper curls. She'd loosened her hair from its braid and it flowed in rich waves over her shoulders and down her back. She stroked a lock away from her lips. He caught himself staring at her and shifted his attention back to the wine.

How often in the past five years had he longed to sink his fingers into her tempestuous red locks and lose himself in the chaotic tangle? He'd imagined the texture would feel like the finest Chinese silk sliding along his bare chest. He'd been right.

Nic extended a glass of wine toward her. She shook her head.

"Something nonalcoholic if you have it."

He found a container of orange juice and poured her a glass. She sipped at it, her eyes smiling at him over the edge of the glass. Expecting a whole new round of verbal fencing, Nic was surprised when she said, "You mentioned that your sister paints here. Could I see her studio?"

"Sure."

He led the way onto the terrace and around the villa in the opposite direction of the guesthouse. A small building with broad windows facing north sat on a little rise overlooking the harbor mouth. Nic unlocked the door and gestured for Brooke to go inside.

"Oh, these are all wonderful," she said the minute she walked in.

Though Brooke was always generous with her praise, Nic thought she was going a little overboard in talking about Ariana's work. Nic was proud of what his sister had accomplished with her paintings but didn't really get her modern style. She had often accused him of being stuck in the Middle Ages in terms of his taste. Brooke, on the other hand, seemed to get exactly what his sister was trying to do.

He enjoyed watching her stroll through his sister's art studio and study each canvas in turn, treating every painting like a masterpiece. By the time Brooke returned to where he stood just inside the door, her delighted grin had Nic smiling, as well. The next time he saw Ariana, he would be sure to tell her what an accomplished artist she was.

"I never looked at Ariana's art that way before," Nic said as he relocked the studio and escorted Brooke back toward the main house. "Thank you for opening my eyes."

She looked caught off guard by his compliment. "You're welcome."

At that moment Nic realized how rarely he'd ever offered Brooke any encouragement or a reason to believe he appreciated her. How had she stayed so relentlessly positive as he'd thrown one obstacle after another in her path? All she'd ever asked was for him to like her and treat her with civility. Was it her fault that she agitated his emotions and incited his hormones?

"What are you thinking about?" she asked as they stepped back into the main house. She gathered her hair into a twist and secured it into a topknot.

"Regrets. I spent so much time keeping you at bay."

Again he'd startled her. "You did, but to be fair, I am a little overwhelming."

"And very distracting. I had a hard time concentrating when you were around."

She narrowed her eyes. "Why are you being so nice to me all of a sudden?"

"I had a call from my brother while you were resting and I have to leave for Sherdana the day after tomorrow."

"So soon?" Her lips curved downward.

Nic wanted to put his arms around her, but it would do neither of them any good to deepen their connection when the time to part was so near. "Apparently my mother has planned several events she'd like me to attend in the next week, culminating in Gabriel and Olivia's wedding."

"But I thought they were already married."

"They are. Actually…" Nic stared out the window at Kioni in the distance. "He brought her to Ithaca for a surprise wedding ceremony."

"That's very romantic."

"And unlike Gabriel to put his desires before the needs of the country. But he's crazy about Olivia and couldn't bear to live without her."

Something about Brooke's silence caught his attention. She was staring at the floor lost in thought. "So why are they getting married again?"

"The crown prince's wedding is pretty momentous and my parents decided it was better to have a second ceremony than to rob the citizens of the celebration. There will be parties every night leading up to the big event, both at the palace and venues around our capital city of Carone."

"Tell me about the parties at the palace. They must be formal affairs." Brooke's smile bloomed. "Do you have to dance?"

"Only when I can't avoid it."

"So you know how."

"It's part of every prince's training," he intoned, mimicking his dance teacher's severe manner. "I don't have Gabriel's technique or Christian's flair, but I don't step on my partner's toes anymore."

"After dinner tonight you are going to dance with me." She held up a hand when he began to protest. "Don't argue. I remember on three separate occasions when you told me you had no idea how to dance."

"No," he corrected her. "I told you I don't dance. There's a difference."

"Semantics."

"Very well." He knew that taking her in his arms and swaying with her to soft music would lead to trouble. But he could teach her a Sherdanian country dance. The movements were energetic and the only touching required was hand to hand. "After dinner."

"So what are we having that smells so delicious?"

"Elena left us lamb stew and salad for dinner."

Brooke drifted to the stove where a pot simmered on a low flame. "I don't know how I can be hungry after all we ate for lunch, but suddenly I'm starved."

Something about the way she said the word made him grind his teeth. She was hungry for food, but the groan in her voice made him hungry for something else entirely. Directing her toward the refrigerator where Elena had put the salad, he spooned the stew into bowls and tried not to remember Brooke beneath him in bed, her red hair fanned across his pillow, lips curved in lazy satisfaction.

"Can I help?"

He handed her a bowl and a basket of bread, almost pushing it at her in an effort to keep her at bay.

She walked toward the table. "I love the bread here in Greece. That and the desserts. I could live on them."

"I hope you like the stew, as well. Elena is an excellent cook."

"I'm sure it's wonderful."

Nic's housekeeper had set the table earlier so there was little left to do but sit down and enjoy the meal. The patch of late-afternoon sunlight on the tile floor had advanced a good three feet by the time they finished eating. Following his example, Brooke had torn pieces of the fresh-baked bread and dipped them into the stew. He'd lost count how many times her tongue came out to catch a crumb on her lip or a spot of gravy at the corner of her mouth.

For dessert Elena had left baklava, a sticky, sweet concoction made of stacked sheets of phyllo dough spread with butter, sugar, nuts and honey. He couldn't wait to watch Brooke suck the sticky honey from her fingers.

And she didn't disappoint him.

"What's so funny?" she demanded, her tongue darting out to clean the corner of her mouth.

Nic banked a groan and sipped his wine. "I'm trying to remember the last time I enjoyed a pan of baklava this much."

"You haven't had any."

He imagined drizzling honey on her skin and following the trail with his tongue. The bees in Greece made thick sweet honey he couldn't get enough of. Against her skin it would be heaven. The arousal that had taunted him all through the meal now exploded with fierce determination. Nic sat back in his chair all too aware of the tightness in his pants and the need clawing at him.

"You've enjoyed it enough for both of us."

"It was delicious." Cutting another piece, she held it out. "Sure you don't want some?"

The question was innocent enough, but the light in her gray-green eyes as she peered at him from beneath her lashes was anything but. Avoiding her gaze, he shook his head.

"As much as I'm enjoying your attempt to seduce me, I'm afraid my intentions toward you haven't changed."

"We'll see." Resolve replaced flirtation in her eyes. She sat back and assessed him. "I still have two nights and a day to dishonor you."

Eager to avoid further banter, he cleared the plates from the table and busied himself putting away the remnants of the stew.

"I can hear what you're thinking," Brooke murmured, following him to the sink. "You're thinking it took me five years to wear you down the first time." She set the pan of baklava on the counter and swept a finger over a patch of honey. "But have you considered that I know a little bit more about what turns you on after all the nights we spent together?"

Out of the corner of his eye Nic watched, his mouth dry, as she stuck her finger into her mouth, closed her eyes in rapt delight and licked off the honey. She was killing him.

"Two nights and a day, Nic." She said again. "Hours and hours of glorious, delirious pleasure as we explore every inch of each other and get lost in deep slow kisses."

But he wasn't free to have the sort of fun Brooke suggested. And one way or another, he intended to make her understand.

"And then what?" he demanded, his voice more curt than he'd intended.

She blinked. "What do you mean?"

"What happens after the fun?" While hot water ran into the sink, he propped his hip against the counter and crossed his arms. "Have you thought about what happens when we leave this island and go our separate ways?"

Her shoulders sagged. "I head back to California and my dream job."

"And I start looking for a wife." To his surprise, he'd managed to get the last word in.

Deciding to capitalize on his advantage, he scrounged up the CD with Sherdanian folk music Ariana had given him for his birthday several years earlier. As the first notes filled the air, he extended his hand in Brooke's direction. "Get over here. It's time for you to learn a traditional Sherdanian country dance."

Five

Nic woke to the smell of coffee and tickle of something in his ear. He reached up to brush away the irritation and heard a soft chuckle. The mattress behind him dipped. His eyes flew open as a hand drifted over his shoulder and a pair of lips slid into the erogenous zone behind his earlobe.

"You sleep like the dead," Brooke murmured. "I have been taking advantage of you for the last fifteen minutes."

"I doubt that." But oh, the idea that she might have hastened his body's awakening.

"Don't be so sure." She sounded awfully damned confident as she snuggled onto the bed behind him, a thin sheet the only barrier between them as she traced the curve of his backside with her knee, running it down along the back of his thigh. As if this caress wasn't provocative enough, she wiggled her pelvis against his butt, aligning her delicious curves against his back from heel to shoulders. "I know you're not wearing any underwear."

"You're guessing."

"Am not." Her palm drifted along his arm, riding the curve of his biceps. Her touch wasn't sexual; she was more like a sculptor admiring a fine marble statue. "I peeked."

He couldn't even gather enough breath to object. What the hell was she doing to him? Reminded of her threat the night before, Nic knew that letting her get her fill of touching him would only lead to further frustration on his part and more boldness on hers. Yet, he couldn't prevent his curiosity from seeing how far she intended to go.

"How long have you been awake?" he asked as her fingers stole up his neck and into his hair. He closed his eyes and savored the soothing caress.

"A couple hours. I went for a swim, started the coffee and grew bored with my own company, so I decided it was time to wake you. How am I doing?"

Brat.

"I'm fully awake," he growled. "Thank you. Now, why don't you run along and fix breakfast while I take a shower."

"Want some company?"

Her mouth opened in a wet kiss on his shoulder. Nic bit back a curse. The swirl of her tongue on his skin caused his hips to twitch. The erection he'd been trying to ignore grew painfully hard.

"Didn't we come to an understanding last night about this being a bad idea?"

"That was your opinion," she corrected. "I think we wasted a perfectly lovely night dancing around your living room when we could have set fire to this big bed of yours."

"Set fire?" Amusement momentarily clouded his desire to roll her beneath him and make her come over and over. She had the damnedest knack for tickling his funny bone.

"Set fire. Tear up the sheets."

He shifted onto his back so he could see her face. Bare of makeup, lips soft with invitation, eyes shadowed by long reddish lashes, her beauty stopped his breath. He cupped her pale cheek in his palm while his heart contracted in remorse. For five months he'd savored the notion of spending the rest of his life with her. He'd claimed her body and given her his heart. At the time, with Gabriel's wedding to Olivia fast approaching and the future of Sherdana safely in their hands, Nic believed he could at last have the life he wanted with the woman who made him happy. It wasn't fair that circumstances had interfered with his plans for the future, but that's the way it was.

His hand fell away from her soft skin. "You know we can't do this."

"Damn it, Nic."

The next thing he knew, she'd straddled him. Astonished by her swift attack and trapped between her strong, supple thighs, Nic reached for the pillow behind his head and dug his fingers in. The challenge in her green-gray gaze helped him maintain control—barely. She settled her hot center firmly over his erection and smirked as his hips lifted off the mattress to meet her partway. She obviously intended to push him past his limits. To incite him to act. He clenched his teeth and held himself immobile.

She put her palms on his chest and leaned forward. "I'm sad and I hate feeling this way. I want to be blissfully happy for just a little while. To forget about the future and just live in the moment."

Where she touched him, he burned. The curtain of her hair swung forward. Still damp from her swim, it brushed against his cheek. He gathered a handful and gently tugged.

"It's not that I don't want that, too," he began and stopped. She couldn't know that what he felt for her went way beyond physical attraction. "I just can't see where that's going to be good for either of us."

Her hands stalked from his chest to his stomach. His muscles twitched in reaction to her touch, betraying him.

He grit his teeth and focused on something less tantalizing than the slender thighs bracketing his hips or the heat of her burning into him through layers of cotton. Unfortunately with her current position, she dominated his field of vision.

"Is that my shirt?"

The last time he'd seen the white button-down, she'd been driving away from his house after they spent the night together. In his eagerness to get her naked the evening before, he'd torn the delicate fabric of her blouse and rendered the garment unwearable. Today, where her damp hair touched the fabric, transparent patches bloomed on her shoulder and chest.

"It is. Every time I wear it I think about you and the nights we spent together."

Nic gripped the bedsheets, endeavoring to stay true to his word and keep his hands off her. Even if his position didn't lend itself to a series of casual affairs, leaving a trail of broken hearts in his wake was not his style. On the other hand, he didn't need the sort of complication a romance with Brooke would bring to his life right now. But since yesterday afternoon he'd become obsessed with all the ways he could touch her without using his hands, and since she'd arrived, he hadn't brooded over the accident for more than five minutes.

"Tell me about the women who are dying to become your princess," she said in a tone as dry as the California desert near the airport test facility. "Are they all beautiful and rich?"

"Do you really want to talk about this?"

"Not really." Her fingers tickled up his sides toward his armpits.

In an effort to stop her before she made him squirm, Nic snagged her wrists and rolled her over. She ended up beneath him, her legs tangled in the sheets. Now that she was trapped in a web of her own making, this was his chance to escape. He should have immediately shifted away from her and put a safe distance between them, but her expression took on a look of such vulnerability that he was transfixed. Pressed chest to groin, they stared at each other.

"Touch me," she whispered, digging her fingers into his biceps.

He flexed his spine, driving his hips tight into hers. She shifted beneath him, rubbing her body against his in a tension-filled rhythm. A groan ripped from his throat as her heat called to him. Today she smelled like pink grapefruit, stimulating with a sweet bitterness. His mouth watered.

"I promised I wouldn't."

"Then, kiss me. You didn't promise not to do that."

That would be following the letter of the law instead of the intent. "You should have been a lawyer," he groused, surrendering to what they both wanted.

His lips lowered to hers. She opened for him like a rose on a warm summer afternoon. He kept the pace slow, concentrating on her mouth while ruthlessly suppressing the urgent thrumming in his groin. Her heart beat in time with his until Nic wasn't sure where he left off and she began. Time was suspended. The room fell away. There was only the softness of her skin beneath his lips, her soft sighs and the growing tension in his body.

This deviation from his intention wouldn't benefit either of them, but he'd grown sick to death of thinking in terms of what he couldn't do, what didn't work, what he stood to lose. He wanted to take joy in this moment and put the future on hold. Brooke had offered him a gift with no strings attached. He would face a lifetime of limits and restrictions soon enough. Why not go wild for a few minutes? Enjoy this exhilarating, vivacious woman who brought joy and laughter into his stolid existence. Who confounded him with her sassy attitude and liberated his emotions. For five years he'd fought against falling for her, afraid if he let her in he might one day have to leave her.

And he'd been right. No sooner had he risked his heart than he'd been forced to make a terrible choice.

"See, that wasn't so hard," she murmured as he broke off the kiss to trail his lips down her neck to the madly beating pulse in her throat.

"I've never met anyone like you. No one knocks me off my game faster."

"It's my dazzling personality."

"It's your damned stubbornness. If Berkeley doesn't work out, you could always teach seminars to salesmen on the art of not taking no for an answer."

Her rock hard nipples burned his chest through the thin cloth, branding him with each impassioned breath she took.

"Unbutton your shirt."

She hesitated at his demand as if unsure what his change of mind might mean. After a long moment, she raised her hands and slipped the first button free. As the top curve of her breast came into view, he lowered his head and tasted her skin. Her gasp made him smile. What he intended to do next would render her breathless.

"Another."

She obliged. He nudged into the ever-widening V, grazing her sensitive skin with the stubble on his chin. A shudder captured her. Nic smiled.

"Keep going."

She unbuttoned the next two buttons in rapid succession, but held on to the edges of the shirt, keeping the material closed. Sensing what he wanted, she peered at him from beneath her lashes. Nic eyed the pink tone in her cheeks.

"Spread the shirt open. I want to look at you."

"Nic, this is—" She broke off as he nudged the material off one breast.

"Not what you had in mind?" His tongue circled her tight nipple.

"It's exactly what I want." She arched her back, her fingers tightening convulsively. "I feel…"

"Tell me," he urged, eager to hear what effect his mouth was having on her body. He flicked his tongue across her nipple. She jerked in surprise. "I want to know everything. What do you like? What drives you wild?"

At last she unclenched her fingers and spread the shirt wide. Now it was Nic's turn to suck in his breath. She was beautiful. Breathtaking. Perfect. Her small round breasts, topped with dark pink nipples, were a perfect fit in his palm. Pity his mouth would be the only part of him to enjoy all that silky skin. And yet, as he pulled one bud into his mouth and sucked, perhaps that wasn't so bad after all.

She was mewling with gratifying abandon by the time he finished with one breast and moved to the other.

The situation was swiftly disintegrating. Nic felt his control slipping. Heaving a sigh, he caught the edges of her shirt and pulled them together, hiding her gorgeous breasts from his greedy eyes.

"You're stopping?" She sounded appalled. "But things were just starting to get interesting."

His muscles clenched at her frustrated wail. He levered himself out of bed and kept his eyes averted from her. He'd survived temptation once. He wasn't sure he could do it twice.

"You still don't get it, do you? I can't offer you anything beyond this bed."

"I know."

She rolled onto her side, her gaze steady on him. Accusations darted like deer through her gray-green eyes. Anger surged in his chest. Damn her for coming here and littering the clear path to his future with enticement and regret. He retreated to the bathroom. Just before closing the door, he shot a last glance in her direction. She had propped her head on her hand and lay watching him through half-closed lids.

She'd left the edges of her shirt unfastened and the three-inch gap gave him an eye-popping view of the curve of her right breast, almost to the nipple. Aphrodite in all her glory could not have appealed to him more than Brooke's slim form in his bed.

Nic shut the bathroom door with more force than necessary and started the shower. A cold shower, he decided.

As she heard the water start, Brooke exhaled raggedly and rolled onto her back. The empty bed mocked her. Frustration bubbled in her chest and rose into her throat, building into a shriek. She clamped her teeth to prevent any sound from escaping, but it was an effort to hold so much emotion in. So she grabbed one of Nic's pillows and covered her face in it to prevent him from hearing her shrill curses.

Once the tantrum had passed, she lay with her nose buried in the cool cotton, absorbing Nic's scent and reliving the moment when his control had broken. Heat wafted off her skin in surging waves, the source the smoking hot place between her thighs that pulsed and throbbed with frustrated longing. The man had a gift for turning her world upside down.

He only had to give her the slightest bit of encouragement and she went all in. How many times since she'd first discovered she had feelings for him had he crushed her hopes by deflecting her overtures or chasing her away when she'd tried to get him to take a break from a problem so he could gain some perspective on it?

Not for the first time an ache built in her chest. What had started out as a whim, a crush, a foolish game had escalated into something she couldn't break free from.

Her mother, Theresa, even Glen, had warned her she was better off with a man who appreciated her. But she hadn't wanted to hear the good advice from her friends and family. And for a while things had been perfect.

The way she'd felt about him the first time he'd kissed her six months ago was nothing compared to the growing connection she felt now. Each day in his presence it grew stronger. How was she supposed to just let him go and move forward? To raise this child on her own? To spend the rest of her life without him? Panic assailed her, causing dark spots in her vision and making it hard to draw a full breath for several minutes.

She rode the paralyzing fear until her emotions calmed. Able to think rationally again, Brooke was mortified by how badly she wanted to cling to Nic and beg him to give up his responsibilities and be with her. Once upon a time she'd prided herself on being an independent woman, capable of living abroad for a year in Italy while she worked on her doctoral thesis on Italian literature. She might make decisions based on emotion rather than logic, but she ruled her finances with a miser's tight fist and had a knack for avoiding bad relationships.

These days she was a rickety ladder of vulnerability and loose screws. What else could explain why she'd charged a fifteen-hundred-dollar airplane ticket on her credit card to chase after a man who'd vanished from her life without even a goodbye? If she'd picked up the phone and delivered her news about the pregnancy she could have saved herself a bucketful of heartache and said to hell with closure.

Brooke sat up and buttoned Nic's shirt once more. A sudden bout of nausea caught her off guard. If the positive pregnancy test result had seemed surreal, here was tangible proof that her body was irrevocably changed. Brooke slipped off the bed and fled the room, afraid Nic would exit the bathroom and catch her looking green and out of sorts, then demand to know what was wrong with her.

On her way to the guesthouse, she snagged a bit of bread and a bottle of water. Once there, she nibbled at the crust, put the chilled bottle to her warm forehead and willed her stomach to settle down. As the nausea subsided, Brooke's confidence ebbed away, as well.

In twenty-four hours Nic was heading home to find a wife. He would be forever lost to her. Maybe she should give up this madness today and run back to California.

Because she still hadn't done what she'd come here to do: tell Nic she was pregnant.

And yet, on the heels of all she'd learned, did it make sense to burden him with the news that his illegitimate child would be living far from him in California? He was returning home to find a bride and start a family. His future wife wouldn't be happy to find out Nic had already gotten another woman pregnant.

Then, too, he'd proved himself an honorable man. It would tear him apart to know he wouldn't be a part of his child's life? What if he demanded partial custody? Was she going to spend the next eighteen years shuffling their child across the Atlantic Ocean so that he or she could know Nic? And what about the scandal this would mean for the royal family? Maybe in America no one thought twice when celebrities had children without being married, but that wouldn't sit well where European nobility were concerned.

Yet morally was it right to keep the information from him? It would certainly be easier on her. Nic had turned his back on Glen and their dream of getting *Griffin* off the ground. Brooke knew she could count on her brother to keep her secret. Her life going forward would be quiet and routine. She would teach at Berkeley or UCLA and throw herself into raising her child. No one would ever know that she'd had a brief affair with a European prince.

Both options had their positives and negatives. And it was early in her pregnancy. So many things could go wrong in the first trimester. She could take another month to decide. The discovery that she was pregnant was only a week old. Maybe if she gave the situation some more thought she could arrive at a decision that she could live with.

Knowing that avoiding a decision was not the best answer, she dressed in black shorts and a white T-shirt. Maybe she would take a hike to the windmills a little later. Although her stomach wasn't back to normal, she had to act as if nothing was wrong.

Half an hour after her encounter with Nic, she returned to the house and found him standing in the kitchen drinking coffee. He was staring out the window as Brooke drew near and when she saw the expression on his face, all the energy drained from her body.

"Don't." Her throat contracted before she could finish.

He swiveled his head in her direction. His gaze was hollow. "Don't what?"

Hearing his tight, unhappy tone, frustration replaced anxiety. Brooke stamped her foot. "Don't regret what just happened."

"Brooke, you don't understand—"

"Don't," she interrupted, despair clutching at her chest. She didn't need to be psychic to know what ran through Nic's mind. "Don't you dare spew platitudes at me. I've known you too long."

"You don't know me at all."

And whose fault was that? She sucked in a breath. Harsh words gathered in her head. She squeezed her eyes shut, moderated her tone. "I wish we had time to change that."

The umber eyes that turned in her direction were a

stark landscape of cynicism and regret. "But we don't." Although he pushed her away with his words, the muscle jumping in his jaw proclaimed he wasn't happy to do so. His agonized expression matched the pain throbbing in his voice. "My family needs me."

I need you. Your child needs you.

But all of a sudden she knew she wasn't going to put that burden on him. What he felt for her wasn't casual. She was finding it hard to let go. He was going through something similar. But they each had their ways of coping and she should respect that.

Brooke retreated to the opposite side of the room and picked up her sandals. The silence in the house went unbroken for several moments while she reorganized her emotions and set aside her disappointment.

"Are these okay for a hike up to the windmills?" she asked, indicating the footwear. "I'm afraid I don't have anything more sturdy."

"They should be fine." He assessed her feet. "There's a well-defined path up to get there."

"Great."

His brow creased at her flat tone. "Are you okay?"

"Fine. Just feeling a little off all of a sudden. Nothing breakfast won't cure."

Brooke was glad that Elena picked that moment to enter the house with bags of groceries. It kept her and Nic from plunging back into heated waters. With Elena bustling around the kitchen they had little need to exchange more than a few words over a meal of eggs and pastries.

An hour later, they were heading to the windmill. The paved road that led from the town past Nic's villa gave out two miles farther. Ahead was the narrow path cluttered with large rocks and tree roots that led to the three windmills she'd seen on arriving at Ithaca. Nic set a moderate pace through the irregular terrain, forcing Brooke to focus on where she stepped, and silence filled the space between them. For once she was grateful for the lack of conversation because she had too many conflicting thoughts circling her mind.

"There are a number of windmills on Ithaca," Nic began as the brush lining the path ahead of them gave way to a flat, rocky expanse. Brooke was glad for her sunglasses as they emerged from the vegetation onto the rocky plateau.

Before them lay the three disused windmills. Twenty feet in diameter, thirty feet tall, their squat, round shapes stood sentinel over all the boats coming and going from the harbor. Their walls once would have been whitewashed, but years of wind and weather had scoured the brick, returning it to shades of gray and tan.

Nic headed toward the structures, his words drifting back to her on the strong breeze. "Corn and wheat would come from all over the islands to be ground here because of the constant winds in this area."

In the lee of the squat towers, Nic gestured to direct her attention through a curved doorway into the windmill's interior. "As you can see, the 1953 earthquake caused the grinding wheel and shaft to break and tumble to the bottom."

"Fascinating." But her attention was only half on the scene before her. A moment earlier she'd stumbled when her toe caught on a half-buried rock and he'd caught her arm to steady her. His hand had not yet fallen away. "Thank you for bringing me here. The view is amazing. I can see why you enjoy coming to the island."

"After this we should take the boat to Vathay and have lunch." He was obviously hoping that by keeping busy they could avoid a repeat of the morning's events.

Brooke wasn't sure she could spend a fun-filled afternoon with him while her heart was in the process of shattering. For the first time since her interest in him had sparked, she was bereft of hope. Even after he'd broken things off a month ago, she hadn't really believed it was over. This morning, she'd finally faced up to reality.

Nic was going to marry someone else and build a life with that person.

"If you don't mind," Brooke said, "I think I'd rather just hang out on the terrace and do a little reading. But you go ahead and do whatever it is you've been doing before I got here."

He frowned, obviously unsure what to make of her abrupt about-face. "If that's what you want to do."

"It is." The words sounded heavy.

"Very well."

For the next fifteen minutes, he inundated her with facts about the area, the aftereffects of the 1953 earthquake and other interesting tidbits about the island. Brooke responded with nods and polite smiles when he paused to see if she was listening. Eventually, he ran out of things to say and they headed back down the path. They had to walk single file until they reached the road. Once they got there they strode side by side without speaking. When Nic's villa was less than a mile away, to Brooke's surprise, it was Nic who broke the silence.

"About this morning."

"Please don't," Brooke murmured, expelling her breath in a weary sigh.

"I was wrong to kiss you," he continued, either not hearing her protest or ignoring it. "I'm sending you mixed messages and that isn't fair."

"It was my fault. I shouldn't have intruded on your sleep and thrown myself at you. Most men would have taken advantage of the situation. You showed great restraint."

"Nevertheless." His frown indicated he wasn't happy she'd taken the blame. "I haven't been fair to you. If I'd told you from the start who I really was, you'd never have developed feelings for me."

Brooke couldn't believe what she was hearing. She'd chased this man for five years, teased him, flattered him, poured her heart out to him and received nothing in return until six months ago when he'd kissed her. *He'd* kissed *her*. She hadn't plunked herself onto his lap and tormented him the way she'd done the day before. In fact, she hadn't even flirted with him that night. He'd been the one to draw her away from Glen's party and kiss her senseless.

"I never meant to hurt you."

"You haven't." She wasn't upset with him. She was disappointed in herself. How could she have been such a fool for so long? "If I hurt right now it's because I didn't listen when you told me over and over that we weren't right for each other. I created my own troubles. Your conscience should be clear."

She walked faster, needing some space from Nic. He matched her stride for stride.

"Is this some sort of ploy—?"

She erupted in exasperation. "Get over yourself already. I'm done." She gestured broadly with her arms as her temper flared. "You've convinced me that it's stupid to keep holding on for something that can never be. So, congratulations, I'm never going to ask you for anything ever again."

Her anger wasn't reasonable, but at that moment it was the only way to cope with her deep sadness. She couldn't cry, not yet, so she took refuge in ferocity. This was a side of her she'd never let Nic see. She always kept things light and fun around him. Even when she showed him her temper, it was followed by a quicksilver smile.

Right now she had no lightness inside her, only shadow.

Nic caught her arm to slow her as she surged forward. "I don't want us to end like this."

She was not going to say nice things so he could ease his

conscience about her. "End like what? Me being upset with you? How do you think I felt a month ago when you told me that sleeping together had been the wrong thing to do?"

"I was wrong not to tell you the truth about what was really going on." The intense light in his eyes seared through her defenses. "I'm sorry."

Unbidden, sympathy rose in her. Brooke cast it aside. She didn't want to accept that he was as much a victim of circumstances as she. With a vigorous shake of her head she pulled free and began walking once again.

"What happened isn't fair to either one of us," he called after her. "Don't you think if I could choose you I would?"

She swung around and walked backward as she spoke. "The trouble is, you didn't choose me. Nothing is really forcing you to go home and make this huge sacrifice for your country. This is your decision. You feel honor bound. It's who you are. It's why I love you. But don't blame circumstances or your family's expectations for the choice you are making."

Leaving him standing in the middle of the road, Brooke ran the rest of the way back to the villa.

Six

Nic lay on his back, forearm thrown over his eyes. Moonlight streamed into his room like a searchlight, but he couldn't be bothered to close the shutters. A soft breeze trailed across his bare chest, teasing him with the memory of Brooke's fingers tantalizing his skin this morning.

The regret he'd been trying unsuccessfully to contain for the past twelve hours pounded him as relentlessly as the Ionian Sea against the cliff below the villa. Any sensible man would have taken Brooke to bed rather than inflict on her a long sightseeing adventure to busted-up windmills. Instead he'd rejected her not once but twice this morning, and then disregarded the pain he'd caused.

She'd eaten lunch by herself on the terrace and barely spoken to him during dinner. When she did speak, her tone had been stiff. He didn't blame her for being upset. Any apology he might make would've been way too little and far too late. But he'd been relieved when she'd escaped as soon as the dishes had been piled in the sink.

He gusted out an impatient breath and sat up. Sleeping without the benefit of too much alcohol had been hard enough before Brooke arrived. Knowing she slept thirty feet away made unconsciousness completely impossible. Hell. It used to be that if he couldn't sleep, he would work. That outlet was lost to him now. Still, he hadn't yet looked at the forty emails restored to his inbox. Maybe a few hours of technical questions would take his mind off his problems.

Padding barefoot downstairs, he stopped short as he neared the bottom, his skin tingling in awareness that he wasn't alone.

Beyond the open French doors, the full moon slanted a stripe of ethereal white across the harbor's smooth surface and reached into the living room to touch the couch. Beside the shaft of moonlight, a dark shadow huddled, an ink spot on the pristine fabric.

Brooke.

His breath lodged in his throat and her name came out of him in a hoarse whisper. His body went into full alert. This was bad. Very bad. A late-night encounter with her was more temptation than he was prepared to handle.

"How come you're not in bed?" he demanded, stepping onto the limestone tile. He took two steps toward the couch, his impulses getting the upper hand. He'd come close enough to smell vanilla and hear her unsteady breathing. He set one hand on his hip and rubbed the back of his neck with the other.

"I couldn't sleep." Her voice emerged from shadow, low and passionless with a slight waver. "I haven't been able to stop thinking about what I said to you earlier. You're doing the right thing where your family and country are concerned."

"This whole thing is my fault. You came a long way

not knowing who I was or what my family has been going through."

If circumstances were different...

But it wasn't fair to patronize her with meaningless platitudes. Circumstances were exactly what they were and he'd made his decision based on what he'd been taught to do.

"Still, I shouldn't have hit you with a guilt trip."

"You didn't." Nic took another two steps and stopped. His breath hissed through clenched teeth. What was he doing? The longing to gather her into his arms and comfort her stunned him with its power. His body ached to feel her soft body melt against him. Madness.

"I just wanted you to choose me for once."

Her words slammed into his gut and rocked him backward. He'd been a first-class bastard where she was concerned. How many times had he rebuffed her when all she wanted was to help him work through a problem? So what if her methods sounded illogical and ineffective? She'd been right the time she'd badgered him into playing miniature golf with her when he was busy trying to solve a difficult technical problem. On the fourth hole the solution had popped into his head with no prompting. Had he bothered to thank her before rushing back to his workroom at the hangar and burying himself in the project once more?

And now, it was too late to make everything up to her.

"You should head back to bed. You have a long flight back to California tomorrow."

Her shadow moved as she shook her head. "I'm not going home tomorrow."

"Where are you going?"

"I don't know yet. I have a few weeks before I have to be back at UC Santa Cruz. I thought maybe I'd head to Rome and meet up with some friends."

"What about your Berkeley interview?"

"It's the day after tomorrow."

"But you said it was in a few weeks."

"It was rescheduled."

"Why didn't you tell me?" Annoyance flared, banishing all thoughts of comforting her.

"I thought if you knew, you'd put me on a plane right away and I wanted these two days with you."

Two days during which they'd argued and he'd done nothing but push her away. Irritation welled.

"But why aren't you going right home for the interview? Teaching at Berkeley is all you've talked about since I've known you."

Her temper sparked in response to his scolding. "Plans change. It's just not the right time for me to take the position."

"Are you giving up something as important as Berkeley because of me?"

"Seems foolish, doesn't it?" she countered without a trace of bitterness.

Nic clenched his fists. She was going to be so much better without him.

And he was going to be so much worse.

"You should take your own advice about going to bed," she told him. "Sounds like your mother planned a grueling week for you. It will be better if you're well rested."

Nic had the distinct impression he'd just been dismissed. His lips twitched. He could always count on Brooke to do the last thing he expected. After her assault on his willpower this morning, he'd been lying awake half expecting her to launch another all-out attack tonight.

From the way he'd been with her this morning, she had to know he was having a harder and harder time resisting her. Resisting what he wanted more than anything. With each beat of his heart, the idea of taking her back upstairs and tumbling her into his bed seemed less like a huge mistake and more like the right thing to do.

Walk away.

"What are you going to do?" he asked, knowing that prolonging this conversation was the height of idiocy. It would only make going back to bed alone that much harder.

"Sit here."

"I won't be able to sleep knowing you're down here in the dark."

A small smile filled her voice as she said, "You've never had trouble putting me out of your mind before."

If she only knew. "You weren't sitting on my couch in your pajamas before."

Her sigh was barely audible over the blood thundering in his ears.

"Good night." Calling himself every sort of fool, he headed back upstairs. Leaving his bedroom door open in a halfhearted invitation, he fell onto the mattress. Hands behind his head, eyes on the ceiling, he strained to hear footfalls on the stairs. The house was completely silent except for the breeze stirring the curtains on either side of his window.

His nerves stretched and twisted, but she didn't appear. He caught himself glancing at the doorway, expecting her silhouette. As the minutes ticked by, Nic forced his eyes shut, but he couldn't quiet his mind and the past two days played through his thoughts with unrelenting starkness.

With a heated curse, he rolled off the bed and stalked downstairs. It didn't surprise him to find her exactly where he'd left her.

"You are the most stubborn woman I've ever known," he complained. "I don't know what the hell you expect from me."

Even his mother had given up trying to keep him in Sherdana when his heart belonged in an airplane hangar in the Mojave Desert. But for years Brooke had relentlessly pushed herself into his life until he couldn't celebrate achievements or face failures without thinking about her.

"My expectations are all in the past," she said, pushing to her feet.

And that's what was eating him alive.

They stared at each other in motionless silence until Brooke heaved a huge sigh. The dramatic rise and fall of her chest snagged Nic's attention. The tank top she wore scooped low in front, offering him the tiniest hint of cleavage. Recalling the way her breasts had tasted this morning, he repressed a groan.

"Brooke."

"Don't." She started past him. Nic caught her wrist. At his touch, she stilled. "I thought I was pretty clear this afternoon when I said that I've given up on you."

"Crystal clear." Nic cupped her face, his fingers sliding into the silky strands of russet near her ear.

"Then what are you doing?"

"Wishing you didn't have to."

He brought his mouth down to hers, catching her lips in a searing kiss that held nothing back. She stiffened, her body bracing to recoil. He couldn't let that happen. Not now. Not when he'd stopped being principled and noble. Not when he wanted her with a hunger that ate at him like acid.

Taking a tighter grip on her wrist, he slowly levered it behind her back, compelling her hips forward until her pelvis brushed against the jut of his erection. The contact made him moan. He deepened the kiss, sweeping his tongue forward to taste her. Her lips parted for him. A soft whimper escaped her throat as she writhed in his grasp, but whether she fought to escape or move closer he couldn't be sure.

"I want you," he murmured, setting his mouth on her throat and sucking gently.

Her body trembled, but her muscles remained tense. Labored, uneven breaths pushed her breasts against his bare chest.

"Damn you, Nic." It was in her voice, in the way she tilted her head to allow him better access to her neck. She was furious and aroused. "It's too late for you to change your mind."

"It's too late when I say it is." He released her wrist and cupped her small, round butt in his palm. The cotton pajama bottoms bunched as he gave a light squeeze.

She gasped, set both hands on his chest and shoved. It was like a kitten batting at a mastiff. "This isn't fair."

"Fair?" He growled the word. "Do you want to talk about fair? You've tormented me for five years. Strutting around the hangar in your barely there denim shorts. Coming to peer over my shoulder and letting your hair tickle my skin. How hard do you think it was for me to keep from pulling you into my lap and putting my hands all over you?"

"You never..." She arched back and stared up into his face. "I had no idea."

"I made sure you didn't. But it wasn't easy." He wrapped his fingers around her red curls and gave a gentle but firm tug. "And it wasn't fun."

Brooke was electrified by Nic's admission; the twinge in her scalp when he pulled her hair merely enhanced her already overstimulated nerves. She welcomed the discomfort. The fleeting pain chased the last vestiges of self-pity from her mind and grounded her in the moment.

Taking her silence and stillness as surrender, Nic bent to kiss her again, but Brooke turned aside at the last minute. Even though this was what she'd wanted when she'd bought her plane ticket, she wasn't the same woman who'd gotten on the plane in San Francisco.

Nic wasn't deterred by her evasion. He kissed his way across her cheek and seized her earlobe between his teeth. Her knees wavered as his unsteady breath filled her ear. Meanwhile, his hands moved over her back, gliding beneath her tank top to find her hot skin and trace each bump of her spine.

"What's wrong?" he murmured as his lips investigated the hollow made by her collarbone.

"You want me to give in." He was doing whatever it took to make her putty in his hand. "Just like you used to want me to leave you alone. It's always about what you want."

She felt as much as heard his sigh. His hands left her body and bracketed his hips. He regarded her solemnly.

"I thought this was what we both wanted."

A breeze puffed in from the terrace, chilling Brooke. Where a second earlier the room had been dark, moonlight now poured over the tiled floor and bathed Nic's splendid torso in a white glow. Her mouth went dry as her gaze traced the rise and fall of his pecs and abs, the perfect ratio of broad shoulders to narrow hips. Although still in shadow, the planes of his face seemed more chiseled, his jaw sharper.

Her pulse began to slam harder, throbbing in her wrist, her throat and between her thighs. She found his eyes in the dimness, fell beneath the hypnotic power of his gaze. A rushing filled her ears, the incessant movement of a stream as it surges past boulders and fallen trees, unstoppable. Once upon a time, she'd been like that, full of purpose and joy. Then she'd let her doubts bottle her up.

Was she really going to stand here being annoyed with him and waste another second of the limited time she had left bemoaning the cards fate had dealt?

She held out her hand to Nic. He linked his fingers with hers and drew her toward the stairs. Without saying a word they entered his bedroom and came together in a slow, effortless dance of hands, lips and tongue. Pajamas landed on the floor and Brooke stretched out on Nic's king-size bed, his strong body pressing her hard into the mattress as they kissed and explored.

Words were lost to Brooke as Nic's fingertips rode her rib cage to the undersides of her breasts. She couldn't remember ever feeling so heavy and so light at the same time. Arching her spine, she pushed her nipples against his palms. Stars burst behind her eyelids as he circled the hard buds, making them ache with pleasure before at long last drawing one, then the other, into his hot mouth.

The sensations snapping along her nerves made Brooke quiver and gasp. She was hungry for Nic to touch her more intimately, but her senses had gone fuzzy, her body languid. His hand rode upward along her inner thigh with torturous precision and she followed its progress with breaths growing ever more faint. By the time his finger dipped into her wet heat, her lungs had forgotten how to function. She lay with her eyes closed, her head spinning as he filled her first with one, then two fingers, stretching her, finding the spot that caused her hips to jerk and the first shuddering moan to escape her throat.

And then he replaced his hand with his mouth and adored her with tongue and teeth. Sliding his hands beneath her butt, he lifted her against the press and retreat of his kiss. She tried to squirm, to escape the tongue that drove her relentlessly toward pleasure so acute it hurt, but Nic dug his fingers into her skin and held her captive. Mewling, Brooke surrendered to the slow, tantalizing rise of ecstasy.

Nic hadn't made love to her like this the first time they were together. Five years of anticipation had made their lovemaking passionate and impatient. Nic had satisfied her three times that night, his large body surging into hers, filling her completely. She'd come with desperate cries, unable to articulate the incandescent heights to which he'd lifted her.

But the rush upward had been followed by only a brief respite to catch her breath and savor the afterglow. Nic had proved insatiable that night and when at last they'd spent the last of their passion, she'd fallen into a deep, dreamless slumber.

This was different. As if recognizing this was their last time together, he made love to her with his eyes first and then his hands. Languid sweeps of his lips across her skin soothed her soul and set her skin aflame. Words of appreciation and praise poured over her while his fingers reverently grazed the lines of her body.

By the time he slipped on a condom and settled between her thighs, Brooke wasn't sure where she ended and he began. He moved slowly into her, easing in just the head of his erection, giving her time she didn't need to adjust to him.

Tipping her hips as he began his second thrust, she ensured that his forward progress didn't end until he was fully seated inside her. He groaned and buried his face in her neck. She dug her fingernails into his back, reveling in the fullness of his possession. For a long moment neither of them moved. Brooke filled her lungs with the spicy tang of his aftershave and the musk of their lovemaking. She closed her eyes to memorize the feel of his powerful body as he began moving.

Measured and deliberate, Nic rocked against her, thrusting in and out while pleasure built. He kissed her hard, his tongue plunging to tangle with hers. Their hips came together with increased urgency. Brooke let her teeth glide along Nic's neck. He bucked hard against her when she nipped at his skin. The thrust rapped her womb where their child grew and sent her spiraling toward climax. She must have clenched around him because suddenly Nic picked up the pace. Together they climbed, hands pleasuring, bodies striving for closeness. Brooke came first, Nic's name on her lips. He drove into her more urgently and reached orgasm moments later.

His strong body shook with the intensity of his release and a hoarse cry spilled out of him. What followed was the deepest, most emotionally charged kiss he'd ever given her. Brooke clung to him while her body pulsed with aftershocks and surrendered to the tempest raging in Nic. If she'd thought their lovemaking had forever branded her as his, the kiss, tender one moment, joyous the next, stole the heart right out of her body.

"Incredible." He buried his face in her neck, his breath heavy and uneven, body limp and powerless.

Brooke wrapped her arms around his shoulders, marveling that this formidable man had been reduced to overcooked noodles in her arms. Grinning, she stroked the bumpy length of his spine and ran her nails through his hair in a soothing caress.

"Am I too heavy?" he murmured, lips moving against her shoulder as he spoke.

"A little, but I don't want you to move just yet." She was afraid any shift would disrupt this moment of perfect harmony.

"Good. I like it just where I am."

They stayed that way for a long time. Legs entwined, his breath soft and steady on her neck, his fingers playing idly in her tangled curls. Brooke couldn't recall if she'd ever enjoyed being so utterly still before. She didn't want to talk or to think. Only to be.

But as with all things, change is inevitable. Nic heaved a mighty sigh and rolled away from her to dispose of the condom and pull a sheet over their cooling bodies. The breeze had shifted direction and the air that had seemed dense and sultry an hour earlier was swept away.

With her head pillowed on his shoulder and Nic's fingers absently gliding across the small of her back, the lethargy she'd experienced earlier didn't return.

"I can feel you thinking," Nic said, his eyes closed, a half smile curving his lips.

"That's illogical."

His chest moved up and down with his sigh. "If I was in a logical frame of mind, I wouldn't be lying naked with you in my arms."

"I suppose not."

"What's on your mind?"

Not wanting to share her true thoughts, she said the first thing that popped into her head. "If you must know I was thinking about getting a cat when I get home."

"Really?" He sounded genuinely surprised. "I thought Glen said you guys grew up with dogs."

"We did, but dogs are so needy and some of my days can go really long with classes and office hours. I think a cat would be a wiser choice."

"I like cats."

"You do?" She couldn't imagine Nic owning anything that needed regular feeding or care. "Wouldn't a snake be a more suitable pet for you?"

"A snake?"

"Sure, something you only had to feed once a week." She chuckled when he growled at her.

"No snakes." He yawned. "A cat. Definitely."

Brooke could tell by the sleepiness of his voice that she was losing him. "But a cat is going to jump on your worktable and knock things off. It's going to wake you in the middle of the night wanting to be petted and yowling at you for attention. They ignore you when you give them commands and never come when they're called."

Nic cracked open one eye and smirked at her. "Yeah, a cat. They're definitely my favorite kind of nuisance."

It took Brooke a couple seconds to realize he had connected her behavior to what she'd just said about cats. In retaliation, she poked him hard in the ribs and he located the ticklish spot behind her knees that had her squirming. It didn't take long for their good-natured tussling to spark another round of lovemaking.

Much later, while Nic's breathing deepened into sleep, Brooke lay awake in the predawn stillness and tried to keep her thoughts from rushing into the future. The hours she had with him grew shorter every second. So instead of sleeping, as the sky grew lighter, Brooke lost herself in Nic's snug embrace, savored the way his warmth seeped through her skin and awaited the day.

The nausea that had plagued her the day before began as the sun peeked over the horizon and gilded the window ledge. She breathed through the first wave and sagged with relief when her stomach settled down. Remembering how the previous morning had gone, Brooke knew she had to get back to her room. Nic might not be the most observant of men, but even he'd be hard-pressed not to notice if she was throwing up in his bathroom.

Last night while in the grip of insomnia, she'd decided not to tell him she was pregnant. If he hadn't made love to her with such all-consuming emotion, she might have accepted that they could go back to being friends, affectionate but disconnected by distance and circumstances. But now she realized that they had to make a clean break of it. It would be best for both of them if he didn't know the truth.

Before her stomach began to pitch and roll again, Brooke untangled herself from Nic's embrace and eased from his bed. Her head spun sickeningly as she got to her feet and snatched up her pajamas. Naked, the soft cotton pressed to her mouth, she raced from the room and down the stairs.

If Elena was shocked to see her streak by, Brooke never knew because her focus was fixed on crossing the twenty feet of terrace to the guesthouse and reaching the bathroom in the nick of time. Panting in the aftermath, she splashed cold water on her face and waited to see if the nausea had passed. When it appeared the worst was over, Brooke climbed into the shower.

She was dressed and repacking her suitcase when a soft knock sounded. Heart jumping, she eased the door open, expecting to see Nic standing there, and was surprised to see Elena bearing a tray with a teapot and a plate of bread and assorted preserves.

"Ginger tea is good for nausea," she announced, slipping the tray onto the dresser. "I understand you are leaving for Sherdana today."

"Nic is going. I'm heading for Italy." But her plan to visit friends in Rome had lost its appeal. More than anything she wanted to head home to family and friends and start the process of healing in their comforting embrace.

Elena's eyes narrowed. "You let me know if you need anything before you leave."

Seven

Awaking to an empty bed hadn't been the best start to Nic's day, but he reasoned he might as well get used to disappointment because he wouldn't ever wake to Brooke's smile again. The sun was high by the time Nic finished his shower and headed to the first floor. Elena was dusting the already immaculate furniture. She shot him an intensely unhappy look as he poured himself a cup of coffee and he wondered at her barely veiled hostility.

"Have you seen Brooke this morning?" he asked, carrying his cup to the terrace doorway and peering in the direction of the guesthouse. The trip to Kefalonia's airport would take forty-five minutes by boat and another hour over land. They would need to leave soon.

"She has eaten breakfast and had some last minute packing to do."

"Is Thasos ready with the boat?"

Elena nodded. "She is a nice girl. You shouldn't let her go to Italy by herself."

"She is going to visit friends," he explained to the housekeeper, while guilt nibbled at the edges of his conscience. "She knows her way around. She lived in Rome and Florence for a year."

"You should take her home."

Nic was startled by Elena's remark. He'd been thinking the same thing all morning. Unfortunately that wasn't possible. Reality dictated he should distance himself from Brooke as soon as possible, but the thought of letting her go off by herself disturbed him.

If she didn't get on a plane bound for California, he would spend the next two weeks worrying about her traveling alone in Europe instead of focusing on the issues at home and the necessity of finding a wife. Nor did he have time to escort her to the gate and satisfy himself that she was heading to San Francisco. He was expected back in Sherdana this afternoon.

Nic's chest tightened. He was doing a terrible job of lying to himself. In truth he wasn't ready to say goodbye. It was selfish and stupid.

"I need to make a phone call," Nic told Elena. "Will you let Brooke know we'll be leaving in ten minutes?"

Calling himself every sort of idiot, Nic dialed Gabriel. When he answered, Nic got right to the point. "I'm bringing someone home with me. She's come a long way to see me and I don't feel right leaving her alone in Greece."

"She?" Gabriel echoed, not quite able to keep curiosity out of his voice. "Is this going to cause problems?"

Nic knew exactly what Gabriel meant and decided not to sugarcoat it. "That's not my intention. She's Glen's sister. I think I've mentioned her a few times."

"The one who drives you crazy?" Gabriel sounded intrigued.

"The interfering one who flew here to convince me to come back to the *Griffin* project."

"Just the project?"

"What's that supposed to mean?" Nic didn't intend to be defensive, but with last night's events still reverberating across his emotions, he wasn't in the best shape to fence with a diplomat as savvy as Gabriel. "She's Glen's little sister."

"And you talk about her more than any woman you've ever known."

"I know what you're getting at, but it's not an issue. Things got a little complicated between us recently, but everything is sorted out."

"Complicated how?"

"I didn't tell her who I was until she came here looking for me and that upset her. I shouldn't have left her in the dark. We've been...friends...for a long time."

"Why didn't you tell her?"

Nic rubbed his temples where an ache had begun. "I know this is going to be hard for you to understand but I liked being an ordinary scientist, anonymously doing the work I'm really good at."

"You're right. I don't understand. I grew up knowing I belonged to the country. You never did like being in the spotlight. So you didn't tell her you're a prince. Do you think she would have looked at you differently if she'd known all along?"

"Brooke values a person for how they behave not who they are or what they have."

Gabriel laughed. "She sounds like your sort of girl. I can't wait to meet her."

"Honestly, it's not like that." He didn't want his brother giving the wrong idea to their parents. "She understands my situation."

"She knows that you're coming home to find a bride? And she wants to accompany you, anyway?"

"I haven't spoken with her this morning." Not exactly a

lie. "She doesn't know I'm bringing her with me to Sherdana yet."

"Well, this should make for an interesting family dinner," Gabriel said. "I'll make sure there's a place set at the table for her beside Mother."

And before Nic could protest that arrangement, Gabriel hung up. Nic debated calling him back, but decided it would only exacerbate his brother's suspicions about Brooke. Playing it cool and calm around his family would be the best way to handle any and all speculation.

Grabbing his bag from his bedroom, Nic made his way toward the steps that Brooke had used to access the terrace two days ago. They led down the steep hillside in a zigzag that ended at a private dock. Brooke had already arrived at the boat and was settled onto the seat opposite the pilot's chair. The smile she offered Nic was bright if a little ragged around the edges.

Thasos started the engine as soon as Nic stepped aboard and quickly untied the mooring ropes. Nic settled into the bench seat at the back of the boat and watched Brooke pretend not to be interested in him. He knew the signs. He'd spent years giving her the impression he was oblivious to her presence. Yet how could he be? She lit up every room she entered. Her personality set the very air to buzzing. Sitting still was probably the hardest thing she did. Yet when her brain engaged, she could get lost in a book or her writing for hours.

They'd shared many companionable afternoons while she was working on her second doctorate. Not surprisingly, she enjoyed sitting cross-legged on the couch in his workroom, tapping away at her computer keyboard or with her nose buried in a book. If he managed to accomplish any work on the weekends she visited, it was a miracle. Most of the time, he'd pretended to be productive while he watched her surreptitiously.

Forty-five minutes after leaving Ithaca, the boat maneuvered into an open space at the Fiskardo quay. A car would be waiting to carry them on the thirty-one-kilometer journey to the airport outside Kefalonia's capital, Argostoli. If traffic was good, they would get there in a little less than an hour.

Thasos carried their bags to the waiting car and with a jaunty wave turned back to the boat. As soon as he'd driven out of sight, Nic turned to Brooke.

"I don't feel comfortable heading home to Sherdana and leaving you on your own."

"Good Lord, Nic." She shot him a dry look. "I'm perfectly capable of taking care of myself."

"I agree. It's just that with everything that has happened in the last few days—"

"Stop right there." All trace of amusement vanished from her tone as she interrupted him. "After everything that's happened...? I am not some delicate flower that has been crushed by disappointment."

"Nevertheless. I'm not going to leave you stranded in Greece. You are coming home with me."

After five years of teasing and cajoling, bullying and begging, Brooke thought she had Nic all figured out. He preferred working in solitude, hated drama and rarely veered from a goal once he'd set his mind to something. But this announcement left her floundering. Had she ever really known him at all?

"What do you mean you're taking me home with you?" The notion thrilled and terrified her.

"Exactly what I said." Nic's jaw was set in uncompromising lines. "You will fly with me to Sherdana and from there I will make sure you get a flight back to California."

The knot in Brooke's stomach didn't ease with his clarification. "I assure you I'm perfectly capable of getting a

flight home from Greece." With morning sickness plagu-
ing her, she'd given up the idea of a summer holiday in
Italy. She wanted to be surrounded by familiar things and
her favorite people. Maybe she'd spend a week in LA visiting her parents.

"Don't make this difficult on yourself."

"Isn't that what I should be saying to you?" Seeing he
didn't comprehend her meaning, Brooke clarified. "Have
you considered what happens when we land? How fast can
you get me on a plane to the States? In the meantime are
you planning on leaving me waiting at the airport? Putting me up in a hotel? Or perhaps you think I'd be more
comfortable at the palace?"

Expecting her sarcasm to be lost on him the way it usually was, Brooke was stunned by his matter-of-fact retort.

"My brother said he'll make sure the staff sets an extra
place for you at dinner next to my mother." Lighthearted
mischief lit his eyes as her mouth dropped open.

"I can't have dinner with your family." Her throat
clenched around a lump of panic.

"Why not?"

"I have nothing to wear."

"You look perfect to me."

With lids half-closed, his gaze roamed over her body,
setting off a chain reaction of longing and need. The July
morning had gone from warm to hot as the sun had crested
the horizon and Brooke had dressed accordingly in a loose-
fitting blue-and-white cotton peasant dress with a thigh-
baring hem and a plunging neckline. The look was fine
for traveling from one Greek Island to another or catching a short flight to Rome, London or anywhere else she
could snag a connection home to California. But to go to
Sherdana and be introduced to Nic's family?

"Why are you really bringing me along?"

"Because I'm not ready to let you go." As light as a

feather, he slid his forefinger along her jaw. It fell away when it reached her chin. "Not yet."

But let her go he would. Her skin tingled where he'd touched her. Brooke saw the regret in his eyes and her heart jerked. Heat kindled in her midsection as she recalled what had taken place between them the night before, but desire tangled with anxiety and sadness. How was she supposed to just walk away?

She jammed her balled fists behind her to hide their shaking and estimated she had half an hour to talk him out of his madness. "Have you considered how unhappy your parents are going to be if you show up with some strange girl in tow?"

"You're not a strange girl. You're Glen's sister."

"And how are you going to explain what I was doing on the island with you?"

"I've already contacted Gabriel and briefed him."

Briefed him with the truth or a diplomatic runaround? "You don't think anyone is going to be suspicious about the nature of our relationship?

"Why would they be? I've spoken of you often to my family. They know you're Glen's annoying baby sister whom I've known for the last five years."

Seeing his wicked smile, she relaxed a little. "Okay, maybe we can do this. After all, Glen knows us better than anyone and he has no idea anything changed between us." If they could fool Glen, they could keep his family from guessing the true nature of their relationship.

"He knows."

Brooke shook her head. "Impossible." Her mind raced over every conversation she'd had with her brother in the past month. "He hasn't said a word."

"He had plenty to say to me," Nic replied in a tight voice, and Brooke suddenly had no trouble imagining how that conversation had gone.

Glen was the best older brother a girl could have. Born eighteen months before her, he'd never minded when she'd tagged after him and his buddies. The guys had accepted her as one of them and taught her how to surf and water-ski. She'd grown up half tomboy, half girlie-girl. They'd all had a great time until Glen graduated high school two years early and headed off to MIT where he'd met Nic.

"The morning after we were together," Nic continued, "your brother cornered me in the lab and threatened to send me up strapped to the rocket if I hurt you."

"No wonder you got out of town so fast after breaking things off with me." Her words were meant to be funny, but when Nic grimaced, she realized her insensitivity. He'd actually left not long after the rocket blew up. "I'm sorry." She looked down at her hands. "I shouldn't have said that."

Nic set his fingers beneath her chin and adjusted the angle of her head until their eyes met. "I'd like to show you my country."

And then what? She received the royal treatment and another goodbye? Already her heart was behaving rashly. She'd opened herself to heartache when she'd surrendered to one last night in his arms. To linger meant parting from him would be that much harder. Did she have no self-control? No self-respect? Hadn't she already learned several difficult lessons?

The need in his gaze echoed the longing in her heart. "Sure," she murmured, surrendering to what they both wanted. "Why not."

"Then that's settled."

An hour later, Nic led her onto a luxurious private plane and guided her into a comfortable leather seat beside the window. With his warm, solid presence bolstering her confidence, Brooke buckled her seat belt and listened to the jet's engine rev. As the plane began to taxi, her chest compressed. Try as she might, she couldn't shake the notion that she should have refused Nic's invitation and just gone home to California.

The instant he'd set foot on the plane his demeanor had changed. Tension rode his broad shoulders and he seemed more distant than ever, his bearing more formal, his expression set into aloof lines. Before leaving Ithaca he'd donned a pair of light beige dress pants and a pale blue dress shirt that set off his tanned skin. On the seat opposite him, he'd placed a beige blazer that bore a blue pocket square. Brooke stared at the oddity.

Nic in stylish clothes. And a coordinating pocket square.

He'd always been sexy, handsome and confident, but he now wore a mantle of überwealthy, ultrasophistication. Ensconced in the luxurious plane, his big hands linked loosely in his lap, he looked utterly confident, poised and...regal. For the first time she truly accepted that Nic was no longer the rocket scientist she knew. Nor was he the ardent lover of last night. Swallowed by helplessness, Brooke stared straight ahead unsure who he'd become.

Maybe leaving him behind in Sherdana was going to be easier than she realized. This Nic wasn't the man she'd fallen in love with. A shiver raced up her spine as his hand covered hers and squeezed gently. Obviously, her heart had no problem with the changes in Nic's appearance. Her pulse fluttered and skipped along just as foolishly as ever.

"Are you okay?" he asked.

Did she explain how his transformation bothered her? To what end? He could never be hers. He belonged to a nation.

"This is quite a plane." Feeling out of place sitting beside such an aristocratic dreamboat on his multimillion-dollar aircraft, Brooke babbled the first thought that entered her head. "Is it yours?"

"If by 'yours' you are asking if it belongs to Sherdana's royal family, then yes."

"Well, that's pretty convenient for you, I guess." She mustered a wry grin. "I suppose the press knows the plane pretty well and that your arrival won't exactly be a state secret."

"Your point?"

"Aside from the fact that we're trying to maintain a low profile on our whole relationship thing, I'm dressed like someone's poor relation. The press is bound to be curious about me. Please can I stay on the plane after you get off until the coast is clear?"

He looked ready to protest, but shook his head and sighed. "If you wish. I'll arrange for someone to meet you at the hangar. That way there won't be any press asking questions you don't want to answer."

It hit Brooke what some of those questions might be and her brain grew sluggish. She'd spent most of her life with her nose buried in books. Glen was the sibling who relished the spotlight. He didn't freeze up in front of large crowds, but put people at ease with his charismatic charm and dazzled them with his intelligence. Numerous times she'd stood back during press events and marveled at his confidence. Not even the difficult questions fired at him after the rocket blew up had rattled him. He'd demonstrated the perfect blend of sadness and determination.

"As for clothes," Nic continued, "I'm sure either my sister, Ariana, or Olivia, Gabriel's wife, will be able to lend you some things."

Brooke would be borrowing clothes from princesses. This wasn't an ordinary family he was taking her home to meet. His mother was a queen. His father was a king. Nic was a prince. What the hell was she doing? She clutched at the armrests, suddenly unable to breathe.

The whirr and clunk of landing gear being locked into place startled her. They were minutes from landing. Nothing about this trip was working out the way she'd planned.

She'd stepped onto the plane in San Francisco thinking she would fly to Greece, tell him about the baby and bring Nic back with her so they could be one big happy family.

The full impact of her foolishness now hit her like a mace. Even if Nic were madly in love with her, he couldn't offer her anything permanent. In fact, he was so far out of her league that they could be living on separate planets.

"I need to know details about your family so I'm prepared," she blurted out, her stomach flipping as the plane lost altitude.

"Sure. Where would you like to start?"

So many questions whirled in her mind that it took her a moment to prioritize them. "Your parents. How do I address them?"

Eight

Nic emerged from the plane and hesitated before descending the stairs to the tarmac. In a tight knot, thirty feet away, a dozen reporters held up cameras and microphones all focused on him. He approached the assembled crowd—the prodigal son returning to the bosom of his family—and answered several questions before heading toward the black Mercedes that awaited him.

Although he'd known it was the sensible thing to do, separating from Brooke even for a short period of time didn't feel right. It wasn't as if he expected her to run off and hop a plane back to California. Enough security surrounded the royal aircraft hangar that she wouldn't get five feet from the plane before she was stopped and questioned.

No, it was more the sense that by traveling separately to the palace, he was acknowledging that there was something to hide. And yet, wasn't there? During the car ride to the airport when she'd asked him why he wanted her to come home with him, he'd told her the truth. He wasn't ready to let her go. The answer had distressed her.

Last night she'd accused him of always demanding things be his way. Now, once again he was acting selfishly.

Nic passed the crowd of reporters without another glance. A familiar figure stood beside the car's rear door. Stewart Barnes, Gabriel's private secretary, offered a smile and a nod as Nic approached.

"Good afternoon, Your Highness. I hope you had a good flight from Greece." The secretary's keen blue eyes darted toward the plane. "Prince Gabriel mentioned you were bringing someone with you. Did she change her mind?"

"No. She's just a little skittish about public appearances. Could you arrange a car to pick her up at the hangar?"

If Stewart was surprised that Nic was sneaking a girl into the country, his expression didn't show it. "Of course." He bowed and opened the car door.

Because the car windows were tinted, Nic had no idea anyone besides the driver was in the vehicle. Therefore, when he spotted Gabriel sitting in the backseat and grinning at him, Nic was overcome by an unexpected rush of joy.

"Good heavens, what are you doing here?" Nic embraced his brother as Stewart closed the door, encasing the princes in privacy.

"It's been three years since you've come home and you have to ask? I've missed you."

The genuine thrum of affection in Gabriel's voice caught Nic off guard. As tight as the triplets had been as children, once on their divergent paths, circumstances and distance had caused them to drift apart. Nic hadn't realized how much he'd missed his older brother until this moment.

"I've missed you, too." The car began to move as Nic asked after the youngest of the three brothers. "How's Christian?"

"Unpredictable as always. Right now he's in Switzerland talking to a company that might be interested in bringing a nanotechnology manufacturing plant here."

"That's wonderful." Nic couldn't help but wonder at the timing of Christian's absence given the series of events his mother had designed for the purpose of finding brides for her sons. "When is he due back?"

"In time for the wedding or Mother will skin him alive."

"And the rest of the parties and receptions?"

Gabriel laughed. "All eyes will be on you."

Nic marveled at the change in his earnest brother. Although young Gabriel had been as full of curiosity and mischief as Nic and Christian, somewhere around his tenth birthday it had hit him that the leadership of the country would one day be his. Almost overnight, while his inquisitive nature had remained, he'd become overly serious and all too responsible.

"You're different," Nic observed. "I don't remember the last time you were this…"

"Happy?" Gabriel's eyes glinted. "It's called wedded bliss. You should try it."

A woman had done this to Gabriel? "I'm looking forward to meeting your wife."

"And speaking of fair women, what happened to your Brooke?"

"She's not my Brooke." Nic heard gravel in his voice and moderated his tone. "And she's staying in the plane until it's taxied into the hangar."

"Your idea or hers?"

"Hers. She was concerned that she wasn't dressed properly and wanted to maintain a low profile."

Gabriel's eyes widened in feigned shock. "What was she wearing that she was so unpresentable?"

"I don't know. Some sort of cotton dress. She thought she looked like someone's poor relation."

"Did she?"

Nic thought she looked carefree and sexy. "Not at all, but what do I know about women's fashion?"

The two men fell to talking about recent events including the incident where the vengeful aunt of Gabriel's twin daughters had infiltrated the palace intending to stop him from marrying Olivia.

"And you have no idea where she's gone?" Nic quizzed, amazed how much chaos one woman had created.

"Interpol has interviewed her former employer and visited her flat in Milan, but for now she's on the run."

As the car entered the palace grounds, Nic's mind circled back to the woman he'd left at the airport. "Have you told anyone besides Stewart that I brought Brooke with me?"

"Olivia and her secretary, Libby, know. They are prepared to take charge of her as soon as she arrives."

"Thank you." Nic was relieved that Brooke would be taken care of.

"Oh, and Mother is expecting you in the blue drawing room for tea. She has an hour blocked out for you to view the first round of potential wives. Stewart interviewed several secretary candidates for you. Their résumés will be waiting in your room. Look them over and let Stewart know which you'd like to meet."

"A secretary?"

"Now that you're back, we've packed your agenda with meetings and appearances. You'll need someone to keep you on schedule."

Nic's head spun. "Damn," he muttered. "It feels as if I never left."

Gabriel clapped him on the shoulder. "It's good to have you back."

From the backseat of a luxurious Mercedes, Brooke clutched her worn travel bag and watched the town of

Carone slip past. In the many years she'd known Nic, which she'd spent alternately being ignored and rejected, she'd never once been as angry with him as she was at this moment.

What had he been thinking to bring her to Sherdana? She didn't belong here. She didn't fit into his world the way he'd fit into hers. No doctorate degrees could prepare her for the pitfalls of palace life. She'd be dining with his family. What fork did she use? She would stand out as the uncouth American accustomed to eating burgers and fries with her fingers. Brooke frowned as she considered how many of her favorite foods didn't require a knife and fork. Pizza. Tacos. Pulled pork sandwiches.

And what if she couldn't get a flight out in the next day or two? As Nic's guest, would she be expected to attend any of the parties his mother had arranged? Were they the sort of parties where people danced? Nic had already shown her a dance specific to the country. They'd laughed over her inability to master the simplest of steps. She'd never imagined a time when she'd be expected to perform them.

And the biggest worry of all: What if someone discovered she was pregnant? Now that morning sickness was hitting her hard, what excuse could she make to explain away the nausea?

Brooke gawked like any tourist as the car swung through a gate and the palace appeared. Nic had grown up here. The chasm between them widened even further. It was one thing to rationalize that her brother's business partner was in reality the prince of a small European country. It was another to see for herself.

During her year abroad in Italy she'd been fortunate enough to be invited to several palaces. A few of the older volumes of Italian literature she'd used in her doctoral thesis had been housed in private collections and she'd been lucky enough to be allowed the opportunity to study them. But those residences had been far less grand and much smaller than the enormous palace she was heading toward right now.

The car followed a circular driveway around a massive fountain and drew up in front of the palace's wide double doors. Surprise held Brooke in place. Given her stealthy transfer from the royal private plane to this car, she'd half expected to be dropped off at the servants' back entrance.

A man in a dark blue suit stepped forward and opened the car door. Brooke stared at the palace doors, unable to make her legs work. One of the tall doors moved, opening enough to let a slim woman in a burgundy suit slip through. Still unsure of her circumstances, Brooke waited as the woman approached.

"Dr. Davis?" She had a lovely soft voice and a British accent. "I'm Libby Marshall, Princess Olivia's private secretary."

"Nice to meet you." Brooke still hadn't budged from the car. "Nic didn't mention he intended to bring me here when we left his villa this morning so I'm not really sure about all this."

The princess's secretary smiled. "Don't worry, all has been arranged. Princess Olivia is looking forward to meeting you. Armando will take your bag. If you will follow me."

If she hadn't flown hundreds of miles in a private jet, Brooke might have been giddy at the thought that a princess was looking forward to meeting her. Instead, it was just one more in a series of surreal experiences.

Brooke slipped from the car and let herself gawk at the sheer size of the palace. Her escort moved like someone who knew better than to keep people waiting and had disappeared through the tall doors by the time Brooke surrendered her meager possessions to Armando. She trotted to catch up, but slowed as soon as she stepped inside.

The palace was everything she'd expected. Thirty feet before her a black-and-white marble floor ended in a wide staircase covered in royal blue carpet. The stairs were wide enough to let an SUV pass. They were split into two sections. The first flight ascended to a landing that then split into separate stairs that continued their climb to the second floor.

She envisioned dozens of women dressed in ball gowns of every color, gliding down that staircase, hands trailing along the polished banister, all coming to meet Nic as he stood, formally dressed, on the polished marble at the bottom of the stairs awaiting them. His gaze would run along the line of women, his expression stern and unyielding as he searched for his perfect bride.

Brooke saw herself bringing up the rear. She was late and the borrowed dress she wore would be too long. As she descended, her heel would catch on her hem. Two steps from the bottom, she'd trip, but there would be no Nic to catch her. He was surrounded by five women each vying for his attention. Without him to save her, she would make a grab for the banister and miss.

Flashes would explode in her eyes like fireworks as dozens of press cameras captured her ignominy at a hundred frames per second.

"Dr. Davis?" Libby peered at her in concern. "Is something amiss?"

Brooke shook herself out of the horrifying daydream and swallowed the lump that had appeared in her throat. "Call me Brooke. This is—" Her gaze roved around the space as maids bustled past with vases of flowers and two well-dressed gentlemen strode by carrying briefcases and speaking in low tones. "Really big. And very beautiful," she rushed to add.

"Come. Princess Olivia is in her office."

Normally nervous energy would have prompted Brooke to chatter uncontrollably. But as she followed Libby past the stairs and into a corridor, she was too overwhelmed. They walked past half a dozen rooms and took a couple more turns. In seconds, her sense of direction had completely failed her.

"You really know your way around." She'd lost the battle with her nerves. "How long have you worked in the palace?"

"A few months. I arrived with Princess Olivia."

"Be honest. How long did it take until you no longer got lost?"

Libby shot a wry smile over her shoulder. "Three weeks."

"I'm only expecting to be here a couple days. I don't suppose there's a map or something."

"I'm afraid not. And I was under the impression that you'd be with us until after the wedding."

Brooke stumbled as she caught the edge of her sandal on the marble floor. "That's not what Nic and I agreed to." But in fact, she wasn't sure if they'd discussed the length of her stay. It certainly couldn't stretch to include a royal wedding.

"I could be mistaken," Libby told her, turning into an open doorway.

The office into which Brooke stepped was decorated in feminine shades of cream and peach, but the functional layout spoke of productivity. On her entrance, a stunning blonde looked up from her laptop and smiled.

"You must be Dr. Davis," the woman exclaimed, rising to greet her. She held out a manicured hand. "Lovely to meet you. I'm Olivia Alessandro."

"It's nice to meet you, as well." The urge to curtsy overwhelmed Brooke and only the knowledge that she'd fall flat on her face if she tried kept her from acting like an idiot. "Your Highness."

"Oh, please call me Olivia. You're Nic's friend and that makes you like family."

It was impossible not to relax beneath Olivia's warm smile. "Please call me Brooke. I have to tell you that I'm a little overwhelmed to be here. This morning I was on a Greek island with no real destination in mind. And then Nic informs me that he intends to bring me to Sherdana."

"Something tells me he didn't plan much in advance, either." The way Olivia shook her head gave Brooke the impression that the future queen of Sherdana believed strongly in preparation and organization.

"Your secretary mentioned something about me staying until after your wedding," Brooke said, perching on the edge of the cream brocade chair Olivia gestured her into. "But I think it would be better if I caught a flight to California as soon as possible."

"I'm sure that could be arranged, but couldn't you stay for a while and see a little of the country? Gabriel and I have plans to tour some of the vineyards in a couple days and it would be lovely if you and Nic could join us."

"As nice as that sounds…" Brooke trailed off. Never before had she hesitated to speak her mind, but being blunt with Nic's sister-in-law seemed the wrong thing to do. "I'm just worried about overstaying my welcome."

"Nonsense."

Brooke tried again. "I got the impression from Nic that his mother had arranged quite a few events in the next week or so that he's expected to attend. I wouldn't want to distract Nic from what he needs to do."

Olivia looked surprised. "You know why he came home?"

"He needs to get married so there can be…" It suddenly occurred to Brooke that the woman who was supposed to produce Sherdana's next generation of heirs but couldn't was seated across from her.

"It's okay." Olivia's smile was a study in tranquillity. "I've made peace with what happened to me. And I consider myself the luckiest woman alive that Gabriel wanted to marry me even though I wasn't the best choice for the country."

"I think you're the perfect princess. Sherdana is damned lucky to have you." Brooke grimaced at her less than eloquent language. "Sorry. I have a tendency to be blunt even when I'm trying not to."

"Don't be sorry. It was a lovely compliment and I like your directness. I can't wait for you to meet Ariana. She has a knack for speaking her mind, as well."

"I saw her artwork at the villa. She's very talented. I'm looking forward to talking with her about it."

"She's been vacationing with friends in Monaco for a few days and is expected home late tonight. She's very excited that you've come to visit. When I spoke with her earlier today, she told me she'd met your brother when he and Nic stayed at the villa."

That was something else Glen had neglected to mention. Brooke intended to have a long chat with her brother when she returned to California.

"And now, I expect you would like to go to your room and get settled. Dinner will be served at seven. If you need anything let a maid know and she can get it for you."

Brooke gave a shaky laugh. "Like a whole new wardrobe? I'm afraid I packed to visit a Greek island. Casual things." She imagined showing up to dinner in her tribal print maxi and winced. "I really don't have anything I could wear to dine in a palace."

"Oh." Olivia nodded. "I should have realized that from the little Gabriel told me. It looks like you and I are the same size, I'll send some things down for you to choose from."

Unsure whether to be horrified or grateful, Brooke could see protesting was foolish so she thanked Olivia. Then she followed a maid through the palace in a journey from the royal family's private wing to the rooms set aside for guest use. After five minutes of walking Brooke knew she'd never find her way back to Olivia's office and hoped someone would be sent to fetch her for dinner. If her presence in the palace was forgotten and she starved to death, how long would it take before her body was discovered? She lost count how many doors they passed before the maid stopped and gestured for Brooke to enter a room.

"Thank you."

The instant Brooke stepped into the bedroom she'd been given, she fell instantly in love. The wallpaper was a gold-and-white floral design while the curtains and bedding were a pale blue green that made her think of an Amer-aucana chicken egg. In addition to a bed and a writing desk, the room held a settee and a small table flanked by chairs against the wall between two enormous windows. The room had enough furniture to comfortably seat the students in her class on Italian Renaissance poetry.

On the bench at the foot of her bed sat her well-worn luggage. To say it looked shabby among the opulent furnishings was an understatement.

"Can I unpack that for you, Dr. Davis?" The maid who'd brought Brooke here had followed her into the room.

"I've been traveling for quite a few days already and most of what's in here is dirty."

Brooke sensed that she would scandalize the maid by inquiring if there was a laundry machine she could use.

"I'll sort through everything and have it back to you by evening."

Brooke dug through the bag and pulled out her toiletries

and the notebook she always kept close by to write down the things that popped into her head. Her mother was fond of saying you never knew when inspiration would strike and some of Brooke's best ideas came when she was in the shower or grabbing a bite to eat.

Once the maid had left, Brooke picked up her cell phone and checked the time in California. At four o'clock in Sherdana it would be 7:00 a.m. in LA. Theresa would be halfway to work. Brooke dialed.

When Theresa answered, Brooke said, "Guess where I am now…"

Nic hadn't been in the palace more than fifteen minutes before his mother's private secretary tracked him down in the billiards room where he and Gabriel were drinking Scotch and catching up. The room had four enormous paintings depicting pivotal scenes in Sherdana's history, including the ratification of the 1749 constitution that was creating such chaos in Nic's personal life.

"Good afternoon, Your Highnesses." A petite woman in her midfifties stood just inside the door with her hands clasped at her waist.

Gwen had come to work for the queen as her personal assistant not long before the three princes had been born and more often than not, regarded the triplets as errant children rather than remarkable men.

"Hello, Gweny."

"None of that."

Nic crossed the room to kiss her cheek. "I missed you."

Her gaze grew even sterner, although a hint of softness developed near the edges of her lips. "You missed tea."

"I needed something a little stronger." Nic held up his mostly empty crystal tumbler.

"The queen expected you to attend her as soon as you arrived in the palace. She's in the rose garden. You'd better go immediately." Gwen's tone was a whip, driving him from the room.

Knowing better than to dawdle, Nic went straight outside and found his mother in her favorite part of the garden. Thanks to the queen's unwavering devotion, the half acre flourished with a mixture of difficult-to-find antique rose varieties as well as some that had been recently engineered to produce an unusual color or enhanced fragrance.

"It's about time you got around to saying hello," the queen declared, peering at him from beneath the wide brim of her sun hat.

"Good afternoon, Mother." Nic kissed the cheek his mother offered him and fell into step beside her. He didn't bother to offer her an explanation of what he'd been doing. She had no tolerance for excuses. "The roses look beautiful."

"I understand you brought a girl home with you. She's the sister of your California friend." She paused only briefly before continuing, obviously not expecting Nic to confirm what she'd said. "What is your relationship to her?"

"We're friends."

"Don't treat me like an idiot. I need to know if she's going to present a problem."

"No." At least not to anyone but him.

"Does she understand that you have come home to find a wife?"

"She does. It's not an issue. She's planning on heading home after the wedding."

"I understand you are taking her along with Gabriel and Olivia on a trip to the vineyards?"

"Gabriel mentioned something about it, but I haven't spoken with Brooke."

"I don't think it's a good idea that you get any more involved with this girl than you already are."

"We're not involved," Nic assured her.

"Is she in love with you?" Nic waited too long to answer and his mother made a disgusted sound. "Do you love her?"

"It doesn't matter how we feel about each other," Nic said, his voice tense and impatient. "I know my duty to Sherdana and nothing will get in the way of that." From his conversation with Gabriel, Nic knew she hadn't gone this hard at Christian. Why was Nic alone feeling the pressure to marry? Christian was just as much a prince of Sherdana. His son could just as easily rule. "I assume you have several matrimonial candidates for me to consider."

"I've sent their dossiers to your room in the visitors' wing. Did Gabriel mention the problem in your suite earlier today? Apparently your bathtub overflowed and flooded the room."

"Gabriel thought it might have been the twins although no one caught them at it."

His mother shook her head. "I don't know why we're paying a nanny if the girl can't keep track of them."

"From what I understand they are a handful."

"There are only two of them. I had three of you to contend with." His mother took Nic's hand in hers and squeezed hard. "It's good to have you home." She blinked rapidly a few times and released her grip on him. "Now, run along and look over the files I sent to your room. I expect you to share your thoughts with me after dinner tonight."

"Of course." He bent and kissed her cheek again. "First I'm off to see Father. I understand he has a ten-minute gap in his schedule shortly before five."

After reconnecting briefly with his father, Nic headed to the room he'd been given until his suite could be dried out. The oddity of the incident left him shaking his head.

How could a pair of two-year-old girls be as much trouble as everyone said?

As his mother had promised, a pile of dossiers had been left on the desk. Shrugging out of his blazer, Nic picked up the stack and counted. There were eight. He had twenty minutes before the tailor arrived to measure him for a whole new wardrobe. The clothes he'd traveled in today had belonged to Christian, as had most of what he'd worn the past ten days. Of the three brothers, Christian spent the most time at the Greek villa.

Nic settled into a chair in front of the unlit fireplace and selected a file at random. The photo clipped to the inside showed a stunning brunette with vivacious blue eyes and full lips. She was the twenty-five-year-old daughter of an Italian count, had gotten her MBA at Harvard and now worked for a global conglomerate headquartered in Paris. She spoke four languages and was admired for being fashionable as well as active on the charity circuit. In short, she was perfect.

He dropped the file onto the floor at his feet and opened the next one. This one was a blonde. Again beautiful. British born. The sister of a viscount. A human rights lawyer.

The next. Brunette. Pretty with big brown eyes and an alluring smile. A local girl. Her family owned the largest winery in Sherdana. She played cello for the Vienna Philharmonic.

Then another blonde. Bewitching green eyes. Daughter of a Danish baron. A model and television personality.

On and on. Each woman strikingly beautiful, accomplished and with a flawless pedigree.

Nic felt like a prize bull.

Replaying the conversation with his mother, he recognized he shouldn't have ignored Brooke's concerns that their relationship would come under scrutiny. He'd deliberately underestimated his mother's perceptiveness. But he didn't regret bringing Brooke to meet his family.

What he wasn't so happy about, however, was how little time they would have together in the days between now and her eventual departure. Being forced by propriety to keep his distance would be much more difficult now that he'd opened the door to what could have been if only he wasn't bound to his country.

At the same moment he threw the last folder onto the floor, a knock sounded on his door. Calling permission to enter, Nic got to his feet and scooped up the dossiers, depositing them back on the desk before turning to face the tailor and his small army of assistants who were to dress Nic.

While the suits he tried on were marked and pinned, Nic fell to thinking about Brooke. He hadn't seen her since leaving the plane and wondered how she'd coped in the hours they'd been apart. Despite the nervousness she'd shown during the flight, he suspected she'd figured out a way to charm everyone she'd encountered. He knew she was supposed to meet with Gabriel's wife right away and wondered how that had gone.

He was eager to meet Olivia. He already knew she was beautiful, intelligent and a strong crusader for children's health and welfare. The citizens loved her and after the drama surrounding her emergency hysterectomy and her subsequent secret elopement with Gabriel so did the media. But Nic was fascinated by how she'd caused such drastic changes in his brother.

The tailor finished his preliminary work and departed. Alone once more, Nic dressed for dinner. Family evenings were for the most part casual and Nic left his room wearing navy slacks and a crisp white shirt he'd purchased at a department store in California. His fashionable younger brother would be appalled that Nic was dressing *off the rack*. Nic was smiling at the thought as he joined Gabriel and his new bride in the family's private drawing room.

"You've made my brother a very happy man," Nic told Olivia, kissing her cheek in greeting. "I haven't seen him smile this much since we were children."

From her location snuggled beneath her husband's possessive arm, the blonde stared up at Gabriel with eyes filled with such love that a knot formed in Nic's gut. At that instant, any lingering resentment he'd felt at the uncomfortable position Gabriel's choice had put him in vanished. His brother deserved to be happy. The responsibility of the country would one day rest on Gabriel's shoulders and being married to the woman he loved would make his burden lighter.

This drew Nic's thoughts back to the dossiers in his room. He was glad there hadn't been a redhead among them. Brooke was a singular marvel in his mind. Marrying a woman with similar hair color was out of the question. He couldn't spend the rest of his life wishing his wife's red hair framed a different face.

Brooke hadn't made an appearance by the time Nic's parents entered the drawing room and he wondered for one brief moment if she'd let her anxiety get the better of her. He was seconds away from sending a maid to check on her when the door opened and Brooke stumbled in, unsteady in heels that appeared too large for her.

She wore a long-sleeved, gold, lace dress that flattered her curves, but conflicted with her usual carefree style. She wasn't wearing her usual long necklace that drew attention to the swell of her breasts, and she'd left her collection of bracelets behind. The look was sophisticated, elegant and formal, except for her hair, which spiraled and bounced around her shoulders like a living thing.

"Dr. Davis, welcome." Gabriel and Olivia had approached her while Nic stood there gaping at her transformation.

"I'm so sorry I'm late," Brooke was saying as he finally approached. "I only meant to close my eyes for fifteen minutes. Then next thing I know it's six-thirty. Thank heavens I showered before I sacked out. Of course this is what happens to my hair when I just let it go. If I'd had a few more minutes, I could have done something to it but I had such a hard time deciding which dress to wear. They were all so beautiful."

"You look lovely." Olivia gave her a warm smile and drew her arm through Brooke's in a show of affection and support. "Why don't I introduce you to Gabriel and Nic's parents."

"You mean the king and queen?" Brooke whispered, her gaze shooting to the couple enjoying a predinner cocktail. They appeared to be ignoring the knot of young people.

"They are eager to meet you," Gabriel said.

Brooke's lips quirked in a wry smile. "That's sweet of you to say." She took a clumsy step and smiled apologetically at Olivia. "I'm usually less awkward than this."

"The shoes are a little large for you," Olivia said, giving the gold laser-cut pumps a critical look. "I didn't realize your feet were so much smaller than mine. Perhaps you have something of your own that would fit better? I could send a maid to fetch something."

"Are you kidding me?" Brooke retorted, her voice feverish as she took her next step with more deliberation and improved grace. "These are *Louboutin glass slippers*. I'm Cinderella."

Gabriel waited a beat before following his wife. He caught Nic's eye and smirked. "I like her."

"So do I," Nic replied, his voice low and subdued.

Not that it should have mattered to Nic, but his brother's words sent gratitude and relief rushing into his chest. It was good to know he had at least two people in the palace, Gabriel and Olivia, who would understand how wretched doing the right thing could feel.

"It's very nice to meet you," Brooke was saying to his parents as Nic and Gabriel caught up to the women. "Thank you for letting me stay at the palace for a few days."

Nic felt the impact of his mother's gaze as he drew up beside Brooke. He set his palm on her back and through her dress felt the tension quivering in her muscles.

"We are happy to have you," Nic's father said, his broad smile genuine.

When it came to matters affecting his country, the king was a mighty warrior defending his realm from all threats social, economic and diplomatic. However, he was a teddy bear when it came to his wife and children. But the queen ruled her family with an iron fist in a velvet glove. All four of her children knew the strength of her will and respected it. In exchange she allowed them the opportunity to figure out their place in the world.

This meant Nic had been allowed to attend university in the United States and stay there living his dream of space travel until Sherdana had needed him to come home. But while he'd appreciated his ten years of freedom from responsibility, it made his return that much harder.

"Very happy," the queen echoed. "I understand, Miss Davis, that you are the sister of the man Nic has been working with for the last five years."

"Yes, my brother is in charge of the *Griffin* project."

"Perhaps you will join me for breakfast tomorrow. I'd like to hear more about the project Nic has been working on with your brother."

"I would be happy to have breakfast with you."

"Wonderful. Is eight o'clock too early for you?"

"Not at all. Unlike Nic, I'm an early riser."

Nic knew she'd meant the jab for him. It was an old joke between them on the mornings when he'd worked late into the night and then crashed on the couch in his workroom. But he could see at once that his mother was wondering how Brooke knew what time Nic got out of bed in the morning.

Even without glancing toward his brother, Gabriel's amusement was apparent. Nic kept his own expression bland as he met his mother's steely gaze.

Olivia saved the moment from further awkwardness. "And after breakfast perhaps you could come to the stables and watch the twins take a riding lesson. They are showing great promise as equestrians. Do you ride, Brooke?"

"I did when I was younger, but school has kept me far too busy in recent years."

"Brooke has two doctorates," Nic interjected smoothly. "She teaches Italian language and literature at the University of California, Santa Cruz."

"You're young to have accomplished that much," Gabriel said.

Brooke nodded. "I graduated high school with two years of college credits and spent the next ten years immersed in academia. After my brother went off to college my parents hosted a girl from Italy. She stayed with us a year and by the time she went home, I was fluent in Italian and learning to read it, as well."

Olivia spoke up. "Have you spent much time in Italy?"

"While I was working on my second doctorate, I spent a year in Florence and Rome. Before that my mother and I would visit for a week or two during the summer depending on her deadlines. She writes for television and has penned a mystery series set in sixteenth-century Venice that does very well." Talking about her mother's accomplishments had relaxed Brooke. Her eyes sparkled with pride.

This relaxed Nic as well, but as the family made their way toward the dining room, the queen pulled him aside.

"Lovely girl, your Miss Davis."

"Actually it's Dr. Davis." Although he had a feeling his mother already knew that and had spoken incorrectly to get a rise out of her son. And since Nic had already denied that he and Brooke were anything but friends, why did his mother put the emphasis on *your*? "I'm glad you like her."

"Did you look at the files I gave you?"

"Yes. Any one of them would be a fine princess." He couldn't bring himself to use the word *wife* yet. "You and your team did a fine job of choosing candidates that lined up with my needs."

"Yes we did. Now, let's see if you can do an equally fine job choosing a wife."

Nine

At her first dinner with Nic's family, Brooke sat beside Nic on the king's left hand and ate little. Part of the reason she'd been late to dinner was another bout of nausea that struck her shortly after she'd risen. So much for morning sickness. Brooke wasn't sure why it was called that when it seemed to strike her at random times throughout the day.

"You're not eating," Nic murmured, the first words he'd spoken directly to her since the meal had begun.

"I'm dining with royalty," she muttered back. "My stomach is in knots."

"They're just people."

"Important people." Wealthy, sophisticated, intelligent people. "Normally I wouldn't get unsettled by this sort of thing, but this is your family and I want them to like me."

"I assure you they do."

"Sure." Brooke resisted the urge to roll her eyes. His mother had been observing her through most of the meal, making each swallow of the delicious salmon more trial than pleasure. Brooke sensed that the queen had a long list of questions she wanted to ask, starting with: When are you going home? Not that Brooke blamed her. Nic's mother had plans for her son. Plans that she must perceive as being threatened by an uncouth redhead who regarded Nic with adoring eyes.

Despite the fact that the meal was a relaxed family affair and not the formal ordeal Brooke had feared, by the time the dessert course concluded, she was more than ready to escape. She was relieved, therefore, when Gabriel and Olivia offered her a quick tour of the public areas of the palace before escorting her back to her room.

Strolling the hall of portraits, Brooke realized the extent of Sherdana's history. Some of the paintings dated back to the late-fifteenth century. Thanks to all those years when she'd accompanied her mother to Italy and helped her research the Italian Renaissance period, Brooke had developed a love of history that partially explained why she'd chosen the same time period for her second doctorate.

"I imagine you have a library with books on Sherdana's history," she said to Gabriel as he and Olivia led the way to the ballroom.

"An extensive one. We'll make that our next stop."

A half an hour later the trio arrived at Brooke's door. She was feeling a touch giddy at the idea that she could return to the library the next day and check out the collection more thoroughly. The vast amount of books contained in the two-story room was an academic's dream come true. She could probably spend an entire year in Sherdana's palace library and never need to leave.

"Thank you for the tour."

"You are very welcome," Olivia said. "If you need anything else tonight, let one of the maids know. There is always someone on call."

Brooke bid the prince and princess good-night and entered her room. As she did, she noticed the store of crackers she'd nibbled on prior to dinner had been replenished. With a grateful sigh, Brooke grabbed a handful and went to the wardrobe. As the maid had promised earlier, her clothes had been laundered and returned. Brooke grinned as she slipped off her borrowed shoes, guessing the staff wasn't accustomed to washing ragged denim shorts and cotton peasant blouses. Regardless, they'd done a marvelous job. Her clothes looked brand-new.

A knock sounded on her door. Brooke's pulse kicked up. Could Nic have come by to wish her good-night? But it wasn't her handsome prince in the hall. Instead, her visitor was a beautiful, tall girl with long chocolate-brown hair and a welcoming smile.

"I'm Ariana." Behind Nic's sister were two maids loaded down with six shoe boxes and four overstuffed garment bags.

"Brooke Davis."

"I know that." Ariana laughed. "Even if the palace wasn't buzzing about the girl Nic brought home, I would have recognized you from the pictures Glen emailed me from time to time. He's very proud of you."

"You and Glen email?" Earlier Brooke had learned that Nic's sister had met Glen in Greece, but an ongoing correspondence was something else entirely. "I thought you'd just met the one time."

"Yeees." She drew the word out. "But it was *quite* a meeting."

Brooke didn't know what to make of the other girl's innuendo and made a note to question Glen about Nic's sister.

"Olivia told me her shoes were too big for you, so I brought you a few pairs of mine," Ariana said, indicating the maids behind her. "They should fit you better—and I included some dresses, as well. That's one of Olivia's, isn't it?"

Brooke couldn't figure out what about the gold lace could possibly have caused Ariana to wrinkle her nose. "Nothing I brought with me is suitable for palace wear. I had no plans to come here with Nic."

For a moment Ariana's eyes narrowed in the same sharp expression of assessment her mother had aimed at Brooke all evening. At last the princess smiled. "Well, I'm glad you did."

"So am I." And for the first time in eight hours, Brooke meant it. "I've really been looking forward to meeting you. I thought your artwork at the villa was amazing."

"Then you'd be the first." With a self-deprecating hair flip, Ariana slipped her arm through Brooke's and drew her into the bedroom.

"What do you mean?" Brooke let herself be led. From the way Nic had talked about his sister and from studying Ariana's art, Brooke felt as if she and the younger woman might be kindred spirits. "Your use of color gave the paintings such energy and depth."

Ariana's eyebrows drew together. "You're serious." She sounded surprised and more than a little hopeful.

"Very." Brooke didn't understand the princess's reaction. "I did my undergrad work in visual and critical studies."

"My family doesn't understand what I paint. They see it all as random splashes of color on canvas."

"I'm sure it's just that they are accustomed to a more traditional style of painting. Have you ever had your work exhibited anywhere?"

"No." A laugh bubbled out of her. "I paint for myself."

"Of course. But if you're ever interested in getting an expert's opinion, I have a friend in San Francisco who runs a gallery. He likes finding new talent. I took some pictures of your work. With your permission I could send him the photos."

"I've never thought…" Ariana shook her head in bemusement. "I guess this is the moment every artist faces at some point. Do I take a chance and risk failing or play it safe and never know if I'm any good."

"Oh, you're good," Brooke assured her. "But art is very subjective and not everyone is going to like what you do."

"I guess I've already faced my worst critics. My family. So why not see what your friend thinks."

"Wonderful, I'll send him the pictures tomorrow morning."

"And in the meantime—" Ariana gestured toward the wardrobe "—show me what you brought from home and let's see if I have anything that will appeal to you."

Brooke suspected the stylish princess wouldn't be at all impressed with the limited contents of her closet, but she knew her fine speech about art being subjective would be hypocritical if she couldn't back it up with action. For what was fashion but wearable art and even though Brooke's wardrobe wasn't suitable for a palace, it worked perfectly in her academic world.

The maids who'd entered behind Ariana deposited their burdens on Brooke's bed. If the princess had brought anything like what she was wearing—a sophisticated but fun plum dress with gold circles embroidered around the neckline and dotted over the skirt—Brooke braced herself to be wowed.

"It feels like every day is Christmas around here," Brooke said as dress after gorgeous dress came free of the garment bags. The variety of colors and styles dazzled Brooke. Of course, with her skin tone, Ariana could wear just about anything.

When the maids finished, Brooke pulled out her own dresses, shorts, skirts and her favorite kimono. Ariana narrowed her eyes in thought and surveyed each item.

"You have a great eye for color and know exactly what suits you."

Coming from the princess, this was a huge compliment. Ariana wasn't at all what Brooke imagined a princess would be like. She was warm and approachable. Not at all stuffy or formal. Brooke warmed to her quickly, feeling as if they had known each other for years instead of minutes.

"In California I blend in dressed like this." Brooke slipped into the tie-dyed kimono. It looked odd over the gold lace dress she'd borrowed from Olivia. "Here I stick out like a sore thumb."

"Hardly a sore thumb, although definitely a standout. No matter how you dress, your unique hair color will keep you from being a wallflower. No wonder my brother finds you irresistible."

Brooke felt Ariana's comment like a blow. "We're just friends," she explained in a rush, but her cheeks heated as the princess arched one slim eyebrow.

"But he talks about you all the time and he brought you to meet us."

"It's not what you're thinking. I went to the island to convince him to return to California. To Glen and the *Griffin* project. And when he was summoned back here sooner than expected, he didn't want to leave me alone in Greece."

"He must be in love with you. He's never brought a woman home before."

Brooke relaxed a little. "That's because the love of his life wouldn't fit inside an airplane." Seeing she had confused Ariana, Brooke explained. "As long as I've known him, Nic has been committed to the rocket he and my brother hope will one day carry people into space. There's been no room for an emotional connection with any woman."

"And yet here you are."

"Until a few days ago I didn't know he was a prince or that he needs to marry a citizen of the country or an aristocrat so his children can rule someday. Obviously I'm neither."

"He wouldn't have kept something like that from you unless he was worried about hurting you."

"That much is true." Here Brooke hesitated, unsure how much to explain. In the end, she decided to trust Ariana. "I've had a crush on him for years. When I showed up on Ithaca, he told me everything. He didn't want me to hope for a future we could never have together."

"Did it work? Did you stop hoping?"

"I'd be crazy if I didn't."

Like her brothers, Ariana had her father's warm brown eyes flecked with gold, but she'd inherited the intensity of her gaze from her mother. "But you two have been intimate."

Hating to lie, Brooke pretended she hadn't heard the soft question. Instead she chose a dress at random and announced, "I love this."

Luckily her selection was a flirty emerald-green dress that she could see herself wearing. Brooke held it against her body. As she looked at her reflection, she noticed the dress had no tags, but Brooke doubted it had ever been worn.

"I'll take your nonanswer as an affirmative." Ariana's musical laughter filled the room. "Try on the dress." While Brooke obeyed her, the princess continued, "I'm sorry if I was blunt and please don't be embarrassed." The gold bracelets on her slender wrists chimed. "My brothers are very hard for the opposite sex to resist. Thank goodness Gabriel and Nic are honorable and not ones to take advantage. Christian is like a child in a toy store wanting everything he sees."

And getting it, too, Brooke guessed. "Please don't tell

anyone about Nic and me. It's over and I wouldn't want to cause any needless problems."

Ariana nodded. "That dress is amazing on you."

The empire bodice cupped her breasts, the fabric ending in a narrow band of a darker green ribbon. From there, the layers of chiffon material flowed over her hips, the hem ending just above her knee. Brooke stared at herself in the mirror as Ariana guided her feet into strappy black sandals.

"It brings out the green in your eyes."

"I feel like a princess." Brooke laughed. "I guess I should because it's a dress fit for a princess. You."

Next, Ariana urged Brooke into a hot-pink sheath with a V-shaped neckline and bands of fabric that crisscrossed diagonally to create an interesting and figure-slimming pattern. It had a sophisticated, elegant vibe that Brooke wasn't sure she could pull off.

"I understand you are having breakfast with my mother tomorrow. This will be perfect, and I think you should pair it with these."

Ariana grabbed a box and pulled out a pair of white suede and black velvet lace ankle boots that were amazing, Brooke waved her hands in protest. "I can't. Those are just too much."

"You must wear them or the outfit will not be complete."

At Ariana's relentless urging, Brooke slipped her feet into the boots and faced the mirror, accepting immediately that she'd lost the battle. "I never imagined I could look like this."

Ariana's eyebrows lifted in surprise. "Why not? You are very beautiful."

"But not refined and effortless like you and Olivia."

With a very unladylike snort, Ariana rolled her eyes. "This is just how I appear here in the palace. When I go to Ithaca, I assure you, I'm so different you'd never recognize me."

"Do you spend a lot of time on the island?"

"Not as much as I'd like. It's an escape. I go to paint. To forget about the responsibilities of being a princess."

"I imagine there's a lot that keeps you busy."

"It's less now that Olivia is here." Ariana selected five more dresses and put them into Olivia's wardrobe with three more pairs of shoes. "That will do for now, but you will need a long dress for a party we must attend the day after tomorrow. It's the prime minister's birthday."

"Are you sure I will be going?"

"Absolutely. The event is always deadly dull and having you along will make the whole thing bearable."

While the maids returned the rest of the dresses to the garment bags, Ariana squeezed Brooke's shoulder. "I am sorry you and Nic cannot see where things might lead between you. I think you would make him very happy."

"Actually, I drive him crazy."

"Good. He has always been too serious. He needs a little crazy in his life." And with that, Ariana said good-night and left Brooke to her thoughts.

The corridors of the visitors' wing were quiet as Nic made his way back to his temporary quarters. The tranquillity would vanish over the next few days as guests began to arrive for the week of festivities leading up to the royal wedding. The conversation he'd had with his parents after dinner had highlighted their expectations for him. The women in the dossiers had been invited to the palace. He was to get to know each of them and make his selection.

As he'd listened to his mother, Nic realized he'd been in America too long. Although he'd grown up in a world where marriages sometimes were arranged, he'd grown accustomed to the notion of dating freely without any expectation that it might end in marriage.

He'd almost reached his suite when the door to the room

beside his opened and two maids emerged carrying garment bags. Their appearance could only mean he had company next door. It hadn't occurred to Nic that Brooke had
been placed on this floor, much less in the room beside
his, and his suspicion was confirmed when his sister came
out of the room a few seconds later.

"Nic!" She raced across the few feet that separated them
and threw herself into his arms. "How good that you're
home."

She smelled of the light floral perfume he'd sent her
the previous Christmas. He'd asked Brooke to help him
pick out the perfume because he'd sensed the two women
were a lot alike. Seeing his sister's good mood upon leaving Brooke, he knew he'd been right.

"I'm happy to be here."

Ariana pushed back until she could see his expression,
and then clicked her tongue. "No you're not. You'd much
rather be in California playing with your rocket."

"I'm done with that." The accident and Gabriel's marriage had seen to that.

"It's not like you to give up."

Her remark sent a wave of anger rushing through him.
The emotion was so sharp and so immediate that he could
do nothing more than stand frozen in astonishment. The
loss of *Griffin*. His obligation to give up his dream and
come home to marry a woman he didn't love. None of it
was of his choosing.

But without this call to duty, would he have stayed in
California and started over? The accident had been a disaster and his confidence was in shreds. Was that why
he wasn't fighting his fate or figuring out a way around
the laws that were in place so he could choose whom he
married?

"Nic?"

As quickly as it had risen, his rage subsided. He shook

himself in the numb aftermath. "Sorry. I'm just tired. It's been a long day. And I didn't give up." He gave her nose an affectionate tweak the way he used to when she was an adorable toddler and he an oh-so-knowing big brother of ten. "I was called home to do my duty."

Ariana winced. "You're right. I'm sorry." Her contrite expression vanished with her next breath. "I met Brooke tonight. She's wonderful."

He was starting to wish his siblings would find something about Brooke to criticize. It was going to be hell bidding her goodbye and it would have been easier on him if they behaved as if falling for her was a huge error in his judgment.

"I'm glad you think so."

"If you're going to visit her, you might want to hurry. I think she was getting ready for bed."

For a second Nic wasn't sure if he should take his sister's statement at face value or if she was trying to get a reaction out of him. He decided it was the latter.

"This is my room." He indicated the door to his left. "I didn't know where she was staying in the palace."

"Why are you in the visitors' wing?"

"Something about my room flooding."

She gave him an incredulous look. "Who told you that?"

"Gabriel." Nic was starting to suspect something might be up. "Why?"

"Because I stopped by your suite earlier and it looked fine to me." She smirked. "I think our brother is trying to play matchmaker. You and Brooke all alone in the visitors' wing with no one to know if you snuck into each other's rooms. Very romantic."

"Damn it." Now he had another dilemma facing him. Confront Gabriel and return to his suite in the family wing or pretend he and Ariana never had this conversation and do what his heart wanted but his brain protested against.

"Honestly, stop being so noble." It was as if Ariana had read his mind. "Gabriel followed his heart. I think he wants the same for you."

"And then who will produce the legitimate heirs to ascend the throne?"

His sister shrugged. "There's always Christian. He isn't in love with anyone. Let him be the sacrificial lamb."

Nic hugged his sister and kissed the top of her head. "You are the best sister in the world."

"So are you going to choose Brooke?"

"You know I can't and you know why."

With a huge sigh, Ariana pushed him away. "You are too honorable for your own good."

"I know how this whole thing is making me feel. I can't do that to Christian." He paused and looked down at her. "Or to you."

"Me?"

"Have you considered what would happen if both Christian and I failed to produce a son? The whole burden shifts to your shoulders."

Ariana obviously hadn't considered this. Even though the constitution wouldn't allow her to rule as queen, she was still a direct descendant of the ruling king and that meant her son could one day succeed.

"Okay, I see your point, but I think it's terrible that you and Brooke can't be together."

"So do I."

Nic watched as his sister retreated down the corridor. For several heartbeats he stood with his hand on the doorknob to his room, willing himself to open the door and step inside, while Ariana's words rang in his head. *Brooke was getting ready for bed.* They were isolated in this wing of the palace. He could spend the night with her and sneak out before anyone discovered them. But how many times could he tell himself this was their last time together? Just that morning he'd been on the verge of saying goodbye.

He pushed open the door to his room, but didn't step across the threshold. He'd invited Brooke to Sherdana; it would only be polite to stop by and find out how her day had gone. If he stood in the hall, they could have a quick conversation without fear that either of them would be overcome with passion. That decided, Nic strode over and rapped on Brooke's door. If he'd expected her to answer his summons looking disheveled and adorable in her pajamas, he was doomed to disappointment.

The stylish creature that stood before him was nothing like the Brooke he'd grown accustomed to. Even the dress she'd worn at dinner tonight, as beautiful as she'd looked in it, hadn't stretched his perception of her as much as this strapless pale pink ball gown that turned her into a Disney princess.

Obviously enjoying herself, Brooke twirled twice and then paused for his opinion. "What do you think?"

"That's quite a dress."

She laughed, a bright silvery sound he hadn't heard since before the day he'd put an end to their fledgling romance. His heart lifted at her joy.

"I never imagined dressing like a princess would be so much fun."

His gut clenched at her words. She didn't mean them the way they'd sounded. The last thing she'd ever do was pick on him for rejecting her as unsuitable. Brooke wasn't the sort to play games or come at a problem sideways. It was one of the things he appreciated about her.

But that didn't stop regret from choking him.

"You look incredibly beautiful."

She shot him a flirtatious grin. "Aw, you're just saying that because it's true. Ariana brought the dress. I simply had to try it on since I'll never get the chance to wear it in public."

"Why not?"

"We both know the answer to that."

She drew him into the room and closed the door. Her actions had a dangerous effect on Nic's libido. He really hadn't come to her suite to make love to her, but it wouldn't take more than another one of her delicious smiles for him to snatch her into his arms and carry her to the bed.

"I don't think I follow you," Nic said, crossing his arms over his chest, his gaze tracking her every move as she enjoyed her reflection. He caught himself smiling as she shifted from side to side to make the skirt swish.

"Your mother and I are having breakfast tomorrow. I'm certain she's going to politely but firmly give me the heave-ho."

"She'd never be that rude."

"Of course not. But she can't be happy that her son brought home some inappropriate girl when he's supposed to be focused on selecting a bride."

"You're not inappropriate."

"I am where your future is concerned." Brooke reached for the dress's side zipper and gave Nic a stern look. "Turn around. I need to get out of this dress."

Blood pounded in his ears. "You are aware that I've seen you naked many, many times."

"That was before I was staying beneath your parents' roof. I think it would be rude of us to take advantage of their hospitality by getting swept up in a passionate moment. Don't you?" She set her hands on her hips. "So, turn around."

"My not watching you strip out of your clothes isn't going to prevent us from getting swept up in a passionate moment. I have memorized every inch of your gorgeous body."

"Turn around." Although her color was high, her firm tone deterred further argument.

At last Nic did as she'd asked. For several minutes the only sound in the room was the slide and crinkle of fabric as she undressed and the harsh rasp of his breath. He berated himself for acquiescing. If she was going to return to California in a few days, they were fools not to steal every moment they could to be together.

Bursting with conviction, Nic started to turn back around. "Brooke, we should..." He didn't finish because she gave him a sharp shove toward the door.

"No we shouldn't."

"One kiss." The irony of his demand wasn't lost on Nic. How many times had she teased, tormented and begged for any little bit of attention from him over the years? Time after time he'd refused her. "I missed waking up with you this morning."

"Whose fault was that?"

"Mine." It was all his fault. The five years when they could have been together if he hadn't been so obsessively focused on work. The way he'd hurt her because he'd chosen duty to his country over her. The emotional intimacy he couldn't give her because he was afraid his heart would break if he opened up.

"One kiss." He was pleading now.

"Fine. But you need to be in the hall with your hands behind your back."

A muscle ticked in his cheek. If she wanted to be in control, he would do his best to let that happen. "Agreed," he said and stepped out of her room.

Given the way he'd yielded to her conditions, Nic expected more demands from her.

"Close your eyes. I can't do this with you glaring at me."

In perfect stillness she waited him out. At last Nic let his lashes drift down. Years of working toward a single possibly unattainable goal would have been impossible without a great deal of fortitude, but Nic had recently discovered a shortage of patience where Brooke was concerned.

"Dear Nic." Her fingertips swept into his hair and tugged his head downward until their lips met.

Sweetness.

The tenderness of her kiss sent his heartbeat into overdrive. The desire previously driving through his body eased beneath her gentle touch. For the first time he acknowledged what existed between them wasn't born out of passion alone, but had its origins in something far deeper and lasting. A sigh fluttered in his chest as she lifted her lips from his and grazed them across his cheek.

"Good night, sweet prince."

Before he'd recovered enough to open his eyes, she was gone.

Ten

Thanks to Ariana's help with her wardrobe, Brooke had gone to bed feeling confident about her breakfast meeting with the queen. However, when she woke at dawn plagued by the increasingly familiar nausea, she plodded through her morning routine, burdened by anxiety.

By the time she'd swept her straightened hair into a smooth French roll, Brooke had consumed half a package of crackers in an effort to calm her roiling stomach. It seemed to be working because by the time she finished applying mascara and lipstick, she was feeling like her old self.

A maid appeared promptly at ten minutes to eight and Brooke dredged up her polite interview face as she followed her downstairs and into the garden. The girl pointed to a grassy path that curved past flower beds overflowing with shades of pink and purple. Brooke's destination—a white gazebo overlooking a small pond—appeared to be about fifty feet away. As she neared the structure, she noted that the queen had already arrived and was seated at the table placed in the center of the space. Rose-patterned china and crystal goblets were carefully arranged on a white tablecloth. The whole display reminded Brooke of a storybook tea party.

"Good morning, Your Majesty," Brooke said cheerfully as she neared.

The queen turned her attention from the electronic tablet in her hand and her keen gaze swept over Brooke, lingering for a long moment on the low boots. Brooke withstood the queen's assessment in silence, wondering if custom required her to curtsy.

"Hello, Dr. Davis. Don't you look lovely. Please sit down."

Noticing the change from last night in the way the queen addressed her, Brooke perched on the edge of a mint-green damask chair and dropped her napkin on her lap. Two maids stood by to wait on them. Brooke accepted a glass of orange juice and a cup of very dark coffee lightened with cream which she sipped until her stomach gurgled quietly. To cover the noise, Brooke began to speak.

"Your garden is beautiful." Ariana had offered Brooke several safe subjects on which to converse. "I understand you have several rare varieties of roses."

"Are you interested in gardening?" the queen asked, offering a polite smile. A diplomat's smile.

Brooke's whole digestive track picked that moment to complain. She pinched her lips tight in response. After a second she took a deep breath. "I love flowers, but I don't have much of a green thumb."

"I suppose you've been busy earning your two doctorates. That's quite impressive for someone your age." Most people thought it was impressive, period, but it made sense that the queen of a country would be hard to impress. "And now you teach at a university."

"Italian language and literature."

"Olivia tells me you've traveled around Italy quite a bit."

"As well as France, Austria and Switzerland. I love this part of the world."

"Have you ever wanted to live in Europe?"

At that moment Brooke wished she'd never agreed to come. Nic's mother obviously regarded her as an intruder, or worse, an opportunist. Should she explain that she understood Nic was off-limits? She couldn't imagine that was the sort of polite conversation one made with the elegant queen of Sherdana.

"I love California. I did my undergraduate work in New York City." Brooke knit her fingers together in her lap lest she surrender to the urge to play with her silverware. "I couldn't wait to get back home."

"Home is a wonderful place to be. Are you hungry?" The queen gestured to the maids and one of them lifted the lid off the serving dish. "Crepes are my weakness," the queen said. "There are also omelets made with spinach and mushrooms or the chef would be happy to prepare something else if you'd prefer."

"I don't want to be any trouble." The crepes looked marvelous. Some were filled with strawberries, others with something creamy and covered in apples or...

"Pears roasted in butter and honey over crepes filled with ricotta cheese," the queen said, her eyes softening for the first time in Brooke's company.

If Brooke hadn't been so queasy, she could have easily eaten her way through half a dozen of the thin fluffy pancakes. As it was, she took one of each kind and nibbled at them.

"Olivia tells me you spoke of leaving in the next few days," the queen remarked in her delightfully accented English. "But when I spoke with Nicolas last night, he wishes you to remain through the wedding." She tucked into her breakfast with relish, obviously enjoying herself. "I think my son believes himself in love with you."

Brooke's coffee cup rattled against the saucer as she set it down too abruptly. Her stomach seized and suddenly eating the crepes didn't strike her as the smartest idea. The queen's words repeated themselves several times in Brooke's head. *He believes himself in love with you.* Not *he's in love with you.* Brooke recognized the difference. In high school and college she'd believed herself in love any number of times. Then she'd met Nic and began the discovery of what love truly was.

"I'm sorry, but you're wrong." Brooke put her napkin to her lips as her body flushed hot. It wasn't embarrassment or guilt, but her system reacting to stress and being pregnant. "Nic knows his mind like no man I've ever met. His heart belongs to this country and his family."

The queen sighed. "And you are in love with him."

The edges of Brooke's vision darkened. What was Nic's mother trying to establish? Already Brooke had accepted that she and Nic had no future. She knew he would never give his mother any cause to believe otherwise so she guessed the queen's protective instincts were kicking in. She understood. In a little more than seven months she would have her own child to keep from harm. Heaven help anyone who got in her way.

"He's my brother's best friend..." Brooke said, her voice trailing off. "I've known Nic for years. Did I once want something more? Yes. But that was before I knew who he was and what was expected of him."

"Are you trying to tell me you didn't know he was a prince?"

Brooke held still beneath the queen's penetrating regard. The older woman's face became difficult to stay focused on. Brooke wanted nothing more than to lie down until the spinning stopped.

"I didn't know until a few days ago. He left California without a word after the accident. I tracked him down to Ithaca because he wouldn't return my phone calls or emails. I was worried about how he was coping in the aftermath." She hoped the queen was satisfied with her reason for following Nic to Greece and would refrain from probing further.

The queen nodded. "The rocket ship was very important to him. But it's gone and he needs to put it behind him." Her tone was matter-of-fact as she dismissed her son's driving passion.

"He can't just put it behind him. He feels responsible for the death of one of his fellow scientists." Brooke endured a sharp pinch of sadness that Nic's mother didn't understand this about her son. "Walter hadn't been with the team long, but he worked closely with Nic. I think part of the reason why Nic was so willing to come home and let you marry him off was because he felt as if he'd failed Walter and Glen and even you and the king. I think the reason he worked so hard was to justify being away from Sherdana. He spent every day proving that his work would benefit future generations, driving himself beyond exhaustion in order to contribute something amazing to the world. So that his absence from you had meaning."

Brooke didn't realize she'd gotten to her feet until the gazebo began to sway around her. She clamped a hand over her mouth as the unsettled feeling in her stomach increased. She couldn't throw up. Not now. Not here. Sweat broke out on her body. She was about to ruin Ariana's gorgeous dress in an inglorious way the palace would be talking about for weeks. Brooke blinked and gulped air to regain her equilibrium. But she was too hot. Too dizzy.

"I have to…" *Go.* She didn't belong here. She'd been unbearably rude to Nic's mother, who was the queen of a nation. But she could no longer tell in which direction lay escape.

"Dr. Davis, are you all right?" The queen sounded very far away.

Brooke tried to focus on the queen's voice but she stumbled. Abruptly a wood column was beneath her fingers and she clutched the rough surface like a lifeline as darkness rushed up to claim her.

Nic exploded through the green salon's French doors and raced toward the gazebo as soon as Brooke stood and began to weave like a drunken woman. For the past fifteen minutes he'd been positioned by the windows that overlooked the garden so he could observe the exchange between his mother and Brooke and step in if things appeared as if they were going badly. Like Brooke, he'd expected his mother to diplomatically encourage her to leave as soon as possible and he was worried that Brooke might say something she'd immediately regret. Never could he have predicted that he'd be just in time to catch Brooke's limp body before it hit the gazebo floor.

"What happened?"

For once his mother looked utterly confounded. "She was going on and on about you and the rocket and then she turned bright pink and collapsed."

Nic scooped Brooke into his arms and headed toward the palace. Whereas she'd been flushed a moment earlier, her skin was now deathly pale. He entered the green salon and crossed the room in several ground-eating strides. His heart hammered harder in his chest each time he glanced down at Brooke's unconscious face. What was wrong with her? As far as he recalled she'd been sick a mere handful of times and it had certainly never been this drastic. A cold. Sinus infection. Once a bad case of food poisoning.

He didn't realize his mother had followed him until he

pushed open the door to Brooke's suite and carried her to the bed.

"Is there something wrong with her that caused her to pass out?" the queen demanded, sitting on the bed to feel Brooke's skin. "She's clammy."

"She's perfectly healthy." He pulled out his phone, unsure if this was a true emergency. "She was anxious about coming here, but seemed all right at dinner last night. What did you say to her at breakfast? She seemed agitated before she passed out."

"You were watching us?"

"I was worried about how you two would get along. Seems I was right to be."

"I merely told her that I thought you believed yourself in love with her."

Nic closed his eyes briefly and shook his head. "What would possess you to tell her that?"

"I needed her to understand that what was between you wasn't real."

"How would you know? You barely know her and I haven't been around for ten years so you scarcely know me, either."

His mother looked shocked. "You are my son. I raised you."

With effort, Nic reeled in his temper. "None of this is helping Brooke. She hasn't awakened yet. I think she needs a doctor."

He was texting Gabriel when a single word from his mother stopped him.

"Wait."

"Why?"

She pointed at a package of crackers on the nightstand. "How long has she been eating these?"

"I have no idea." And what did it matter? "Do you think there's something wrong with them?"

"No, but when I was pregnant I used to eat crackers to fight nausea." His mother looked thoughtful. "She barely ate any of her dinner last night and she was picking at breakfast today. Pregnancy could explain her fainting spell."

"Pregnant?" Nic shook his head to clear the sudden rushing in his ears. "Impossible."

"Impossible because you haven't been intimate or because you thought you were being careful."

The blunt question shocked him for a moment before comprehension struck. Of course his mother knew he'd been involved with Brooke. They hadn't kept their relationship secret and no doubt Ariana had mentioned that he was seeing someone in California.

"We've been very careful."

"Then perhaps she has someone else in her life."

Nic glared at his mother. "There's no one else."

The queen pressed her lips together and didn't argue further. "I suggest we wait for her to come around and ask her. If there's something more serious going on, we can call the doctor then." His mother stood and smoothed her skirt. "I'll give you some privacy. Please let me know how she's doing when she wakes."

And with that, the queen left and Nic was alone with Brooke.

Pregnant.

With his child. The thought of it filled him with warmth. But all too quickly questions formed. Had she realized it yet? She wasn't showing and he guessed that she was between five and eight weeks along. Was that too early for her to suspect? Yet she'd obviously been queasy and had to wonder why.

Brooke began to stir and Nic went to sit beside her. She blinked and slowly focused on him.

"What happened?"

"You passed out."

"Damn." She rubbed her eyes. "I yelled at your mother. She must hate me."

"She doesn't." He skimmed his knuckles against her cheek. "What's going on with you? I've never known you to be sick."

She avoided his gaze. "Nothing, I'm just really overwrought and I think my blood sugar is low because I was too nervous to eat much at dinner."

"Is that why you were eating these?" He picked up the crackers and held them before her.

"Whenever my stomach gets upset, I eat crackers to absorb the acid." Her words made sense, but something about her tone told him she wasn't giving him full disclosure.

"My mother told me she used to eat crackers when she was pregnant," he said. "She claimed it helped with nausea."

Brooke's body tensed. "I've heard that before. I think if you keep something bland in your stomach it settles it."

Nic's irritation was growing by the second. Brooke was a terrible liar because she believed in being honest. So much so it had gotten her into trouble a number of times. Her behavior while answering his questions demonstrated that while she hadn't actually said anything false, she was keeping things from him.

"Are you pregnant?"

"We've been careful."

"That didn't answer my question." He leaned down and grabbed her chin, pinning her with his gaze. "Are you pregnant?"

"Yes." Her voice came out small and unsure.

He sat back with a muffled curse. "Why didn't you tell me?"

"That was the plan when I came to Ithaca." She pushed into a sitting position and retreated away from him as far as the headboard would allow. "I couldn't tell you some-thing like that over the phone, but then I showed up and you were so unhappy to see me." She wrapped her arms around herself and stared at her shoes. "And then you an-nounce that you are a prince and you need to get married so your country could have an heir and that your wife needed to be an aristocrat or a citizen of Sherdana."

"So you were planning on leaving without ever telling me?" Outrage gave his voice a sharp edge.

"Don't say it like that. You made a choice to come back here and do the honorable thing. I made a decision that would save you from regret."

"But to never see my child?"

She put her hands over the lower half of her face and closed her eyes. After a long moment she spoke. "Don't you think I considered that? But I knew you would have other children, hopefully lots of them."

Her every word slashed his heart into ribbons. The woman he loved was having his child and he'd been days away from never knowing the truth. "Well, there's no ques-tion of you going home now."

"What? You can't make that decision for me. My job, friends and family are in California. That's where I be-long. Just like you belong here in Sherdana with your fam-ily and your future *wife*."

She was crazy if she thought he was just going to let her vanish out of his life. "You belong with me just like I belong with you and our child."

"Maybe if you were the ordinary scientist I first fell in love with, but you are a prince with responsibilities that are bigger than both of us combined. Do the right thing and let me go. It's the only thing that makes sense."

"I refuse to accept that." Nic got to his feet and stared down at her. Where a moment earlier she'd seemed frag-ile and lost, her passionate determination to do what she perceived as the honorable thing gave her the look of a Valkyrie. "Get some rest. We will talk at length later."

Nic should have gone straight to his mother to deliver the confirmation of Brooke's condition as he'd promised, but found he needed some privacy to absorb what he'd just learned. He headed to his suite in the royal wing, curious to see if it was in the condition Gabriel had said. But just as Ariana had said, there was no leak.

The rooms that had been his growing up couldn't feel any less familiar than if he'd never seen them before. The past ten years of his life, first living in Boston, then California, felt much more real to him than the first twenty-two being Sherdana's prince. But that had been the case before he'd found out Brooke was pregnant. If he put aside duty and engaged in an honest conversation with himself, he'd accept that he no longer felt connected to his birth country. Yet his failure in the Mojave Desert meant that California was no longer a welcoming destination, either.

Never had he felt so conflicted about his future path. No matter what direction he chose, he was destined to leave disappointment and regret in his wake. Staying in Sherdana and marrying a suitable bride would require him to give up the woman he loved and abandon his child. But if he chose to make a life with Brooke could he convince her that he would never regret turning his back on his country when he knew it would always haunt him? And what would he do in California without the *Griffin* to work on? Teach at a university? He frowned.

When an hour of self-reflection passed without a clear solution presenting itself, Nic left his suite and sought his mother. He found her and his father in the king's private office deep in discussion.

"Well?" the king demanded, his eyes reflecting disappointment. He was seated behind a large mahogany desk that had been a gift from the king of Spain back in the early eighteenth century. "Is Dr. Davis pregnant?"

"Yes." Nic refused to feel like a chastised teenager. "And the child is mine." This last he directed to his mother, who sat on one of the burgundy sofas in the office's sitting area.

She was in the process of pouring a cup of tea and sent a pained look to her husband. "It seems as if none of my grandchildren are going to be legitimate."

"I won't apologize for what happened," he told his parents. "And I won't shirk my responsibility to Brooke."

"What does that mean?" his father said, his deep voice charged with warning.

"I don't have all the details worked out yet."

"You're not planning to marry her."

"It would take both of us to be on board for that to happen and at this point she's determined to return to California alone."

"You must let her," his mother said. "We will make sure she and the child are well taken of, but news of this must not get out. You need to marry and produce children that can one day succeed Gabriel."

The press of duty had never felt more overwhelming. Nic wanted to struggle free of the smothering net of responsibility that his parents cast over him.

"And what about Christian?" Nic asked, his heart burning with bitterness. "Will he not be expected to do the same?"

"Of course." The king nodded. "We are calling on both of you."

And with that, Nic accepted that one decision had been made for him.

Embarrassment and remorse kept Brooke from venturing out of her room the rest of the day. She put her pajamas back on, pulled the curtains closed and huddled in bed. A maid brought her lunch, which she barely touched, and when Ariana poked her head in the room sometime in the late afternoon, Brooke pretended to be sleeping.

She couldn't hide like this forever. For one thing it wasn't her style to avoid problems, and she really wouldn't shake the despair gnawing at her until she apologized to the queen for her outburst.

Around five she roused and phoned Theresa, needing to pour her heart out to someone who was 100 percent on her side. Unfortunately, the call rolled to voice mail and Brooke hung up without leaving a message. This was her problem to solve and the sooner she faced the music, the better.

A maid came by around six and found Brooke dressed in her tribal print maxi dress and sandals. Wearing her own clothes was like wrapping herself in a little piece of home. She didn't fit into Nic's world and trying to appear as if she did had been silly. Better to face the queen's displeasure as her authentic self, a woman who knew her own mind and was determined to do what was best for her and for Nic.

"Princess Olivia sent me to ask if you felt well enough to have dinner with her in half an hour," the maid said.

"Tell her yes."

When Brooke entered Prince Gabriel and Princess Olivia's private suite thirty minutes later, she wasn't surprised to discover Olivia had heard all about the morning's events. Up until now the princess had seemed like an ally, but would that continue? Brooke regarded Olivia warily as the princess indicated a spot on the gold couch. Brooke sat down while Olivia poured a cup of something that smelled like peppermint from a silver tea set.

The princess's kindness brought tears to Brooke's eyes. "How badly have I messed everything up?"

Olivia's eyes grew thoughtful. "Your pregnancy has

created quite a stir as you can imagine, but you shouldn't feel responsible. I doubt either you or Nic planned this."

"I don't mean that. I mean how mad is the queen that I yelled at her?"

"I didn't hear anything about that." Olivia's lips twitched and her eyes glinted with merriment. "What happened?"

"It's a bit of a blur. She said something dismissive about Nic needing to forget about the rocket and I straight up lost it." Brooke cradled the teacup, hoping the warmth would penetrate her icy fingers. "I started ranting about how he worked so hard because he wanted to justify his being away from his country for so long." Brooke shook her head as her heart contracted in shame. "It's none of my business. I shouldn't have said anything."

"You were defending the man you love. I think the queen understands."

"You didn't see her face." Brooke squinted and tried to summon a memory of the queen's reaction, but all she recalled was the garden pitching around her and the descent into darkness. "I was so rude."

"You are being too hard on yourself," Olivia said. "No wonder you and Nic get along so well. You're both such honorable people."

"I don't feel very honorable at the moment. But I'd like to change that. I made arrangements for a flight leaving the day after tomorrow at nine in the morning. I could use some help getting to the airport."

"You can't really mean to leave."

"You can't possibly think it's a good idea for me to stay. The longer I'm here the more likely it will leak that I'm pregnant. Better if I disappear from Sherdana so Nic can move forward with his life."

"What makes you think he's just going to let you go? When faced with the same choice, Gabriel fought for me.

Nic is no less an Alessandro and I don't think he's any less in love."

Olivia's words provoked many questions as Brooke realized that the princess had been confronted by a similar choice of whether to marry her prince when doing so put the future line of Alessandros at risk. But as much as curiosity nipped at her, Brooke feared asking would insult the princess.

"I think Gabriel is more of a romantic than Nic," Brooke said. "Your husband's heart led him to choose you and he will never question whether he made the right decision. Nic approaches matters with logic, listing the pros and cons, assigning values so he can rank what's most important. I think he takes after his mother in that respect."

Olivia's beautiful blue eyes clouded. "You know him well so I will just have to accept that you're right, but I hope for your sake that you're wrong."

Eleven

Both Olivia and Ariana had ganged up on Brooke and convinced her to go to the prime minister's birthday party the next evening. As it was her last night in Sherdana—she was due to fly out the next morning—the princesses were opposed to her spending any more time alone. Their concern was a balm to Brooke's battered spirit and because Ariana had tapped into her contacts in the fashion world and found Brooke the perfect Jean-Louis Scherrer gown to wear, she'd caved with barely a whimper.

Trailing into the party behind the crown prince and princess with Ariana beside her for support, Brooke experienced a sense of wonder that made her glad she'd come. The gown Ariana had found for her had the empire waist Brooke loved and a free flowing skirt. With every stride, the skirt's bright gold lining flashed and showed off the most perfect pair of Manolo Blahnik shoes with tasseled straps. The bodice was crusted with bronze beading that made her think of Moroccan embellishment and the gown's material was a subdued orange, gold and pink paisley pattern that exhibited Brooke's bohemian style.

After meeting the prime minister and wishing him a happy birthday, Brooke relaxed enough to gaze around at the guests. With Ariana at her side, no one seemed overly interested in her. It wasn't that she was ignored. Each person she was introduced to was polite and cordial, but no one seemed overly curious about the stranger from California. Brooke suspected that Ariana's social nature brought all sorts of individuals into her sphere.

Of Nic she saw nothing. The party was crowded with Sherdanian dignitaries and Brooke was determined not to spend the entire evening wondering which of the women Nic might choose to become his wife.

"Do you see what I mean about dull?" Ariana murmured to her an hour into the party. "We've made an appearance. Anytime you're ready to leave, just say the word. A friend of mine owns a club. It's opening night and he'd love to have me show up."

Brooke had been finding the party anything but dull. Unlike Nic, she liked to balance hours of study and research with socializing. People-watching was the best way to get out of her head and the prime minister's party was populated by characters.

"Sure, we can leave, but this isn't as dull as you say."

"I'm sorry, I forget that you are new to all this."

"I suppose you're right. Who is the woman in the black gown and the one over there in blue?" Each of them negotiated the room on the arm of an older gentleman, but Brooke had observed several telling glances passing between them.

"That's Countess Venuto." Ariana indicated the woman wearing blue. "And Renanta Arazzi. Her husband is the minister of trade. The men hate each other."

"Their wives don't share their husbands' antagonism."

"What do you mean?"

"I think they're having an affair." Brooke grinned. "Or they're just about to."

Ariana gasped, obviously shocked. "Tell me how you know."

Brooke spent the next hour explaining her reasoning to Ariana and then commented on several other things she'd picked up, astonishing the princess with her observations and guesses.

"You have an uncanny knack for reading people," Ariana exclaimed. "Gabriel should hire you to sit in on his meetings and advise him on people's motives."

Flattered, Brooke laughed. "I'm trained as an analyst. Whether it's art, literature or people, I guess I just dig until I locate meaning. Just don't ask me about anything having to do with numbers or technology. That's where I fail miserably."

"But that's what makes you and my brother such a perfect pairing. You complement each other."

At the mention of Nic, Brooke's good mood fled. "If only he wasn't a prince and I wasn't an ordinary girl from California." She kept her voice light, but in her chest, her heart thumped dully. "I didn't tell you earlier, but I made arrangements to fly home tomorrow morning."

"You can't leave." Ariana looked distressed. "At least stay through the wedding."

The thought of delaying the inevitable for another week made Brooke shudder. Plus, she hadn't yet been offered the opportunity to apologize to the queen in person and didn't feel right taking advantage of the king and queen's hospitality with that hanging over her. "I can't stay. Coming here in the first place was a mistake."

"But then I'd never have met you and that would have been a tragedy."

Brooke appreciated Ariana's attempt to make her feel

special. "I feel the same way about you. I just wish I'd handled things better." By which she meant the incident with the queen and Nic's discovering that she was pregnant.

She hadn't spoken to him since he'd left her room the day before. She'd dined that night with Olivia and taken both breakfast and lunch in her room. Ariana had joined her for the midday meal, bringing with her the gown Brooke was wearing tonight and reminding her of the promise she'd made to attend the birthday party.

Suddenly the crowd parted and Nic appeared, looking imposing and very princely as he strode through the room. Brooke stared at him in hopeless adoration, still unaccustomed to the effortless aura of power he assumed in his native environment. What was so different about him? He'd always radiated strength and confidence, but he'd been approachable despite his often inherent aloofness. What made him seem so inaccessible now? Was it the arrogant tilt of his head? The way he wore the expensive, custom tuxedo as easily as a T-shirt and jeans? The cool disdain in his burnished gold eyes?

And then he caught sight of her and the possessive glow of his gaze melted the chill from his features. Brooke's heart exploded in her chest and she abandoned Ariana with a quick apology, slipping through the party guests in Nic's direction before she considered what she would say. When she'd drawn to within five feet of him, her path was blocked by a petite brunette in a shimmering black mini.

"Nicolas Alessandro, I heard you returned home." The woman's cultured voice stopped Brooke dead in her tracks.

She turned aside and spotted French doors leading onto a terrace. Moving in that direction with as much haste as she dared, Brooke chastised herself. What had she been thinking? She and Nic couldn't act as friends or even acquaintances at this public event. All eyes were on the returning prince. During her self-imposed incarceration, she'd pored over the local gossip blogs and read several news articles speculating on Nic's abrupt return. The media were having a field day detailing all the women who'd been invited to the royal wedding the following week and speculating on who might be the front-runner to become the next Sherdanian princess.

Not one of the news sources had mentioned a girl from California. For that Brooke was grateful, but if she threw herself at Nic during this party, how long would it be before someone started wondering who she was.

Brooke had about five minutes of solitude on the terrace before she was joined by Olivia.

"Are you all right?" the princess inquired, her concern bringing tears to Brooke's eyes.

"I almost made a huge mistake out there. I saw Nic and raced through the crowd to get to him." Her story came out in uneven bursts as her heart continued to pound erratically. "If someone hadn't beaten me to him, I don't know what I would have done." Brooke braced herself on the metal railing as hysterical laughter bubbled up, making her knees wobble. "I am such an idiot."

"Not at all. You are in love. It makes us behave in strange and mysterious ways."

Brooke loved Olivia's British accent. It made even the most impossible statements sound plausible. Already calm was settling back over her.

"I'm so glad I had the chance to get to know you," Brooke said. "Ariana, too. Nic is lucky to have you."

"He'd be lucky to have you as well if only you wouldn't be so eager to rush off."

"I know you mean well." Brooke shook her head. "But Nic needs me to go."

"What if instead he really needs you to stay? He's been locked in the library since yesterday morning. His mind is a hundred miles away from anyone trying to have a conversation with him. He called Christian and could be heard yelling at him to get home all the way across the palace."

That didn't sound much like the Nic she knew, but then he'd been through a lot in the past month. Was it any surprise that having his entire world turned upside down would cause a crack in his relentless confidence?

"It's my fault," Brooke said, her own confidence returning. "I dropped a huge bomb on him yesterday when I said I was going back to California without consulting him."

"You should speak to him. He wants badly to do right by everyone and it's tearing him apart."

As it had torn Brooke apart, until she'd concluded that Nic would be better off not knowing about her pregnancy. "But I'm leaving in the morning. It will have to be tonight." Brooke considered. "Ariana's friend has a club opening tonight and she wants to go. I'll have her drop me at the palace. If you'll let Nic know, I'll be waiting for him in the library at midnight."

She didn't want him to leave the party early. His mother would expect him to spend the evening getting acquainted with all the available women there. Brooke turned to go, but Olivia stopped her.

"If Nic could marry you, would you accept?"

The princess asked the question with such poignant sincerity that Brooke faced her and answered in kind. "I love him with everything I am. Which is why it's both incredibly simple and impossibly hard to let him go so he can be the prince his family needs him to be."

Olivia wrapped her in a fierce hug and whispered, "If he asks you to stay, please say yes."

Brooke smiled at the beautiful princess without answering and then squared her shoulders and went to find Ariana.

* * *

Trapped in a tedious conversation with one of Christian's former girlfriends, Alexia Le Mans, Nic watched Brooke exit the ballroom for the less populated terrace and was just extricating himself to go after her when Olivia beat him to it. He'd only come to the party tonight in the hopes of seeing Brooke and demanding they have a conversation about the child she carried. He might not be able to marry her, but he'd be damned if the child would disappear out of his life. Nic had seen Gabriel's regret at not knowing his daughters during their first two years and Nic wasn't going to let that happen to him.

Ten minutes after Brooke left the room, she was back, and almost immediately he lost her in the crush. He moved to intercept her, but was stopped three times before he reached where he thought Brooke had been headed.

"Nic."

He turned at Olivia's voice and saw that she and Gabriel were coming up behind him. "I can't talk right now, I'm looking for Brooke."

Olivia exchanged a wordless look with her husband. "Ariana was heading to a club opening and she offered to give Brooke a lift back to the palace. But before she left, she gave me a message for you. She said she'll be waiting to speak to you in the library at midnight."

"Thank you." Nic had no intention of waiting until then to talk with Brooke. "And thank you for all you've done for her."

"No need to thank me," Olivia said, her smile affectionate. "She's lovely and I've enjoyed being her friend."

"Yes," Gabriel added. "Too bad she couldn't become a permanent fixture in the palace. I think she'd make an outstanding princess."

The temptation to say something disrespectful to the future king sizzled in Nic's mind, but he quelled his frustration and thanked Olivia with as much courtesy as he could muster. Bidding them goodbye, Nic headed downstairs to reclaim his car and follow Brooke to the palace.

The drive from the hotel where the prime minister's party had taken place back to the palace only took ten minutes, but Nic discovered Brooke had already disappeared into the visitors' wing by the time he arrived. He'd hoped to catch her before she went upstairs so they could have their conversation someplace that wouldn't invite gossip, but that wasn't going to stop him from tracking her down.

As he knocked on her door, he was a little out of breath from his rush up the stairs to the third floor. Listening to his heart thunder in his chest as he waited for her to answer, he made a note to drink less and exercise more than had been his habit in the past month. But when Brooke answered the door, snatching his breath away as he stared down into her soft gray-green eyes, he knew it wasn't stamina that had caused his heart and lungs to labor, but excitement at being close to her again.

"Nic? What are you doing here?"

"You wanted to talk." He stepped forward, forcing her to retreat into her room. As soon as he cleared the door, he shut it behind him. His hands made short work of his tie and slipped the first buttons of his shirt free. "Let's talk."

Brooke's body immediately began to thrum with arousal at Nic's apparent intent in entering her room. Her lips couldn't form protests as he removed his tuxedo jacket and unfastened his gold cuff links. Those went into his pocket before he set the jacket on a convenient chair while still advancing on her.

"Didn't Olivia tell you midnight in the library?"

"I considered it a suggested time and place." He pulled his shirt free of his pants and went back to work on the buttons. Each one he freed gave her a more evocative glimpse of the impressive chest beneath. "I prefer this one."

The gold shards in Nic's eyes brightened perceivably when his temper was aroused. Because she enjoyed riling him, Brooke had noticed this phenomenon a lot. She could judge the level of his agitation by the degree of the sparkle. At the moment his gaze was almost too intense to meet.

She thought about Olivia's words and wished he'd ask her to stay in Sherdana. No, she didn't. She ached for him to ask her. But he wouldn't. He shouldn't. From the start he'd been right to keep her at bay.

Nic closed the distance between them and swept her into his arms. As he bent her backward, his lips gliding along her temple, Brooke's senses spun.

"Stay in Sherdana a while longer."

He wasn't asking for forever, but every second with him was precious. "I don't belong here."

"Neither do I," he whispered an instant before his lips met hers.

With a moan, she sank her fingers into his thick black hair and held on as he fed off her mouth. Desire lashed at her, setting her pent-up emotions free. She met him kiss for kiss, claiming him as he sought to brand her with his passion.

Both were breathing unevenly when he lifted his lips from hers and captured her gaze. With her heart thundering in her ears, Brooke barely heard his words.

"You and I belong together."

"In another life. As different people. I'd give up everything to be with you," she murmured, the last of her resistance crumbling as he slid his hands down her back and aligned her curves to his granite muscles. "But not here and now."

"Yes to here and now," he growled. "It's tomorrow and

all the days beyond we can't have. Don't deny either of us this last night of happiness."

Brooke surrendered to the flood of longing and the demanding pressure of his arms banded around her body. Tomorrow would come all too soon. She wanted him for as long as possible.

With her face pressed against his bare chest, her ear tuned to the steady beat of his heart, she said, "I love you."

His arms crushed her, preventing any further words. For a long moment his grip stopped her from breathing, and then his hold gentled.

"You are the only woman I'll ever love."

Brooke lifted up on tiptoe and pushed her lips against his. He immediately opened to her and she matched the fierce hunger of his kiss with a desperation she couldn't hide. He loved her.

Working with deliberation that made her ache, he eased down the zipper of her dress, his lips sending a line of fire along her skin as he went. She'd never felt so adored as he unwrapped her body, treating her as if she was a precious gift. By the time his fingers lifted away the exquisite designer gown, exposing all of her, she was quivering uncontrollably.

Nic stripped away the last of her clothes, pushed her to arm's length and stared. Looking at her excited him and that set her blood on fire. She licked her dry lips and his pupils flared, almost vanquishing his gold irises. Her legs trembled. She couldn't take much more without ending up in a heap at his feet.

Without warning he surged back to life, lifting her into his arms and carrying her to the bed. As she floated down to land on the mattress, Brooke's thighs parted in welcome and Nic quickly stripped off the rest of his clothes and covered her with his body. She expected him to surge inside her, such was the intensity of his erection, but instead, he went back to work on her body with lips and hands, driving her to impossible levels of hunger.

At long last, she'd gone light-years past the point of readiness and gathered handfuls of his hair. "I can't wait any longer to have you inside me."

"Are you asking or commanding?" He sucked hard on her neck and she quaked.

"I'm begging." She reached down and found him. Her firm grip wrenched a satisfying moan from his lips. "Please, Nic."

His hands spanned her hips and in one swift thrust he answered her plea. She flexed her spine and accepted his full length while he devoured her impassioned groan. Before she could grow accustomed to the feel of him filling her, Nic rolled them over until she sat astride his hips.

This new position offered a different set of sensations and freed his hands to cruise across her torso at will. She took charge of their lovemaking and began to move. Whispering words of encouragement, he cupped her breasts, kneading and rolling her hard nipples between his fingers to intensify her pleasure.

When she came, it was hard and fast. If she could have lingered in the moment forever, she would have known perfect happiness, but such profound ecstasy wasn't meant to last. And there was a different sort of joy in the lazy aftermath of being so thoroughly loved. As Nic nuzzled his face in the place where her neck met her shoulder, Brooke savored the synchronized beat of their hearts and knew no matter where her body existed, her soul would stay with Nic where it belonged.

Morning brought rain and the distant rumble of thunder. Nic woke to the soft, fragrant sweetness of Brooke's naked body curved against his and held his breath to keep from disturbing the magic of the moment. Last night had been incredible. And it had been goodbye. He'd tasted it in the desperation of her kisses and felt it in the wildness of his need for her.

"What time is it?" she asked, her voice a contented purr.

"A little before seven."

"Oh." She practically sprang out of bed and began to hunt around for her clothes. "I have to go."

Nic sat up, automatically admiring the fluid movement of her nude form as she dressed. "Where are you going?"

"Home. My flight leaves in two hours."

Shock held him motionless and she'd almost reached the door before he caught up with her. If he hadn't barged into her room and spent the night would he have even known she was gone?

"And if I ask you to stay?" He thought he was ready to set her free, but now that the moment had arrived, he was incapable of saying goodbye.

"Don't you mean command?" Her smile was both wicked and sad.

Despite his solemn mood, Nic's lips twitched. "You aren't Sherdanian. I have no way to make you behave."

"And throwing me in the dungeon would create an international scandal that would upset your mother."

"Is that why you're running away? Because you think either I or my family would be bothered by some adverse publicity?"

Her body stiffened. "I'm not running away. I'm returning to California where I live. Just like you are staying in Sherdana where you belong. Besides, the longer I stay the more I risk becoming fodder for the tabloids and that wouldn't do your marriage hunt any favors."

"No. I suppose it wouldn't. But I still don't want you to go."

"And yet I must."

"You're breaking my heart," he said, carrying her hand to his lips and placing her palm against his bare chest.

"I'm breaking *your* heart?" She tugged her hand from beneath his, but his free arm snaked around her, and pulled her resistant body against him. "Do you have any idea how unfair you're being right now?"

He knew and didn't care. Nic tightened his hold, letting his heat seep into her until there was no more resistance. And then he kissed her, long and slow and deep, while in the back of his mind he acknowledged that this would be their final goodbye. By the time he broke away they were both gasping for breath.

Brooke spoke first. "You were right."

"About?" He nuzzled her cheek, feathering provocative kisses along her skin. His teeth grazed her earlobe, making her shudder.

"Starting something that had no future." Her pain and grief tore at him.

"I didn't want there to be regrets between us."

"I don't regret it."

"But you can't help thinking if we'd never been together that leaving would be easier." His arms tightened. "And you might be right. But for the rest of my life I will cherish every second we've spent together." And now he had to be strong enough to let her go. Only knowing that their child would connect them together forever gave him the courage to set her free. "There's no getting you out of my system," he said. "Or my heart."

"I love you." She kissed him one last time. "Now let me go."

Twelve

"You let her go?" Gabriel Alessandro, crown prince of Sherdana, was furious. "What the hell is the matter with you?"

From her seat behind the ornate writing desk, Olivia watched her husband storm around the living room of their suite, her expression a mask of sadness and resignation.

"Why are you yelling at me?" Nic demanded, pointing at Gabriel's princess. "She's the one who arranged to have a car take her to the airport."

It was shortly before lunch and Brooke's flight had departed Carone International over two hours prior. By now she would be over the Atlantic Ocean on her way to New York's JFK airport and her connecting flight to San Francisco.

"It's not my wife's fault that she was leaving in the first place. You were supposed to stop her before she ever got into the car." Gabriel raked his fingers through his hair in a gesture of acute frustration. "Do you realize what you've done?"

"I did what the country required of me."

Silence greeted his declaration, but Nic refused to feel bad that he'd at long last addressed the elephant in the room. He'd let Brooke get away because Gabriel hadn't acted in the country's best interest when he'd married Olivia.

"For the first time in your life," Gabriel shouted back. "How the hell do you think I felt having to carry the burden of responsibility for both you and Christian all these years? Maybe I would have enjoyed being an irresponsible playboy or playing at an impossible dream like building a rocket ship."

"Playing at—"

"Enough." Olivia's sharp tone sliced through the testosterone thickening the air and silenced both men. "Tossing accusations back and forth is not solving our immediate issue."

Gabriel was the first to back down. He turned to his wife and the love that glowed in his gaze made Nic's heart hurt.

"She's right." Gabriel's attention returned to his brother. "I know you were doing amazing things in California and I wish you were still there doing them. I really don't begrudge you any time you've spent chasing your dream."

Nic was seeing a different side of his brother. Never before had Gabriel spoken so eloquently about what he was feeling. The crown prince could speak passionately about issues relating to the country and he had a fine reputation for diplomacy, but he'd always been a closed book with regard to anything of a personal nature.

"I've lost my nerve." Since Gabriel felt comfortable sharing, Nic decided it was only fair to give a little in return. "Since the accident, I am afraid to even think about what went wrong with *Griffin*. Five years of my life went into designing the fuel delivery system that caused the rocket to blow up. I killed someone. There's no coming back from that for me." Nic's voice was thick with regret as he finished, "It's part of the reason I let Brooke go. Her life is in California and there's no place for me there anymore. I belong here where I can make a difference."

"Oh, Nic." Olivia was at his side, her soft hand gentle on his arm. "I'm sorry you are in so much pain. And what happened to your rocket and that man's death are a horrible tragedy, but you can't let that get in the way of your happiness with Brooke."

Gabriel grabbed his other arm and gave him a shake. "And you really don't belong here."

"Yes, I do. The country needs an heir to the throne." But his protest was cut short as Olivia and Gabriel shared a moment of intense nonverbal communication. "What's going on?"

Olivia shifted her gaze to Nic and offered him a sympathetic head tilt. "We can't get into specifics…"

"About what?" There was obviously an important secret being kept from him and Nic didn't like being left out.

The crown prince's lips quirked in a wry smile. "What if as the future leader of your country I order you to return to California, resume work on your rocket ship and marry the mother of your child?"

Nic spent a long moment grappling with his conscience. He'd come to grips with sacrificing his happiness for the sake of the country and although it had torn him apart to let Brooke go, he'd known it was for the greater good of Sherdana and his family.

Now, however, his brother was offering him a way out. No, Nic amended. Gabriel was directing him to forsake his duty and chase his dreams all the way back to California. The walls he'd erected to garrison his misery began to crumble. He sucked in a ragged breath. Permission to marry Brooke and raise their child with her. The chance to complete his dream of space travel. All on a silver platter compliments of his brother. It was too much.

But as he scrutinized Gabriel's confident posture and observed the secret smile that lit Olivia's eyes, he sensed that whatever was going on, these two were well in control of the country's future.

Nic offered Gabriel a low bow, his throat tight. "Naturally, I'd do whatever my crowned prince commands."

On her way to the Mojave Air and Space Port to visit her brother, Brooke took a familiar detour and drove past the house Nic had rented for the past three years. The place looked as deserted as ever. Nic hadn't spent much time there, sometimes not even sleeping in his own bed for days at a stretch because the couch in his workroom was within arm's reach of his project.

Still, when she could get him to take time off, they'd often had fun barbecuing in the backyard or drinking beer on the front porch while they stared at the stars and Nic opened up about what he and Glen hoped one day to accomplish.

Brooke stomped on the accelerator and her Prius picked up speed. Those days were behind her now that Nic was back in Sherdana, but at least she had the memories.

A ten-minute drive through town brought her to the hangar where Glen and his team were working on the new rocket. Brooke hadn't been here since the day Nic had broken off with her and she was surprised how little work had been done. From what Glen had told her, the inflow of cash hadn't dried up after the first *Griffin* had exploded. In fact, the mishap had alerted several new investors who'd promised funding for the project.

Brooke spent several minutes walking around the platform that held the skeleton of the *Griffin II*, her footsteps echoing around the empty hangar. She wasn't accustomed to this level of inactivity and wondered if she'd misunderstood her brother's text, asking her to meet him at the airfield rather than at his house.

As she made her way to the back of the facility where the workrooms and labs were set up, Brooke detected faint strains of music and figured her brother had gotten caught up in something and lost track of time. Except the music wasn't coming from Glen's office, but from Nic's former workroom.

The wave of sorrow that swarmed over her stopped Brooke in her tracks. Someone had obviously been hired to replace Nic on the team and had been given his office. The shock of it made her dizzy, but she quickly rationalized the unsteadiness away. How could she expect forward progress on the rocket without someone taking on the fuel delivery system Nic had abandoned? With the exception of her brother, no one else on the team could match Nic's brilliance or comprehend the intricacies of his design. Someone new would have to be brought in.

Brooke squared her shoulders and continued down the hallway. She might as well introduce herself to Nic's replacement and start to accept the changes that he'd bring to the team.

"Hi," she called over the music as she first knocked, and then pushed open the unlatched door. "I'm Brooke Davis, Glen's…" Her voice trailed away as the tall man in jeans and a black T-shirt turned to greet her.

"Sister," Nic finished for her. "He told me you might be stopping by today."

Brooke's throat tightened. "What are you doing here?"

"I work here." His smile—at once familiar and utterly different from anything she'd seen before—knocked the breath from her lungs.

"I don't understand." She sagged back against the door frame and drank in Nic's presence. His vibrant, imposing presence made it impossible for her to believe he was a hallucination, but she couldn't let herself trust this amazing turn of fortune until she knew what was going on. "I left you in Sherdana. You were going to get married and make Alessandro heirs."

Nic shook his head. "Turns out I was completely wrong for the job."

"How so?" His wry amusement was beginning to reach through her shock. She was starting to thaw out. The ice water that had filled her veins for the past week heated beneath his sizzling regard. "You're not impotent or something, are you?"

He laughed and reached out to snag her wrist, pulling her away from the wall and up against his hard body. "That was not the problem."

"Then what was?" She wrapped her arms around his neck and arched her back until they were aligned from chest to thigh.

"No one wanted me."

"I can't believe that." And she didn't. Not for a single second.

"It's true. Word got around that a spunky redhead had stolen my heart and left me but a shell of a man."

Brooke purred as he bent his head and nuzzled his lips into her neck. "So you've come here to take it back?"

"No. I've come here to sign it over all legal and such."

Fearing she'd misunderstood what he was saying, Brooke remained silent while her mind worked furiously. He'd left Sherdana and resumed his old position on the team. From the way his lips were exploring her neck, she was pretty sure he intended that their physical relationship would get back on track.

"Brooke?" He cupped her face and stared deep into her eyes. "You're awfully quiet."

"I guess I'm not sure what to say."

"You could start by saying yes."

Relief made her giddy. "You haven't asked me a question."

"You're right." And to her absolute delight, he dropped down on one knee and fished a ring out of his pocket. "Brooke Davis, love of my life and mother of my child, will you marry me?"

She set her hands on her hips and shook her head. "If this is about the baby, I assure you I'm not expecting you—"

"Oh, for heaven sakes," came an explosive shout from the hallway behind them. "Just tell the guy yes."

"Yes," she whispered, leaning down to plant her lips on Nic's.

He wrapped his arms around her and shot to his feet, lifting her into the air and spinning her in circles. She laughed, delirious with joy, and hugged him back. When he let her toes touch the floor once more, Glen was there to pound Nic on the back and offer his congratulations.

Amidst this, Nic slipped an enormous diamond ring onto her left hand. She ogled it while Glen played the brother card and threatened Nic with bodily harm if he didn't take good care of her. Then Glen left her and Nic alone so he could fill her in on what had transpired after she'd left.

"Gabriel almost killed me when he heard that you'd left," Nic explained, sitting on his couch and pulling her onto his lap.

She let her head fall onto his shoulder and savored the contentment that wove through her. "He did?"

"Apparently he decided to play matchmaker and wasn't particularly happy that I failed to do my part."

"Matchmaker?"

"He made sure we were in adjoining rooms in the visitors' wing of the palace and enlisted Olivia and Ariana to convince you not to give up on us."

"They did a pretty good job of that," Brooke agreed, thinking about that last night she'd spent with Nic. "In fact, I almost left without seeing you one final time, but both of them convinced me I owed it to us to say goodbye." But there was something she still didn't understand. "And we did. I left and you didn't stop me. You were determined to do the honorable thing and stay in Sherdana and get married. So what's changed?"

"Two things. First, I thought long and hard about what made me happy. Spending the rest of my life with you and my work. But I couldn't marry you without regretting that I'd decided not to step up when my family needed me and I couldn't see returning to the *Griffin* project when my design had caused a man's death."

"And yet you're here," Brooke pointed out.

"I didn't accept I couldn't live without you until I had to start."

"But what about Sherdana and producing an heir?"

"Gabriel released me from duty. Before I left he explained how it had nearly destroyed him to lose Olivia and he refused to let me go through the same sort of pain."

"But what about an heir for the throne?"

"I guess it's up to Christian."

"And you don't feel bad that he has to carry the full burden of the country's future on his shoulders?" Brooke arched her eyebrow at Nic's poor attempt to conceal a grin.

"If he had to choose between the woman of his dreams and duty to Sherdana, I'd feel horrible." Nic brushed Brooke's hair aside and kissed his way down her neck. "But he's never dated any woman long enough to fall in love and it's time he let someone in."

"Et benedetto il primo dolce affanno ch'i' ebbi ad esser con Amor congiunto."

Nic translated, "And blessed be the first sweet agony I suffered when I found myself bound to Love." He grazed his lips against Brooke's, making her sigh in pleasure. "I only hope the woman who finally breaks through to Christian makes him half as happy as you've made me."

Heart singing, Brooke wrapped her arms around Nic's neck and set her forehead against his. His gaze fastened on hers, letting her glimpse his joy and his need for her. For the first time she truly understood the depth of Nic's love for her. He'd made light of his decision to leave Sherdana, but she suspected even though Gabriel had released him from duty, the king and queen hadn't backed either of their sons' actions.

"I haven't begun to make you happy," she promised, tightening her hold.

"You don't say."

"I do say." And she proceeded to demonstrate how she planned to start.

* * * * *

A ROYAL BABY FOR CHRISTMAS

SCARLET WILSON

This book is dedicated to my fellow authors Kate
Hardy, Tina Beckett and Susanne Hampton. It's been
a pleasure working with you, ladies!

PROLOGUE

May

HIS EYES SCANNED the bar as he ran his fingers through his hair. Six weeks, three countries, ten flights and thousands of miles. He'd been wined and dined by heads of state and consulate staff, negotiated trade agreements, arranged to be part of a water aid initiative, held babies, shaken hands for hours and had a number of tense diplomatic conversations.

All of this while avoiding dozens of calls from his mother about the upcoming royal announcement. His apparent betrothal to his lifelong friend.

All he wanted to do was find a seat, have a drink and clear a little head space. Il Palazzo di Cristallo was one of the few places he could do that. Set in the stunning mountains of Montanari, the exclusive boutique hotel only ever had a select few guests—most of whom were seeking sanctuary from the outside world. The press were banned. The staff were screened and well looked after to ensure all guests' privacy was well respected—including the Crown Prince of Montanari. For the first time in six weeks Sebastian might actually be able to relax.

Except someone was sitting in his favourite seat at the bar.

There. A figure with shoulders slumped and her head

leaning on her hand. Her ash-blonde hair was escaping from its clasp and her blue dress was creased. Two empty glasses of wine sat on the bar in front of her.

The bartender sat down a third and gave Sebastian an almost indiscernible nod. The staff here knew he liked to keep his identity quiet.

Odd. He didn't recognise the figure. Sebastian knew all the movie stars and celebrities who usually stayed here. She wasn't a fellow royal or a visiting dignitary. His curiosity was piqued.

He strode across the room and slid onto the stool next to hers at the bar. She didn't even look up in acknowledgement.

Her fingers were running up and down the stem of the glass and her light brown eyes were unfocused. But it wasn't the drink. It was deep contemplation.

Sebastian sucked in a breath. Whoever she was, she was beautiful. Her skin was flawless. Her features finer than those of some of the movie starlets he'd been exposed to. Being Prince of Montanari meant that a whole host of women had managed to cross his path over the last few years. Not that he'd taken any of them seriously. He had a duty to his future kingdom. A duty to marry an acceptable neighbouring princess. There was no question about it— it had been instilled in him from a young age it was part of his preparations for finally becoming King. Marriage was a business transaction. It wasn't the huge love and undying happiness portrayed in fairy tales. There were no rainbows and flying unicorns. It came down to the most advantageous match for the country and his parents had found her. Theresa Mon Carte, his childhood friend and a princess from the neighbouring principality. They were to be married within the year.

Part of the reason he was here was to get some time to resign himself to his fate. Because that was what it felt like.

But right now, he couldn't think about that at all.

He was entirely distracted by the woman sitting next to him. She looked as if she had the weight of the world on her shoulders. There was no Botox here. Her brow was definitely furrowed and somehow he knew this woman would never be interested in cosmetic procedures.

'Want to tell me about them?'

'What?' She looked up, startled at the sound of his voice.

Light brown eyes that looked as if they'd once had a little dark eyeliner around them. It was smudged now. But that didn't stop the effect.

It was like being speared straight through the heart.

For a second neither of them spoke. It was the weirdest sensation—as if the air around them had just stilled.

He was drinking in everything about her. Her forgotten-about hair. Her crumpled clothes. Her dejected appearance.

But there was something else. Something that wouldn't let him break their gaze. A buzz. An air. He'd never felt something like this before. And she felt it too.

He could tell. Her pupils dilated just a little before his eyes. He didn't have any doubt that his were so big right now the Grand Canyon could fit in them.

There was something about her demeanour. This woman was a professional. She was educated. And she was, oh, so sexy.

He found his tongue. 'Your worries.' He couldn't help but let the corners of his mouth turn upwards.

She gave the briefest rise of her eyebrows and turned back towards the waiting wine glass. Her shoulders straightened a little. He'd definitely caught her attention.

Just as she'd caught his.

He leaned a little closer and nudged her shoulder. 'You're sitting on my favourite bar stool.'

'Didn't have your name on it,' she quipped back.

Her accent. It was unmistakeable. The Scottish twang made the hairs on his arms stand on end. He could listen to that all day. Or all night.

She swung her legs around towards him and leaned one arm on the bar. 'Come to think of it, you must be kind of brave.' She took a sip of her wine. Her eyebrows lifted again. 'Or kind of stupid.'

He liked it. She was flirting back. He leaned his arm on the bar too, so they were closer than ever. 'What makes you think that?'

She licked her lips. 'Because you're trying to get between a Scots girl and the bar.' She smiled as she ran her eyes up and down the length of his body. It was almost as if she'd reached her fingers out and touched him. 'Haven't you heard about Scots girls?'

He smiled and leaned closer. 'I think I might need a little education.' He couldn't think of anything he wanted more.

Instant attraction. He'd never really experienced it before. Not like this. He'd wanted to come in here to hide and get away from things. Now, his sanctuary had become a whole lot more exciting.

A whole lot more distracting.

His stomach flipped over. What if he never felt like this again? Or even worse, what if he felt like this when he was King of Montanari and married?

Right now he was none of those things. The engagement hadn't been announced. He was about to step into a life of duty and constant scrutiny.

Theresa was a friend. Nothing more. Nothing less. They'd never even shared a kiss.

He hadn't come here to meet anyone. He hadn't come here to be attracted to someone.

But right now he was caught in a gaze he didn't want to escape from. The pull was just too strong.

Something flitted across her eyes. It was as if her confidence wavered for a second.

'What's wrong?' He couldn't help himself.

She sucked in a breath. 'Bad day at the office.'

'Anything to do with a man?' It was out before he thought.

She blinked and gave a little smile again, pausing for a second. 'No. Definitely nothing to do with a man.'

It was as if he'd just laid himself bare. Finding out the lie of the land. He couldn't ignore the warm feeling that spread straight through him.

He had no royal duties this weekend. There were no hands he needed to shake. No business he needed to attend to. He'd told Security he was coming here and to keep their distance.

If he lived to be a hundred he'd remember this. He'd remember this meeting and the way it made him feel. The buzz was so strong the air practically sparkled around her.

He was still single. He could do this. Right now he would cross burning coals to see what would happen next.

He leaned even closer. 'I came here to get some peace and quiet. I came here to get some head space.' He gave her a little smile and lowered his voice. 'But, all of a sudden, there's no space in my head at all.'

He took a chance. 'How about I stop searching for some peace and quiet, and you forget all about your bad day?'

She ran her fingers up the stem of her wine glass. He could tell she was thinking. She looked up from beneath heavy eyelids. 'You mean, like a distraction. An interlude?'

The warm glow in his body started to rapidly rise. He nodded. 'A distraction.'

She licked her lips again and he almost groaned out loud. 'I think a distraction might be just what I need,' she said carefully.

He tried to quieten the cheerleader squad currently yelling in his head.

'I've always wanted to meet a Scots girl. Will you teach me how to wear a kilt?' He waved to the barman. 'There are some killer cocktails in here. You look like a Lavender Fizz kind of girl.'

'I'll do better than that.' There was a hint of mischief in her voice. 'I'll teach you how to take it off.'

This wasn't her life. It couldn't be. Things like this didn't happen to Sienna McDonald. But it seemed that in the blink of an eye her miserable, lousy day had just got a whole lot better.

It was the worst kind of day. The kind of day she should have got used to in this line of work.

But a doctor who got used to a baby dying was in the wrong profession.

It had been little Marco's third op. He'd been failing all the time, born into the world too early with undeveloped lungs and a malformed heart; she'd known the odds were stacked against him.

Some people thought it was wrong to operate on premature babies unless there was a guarantee of a good outcome. But Sienna had seen babies who had next to no chance come through an operation, fight like a seasoned soldier and go on to thrive. One of her greatest successes was coming up on his fourth birthday and she couldn't be prouder.

Today had been draining. Telling the parents had been soul-destroying. She didn't usually drown her sorrows in alcohol, but tonight, in a strange country with only herself for company, it was the only thing that would do. She'd already made short work of the accompanying chocolate she'd bought to go with the wine. The empty wrappers were littered around her.

She sensed him as soon as he sat down next to her.

There was a gentle waft of masculine cologne. Her eyes were lowered. It was easy to see the muscled thigh through the probably designer trousers. If he was staying in this hotel—he was probably a millionaire. She was just lucky the royal family were footing her bill.

When he spoke, his lilting Mediterranean accent washed over her. Thank goodness she was sitting down. There was something about the accent of the men of Montanari. It crossed between the Italian, French and Spanish of its surrounding neighbours. It was unmistakeable. Unique. And something she'd never forget.

She glanced sideways and once more sucked in her cheeks.

Nope. The guy who looked as if he'd just walked off some film set was still there. Any second now she'd have to pinch herself. This might actually be real.

Dark hair, killer green eyes with a little sparkle and perfect white teeth. She might not have X-ray vision but his lean and athletic build was clear beneath the perfectly tailored suit. If she were back in Scotland she'd tell him he might as well have *sex on legs* tattooed on his forehead. Too bad she was in a posh kingdom where she had to be a whole lot more polite than that.

He hadn't responded to her cheeky comment. For a millisecond he looked a little stunned, and then his shoulders relaxed a little and he nodded slowly. He was getting comfortable. Did he think the game was over?

She was just settling in for the ride. She didn't do this. She didn't *ever* do this. Pick up a man in a bar? Her friends would think she'd gone crazy. But the palms of her hands were tingling. She wanted to touch him. She wanted to feel his skin against hers. She wanted to know exactly what those lips tasted like.

He was like every erotic dream she'd ever had just handed to her on a plate.

She leaned her head on one hand and turned to face him. 'Who says I'm a cocktail kind of girl?'

He blinked. Her accent did that to people. It took their ears a few seconds to adjust to the Scottish twang. He was no different from every other man she'd ever met. The edges of his mouth turned upwards at the sound of her voice. People just seemed to love the Scottish accent— even if they couldn't understand a word she said.

'It's written all over you,' he shot back. He mirrored her stance, leaning his head on one hand and staring at her.

There was no mistaking the tingling of her skin. Part of her stomach turned over. There was a tiny wash of guilt.

Today wasn't meant to be a happy day. Today was a day to drown her sorrows and contemplate if she could have done anything different to save that little baby. But the truth was she'd already done that. Even if she went back in time she wouldn't do anything different. Clinically, her actions had been everything they should have been. Little Marco's body had just been too weak, too underdeveloped to fight any more.

The late evening sun was streaming in the windows behind him, bathing them both in a luminescence of peaches and purples. Distraction. That was what this was. And right now she could do with a distraction.

Something to help her forget. Something to help her think about something other than work. She was due to go home in a few days. She'd taught the surgeons at Montanari Royal General everything she could.

She let her shoulders relax a little. The first two glasses of wine were starting to kick in.

'I don't know that I'm a Lavender Fizz kind of girl.'

'Well, let's see what kind of girl you are.' The words hung in the air between them, with a hundred alternative meanings circulating in her mind. This guy was good. He was very good.

She half wished she'd changed after work. Or at least pulled a brush through her hair and applied some fresh make-up. This guy was impeccable, which made her wish she were too. He picked up the cocktail menu, pretending to peruse it, while giving her sideways glances. 'No,' he said decidedly. 'Not gin.' He paused a second. 'Hmm, raspberries, maybe. Wait, no, here it is. A peach melba cocktail.'

She couldn't help but smile as she raised her eyebrows. 'And what's in that one?'

He signalled the barman. 'Let's find out.'

Her smile remained fixed on her face. His confidence was tantalising. She sipped at her wine as she waited for the barman to mix the drinks.

'What's your name?' he asked as they waited. He held out his hand towards her. 'I'm Seb.'

Seb. A suitable billionaire-type name. Most of the men in this hotel had a whole host of aristocratic names. Louis. Alexander. Hugo. Augustus.

She reached out to take his hand. 'Sienna.'

His hand enveloped hers. What should have been a firm handshake was something else entirely. It was gentle. Almost like a caress. But there was a purpose to it. He didn't let go. He kept holding, letting the warmth of his hand permeate through her chilled skin. His voice was husky. 'You've been holding on to that wine glass too long.' Before she could reply he continued. 'Sienna. It doesn't seem a particularly Scottish name.'

A furrow appeared on his brow. As if he were trying to connect something. After a second, he shook his head and concentrated on her again.

She tried not to fixate on the fact her hand was still in his. She liked it. She liked the way this man was one of the most direct flirts she'd ever met. He could have scrawled his intentions towards her with her lipstick on the mir-

rored gantry behind the bar and she wouldn't have batted
an eyelid because this was definitely a two-way street.

'It's not.' She let her thumb brush over the back of his
hand. 'It's Italian.' She lifted her eyebrows. 'I was con-
ceived there. By accident—of course,' she added.

A look of confusion swept his face as the barman set
down the drinks, but he didn't call her on her comment.

Sienna had a wave of disappointment as she had to
pull her hand free of his and she turned to the peach concoction on the bar with a glimpse of red near the bottom.
She lifted the tiny straws and gave it a little stir. 'What
is this, exactly?'

Those green eyes fixed on hers again. 'Peach nectar,
raspberry puree, fresh raspberries and champagne.'

She took a sip. Nectar was right. It hit the spot perfectly. Just like something else.

'Are you here on business or pleasure, Sienna?'

She thought for a second. She was proud to be a surgeon. Most men she'd ever met had seemed impressed
by her career. But tonight she didn't want to talk about
being a surgeon. Tonight she wanted to concentrate on
something else entirely.

'Business. But it's almost concluded. I go home in a
few days.'

He nodded carefully. 'Have you enjoyed visiting Montanari?'

She couldn't lie. Even today's events hadn't taken the
shine off the beautiful country that she'd spent the last
few weeks in. The rolling green hills, the spectacular
volcanic mountain peak that overlooked the capital city
and coastline next to the Mediterranean Sea made the
kingdom one of the prettiest places she'd ever visited.
She took another sip of her cocktail. 'I have. It's a beautiful country. I'm only sorry I haven't seen enough of it.'

'You haven't?'

She shook her head. 'Business is business. I've been busy.' She stirred her drink. 'What about you?'

He had an air about him. Something she hadn't encountered before. An aura. She assumed he must be quite enigmatic as a businessman. He could probably charm the birds from the trees. At least, she was assuming he was a businessman. He looked the part and every other man she'd met in this exclusive hotel had been here to do one business deal or another.

But for a charmer, there was something else. An underlying sincerity in the back of his eyes. Somehow she felt if the volcanic peak overlooking the capital erupted right now she would be safe with this guy. Her instincts had always been good and it had been a long time since she'd felt like that.

'I've been abroad on business. I'm just back.'

'You stay here? In this hotel?'

He laughed and shook his head. 'Oh, no. I live...close by. But I conduct much of my business in this hotel.' He gave another gracious nod towards the barman. 'They have the best facilities. The most professional staff. I'm comfortable here.'

It was a slightly odd thing to say. But she forgot about it in seconds as the barman came back to top up their glasses.

She took a deep breath and stared at her glass. 'Maybe I should slow down a little.'

His gaze was steady. 'The drink? Or something else?'

There it was. The hidden question between them. She ran her finger around the rim of the glass. 'I came here to forget,' she said quietly, exposing more of herself than she meant.

Her other hand was on the bar. His slid over the top, intertwining his fingers with hers. 'And so did I. Maybe there are other ways to forget.'

She licked her lips, almost scared to look up and meet

his gaze again. It would be like answering the unspoken question. The one she was sure that she wanted to answer.

His thumb slid under her palm, tracing little circles. In most circumstances it would be calming. But here, and now, it was anything but calming; it was almost erotic.

'Sienna, you have a few days left. Have you seen the mountains yet? How about I show you some of the hidden pleasures that we keep secret from the tourists?'

It was the way he said it. His voice was low and husky, sending a host of tiny shivers of expectation up her spine.

She could almost hear the voices of her friends in her head. She was always the sensible one. Always cautious. If she told this tale a few months later and told them she'd made her excuses and walked away...

The cocktail glass was glistening in the warm sunset. The chandelier hanging above the bar sending a myriad of coloured prisms of light around the room.

The perfect setting. The perfect place. The perfect man.

A whole host of distraction.

Exactly what she'd been looking for.

She threw back her head and tried to remember if she was wearing matching underwear. Not that it mattered. But somehow she wanted all her memories about this to be perfect.

She met his green gaze. There should be rules about eyes like that. Eyes that pulled you in and held you there, while all the time giving a mischievous hint of exactly what he was thinking.

She stood up from her bar stool and moved closer. His hand dropped from the bar to her hip. She brushed her lips against his ear. 'How many of Montanari's pleasures are hidden?'

There it was. The intent.

It didn't matter that her perfect red dress was hanging in the cupboard upstairs. It didn't matter that her matching lipstick was at the bottom of her bag. It didn't matter that her most expensive perfume was in the bathroom in her room.

Mr Sex-on-Legs liked her just the way she was.

He closed his eyes for a second. This time his voice was almost a growl, as if he were bathing in what she'd just said. 'I could listen to your accent all day.'

She put her hand on his shoulder. 'How about you listen to it all night instead?'

And the deed was done.

CHAPTER ONE

SHE STARED AT the stick again.

Yep. The second line was still there.

It wasn't a figment of her imagination. Just as the missing period wasn't a dream and the tender breasts weren't a sign of an ill-fitting bra.

A baby. She was going to have a baby.

She stared out of her house window.

Her mortgage. She'd just moved in here. Her mortgage was huge. As soon as she'd seen the house she'd loved it. It was totally too big for one person—how ironic was that?—but she'd figured she'd have the rest of her life to pay for it. It was five minutes from Teddy's and had the most amazing garden with a pink cherry blossom tree at the bottom of it, and a little paved area at the back for sitting.

It was just like the house she'd dreamed of as a child. The house where she and her husband and children would stay and live happily ever after.

She sighed and put her head in her hands.

She was pregnant. Pregnant to Seb, the liar.

It made her insides twist and curl. She'd never quite worked out when he'd realised who she was, while she'd spent the weekend in blissful ignorance.

A weekend all the while holed up in the most beautiful mountain chalet-style house.

The days had been joyful. She'd never felt an attraction like it—immediate, powerful and totally irresistible. Seb had made her feel like the only woman in the world and for two days she'd relished it.

It was too good. Too perfect. She should have known. Because nobody could ever be *that* perfect. Not really.

She'd been surprised by his security outside the hotel. But then, lots of businessmen had bodyguards nowadays. It wasn't quite so unusual as it could have been.

And she hadn't seen any of the sights of Montanari. Once they'd reached his gorgeous house hidden in the mountains, the only thing she'd seen was his naked body.

For two whole days.

She squeezed her eyes closed for a second. It hurt to remember how much she'd loved it.

How many other woman had been given the same treatment?

She shook her head and shuddered. Finding out who he really was had ruined her memories of those two wonderful days.

Of those two wonderful nights...

She pressed her hand on her non-existent bump. *Oh, wow.* She was pregnant by a prince.

Prince Sebastian Falco of Montanari.

Some women might like that. Some women might think that was amazing. Right now she was wondering exactly why her contraceptive pill had failed. She'd taken it faithfully every day. She hadn't been sick. She hadn't forgotten. This wasn't deliberate. This absolutely wasn't a ploy to get pregnant by a prince. But what if he thought it was?

Her mind jumped back to her house. How much maternity leave would she get? How much maternity pay would she get—would it cover her mortgage? She'd used her savings as the deposit for the house—that, and the little extra she'd had left to update the bathroom and kitchen, meant her rainy-day fund was virtually empty.

She stood up and started pacing. Who would look after her baby when she returned to work? Would she be able to return to work? She had to. She was an independent woman. She loved her career. Having a baby didn't mean giving up the job she loved.

She rested her hand against the wall of her sitting room. Maybe someone at the hospital could give her a recommendation for a childminder? The crèche at the hospital wouldn't be able to cater for on-calls and late night emergency surgeries. She'd need someone ultra flexible. There was so much to think about. So much to organise.

She couldn't concentrate. Her mind kept jumping from one thing to the other. Oh, no—was this the pregnancy brain that women complained about?

She couldn't have that. She didn't have time for that. She was a neonatal cardiothoracic surgeon. She was responsible for tiny lives. She needed to be focused. She needed to have her mind on the job.

She walked through to the kitchen. The calendar was lying on the kitchen table. It was turned to April—showing when she'd had her last period. It had been left there when the realisation had hit her and she'd rushed to the pharmacy for a pregnancy test. She'd bought four.

She wouldn't need them. She flicked forward. Last date of period, twenty-third of April. Forty weeks from then? She turned the calendar over, counting the weeks on the back. January. Her baby was due on the twenty-eighth of January.

She pushed open her back door and walked outside. The previous owners had left a bench seat, carved from an original ancient tree that had been damaged in a lightning strike years ago. She sat down and took some deep breaths.

It was a beautiful day. The flowers in her garden had

all started to emerge. Fragrant red, pink and orange free-sias, blue cornflowers, purple delphinium and multi-coloured peonies blossomed in pretty colours all around her, their scents permeating the air.

She smiled. The deep breathing was beginning to calm her. A baby. She was going to have a baby.

She closed her eyes and pressed her lips together as a wave of determination washed over her. Baby McDonald might not have been planned. But Baby McDonald would certainly be wanted.

He or she would be loved. Be adored.

A familiar remembrance of disappointment and anger made her catch her breath. For as long as she could re-member her parents had made it clear to her that she'd been a 'mistake'. They hadn't put it quite in as few words but the implication was always there. Two people who had never really wanted to be together but had done 'what was right'.

Except it wasn't right. It wasn't right at all. Anger and resentment had simmered from them both. The expres-sion on her father's face when he had left on her eigh-teenth birthday had told her everything she'd ever needed to know—as had the relief on her mother's.

She'd been a burden. An unplanned-for presence.

Whether this baby was planned for or not, it would always feel loved, always feel wanted. She might not know about childcare, she might not know about mater-nity leave, she might not know about her mortgage—but of that one thing, she was absolutely sure.

Her brain skydived somewhere else. Folic acid. She hadn't been taking it. She'd have to get some. Her feet moved automatically. She could grab her bag; the nearest pharmacy was only a five-minute drive. She could pick some up and start taking it immediately. As she crossed the garden her eyes squeezed shut for a second. Darn it. Folic acid was essential for normal development in a baby.

She racked her brains. What had she been eating these last few weeks? Had there been any spinach? Any broccoli? She'd had some, but she just wasn't sure how much. She'd had oranges and grapefruit. Lentils, avocados and peas.

She winced. She'd just remembered her intake of raspberries and strawberries. They'd been doused in champagne in Montanari. Alcohol. Another no-no in pregnancy.

At least she hadn't touched a drop since her return.

Her footsteps slowed as she entered the house again. Seb. She'd need to tell him. She'd need to tell him she was expecting his baby.

A gust of cool air blew in behind her, sending every hair on her arms standing on end. How on earth would she tell him? They hadn't exactly left things on good terms.

She sagged down onto her purple sofa for a few minutes. How did you contact a prince?

Oliver. Oliver Darrington would know. He was Seb's friend, the obstetrician who had arranged for her to go to Montanari and train the other paediatric surgeons. But how on earth could she ask him without giving the game away? Would she sound like some desperate stalker?

Oh, Olly, by the way...can I just phone your friend the Prince, please? Can you give me his number?

She sighed and rested her head backwards on the sofa watching the yellow ticker tape of the news channel stream past.

Her eyes glazed over. Last time she'd seen Seb she'd screamed at him. Hardly the most ladylike response.

It didn't matter that his lie had been by omission. That might even seem a tiny bit excusable now. But then, six weeks ago, rationality had left the luxurious chalet she'd found herself in.

It had been a simple mistake. The car driver—or, let's face it, he was probably a lot more than that—had given a nod and said *Your Highness* to something Seb had asked him.

The poor guy had realised his mistake right away and made a prompt exit. But it was too late. She'd heard it.

At first she'd almost laughed out loud. She'd been so relaxed, so happy, that the truth hadn't even occurred to her. 'Your Highness?' She'd smiled as she'd picked up her bags to go back in the house.

But the look of horror on Seb's face had caused her foot to stop in mid-air.

And just like today, the hairs on her arms had stood on end. Seb. Sebastian. The name of the Prince of Montanari. The person who'd requested she train the surgeons in his hospital. The mystery man that she'd never met—because he was doing business overseas.

Just like Seb.

She might as well have been plunged into a cold pool of glacier ice.

'Tell me you're joking?'

For the first time since she'd met him, his coolness vanished. He started to babble. *Babble.* His eyes darting from side to side but never quite meeting her gaze.

She dropped her bags at her feet on the stony path. 'You're not, are you?' He kept talking but she stopped listening. Her brain trying to make sense of what was going on.

'You're Sebastian Falco? *You're* the Prince?' She walked right up under his nose.

It must have been the way she'd said it. As if it were almost impossible. As if he were the unlikeliest candidate in the world.

He let out a sigh and those forest-green eyes finally met hers. His head gave the barest shake. 'Is that so ridiculous?'

The prickling hairs on her arms spread. Like an infectious disease. Reaching parts of her body that definitely shouldn't feel like that.

Although the rage was building inside her, all that came out was a whisper. 'It's ridiculous to me.'

He blinked. She could see herself reflected in his eyes. Hurt was written all over her face. She hated feeling like that. She hated being emotionally vulnerable.

Her mother and father had lived a lie for eighteen years. She'd always promised herself that would never be her life. That would never be her relationship.

She'd thrown caution to the wind and lost. Big style.

He'd made a fool of her. And she'd let him.

'How could you?' she snapped. 'How could you lie to me? What kind of woman do you think I am?'

As she heard the words out loud she almost wanted to hide. She knew exactly what kind of woman she'd been these last two days. One that acted as though this was nothing. She'd experienced a true weekend of passion and abandon. She'd pushed aside all thoughts of consequences and lost herself totally in him.

Ultimate fail.

Now she was looking into the eyes of a man who'd misled her. Let her think that this was something it was not.

He pulled his gaze away from hers, having the good shame to look embarrassed, and ran his hand through his thick dark hair.

But even that annoyed her. She'd spent all weekend running her own fingers through the same hair and right now she knew she'd never do that again.

He reached up and touched her shoulder. 'Sienna, I'm sorry.'

She pulled back as if he'd stung her and his eyes widened.

'Don't touch me. Don't touch me again. Ever!' She spun around and walked back inside.

She ignored everything around her. Ignored the soft

sofas they'd spent many an hour on. Ignored the thick wooden table that they'd eaten more than their dinner from. Ignored the tangled sheets in the white and gold bedroom that told their own story.

She grabbed the few things she'd brought with her—and the few other things she'd bought—and started throwing them into her bag.

Seb rushed in behind her. 'Sienna, slow down. Things weren't meant to happen like this. I'm sorry. I am. I came to the hotel to get away. I came to think about some things.' He ran his fingers through his hair again. 'And then, when I got there, there was just...' he held his hands up towards her '...you,' he said simply.

She spun back around.

'I didn't realise right away who you were. I'd asked Oliver if he could send a surgeon to help with training. I'm the patron of the hospital and they only come to me when there are big issues. The hospital board were unhappy about all our neonates having to be transferred to France for cardiac surgeries. It was time to train our own surgeons—buy our own equipment. But once I'd made the arrangement with Oliver I hadn't really paid attention to all the details. Our hospital director took care of all those because I knew I wouldn't be here. I didn't even recognise your name straight away.'

She felt numb. 'You knew? You knew exactly who I was?'

He sighed heavily and his tanned face paled. 'Not until yesterday when you mentioned you were a surgeon.'

She gulped. She knew exactly what he wasn't saying. Not until after they'd slept together.

'Why didn't you tell me? Why didn't you tell me you knew Oliver yesterday?'

He shook his head. 'Because we'd already taken things further than either of us probably intended. We were in our own little bubble here. And I won't lie. I liked it, Sienna. I liked the fact it was just you and me and the outside world seemed as far away as possible.' He took a deep breath. 'I didn't want to spoil it.' He started pacing around. 'Do you know what it's like to have the eyes of the world constantly on you? Do you know what it's like when every time you even say hello to a woman it's splashed across the press the next day that she could be the next Queen?' The frustration was clearly spilling over.

'You expect me to feel sorry for you?'

He threw up his hands. 'The only time I've had a bit of a normal life was when I was at university. The press were banned from coming near me then. But every moment before that, and every second after it, I've constantly been on display. Life is never normal around me, Sienna. But here—' he indicated the room '—and in Il Palazzo di Cristallo I get a tiny bit of privacy. Do you know how good it felt to walk in somewhere, see a beautiful woman and be able to act on it? Be able to actually let myself feel something?'

Her throat was dry. Emotion and frustration was written all over his face. He couldn't stop pacing.

It was as if the weight of the world were currently sitting on his shoulders. She had no idea what his life was like. She'd no idea what was expected of him. Her insides squirmed. The thought of constantly being watched by the press? No, thanks.

But the anger still burned inside. The hurt at being deceived. How many other women had he brought here? Was she just another on his list?

She stepped up close to him again, ignoring his delicious aftershave that had wound its way around her over the last few days. 'So, everything was actually a lie?'

He winced. 'It wasn't a lie, Sienna.'

'It was to me.'

He shook his head and straightened his shoulders. 'You're overreacting. Even if I had introduced myself,

what difference would it have made?' He moved clos
his chest just in front of her face. 'Are you telling me
that this wouldn't have happened? That we wouldn't have
been attracted to each other? We wouldn't have ended
up together?'

She clouded out his words—focusing only on the first
part. It had been enough to make the red mist descend.
'I'm overreacting?' She dropped the clothes she had
clutched in her hands. 'I'm overreacting?' She let out an
angry breath as her eyes swept the room.

She shook her head. 'Oh, no, Seb. I'm not overreacting.' She picked up the nearest lamp and flung it at the
wall, shattering it into a million pieces. '*This*. This is
overreacting. This is letting you know how I really feel
about your deception.'

His chin practically hung open.

She stalked back to the bed and stuffed the remaining
few items into her bag, zipping it with an over-zealous tug.

She marched right up under his nose. 'If I never see
you again it will be too soon. Next time find someone else
to train your surgeons. Preferably someone who doesn't
mind being deceived and lied to.'

He drew himself up to his full height. On any other
occasion she might have been impressed. But that day?
Not a chance.

His mouth tightened. 'Have it your own way.'

'I will,' she'd shouted as she'd swept out of the chalet
and back into the waiting car. 'Take me back to my hotel,'
she'd growled at the driver.

Heavens. She hoped she hadn't got that poor man fired.
He hadn't even blinked when she'd spoken. Just put the
car into gear and set off down the mountain road. Her
last view of Seb had been as he'd walked to the door and
watched the car take off.

Now, it seemed all a bit melodramatic.

She'd never admit she'd cried on the plane on the way

home. Not to a single person. And especially not to a person she'd now have to tell she was carrying his baby.

Her eyes came into focus sharply and she leaned forward.

The tickertape stream of news changed constantly. Something had made her focus again.

She waited a few seconds.

Prince Sebastian Falco of Montanari has announced his engagement to his childhood friend Princess Theresa Mon Carte of Peruglea. Although the date of their wedding has not yet been announced it is expected to be in the next calendar year. The royal wedding will unite the two neighbouring kingdoms of Montanari and Peruglea.

Every single tiny bit of breath left her body. Her stomach plummeted as a tidal wave of emotions consumed her.

It was as if the glacier ice pool she'd imagined on the mountain of Montanari had followed her home. Nausea made her bolt to the bathroom.

This wasn't morning sickness.

This was pure and utter shock.

He was engaged. Sebastian was engaged.

As she knelt on the bathroom floor she felt momentarily light-headed. Could this be any worse?

She squeezed her eyes closed. Trying to banish all the memories of that weekend from her mind. Her body responded automatically, curling into a ball on the ground. If she didn't think about him, she couldn't hurt. She couldn't let herself hurt like this. She had a baby. A baby to think about.

She pressed her head against the cool tiles on the wall.

Pregnant by a prince. An *engaged* prince.

Funnily enough, no fairy tale she'd ever heard of ended like this.

CHAPTER TWO

December

SHE WAS LATE. Again. And Sienna was never late. She hated people being late. And now she was turning into that person herself.

It was easy to shift the blame. Her obstetrician's clinic was running nearly an hour behind. How ironic. Even being friends with the Assistant Head of Obstetrics around here didn't give her perks—but she could hardly blame him. Oliver had been dealing with a particularly difficult case. It just meant that now she wouldn't complete her rounds and finish when planned.

She hurried across the main entrance of the hospital and tried not to be distracted by the surroundings. The Royal Cheltenham hospital—or Teddy's, as they all affectionately called it—did Christmas with style.

A huge tree adorned the glass atrium. Red and gold lights twinkled merrily against the already darkening sky. The tea room near the front entrance—staffed by volunteers—had its own display. A complete Santa sleigh and carved wooden reindeers with red Christmas baubles on their noses. Piped music surrounded her. Not loud enough to be intrusive, but just enough to set the scene for Christmas, as an array of traditional carols and favourite pop tunes permeated the air around her.

Sienna couldn't help but smile. Christmas was her absolute favourite time of year. The one time of year her parents actually stopped fighting. Her mother's sister, Aunt Margaret, had always visited at this time of year. Her warmth and love of Christmas had been infectious. As soon as she walked in the house, the frosty atmosphere just seemed to vanish. If Margaret sensed anything, she never acknowledged it. It seemed it wasn't the 'done thing' to fight and argue in front of Aunt Margaret and Sienna loved the fact that for four whole days she didn't have to worry at all.

Aunt Margaret's love of Christmas had continued— for Sienna, at least—long after she'd died. Sienna's own Christmas tree had gone up on the first of December. Multicoloured lights were decorating the now bare cherry blossom at the bottom of her garden. She wasn't even going to admit how they got there.

It seemed that Mother Nature was even trying to get in on the act. A light dusting of snow currently covered the glass atrium at Teddy's.

This time next year would be even more special. This time next year would be her baby's first Christmas. A smile spread across Sienna's face.

Thoughts like that made her forget about her aching back and sore feet. At thirty-four weeks pregnant she was due to start maternity leave some time soon. Oliver had arranged for some maternity cover, and he'd had the good sense to start her replacement early. Max Ainsley was proving more than capable.

He'd picked up the electronic systems and referral pathways of Teddy's easily. It meant that she'd be able to relax at home when the baby arrived instead of fretting over cancelled surgeries and babies and families having to travel for miles to get the same standard of care.

She hurried into the neonatal unit and stuffed her bag into the duty room. She looked up and took a deep breath.

Every cot was full. An influx of winter virus had hit the
unit a few weeks ago. That, along with delivery of a set of
premature quads—one of whom needed surgery—meant
that the staff were run off their feet.

Ruth, one of the neonatal nurses, shot her a sympathetic look. 'You doing okay, Sienna?'

Sienna straightened up and rubbed her back, then her
protruding stomach. She was used to the sideways glances
from members of staff. As she'd never dated anyone from
the hospital and most of the staff knew she lived alone,
speculation about her pregnancy had been rife.

The best rumour that she'd heard was that she'd decided she didn't need a man and had just used a sperm
donor to have a baby on her own. If only it were true.

She'd stopped watching the news channel. Apart from
weather reports and occasional badly behaved sportsmen,
it seemed that her favourite news channel had developed
an obsession with the upcoming royal wedding in Montanari early next year.

News was obviously slow. But if she saw one more shot
of Seb with his arm around the cut-out perfect blonde she
would scream. She didn't care that they looked a little
awkward together. She just didn't want to see them at all.

She smiled at Ruth. 'I'm doing fine, thanks. Just had
my check-up. Six weeks to go.' She waved her hand at the
array of cots. 'I've got three babies to review. I'm hoping
we can get at least two of them home for their first Christmas in the next few days. What do you think?'

As she said the words her Head Neonatal Nurse appeared behind Ruth. She'd worked with Annabelle
Ainsley for the last year and had been more than a little
surprised when it had been revealed that Annabelle was
actually Max's estranged wife. She hadn't been surprised
that it had only taken them a week to reconcile once he'd
started working at Teddy's. For the last couple of weeks

Annabelle hadn't stopped smiling, so she was surprised to see her looking so serious this afternoon.

'There's someone here to see you.' The normally unfazed Annabelle looked a little uncomfortable.

Sienna picked up the nearest tablet to check over one of her patients. 'Who is it? A rep? Tell them I don't have time, I'm sorry.' She gave Annabelle a smile. 'I think I should maybe hand all the reps over to Max now—what do you think?'

Annabelle glanced at Ruth. 'It's not a rep. I don't recognise him and didn't have time to ask his name. He's insisting that he'll only speak to you and…' she took a breath '…he won't be kept waiting.'

Sienna sat the tablet back down, satisfied with the recordings. Her post-surgery baby was doing well. She shook her head. 'Well, who does he think he is?' She looked around the unit and paused. 'Wait? Is it a parent of one of the babies? Or someone with a surgery scheduled for their child? You know that I'll speak to them.'

Annabelle shook her head firmly. 'No. None of those. No parents—or impending parents. It's something else entirely.' She handed a set of notes to Ruth. 'Can you check on little Maisy Allerton? She didn't take much at her last feed.'

Ruth nodded and disappeared. Annabelle pressed her lips together. 'This guy, he says it's personal.'

Sienna felt an uncomfortable prickle across her skin. 'Personal? Who would have something personal to talk to me about?'

The words were out before she even thought about them. Nothing like making herself sound sad and lonely. Did people at Teddy's even think she had a personal life?

Annabelle's eyes darted automatically to Sienna's protruding stomach, then she flushed as she realised Sienna had noticed.

Sienna straightened her shoulders. She'd never been

a fan of anyone trying to push her around. She gave Annabelle a wide smile. 'Oh, he's insisting, is he?'

Annabelle nodded then her eyes narrowed and she folded her arms across her chest. She'd worked with Sienna long enough to sense trouble ahead.

Sienna kept smiling. 'Well, in that case, I'll review my three babies. Talk to all sets of parents. I might make a few phone calls to some parents with babies on my list between Christmas and New Year, and then...' she paused as she picked up the tablet again to start accessing a file '...then, as a heavily pregnant woman, I think I'll go and have something to eat. I missed lunch and—' she raised her eyebrows at Annabelle '—I have a feeling a colleague I work with might *insist* I don't faint at work.'

Annabelle smiled too and nodded knowingly. 'Not that I want to be any influence on you, but the kitchen staff made killer carrot cake today. I think it could count as one of your five a day.'

Sienna threw back her head and laughed. 'You're such a bad influence but I could definitely be persuaded.' Her eyes went straight back to the chart. 'Okay, so let's see Kendall first. Mr I-Insist is just going to have to find out how things work around here.'

Annabelle gave a smile and put an arm at Sienna's back. 'Don't worry. Somehow I think you'll be more than a match for him. Give me a signal when you come back. I can always page you after five minutes to give you an escape.'

Sienna nodded. She didn't really care who was waiting for her—her babies would always come first.

Seb was furious. He kept glancing at his watch. He'd been in this room for over an hour—his security detail waiting outside.

The sister of the neonatal ward had seemed surprised at first by his insistence at seeing Sienna. Then, she'd explained Sienna was at another appointment and would be back soon. What exactly meant *soon* at the Royal Cheltenham?

He'd paced the corridors a few times looking for her with no success. The doors to the neonatal unit had a coded lock, and, from the look of the anxious parents hurrying in and out, it really wasn't a place he wanted to be.

He'd been stunned when Oliver Darrington had phoned him to discuss his own difficult situation—after a one-night stand a colleague was pregnant. A colleague who he had feelings for. Oliver had been Sebastian's friend since they'd attended university together, even though they were destined for completely different lives.

He hadn't told Oliver a thing about his weekend with Sienna, so when Oliver had mentioned that Sienna too was pregnant, Sebastian had felt as if he couldn't breathe.

His tongue had stuck to the roof of his mouth and his brain had scrambled to ask the question he'd wanted to, without giving himself away. According to Oliver she was heavily pregnant—due to have her baby at the end of January.

For a few seconds Seb had felt panicked. The dates fitted perfectly. He didn't have a single doubt that her baby could be his.

He could hardly remember the rest of the conversation with Oliver. That made him cringe now. It was a complete disservice to his friend.

He'd had things to deal with.

Since Sienna had stormed out of his chalet retreat his life had turned upside down. He'd followed his parents' wishes and allowed the announcement of the engagement. Theresa had seemed indifferent. Uniting the kingdoms had been important to her too. But marrying someone she wasn't in love with didn't seem any more appealing to her than it was to him.

If Sienna hadn't happened, maybe, just maybe, he

could have mustered some enthusiasm and tried to persuade Theresa their relationship could work.

But his nights had been haunted with dreams of being tangled in the sheets with a passionate woman with ash-blonde hair, caramel-coloured eyes and a firm, toned body.

She'd ignited a flame inside him. Something that had burned underneath the surface since she'd left. He'd been a fool. A fool to let his country think he would take part in a union he didn't think he could make work.

His parents had been beside themselves with anger at the broken engagement.

Theresa had been remarkably stoic about him breaking the engagement. She'd handed back the yellow diamond ring with a nod of her head. He suspected her heart lay somewhere else. Her voice had been tight. 'I hadn't got around to finalising the design for my wedding dress yet. The designer was furious with me. It's just as well really, isn't it?'

He'd felt bad as he bent to kiss her cheek. Theresa wasn't really upset with him. Not yet, anyway. She might be angrier when she found out about the baby. It could be embarrassing for her. He only hoped she would have moved on to wherever her heart truly lay.

The Head of his PR had nearly had a heart attack. He'd actually put his hand to his chest and turned an alarming shade of grey. And that had given Sebastian instant inspiration. In amongst breaking the news to both Theresa and his parents, Sebastian had spent the last two weeks doing something else—making arrangements to twin the Cheltenham hospital with the Montanari Royal General. He was already a patron of his own hospital; a sizeable donation would make him a patron of Teddy's too.

It was the perfect cover story. He could come to the Royal Cheltenham without people asking too many questions. Oliver had been surprised for around five minutes.

Then, he'd made him an appointment with the board. In the meantime, Sebastian could come freely to the hospital with his security and press team in tow. The announcement was due to be made tomorrow. Seb was hoping he could also make an announcement of his own.

He glanced at his watch again as the anger built in his chest. Sienna hadn't even contacted him. Hadn't even let him know he was going to be a father. Was her intention to leave his child fatherless? For the heir of Montanari not to be acknowledged or have their rightful inheritance?

That could never happen. He wouldn't *allow* that to happen. Not in his lifetime.

He heard a familiar voice drifting down the corridor towards him. It sent every sense on fire. That familiar Scottish twang. The voice she'd invited him to listen to all night...

'No problem. I'll be along to review the chest X-ray in five minutes. Thanks, Max.'

The footsteps neared but he wasn't prepared for the sight. Last time he'd seen Sienna she'd been toned and athletic. This time the rounded belly appeared before she did.

Her footsteps stopped dead in the doorway, her eyes wide. It was clear he was the last person she'd been expecting to see.

She took his breath away. She didn't have on a traditional white coat. Instead she was dressed in what must be a maternity alternative to a suit. Black trousers with a matching black tunic over the top. It was still smart. Still professional. Her hair was gleaming, a bit longer than he remembered and tucked behind her ears. A red stethoscope hung around her neck, matching her bright red lipstick.

'Sebastian.' It was more a breath than a word.

Her hand went automatically to her stomach. His reply stuck in his throat. He hadn't been ready. He hadn't been ready for the sight of her ripe with his child. Even under her smart clothes he could see her lean body had changed totally. Her breasts were much bigger than before—and they suited her. Pregnancy suited her in a way he couldn't even have imagined.

But now he was here, he just didn't even know where to start.

This wasn't happening. Not here. Not now.

She'd planned things so carefully. All her surgeries were over. Any new patients had been seen jointly with Max. He would perform the neonatal surgeries and she would do later follow up once she was back from maternity leave.

But here he was. Right in front of her. The guy she'd spent the last six months half cursing, half pining for.

Those forest-green eyes practically swept up and down her body. Her palm itched. That thick dark hair. The hair she'd spent two days and two nights running her fingers through. Those broad shoulders, filling out the exquisitely cut suit. The pale lilac of the shirt and the shocking pink of his tie with his dark suit and good looks made him look like one of the models adorning the billboards above Times Square in New York. Imagine waking up with that staring in your hotel window every morning.

Her breath had left her lungs. It was unnatural. It was ridiculous. He was just a man. She sucked in a breath and narrowed her gaze. 'Congratulations on your engagement.'

He flinched. What had he expected? That she'd welcome him here with open arms?

Part of her felt a tiny twinge of regret. Her hand had picked up the phone more times than she could count. She'd tried to have that conversation with Oliver on a number of occasions. But it was clear that he'd never realised what was behind her tiny querying questions. The thought that his friend might have had a liaison with his colleague obviously hadn't even entered his mind.

Was it really such a stretch of the imagination?

Sebastian let out a sigh and stepped towards her. She held up her hand automatically to stop him getting too close—last thing she needed was to get a whiff of that familiar aftershave. She didn't need any more memories of the past than she already had. Baby was more than enough.

The royal persona she'd seen on the TV news seemed to be the man in the room with her now. This wasn't the cheeky, flirtatious, incredibly sexy guy that she'd spent two days and two nights with. Maybe her Seb didn't really exist at all?

There was something else. An air about him she hadn't noticed before. Or maybe she hadn't been paying attention. An assurance. A confidence. The kind of persona that actually fitted with being a prince.

He caught the hand she held in front of her.

The effect was instant, a rush of warmth and a pure overload of memories of the last time he'd touched her.

If she hadn't been standing so squarely she might have swayed. Her senses were alight. Now, his aftershave was reaching across the short space between them like a cowboy's rope pulling her in. Her hand tingled from where he held it. His grip initially had been firm but now it changed and his thumb moved under her palm, tracing circles— just as he'd done months ago.

Her breathing stalled. No. No, she wasn't going to go here again.

This was the man that had announced his engagement a few weeks after they'd met. An engagement to a childhood friend. Had he been seeing her the whole time? She'd checked. But the media wasn't sure. Had he been sleeping with them both at the same time?

She had no idea.

But no matter what her senses were doing, thoughts like that coloured her opinion of the man. He hadn't been honest with her. They hadn't promised each other anything, but that didn't matter.

She snatched her hand back.

'I'm not engaged, Sienna. I broke off my engagement when I heard the news you were pregnant.' His voice was as smooth as silk.

She felt herself bristle. 'And what am I supposed to feel—grateful?'

He didn't even blink. He just kept talking. 'I heard the news from Oliver. He called me about something else. A woman. Ella? Do you know her?'

Sienna frowned. 'Yes, yes, I know her. She's a midwife here.' She paused. Did Sebastian know the full story?

'They're engaged,' she said carefully, missing out the part that Ella was pregnant too. She wasn't sure just how much Oliver would have told Sebastian.

A wide smile broke across Sebastian's face. 'Perfect. I'll need to congratulate him.' His focus came back on Sienna. 'Maybe we could have a joint wedding?'

'A what?' Someone walking past the door turned their head at the rise of her voice. 'Are you crazy?'

Sebastian shook his head. 'Why would you think I'm crazy?'

He drew himself up in front of her. 'You're carrying the heir to the Montanari throne. We might still have things to sort out, but I'd prefer it if the heir to the throne was legitimate. Wouldn't you? If you come back with me now we can be married as soon as we get there. We can tell the world we met when you came to work in Montanari Royal General. Everything fits.'

He made it all sound so normal. So rational. So matter-of-fact.

She wasn't hearing this. She wasn't. It was some sick, delusional dream. She thought back to everything she'd eaten today. Maybe she'd been exposed to something weird.

He reached into his pocket and pulled out a ring. 'Here.'

She wasn't thinking straight and held out her hand. 'What is it?'

One of the ward clerks walked past and raised her eyebrows at the sight of the way-too-big diamond. Perfect. Just perfect. She was already the talk of the place and Polly was the world's biggest gossip. She just prayed that Polly hadn't recognised Sebastian.

She flinched and pulled her hand away. 'What am I supposed to do with that?'

'Put it on,' he said simply, glancing at her as if it were a stupid question. 'You need to wear an engagement ring.' He paused for a second and looked at her face. 'Don't you like it? It's a family heirloom.' His forehead wrinkled. 'I'm sure I can find you something else in the family vault.'

She shook her head and started pacing. 'It doesn't matter if I like it. I don't want it. I don't need it. I'm—' She stopped and placed her hand on her stomach. '*We're* going nowhere. I have a job here. A home. The very last place I'm going is Montanari. And the very last thing I'm doing...' she paused again and shook her head, trying to make sense of the craziness around her. She drew in a deep breath and stepped right up to him, poking her finger in her chest. 'The very last thing I'm doing is marrying you.'

Now Sebastian started shaking his head. He had the absolute gall to look surprised. 'Why on earth not? You're expecting our child. You're going to be the mother of the heir to Montanari. We should get married. And as soon as possible.' He said it as if it made perfect sense.

Sienna put her hands on her back and started pacing. 'No. No, we absolutely shouldn't.'

Sebastian held out his hands. 'Sienna, in a few years you get to be the Queen of Montanari. What woman wouldn't want that?'

She shuddered. She actually shuddered. 'Oh, no. Oh, no.'

Sebastian's brow creased. 'What on earth is wrong? We can have a state wedding in Montanari...' he glanced at her stomach and gave a little shrug '...but we'll need to be quick.'

Sienna took a step back. 'Okay, were you really this crazy when I met you in Montanari and I just didn't notice? Because this is nowhere near normal.' She put her hand on her stomach. 'Yes, I'm pregnant. Yes, I'm pregnant with your baby. But that's it, Sebastian. This isn't the Dark Ages. I don't want your help—or need it.' She ran her fingers through her hair, trying to contemplate all the things she hadn't even considered. 'Look at me, Sebastian. I live here. In the Cotswolds. I came here from Edinburgh. I purposely chose to come here. I've bought my dream house. I have a great job and colleagues that I like and admire. I've arranged a childcare for my baby and cover for my maternity leave.' She could feel herself getting agitated. Her voice was getting louder the longer that she spoke. 'I won't keep you from our baby. You can have as much—or as little—contact as you want. But don't expect to waltz in here and take over our lives.' She pressed her hand to her chest. 'This is my life, Sebastian. *My life.* I don't need your money and I don't need your help. I'm perfectly capable of raising this baby on my own.'

Polly walked past again. It was obviously deliberate. Not only was she spying, now she was eavesdropping too.

With a burst of pure frustration Sienna kicked the door closed.

Sebastian raised his eyebrows.

She took a deep breath. 'I need you to go. I need you to leave. I can't deal with this now.'

Her lips pressed tight together and resisted the temptation to say the words she was truly thinking.

Sebastian seemed to have frozen on the spot. The air of assurance had disappeared.

It was then she saw it. The look. The expression.

He'd actually expected her to say yes.

He hadn't expected her to reject him. He hadn't expected a no.

Sebastian Falco was hurt.

Now, it was her that was surprised. It struck her in a way she didn't expect. She could almost see a million things circulating around in his brain—as if he was trying to find a new way to persuade her to go with him.

She could see the little vein pulsing at the base of his throat.

Her mouth was dry.

If she were five years old—this would be her dream. Well, not the pregnancy, but the thought of a prince sweeping in and saying he would marry her, presenting her with a huge diamond ring and the chance to one day be Queen.

But it had been a long time since Sienna had been five.

And her ambitions and dreams had changed so much they could move mountains.

Sebastian folded his arms across his chest. 'Why didn't you call me, Sienna?' His voice was rigid. 'Why didn't you phone and tell me as soon as you knew you were pregnant?'

Oh. That.

She should have expected it to come up.

'I was going to. I meant to. But the day I did my pregnancy test was the day your engagement was announced on the national news.' She looked at him directly, trying to push away the tiny part of guilt curling in her stomach.

'Between that, and finding out I was pregnant, it kind of took the feet out from under me.'

He broke their gaze for a second, his words measured. 'Theresa was a friend. It wasn't going to be a marriage of love. It was going to be a union of kingdoms. Something my parents wanted very much.'

'How romantic.'

She couldn't help herself. She'd been a child of a loveless marriage. She knew the effects it had. She raised her eyes to the ceiling. 'Well, your parents must be delighted about me. I guess I'm going to be the national scandal.'

She'd been delusional. She'd thought she knew this man—even a little. But nothing about this fitted with the two days they'd spent together. The Sebastian she'd known then was a man who actually felt and thought. He'd laughed and joked and made her the coffee she craved. He'd cuddled up beside her in bed and taken her to places she'd never been before. He'd gently stroked the back of her neck as she'd fallen asleep. He was someone she'd loved being around.

Too bad all of it had been a lie.

The man in front of her now was the Sebastian that appeared on the news. The one with a fixed smile and his arm around someone else.

That was what it was. That was what she'd always noticed. Even though she'd tried not to watch him on the news—she'd tried to always switch channel—on the few occasions she had seen pictures of him, something had never seemed quite right.

She'd always tried not to look too closely. Her heart wouldn't let her go there. Not at all.

But little things were falling into place.

The smile had never reached his eyes.

Now, the look in his eyes seemed sincere. His tone much softer. 'You can be whatever you want to be, Sienna. I'd just like you to do it as my wife.'

This look was familiar. She'd seen it so many times on the weekend they'd spent together. In between the flirting, fun and cheekiness there had been flashes of sincerity.

That had been the thing that made his untruthfulness so hard to take.

The room was starting to feel oh-so-small.

'Why didn't you call me later?'

It didn't matter that she'd just sipped some water. Her mouth felt dry. He wasn't going to let this go. He was calling her on it.

She licked her lips. 'I wanted to. I thought about it. But we didn't exactly exchange numbers. How easy is it to call a royal palace and ask to speak to the Prince?'

He shifted a little uncomfortably, then shook his head. 'You could have asked Oliver. You knew we were friends. He was the one who recommended you. He would have given you the number whenever you asked.'

'And how would that work out? "Oh, Oliver? Can you give me Seb's mobile number, please? I want to tell him that I'm going to ruin his engagement by letting him know I'm pregnant. You know, the engagement to his child-hood sweetheart?" At least that's the way it sounded in the media.'

He smiled. He actually smiled.

'You think it's funny?'

'No. Not at all. But that's the first time you've called me Seb since I got here.' He stepped forward.

She sucked in a breath.

She hadn't even noticed.

Seb was too close again. She needed some space, some distance between them.

He touched her arm. Her bare skin almost caught fire. There was no opportunity to flinch or pull away. His palm surrounded her slim wrist. 'I've told you. It was never like that with Theresa. We just didn't think of each other that way. And we'd never been childhood sweethearts. We were friends. Just friends.'

'You've told her about the pregnancy?'

He gave a little grimace. 'Not exactly. Not yet anyway.' He ran his fingers through his hair. 'I wasn't quite sure how to put it.'

'You were sleeping with us both?'

She couldn't help it. It just came out.

'What? No.' Sebastian shook his head again. 'I've never slept with Theresa. I've told you. It wasn't that kind of relationship. I don't sleep with my friends.'

She hated the way that relief flooded through her. The sincerity was written all over his face. He might have lied by omission before but she was certain he wasn't lying now.

She met his gaze. 'How will she feel when she finds out? It will look to the world as if you've made a fool of her. As if *we've* made a fool of her. I hate that. I don't want anyone to think I'd have an affair with someone else's man.'

He sucked in a deep breath and reached up towards her face. 'But I wasn't in a relationship with Theresa. I was single. I was free when we were together. And if I'd known you were pregnant I would never have let my parents force me into announcing an engagement.' His hand brushed her cheek and his fingers tangled in her hair.

This was what he'd done when they'd been together. This was how he'd pulled her into *that* first kiss.

The touch should have been mesmerising. But his words left her cold.

Forced. He'd never really mentioned his parents in their short time together.

'They forced you? I didn't think you'd let anyone force you to do anything.' There was an air of challenge in her voice.

He recognised it and raised his eyebrows. He gave her a half-smile. 'You haven't met my parents—yet.'

It was her first truly uncomfortable feeling. The King and Queen of Montanari. They wouldn't like her. They wouldn't like her at all. She'd ruined the plan to unite the neighbouring kingdoms and was going to give Montanari an illegitimate heir. Her face was probably currently fixed to a dartboard or archery target in their throne room.

'And are they forcing you to do this too?' The words came out in a whisper. Every muscle in her body was tensed.

Duty. That was what she was sensing here.

He might be sincere. But there was no love—no compassion here. Tears threatened to fill her eyes. She licked her dry lips and stepped back, out of his hold. He hadn't answered her question and she couldn't quite believe how hurt she felt.

'I think you should go back to Montanari, Sebastian. I'll let you know when the baby arrives and we can sort things out from there.'

He looked surprised, his hand still in the air from where he'd touched her hair. He stared at it for a second, then shook his head. 'Who says I'm going back to Montanari?'

She concentrated on her shoes. It was easier than looking at him. 'Well, you will, won't you? You'll have—' she waved her hand '—princely duties or something to do. You can't stay here. There's been enough tittle-tattle about who the father of my baby is. The last thing I want is for someone to realise who you are and gossip about us. I'm the talk of the steamie already.'

He shook his head in bewilderment. 'The what?'

'The steamie. You know—the washhouse.'

He shook his head. 'I have no idea what you're talking about. But you know what? Just keep talking. I'd forgotten how much I loved the sound of your voice.'

Ditto.

'The steamie. It's a Scottish term for an old wash-house—the place where people used to go and wash their clothes before everyone had washing machines. It was notorious. The women used to always gossip in there.'

'So, that's what we could be? The talk of the steamie?'

She nodded again. 'And I'd rather not be. It would be easier if you left. We can talk. We can make plans about access arrangements when the baby arrives. We have another six weeks to wait. There's enough time.'

'Oh, no, you don't,' he replied promptly.

She had a bad feeling about this. 'What do you mean?'

'I'm not going anywhere. I've already missed out on things. I'm not missing out on anything else.'

'What do you mean by that?' she asked again.

He leaned against the door jamb and folded his arms across his chest. There was a determined grin on his face. 'I've got work to do here.' He mimicked her hand wave. 'Princely duties. I need to sort out the twinning of our hospitals and iron out all the details. Get used to me being around.' He gave her a little nod. 'I'm your new best friend.'

CHAPTER THREE

IF HE DIDN'T love his friend so much he'd be annoyed by the permanent smile that seemed to have fixed itself to Oliver's face. Even sitting at a desk swamped with paperwork, Oliver still had the smile plastered on his face.

'Sebastian!' Oliver jumped to his feet, strode around the desk and engulfed Sebastian in a bear hug.

Sebastian returned the hug and leaned back. 'You're engaged? Do I get to meet the lucky lady?'

Oliver slapped his arm. 'You get to be my best man!' His smile wavered for a second. 'Are you here for the announcement tomorrow? I thought I would have heard from you.'

Sebastian gave a brief nod. He pushed his hands into his pockets and looked at Oliver. 'Not just that. It seems you and I are about to experience some changes together.'

Oliver's brow furrowed at the cryptic line. 'What do you mean?'

Sebastian glanced around. There was no one hovering near the door. Oliver's office seemed private enough. 'We're both about to be fathers.'

For a few seconds Oliver's expression was pure surprise. 'Theresa's pregnant? Congratulations. I had no idea—'

Sebastian held up his hand to stop him. Of course he

was surprised. He knew Sebastian's real feelings about that engagement.

He shook his head. 'It's not Theresa.'

Oliver paled. 'It's not?'

They were good friends. He'd experienced Sebastian's parents. He knew exactly how focused and overbearing they could be. They'd spent many hours and a number of cases of beer contemplating the pressures of being an heir, along with Sebastian's personal feelings and ambitions.

The grin that spread over Oliver's face took Sebastian by surprise. He let out a laugh and walked back around the desk, pushing his wheeled chair back, putting his feet on the desk and crossing his arms. 'Oh, this is going to be good. Tell me all about it.'

Sebastian shook his head and leaned on the chair opposite Oliver. 'You find this amusing?'

Oliver nodded. 'I find this very amusing. It's only taken you thirty-one years to cause a scandal. I hope it's a good one.'

Sebastian made a face. 'You might change your mind when you find out the rest of it.'

'What's that supposed to mean?'

Sebastian shook his head again. 'Is everything set for the board meeting tomorrow?'

Oliver nodded. 'It's just a formality. They've already agreed to twin the hospitals and develop the training programme. You realise as soon as it's announced there'll be around forty staff queued outside my door trying to get their name on the reciprocal swap programme?'

Sebastian took a deep breath. Was there even a chance in a million that Sienna might consider something like that?

He was still smarting about her reaction earlier. What was wrong with making the heir to the Montanari throne legitimate? It made perfect sense to him.

Why was she so against it? He'd still felt the chemistry in the air between them—even if she wanted to deny it. He could admit that the timing wasn't great. But he'd dealt with things as best he could.

At the end of the day it was his duty to marry the mother of his baby. Maybe he could work on her, get her to reconsider?

'I plan on being around for the next few days—maybe longer.'

Oliver glanced at him. Sebastian's visits were usually only when he flew in and out of the UK on business and usually only lasted a couple of hours.

'Really, why?'

He'd picked up a pen and was scribbling notes.

Sebastian lowered his voice. 'Because I have to convince the mother of my child to marry me.'

The pen froze and oh-so-slowly one of Oliver's eyebrows rose. 'Say that again?'

Sebastian sat back in the chair and relaxed his arms back. He felt better after saying it out loud. It didn't seem quite so ridiculous a thought.

'Sienna—the mother of my child. I have to convince her to marry me.'

The pen flew past his ear. Oliver was on his feet. 'What? What do you mean, Sienna?' His head turned quickly from side to side. 'I mean, you? Her? The baby? It's yours?' It was almost as if he were trying to sort it all out in his mind. Then his eyes widened and he crumpled back down into his seat.

'Oh, no.' He looked as if he were going to be sick on the desk. 'How did you find out?' He didn't even wait for an answer. His head was already in his hands.

Sebastian gave a nod, reached over and clapped the side of one of Oliver's hands. 'Yep. It was you. You phoned about Ella and mentioned Sienna and how pregnant she was.'

Oliver's head shot back up. 'I thought you'd gone quiet

when we spoke but I just assumed it was because you were surprised when I said Ella was pregnant.'

'It wasn't Ella's pregnancy that surprised me.'

Oliver ran his hand through his hair. 'Yeah, obviously.'

He wrinkled his nose and a smile broke out on his face. 'You and Sienna, really?'

Sebastian was curious. 'What's so strange about me and Sienna?'

Oliver threw up his hands. 'It's just…it's just…she's so… *Sienna*.' He shook his head and laughed. 'Your parents will hate her. She'd be their ultimate nightmare for a queen.'

Sebastian felt a little flare of protective anger. 'What's that supposed to mean?'

Oliver shrugged. 'Where will I start? She's a surgeon. She's *always* going to be a surgeon. Sienna would never give up her job—she's just too good and too emotionally connected. Surgery is in her blood.' He was shaking his head. 'As for tactfulness and decorum? Sienna's one of the most straight-talking doctors I've ever known. She doesn't take any prisoners. She wouldn't spend hours trying to butter up some foreign dignitary. She'd tell them exactly what she expected of them and then move on to dessert.' He tapped his fingers on the table and stared up to the left for a second. 'It's almost like you picked the person least like your mother in the whole world. Except for looks, of course. Your mother was probably born knowing she'd one day be Queen. I bet even as a child Sienna never played dress-up princesses or looked for a prince. She'd have been too busy setting up her dolls' hospital.'

Sebastian had been about to interrupt, instead he took a breath. Oliver had absolutely nailed it.

Sienna was a career woman. His mother had always taken a back seat to his father in every way.

Sienna hadn't been scared to shout at him. He'd never heard his mother raise her voice in her life.

Sienna hadn't been afraid to be bold and take him up on his proposition. Her comment *How about you listen to it all night instead?* had haunted his dreams in every erotic way possible. His mother would have a heart attack if she ever knew.

Just as well Sienna was a doctor really.

The reality of his future life was starting to crash all around him. Sebastian didn't panic. He'd never panicked. But he felt wary. If he didn't handle things well this could be a disaster.

Could Sienna McDonald really be the future Queen of Montanari?

He leaned back and folded his arms. 'She's the mother of my child. Montanari needs an heir. It's my duty to marry her.'

Oliver raised his eyebrows. 'Please tell me you didn't just say that?'

When Sebastian didn't answer right away, Oliver shook his head. 'More importantly, please tell me you didn't say that to Sienna?'

Sebastian ignored the comment. 'Montanari needs change. Sienna will be just the breath of fresh air it needs. Who couldn't love her? She's a neonatal surgeon. She eats, breathes and sleeps her job. People will admire her intelligence. They'll admire her dedication. I know I do.'

Oliver started tapping his fingers on the table again. 'And what does Sienna have to say about all this?'

He was good. He was too good. He clearly knew Sienna well.

'Let's just say that Sienna and I are a work in progress.'

Oliver let out something resembling a snort. He stood up again. 'You're my oldest friend, Sebastian, but I'm telling you right now, I'm not choosing sides. She's one of my best doctors. Upset her and you'll upset me.' He gave a little shudder. 'She'll kill me when she finds out it was me that told you.' He leaned against the wall for a second. 'Why didn't she tell you herself?'

Sebastian shrugged slightly. 'Timing, she says. I'd just got engaged.'

Oliver rolled his eyes then narrowed them again. 'And why didn't you tell me that you'd got in a compromising position with one of my doctors?' He wagged his finger at Sebastian. 'Can't trust you for two minutes. I'll need to rethink this whole hospital-twinning thing. Can't have us sending all our doctors over there to get seduced by Montanari men—royal or not.'

Sebastian stood up. 'I have a baby on the way. My priorities have changed.' He headed to the door. 'I'll see you at the board meeting tomorrow—and for the press announcement.'

Oliver gave a nod. He tipped his head to one side. 'So, what's your next plan?'

Sebastian shot him a wide smile. 'Charm. Why else be a prince?'

Sienna stuck her head outside the doors to the paediatric ICU, then ducked back inside, keeping her nose pressed against the glass. The tinsel taped to the window tickled her nose and partially blocked her view.

'What are you doing?' asked an amused Charlie Warren, one of her OBGYN colleagues.

'I'd have thought that was clear. I'm hiding.' Her ever-expanding belly was stopping her from getting a clear view.

Charlie laughed. 'And who are you hiding from?'

'You know. Him.'

'Him, who?'

Sienna sighed and turned around, leaning back against the door.

'Sebastian.'

Charlie nodded slowly. 'Ah…now I see.'

Sienna brushed a lock of loose hair out of her eyes. 'I see the Teddy's super-speed grapevine is working as well as ever. He's been here less than twenty-four hours.'

Charlie leaned against the door with her and gave her a knowing smile.

'What are you grinning at?' she half snapped.

She'd always liked Charlie. They got on well. All her colleagues had been so supportive of her pregnancy. She stared at him again.

'There's something different about you.'

'There is? What?' He had a dopey kind of grin on his face.

She pointed. 'That. You've got the same look that Oliver is wearing.'

'I don't know what you mean.'

She poked her finger in his chest. 'Oh, yes, you do. What's her name?'

She was definitely curious. She'd spent the last week so wrapped up with preparations for Christmas and trying to keep her energy up that she'd obviously missed something important. Charlie was a widower. For as long as she'd known him there had been veiled shadows behind his eyes.

They were gone now. And it made her heart sing a little to see that.

He gave her a sheepish smile. 'It's Juliet.'

Sienna's mouth dropped open. 'No.' Then she couldn't help but grin. 'Really?' She got on well with the Aussie surgeon who'd performed *in-utero* surgery to save the life of a quad born at Teddy's last week.

His smile said it all. 'Really.'

She leaned against the door again. 'Oh, wow.' She flicked her hair back. It was really beginning to annoy her. 'First Oliver and now you. Lovesick people are falling all over the place.' She gave him a wicked glare. 'Better phone Public Health, it looks like we've got an infectious disease here.'

He nodded. 'Don't forget Max and Annabelle. This thing is spreading faster than that winter virus.' He gave her a cheeky wink. 'And from what I saw this morning at breakfast, others might eventually succumb.'

Heat rushed into her cheeks. She'd come in early this morning and walked along to the canteen for breakfast. She'd barely sat down before Sebastian had ambushed her and sat down at the other side of the table with coffee, toast and eggs.

It had been excruciating. She could sense every eye in the canteen on them both and it had been as quick as she could bolt down her porridge and hurry out of there.

Normally she loved breakfast in the canteen at Christmas time. Christmas pop tunes were always playing and the menu food got new names like Rudolph's raisin pancakes or Santa's scrumptious scrambled egg.

'I don't know what you mean,' she said defensively to Charlie, who was obviously trying to wind her up.

He laughed as he pulled open the door and looked out for a second. 'He seems like a nice guy. Maybe you should give him a chance.'

She laid her hand on her large stomach. 'Oh, I think it's pretty obvious I've already given him a chance.'

He just kept laughing. 'Well, he's on the charm offensive. And he's winning. Everyone that's met him thinks he's one version of wonderful or another. Including Juliet's daughter.'

'He's met her daughter?'

Charlie nodded. 'She loves him already. He gave her some kind of doll that the little girls in Montanari love. A special Christmas one with a red and green dress. She was over the moon.'

Sienna wrinkled her nose. 'You shouldn't let her speak to strangers.'

Something flashed over Charlie's face. 'If I didn't know any better, Sienna, I'd think you were a woman reaching that crabby stage just before she delivers.'

She shook her head fiercely and patted her stomach. 'Oh, no. No way. I've got just under six weeks. This baby is not coming out before then.'

'If you say so.' Charlie stuck his head out of the door again. 'Okay, you can go. The coast is clear. Just remember to be on your best behaviour.' He held the door before her as she rushed outside. 'And just remember... I recognise the signs.'

The coast wasn't clear at all.

Sebastian was waiting outside the unit, leaning against the wall with his arms folded.

'I'm going to kill Charlie with my bare hands,' she muttered.

It didn't help that he was looking even sexier than before. When he'd joined her this morning at breakfast he'd been wearing a suit and tie. Something to do with a business meeting. She hadn't really been paying attention.

Now, he'd changed into jeans, a leather jacket and a slim-fitting black T-shirt. His hair was speckled with flecks of snow.

'What are you doing here?' she asked as she made her best attempt to sweep past.

Sebastian was having none of it. He fell into step beside her. 'Waiting for you.'

She stopped walking and turned to face him. She wanted to be angry with him. She wanted to be annoyed. But he had that look on his face, that hint of cheek. He was deliberately taunting her. They'd spent most of the weekend in Montanari batting smart comments back and forth. This felt more like sun-blessed Montanari than the snow-dusted Cotswolds.

She stifled her smile. 'This better not get to be a habit. I'm busy, Seb. I'm at work.'

His grin broadened and she realised her error. She'd called him Seb again.

'When do you finish work?'

'Why?'

'You know why. I'd like us to talk—have dinner maybe. Do something together.'

His phone buzzed in his pocket. He shifted a little on his feet but ignored it.

'Aren't you going to get that?'

He shook his head. 'I'm busy.'

'How long—exactly—have you been standing out here?'

He smiled. 'Around two hours.' He lifted one hand and shrugged. 'But it's fine. The people around here are very friendly. They all like to talk.'

'Talk is exactly what they'll do. You might be a public figure, Seb, but I'm not. I'm a pretty private person. I don't want anyone else knowing about our baby.'

The look on his face was so surprised that she realised he hadn't even considered that.

How far apart were they? Had he not even considered that might put her under stress? Not exactly ideal for a pregnant woman.

And it didn't help that wherever Seb was, men in black were permanently hovering in the background.

He'd already made the assumption that she would want to marry him. Maybe he also thought she would be fine about having their baby in the public eye?

Oh, no.

She gave a sway.

'Sienna? What's wrong? Are you okay?'

He moved right in front of her, catching both her arms with his firm hands. He was close enough for her to see the tiny lines around his eyes and the little flecks in his forest-green eyes.

'You're a prince,' she breathed slowly.

He blinked. There was a look of amusement on his face. 'I'm a prince,' he confirmed in a whisper.

'I slept with a prince.' It was almost as if she were talking to herself. She knew all this. None of it was a surprise. But all of a sudden things were sinking in fast.

Before, Sebastian Falco hadn't featured in her life. Apart from the telltale parting gift that he'd left her, there was really no sign of any connection between them. No one knew about their weekend together. No one knew that they'd even met.

When she'd come back, it was clear that even though Oliver was Sebastian's friend, he'd had no idea about their relationship.

That was the way things were supposed to be. Even though, in her head, she'd known she should tell Seb about the baby, once the engagement was announced she'd pushed those thoughts away.

She'd pushed all memories of Sebastian and their time together—the touch of his hands on her skin, the taste of his lips on hers—away into that castle of his that she'd never seen.

A castle. The man lived in a castle. Not in the mountain retreat he'd taken her to. Her stomach gave a little flip as she wondered once more how many other women had been there.

'Sienna, honey? Are you okay? Do you want to sit down?'

Honey. He'd just called her honey as if it were the most natural thing in the world to do.

He wanted them to get married. A prince wanted to marry her.

Most women would be happy. Most women would be delighted.

Marry a prince. Live in a castle. Wasn't that the basis of every little girl's favourite fairy tale?

Not hers.

She wasn't a Cinderella kind of girl. Well, maybe just a little bit.

She definitely wasn't Rapunzel. She didn't need any guy to save her.

And she so wasn't Sleeping Beauty. She'd never spend her life lying about.

She looked around. They were three floors up. The glass atrium dome above them and the Christmas decorations directly underneath them. People flowed all around them. The Royal Cheltenham Hospital was world renowned. People begged to work here. Posts were fiercely contested. Three other surgeons she respected and admired had interviewed for the job that she'd been appointed to.

That had been the best call of her life.

She sucked in a breath. Teddy's was her life.

She loved her job, loved the kids, loved the surgeries and loved the people.

A gust of icy wind blew up through the open doors downstairs. The chill felt appropriate.

The kids' book character in front of her right now was threatening all that.

Would she really get any peace once people found out her child was the heir of Montanari?

Her hands went protectively to her stomach. 'What happens once he or she arrives?'

He looked confused. 'What do you mean?'

So much was spinning around in her head that the words stuck in her throat. After her childhood experiences she'd always vowed to be in charge of her own life, her own relationships and her own destiny.

Finding out she was pregnant had only made her sway

for a second or two, then it had just put a new edge to her determination to get things right.

She'd made so many plans this Christmas—almost as if she were trying to keep herself busy. Carolling. Helping on the children's ward. Wrapping presents for army troops stationed away from home. Oh, her house was decorated as usual, and she opened the doors on her advent calendar every day. But she'd pictured spending this Christmas alone so was scheduled to be working over the holiday. She hadn't counted on Sebastian being around.

Seb was still standing straight in front of her, looking at her with concern in his eyes. He reached up and brushed her cheek with the gentlest of touches—the most tender of touches. It sent a whole host of memories flooding through her.

Seb. The man she'd shared a bed with. The man who kissed like no other. The man she'd thought was someone else entirely.

The man who'd thought he could walk in here and sweep her off her feet.

She shivered. She actually shivered.

'What are the rules in Montanari? Did you propose to me because an illegitimate child can't inherit the throne?'

He shook his head. 'No. No, of course I didn't. And no. There's no rules like that in Montanari. I'm the heir to the throne, and my firstborn son, or firstborn daughter, will be the heir to the throne once I'm King.' He gave an almost indiscernible shake of his head. 'But let's face it, it would be much better if we were married.'

'Better for who?'

He held up his hands, but she wasn't watching his hands, she was watching his face.

'Better for everyone. I have a duty—a duty to my people and my country. I want to introduce our son or daughter as the heir to the throne.' His gaze softened. 'And I'd like to introduce you as my wife.'

She had an instant dual flashback. One part caused by his word 'duty'. An instant memory of just exactly how both her parents had felt about their 'duty' and the look of absolute relief on her father's face as he'd packed his bags and left. The second part was caused by the first. A memory from months ago—those first few weeks when apparent morning sickness had struck at any second of the day or night. She wanted to be sick right here, right now. Right over his brown boots.

Duty. A word that seemed to have an absolute chilling effect that penetrated right down to her soul. Every time she heard people use the word in everyday life she had to try and hold back her instant response—an involuntary shudder.

Her insides were curled in knots. He'd just told her he wanted to marry her—again.

But not for the right reasons.

It didn't matter that her back had ached these last few days, she drew herself up to her full height and looked him straight in the eye.

It was almost like putting blinkers on. She wouldn't let those forest-green eyes affect her in the way they had before.

'I have a duty. To myself and to my child. We aren't your duty. We belong to ourselves. No one else. Not you. Not your parents. Not your people. I spent my childhood watching two people who should have never got together barely tolerate each other.' Fire was starting to burn inside her. 'What did you get for your eighteenth birthday present, Sebastian?'

The question caught him unawares. He stumbled around for the answer. 'A car, I think. Or a watch.'

'Well, good for you. Do you know what I got? I got my father packing his bags and leaving. But that didn't hurt nearly as much as the look of complete relief on his face. As for my mother? Two months later she moved to

Portugal and found herself a toy boy. I can honestly say I've never seen her happier.' She pressed her hand to her chest. 'I did that to them, Sebastian. I made two people who shouldn't have been together spend eighteen years in what must have been purgatory for them.' She shook her head fiercely. 'I will never, *ever* do that to a child of mine.'

Sebastian pulled back. He actually pulled back a little.

She'd done it again. Twice, in the space of two days, she'd raised her voice to Sebastian in a public place. Perfect. The talk of the steamie again.

But she couldn't help it. She wasn't finished.

There was no way Mr Fancy-Watches-For-His-Birthday could sweep in here and be part of her and her baby's life.

While she might have had a few little day dreams about the guy who was engaged to someone else, her reality plans had been way, way different.

This was why she'd negotiated new hours for the job she loved. This was why she'd visited four different nurseries and interviewed six potential childminders. This was why she'd spoken to her friend Bonnie—a fellow Scot who'd transported to Cambridge—on a number of occasions about how best to handle being a single mum.

This man was messing with her mind. Messing with her plans.

She didn't need this now. She really didn't.

She held up her hand. She knew exactly how to get rid of him. And not a single word would be a lie.

'I don't want this, Sebastian. This isn't my life. This isn't my dream. I will never, ever marry a man out of duty.' She almost spat out the word.

She lifted her hands towards the snow-topped atrium. 'When, and if, I ever get married, I'll get married to the man I love with all my heart. The man I couldn't bear to spend a single day without in my life. The man who would walk in front of a speeding train for me or my child without a single thought for himself—just like I would for him.' She took a few steps away from him. She was aware that a few people had stopped conversations around them to listen but she was past the point of caring.

'You don't know me, Sebastian. I want the whole hog. I want everything. And this, what you're offering? It doesn't even come close. I want a man who loves and adores me, who will walk by my side no matter what direction I take. I want a man who can take my breath away with a single look, a single touch.'

She could see him flinch. It didn't matter she was being unfair. Sebastian had taken more than her breath away with his looks and touches, but he didn't need to know that, not right now.

'I want a husband who will be proud of me and my career. Who won't care that I'm on call and he might need to reorganise his life around me. Who'll help around the house and not expect a wife who'll cook him dinner. Public Health may well have to do investigations into my cooking skills.'

She was enjoying herself now, taking it too far. But he had to know. He had to know just how fast to run.

'I will never accept anything less. I've been the child of a duty marriage. I would never, ever do that to my child. It's a form of torture. Growing up feeling guilty? It's awful.' She pressed her hands on her stomach again. '*My* child—' she emphasised the word '—is going to grow up feeling loved, blessed and, above all, wanted. By me, at least. There will be rules. There will be discipline. But most of all, there will be love.'

She walked back up to stand right in front of him. 'Whoever loves me will know how much I love Christmas, will want to celebrate it with me every year. Will know the songs I love, the crazy carols I love to sing. They won't care that I spend hours wrapping presents that are opened in seconds, they won't care that I buy more Christmas decorations than there is space for on the tree, they won't care that I have to have a special kind of cake every Christmas Eve and spend a fortune trying to find it. They'll know that I would only ever get married at Christmas. They would never even suggest anything else.'

She took a deep breath and finally looked at him—really looked at him.

Yip, she'd done it. He looked as if she'd just run over him with an Edinburgh tram. This time she lowered her voice. 'You might be a prince. You might have a castle. But I want the fairy tale. And you can't give it to me.'

And with that, she turned and walked away.

CHAPTER FOUR

'ARE YOU COMING down with something?' Oliver was staring at him in a way only a doctor could.

'What? No. Don't be ridiculous.'

Oliver gave a slow, careful nod. 'The board paper was excellent. They love the idea. It looks like the Falco charm has done its magic.'

'Except where it counts.'

'What's that supposed to mean?' Oliver rolled his eyes. 'No. Please. I'm not sure I want to know.' He walked around the desk and leaned against the wall.

Sebastian sighed loudly. He couldn't help it. 'I thought once I came here, Sienna might be happy to see me again. I didn't expect her to be quite…quite…'

'Quite so Sienna?' Oliver was looking far too amused for his liking.

Sebastian let out a wry laugh. 'Yeah, exactly. Quite so Sienna. I still can't believe she didn't let me know.'

Oliver shook his head. 'Doesn't sound like her. She's fierce. She's independent. She's stubborn—'

'You're not helping.'

Oliver laughed. 'But she's also one of the kindest-hearted women I know. She's always been professional but I can't tell you how many times I've caught her sobbing in a dark corner somewhere when things aren't going well with one of her patients. Working with neonates is the toughest area for any doctor. They're just getting started at life. They deserve a chance. And Sienna needs to be tough to get through it. She needs to be determined.' He paused for a second and his steady gaze met Sebastian's. 'Sienna puts up walls. She's honest. She's loyal. If she didn't let you know about the baby—she must have had a darn good reason.'

Sebastian bit the inside of his cheek. All of Oliver's words were striking chords with him. 'She said it was the engagement announcement. It put her off. She didn't want to destroy my engagement and cause a scandal.'

Oliver's brow creased. 'That's very considerate of her.' He stood up straight and took a few steps towards Sebastian. 'Quick question, Seb. Did you believe that?'

Sebastian was surprised. It hadn't occurred to him to doubt what Sienna told him. 'What do you mean?'

Oliver started shaking his head. 'I guess I just think it could be something else.'

'What do you mean?'

Oliver began walking around. 'It all sounds very noble. But would Sienna really deny you the chance to know your child? She could have spoken to me—she knows we are friends—I could have found a way to get a discreet message to you.' He gave Sebastian a careful look. 'I wonder if there was something else—a different kind of reason.'

Sebastian shifted in his chair. He couldn't get his head around what Oliver was saying. 'What do you mean? You think the baby might not be mine?'

Oliver held up his hand. 'Oh, no. Sienna wasn't seeing anyone. I couldn't even tell you when she had her last date. She's totally dedicated to her work. You don't need to worry about that.'

Thoughts started swirling around his head as relief flooded through him. Sienna had nailed exactly why he had come here. Duty. That was how he always lived his life.

It had been instilled in him from the youngest age.

He might not have loved Theresa. But she would have fulfilled the role of Queen with grace and dignity.

Sienna? Her personality type was completely different. She was intelligent. She was a brilliant surgeon. But she hadn't been brought up in a royal family. She didn't know traditions and protocols. He wasn't entirely sure she would ever follow them or want to.

He was pushing aside the way his heart skipped a beat when he saw her. The way his body reacted instantly. Passion like that would never last a lifetime no matter how pleasurable.

But that passion had created the baby currently residing inside Sienna. His baby. The heir to the throne of Montanari.

He stared back at Oliver. Knowing there were no other men in Sienna's life was exactly what he needed to hear. His press team were already wondering how to handle the imminent announcement about the baby.

'Then what on earth are you talking about?' He was getting increasingly frustrated by Oliver talking around in circles.

Oliver ran his hand through his hair. 'Let's just say I recognise the signs.'

'The signs of what? By the time you actually tell me what you mean this baby will be an adult.'

Oliver laughed again and started counting off on his fingers. 'Do you know what I've noticed in the last day? Sienna's twitchy. She's on edge. She's different. Throughout this whole pregnancy she's been as cool as a cucumber.'

'You think I'm having a bad effect on her?'

Oliver put his hand on Sebastian's arm. 'I think you're having *some* kind of effect on her. I've never seen her like this.' He gave a little smile. 'If I didn't know any better—I'd say Sienna McDonald likes you a whole lot more than she admits to.'

Sebastian was stunned. 'Really?'

Oliver raised his eyebrows. 'It's such an alien concept to you?'

A warm feeling spread all over Sebastian's skin, as if the sun had penetrated through his shirt and annihilated the winter chill. When he'd proposed marriage the other day it had been an automatic reaction—something he'd planned on the flight over. But it had been precipitated by duty. Their baby would be the heir to the throne in Montanari.

Part of him was worried. She did actually like him? Was that why Sienna was acting the way she did?

He stood up and started pacing. 'She told me outright she'd never marry me. She told me she wanted everything. Love, romance, marriage, a husband who would love and adore her. She told me being a prince wasn't enough—not nearly enough.'

'And you thought it would be?' Oliver's face said it all. 'How come I've known you all these years and never realised how stupid you were?'

He stood up, stepped forward and poked his finger into Sebastian's chest. 'How do you feel about Sienna? How do you feel about her in here?'

His answer came out automatically. 'What does that matter? A marriage in Montanari is usually about a union. On this occasion, it's about a child. Feelings don't come into it.'

It was an uncomfortable question. Memories of Sienna McDonald had swirled around his head for months. The most obscure thing—a smell, a word—could conjure Sienna front and foremost in his mind again. The briefest thought could send blood rushing all around his body. His first sight of her—pregnant with his child—had affected him in ways he hadn't even contemplated.

From the second he'd met her Sienna had got under his skin.

The sight of her, the taste of her, the smell of her was irresistible. The way she responded to his teasing. He did care about her. He did care about this baby. But could it be more?

How would someone like him know what love was anyway? It wasn't as if he'd spent a life exposed to it. He'd had teenage crushes. A few passionate flings. But marrying for love had never really been on his radar. Sienna's words and expectations the other day had taken him by surprise.

Oliver folded his arms and raised his eyebrows. He knew Sebastian far too well to take his glib answer at face value.

'I... I... I...' He threw up his hands in frustration. 'I don't know. She confuses me. I never contemplated having emotional ties to the woman I'd marry. Sienna has just mixed everything up.'

Oliver shook his head. 'Then hurry up and decide. Hurry up and decide how you feel about the mother of your child. A beautiful, headstrong and highly intelligent member of my staff *and* a friend of mine.' He took a step closer and held up his finger and thumb almost pressed together. 'Do you want to know how much Sienna Mc-Donald will care about you being a prince? Do you want to know how much a palace will impress her? This much.'

Oliver walked away and sat down behind his desk. He looked at Sebastian carefully. 'The trouble with you is that you've had too much help in this life.'

'What's that supposed to mean?'

Oliver waved his hand. 'Someone to do this for you, someone to do that. You didn't even do your own grocery shopping when we were students together.'

Sebastian looked embarrassed.

'Sienna doesn't have that. Sienna has never had that. Everything for this baby, she's worked out for herself. She's juggled her schedule. Worked out her maternity leave to the second. Put plans in place for every patient.' He put his elbows on the desk. 'Everything to do with her house—what we'd call a fixer-upper—she's sorted out herself too. She's spent years saving to get the house she really wants. It's not a house to her—it's a home. Do you know how crazy she is about Christmas? Do you know that she's a fabulous baker?' Oliver sighed.

Sebastian shook his head. 'All I know about Sienna is what I learned on that weekend back in Montanari, and what I've learned in the last few days. Everything's a mess. She's still angry with me—angry that I was engaged to someone else. She told me exactly what she wanted in this life and it was the whole fairy tale.' He dropped his voice slightly. 'She also told me I wasn't part of it. I have no idea how to connect with this woman, Oliver. I have no idea how I can manage to persuade her to give the thought of us a chance. Sometimes I think she doesn't even like me.'

Oliver frowned. 'Oh, she likes you—I can tell.'

'She does?' It was the first thing that gave him some hope.

Oliver leaned back again and looked his friend up and down as if he were assessing him. 'In the past she's been very selective. Guys who don't live up to her expectations?' He snapped his fingers and gave Sebastian a wicked grin. 'Gone. Just like that.'

Sebastian had started to feel uncomfortable. But Oliver was his friend—he couldn't keep up his serious face for long. It was obvious he cared about the welfare of Sienna. And Sebastian was glad about that, glad to know that people had her back.

He folded his arms across his chest and leaned against

the wall. Some of the things that Oliver had said had struck a chord. There were so many things about Sienna that he didn't know. Things he wanted to know.

The bottom line was—could Sienna really be Queen material?

One weekend was not enough. It would never be enough. But he wasn't sure he wanted to say that out loud now. At least not to his friend.

'So, how do I get to know the real Sienna McDonald— the one behind the white coat?'

Oliver smiled. 'Eh, I think you've already achieved that.' He raised his eyebrow. 'There is evidence.'

Sebastian started pacing. Things were rushing around in his mind. 'Stop it. What about the other stuff? The Christmas stuff? What she takes in her tea?' His footsteps slowed. 'How she wants to raise our kid?' His voice got quieter. 'If she actually might more than like me...'

He stopped. Sienna. He needed to be around Sienna.

Oliver gave him a smile. 'I guess you should go and find out.'

It was an Aston Martin DB5. She'd seen one in a James Bond movie once. Even she could recognise it. A classic machine. She should have known he'd own something like this. He opened the door of the pale blue car revealing a red leather interior and she sucked in her breath.

She'd never been a show-me-your-money-and-I'll-be-impressed kind of girl. But this was a bit different. This was pure class. She'd watched enough car shows in her time to know that owning a car like this was a labour of pure love.

Just looking at it made her tingle.

The streets were dusted with snow. People were crossing the car park and staring, nudging each other and pointing at the car.

Christmas lights lit up the street opposite. Every shop

had decorations in its windows. She could hear Christmas pop songs drifting out of the pub across the road. At the end of the road was a courtyard where a giant tree was lit with gold and red lights. It was paid for by the local council and the kids on the paediatric ward could see it from their windows. The lights twinkled all night long.

'What are you doing, Sebastian?'

He smiled. He was dressed for the British weather in a pair of jeans, black boots and his black leather jacket. She gave a little gulp as her insides did some weird little flip-flop.

He smiled. Oh, no. The flip-flop turned into a somersault. 'I came to pick you up. Someone told me you had car trouble. I thought I could drive you home.'

She bit her lip. Tempting. Oh, so tempting.

'I can call for roadside assistance. I really need to get my car sorted. It shouldn't take too long.'

He waved his hand. 'Albie, the porter, said if you leave your keys with him he'll get your car started later. It's too cold to hang around and wait for roadside assistance.' He stepped a little closer.

There it was. That familiar aroma. The one that took her back to Montanari, and sun, and cocktails, and...

'We could pick up a little dinner on the way home.'

Her stomach let out a loud growl. It was almost as if her body were conspiring against her. She scrambled to find a suitable excuse but her stubborn brain remained blank. 'Well, I... I...'

'Great. That's sorted, then.' He took her car keys from her hand and walked swiftly back to the hospital, leaving her to stare at the pale blue machine in front of her, gleaming as the sun dipped lower in the sky.

She was still staring a few seconds later when he returned. He stood alongside her and smiled. 'Like it?'

She couldn't help the smile as she met his proud gaze. 'I guess I'm just a little surprised.'

'By what?'

She waved her hand towards the car. 'I guess I thought you might be in something sleek, low-slung and bright red.'

He laughed out loud. 'You think I'm one of *those* kind of guys?'

She nearly laughed herself. He really didn't need to elaborate. But as she kept staring at the car she felt a wave of something else. 'I guess I don't really know, do I?'

She turned to look at him, her warm breath frosting the air between them. Those dark green eyes seemed even more intense in the darkening light. He held her gaze. She could see his chest rise and fall as he watched her, searching her face.

All of a sudden she felt a little self-conscious. Was there any make-up even left on her skin? When was the last time she'd combed her hair?

This time Sebastian wasn't smiling. He was looking at her in a way she couldn't really fathom. As if there were a thousand thoughts spinning around in his head.

He would be King one day. He would be King of his country. She'd tried not to think about any of this. It had been easy before. He was engaged. He was getting married. He was with someone else.

But now he was here.

Here, in the Cotswolds, to see her. Her, and their baby.

He leaned forward and she held her breath, wondering what would happen next.

His arm brushed against hers as he pulled open the car door. 'Then let's do something about that,' he said huskily.

Snowflakes started to fall around her. She looked up at the now dark purple streaked sky. She could almost swear that there was something sparkling in the air between them.

As she took a step towards the car he turned towards her again, his arm settling at the side of her waist.

'In case you haven't noticed, I'm not a flashy kind of guy. I like classics. Things that will last a lifetime. Something that every time you look at it, it makes your heart flutter just a little. Because you know it's a keeper. You know it was made just for you.'

She couldn't breathe. She couldn't actually breathe. Large snowflakes were landing on his head and shoulders. His warm breath touched her cheek as he spoke— he was that close. Her hand rose automatically, resting on his arm. They were face to face. Almost cheek to cheek. If she tilted her chin up just a little...

But she couldn't. Not yet. Maybe not ever. She needed her head to be clear around Sebastian. And right now it was anything but clear.

It was full of intense green eyes framed by dark lashes, a sexy smile and sun-kissed skin. She could smell the leather of his jacket mingling with the familiar scent of his aftershave. She could see the faint shadow along his jaw line. The palm of her hand itched to reach up and touch it.

She hadn't moved. And he hadn't moved either. Being this close was almost hypnotic.

But she had to. She had to look away. She broke his gaze and glanced back at the car. 'It's blue,' she said. 'I thought all these cars were silver.'

Cars. A safe topic. A neutral topic. Something that would stop the swell of emotion currently rising in her chest.

He blinked. His hand hadn't moved from her currently non-existent waist. He gave a nod. 'A lot of them were silver. James Bond's was silver. But mine? Mine is Caribbean blue. As soon as I saw it, and the red leather interior, I knew it was perfect. I had to have it.'

He held her gaze again and she licked her lips anxiously. *I had to have it* echoed in her head. Why did it feel as if he wasn't talking about the car?

There was a screech behind them. A bang. A huge shattering of glass. And they both jumped apart.

Two seconds later the air was filled by a blood-curdling scream.

Sebastian didn't hesitate. He ran instantly towards the scream.

The doctor's instinct in her surged forward. She glanced towards the hospital doors. She could go and ask for help but Teddy's only took maternity and paediatric emergencies. It wasn't a district general and she didn't even know what was wrong yet.

She started running. Running wasn't easy at her current state of pregnancy. The ground was slippery beneath her feet as snow was just starting to settle on the ground.

As she reached the road that ran alongside the hospital she could see immediately what was wrong. One car had skidded and hit a lamp post. Another car had mounted the pavement and was now embedded in the dress shop's window. The Christmas decorations that had decorated the window were scattered across the street. She winced as her foot crunched on a red bauble. Sebastian was trying to talk to the woman who was screaming. He had his hands on both of her shoulders and was trying to calm her down.

Sienna's eyes swept over the scene, trying to make sense of the situation. An air bag had exploded in the car that had hit the lamp post. A young woman was currently slumped against it.

The other driver was slumped too. But there was no airbag. It was an older car and his head and shoulders were over the steering wheel of the car. The windscreen was shattered and shards of glass from the shop's window frame were directly above him.

The woman on the pavement was obviously in shock. She'd stopped screaming and was talking nonstop between sobs to Sebastian.

He turned towards her, his eyes wide. 'Her kid. Her kid is under the car.'

Another bystander stepped forward and put his arm around the woman, nodding towards Sebastian and Sienna. 'I've phoned an ambulance.'

Sienna gulped. She was familiar with obstetric emergencies. She was often called in for a consult if there could be an issue with the baby. Paediatric emergencies took up half of all her days. Neonates had a tendency to become very sick, very quickly and she needed to be available.

But regular emergencies?

She dropped to her knees and peered under the car. There was a mangled pushchair, and further away, out of her reach, a little figure.

Her heart leapt. Sebastian dropped down next to her, his head brushing against hers as he looked under the car.

He pressed his hand over hers. It was the quickest movement. The warmth of his hand barely had time to make an impact on her. 'I'll go.'

She hardly had time to speak before Sebastian was wriggling his way under the car. She opened her mouth to object just as baby gave her an almighty kick. Her hand went automatically to her belly. Of course. There was no way she could possibly fit under the body of the car—Sebastian was already struggling.

She edged around the front of the vehicle, watching the precarious shards of glass hanging above the car and staying on the ground as low as she could. The slush on the ground soaked her knees and legs, her cream winter coat attracting grime that would never be removed. She slid her arms out of the coat and pulled it over her head—at least she'd have some protection if glass fell.

'Can you try and feel for a pulse?' she said quietly to Sebastian, then added, 'Do you know what to do?'

There was a flicker of light. Sebastian had wriggled

his phone from his pocket and turned on the torch, lying it on the ground next to him.

In amongst the darkness and wetness, Sienna thought she could spot something else. The little boy was still tangled in part of the buggy and her view was still partially obscured.

She turned to the people behind her. 'Can someone find out the little boy's name for me, please?'

Sebastian's face was grim; he had a hand up next to the little boy's head. 'Yes, I've got a pulse. It's fast and it feels faint.'

Truth was, so did she.

She nodded. 'What position is he in?'

Right now she so wished she could be under there. Her frustration at not being able to get to the child was building by the second.

'He's on his back. Wait.'

She couldn't see what Sebastian was doing. He was moving his hand and holding up the torch to the little guy's face.

A voice in her ear nearly made her jump out of her skin. 'Gabriel. The little boy's name is Gabriel.'

She sucked in a breath. 'Sebastian, tell me what's wrong. What can you see? His name is Gabriel. Is he conscious?'

The wait must only have been a few seconds but it felt like so much longer.

Sebastian's face was serious. He held up one hand, palm facing towards her, and held his phone with the other so she could see. It was stained red.

'There's blood, Sienna. Lots of it. He's pale but there's something else—his lips are going a funny colour.'

Sienna turned to the crowd again, searching for the man's face she'd seen earlier. 'Any news about the ambulance?'

The man shook his head. 'Someone has run over to the hospital to try and get more help and some supplies.'

She nodded. 'I need swabs. Bandages. Oxygen. A finger monitor if they've got one.'

'I'll go,' said a young woman and ran off towards the hospital entrance.

Sienna felt in her pocket. All she had was an unopened packet of tissues. Not exactly the ideal product—but at least they were clean.

She threw them towards Sebastian. 'It's all I've got. Try and stem the flow of blood. Where is it coming from?'

Sebastian moved his body, blocking her view again, and she almost whimpered in frustration. She felt useless here. Absolutely useless. She couldn't check the child properly, assess any injuries or provide any care. It was the only time in her life she'd regretted being pregnant.

But Sebastian was calm. He wasn't panicking. He hadn't hesitated to slip under the car and help in any way that he could. As she watched he tore open the packet of tissues and tried to stem the flow of blood.

'It's coming from the side of his neck. I think he's been hit by some of the glass.' He paused for a second and she instantly knew something was wrong.

'What is it? Tell me?'

Sebastian kept his voice low. 'His lips are blue, Sienna.'

She hated this. She hated feeling helpless. 'Do you know what the recovery position is? Turn him on his side, Seb. Open his mouth and try and clear his airway. Check there's nothing inside his mouth. He's not getting enough oxygen into his lungs.'

The noise around them was increasing. There was a faint wail of sirens in the distance. The volume of the murmuring voices was increasing. People were always drawn to the scene of an accident. She could hear someone shouting instructions. A voice with some authority attached to it. She could only pray it was a member of the hospital staff dealing with one of the drivers.

The driver. She should really look at him too. But her first priority was this child. If Gabriel didn't breathe he would be dead. If his airway was obstructed he would be dead. She had no idea the extent of his other injuries but no oxygen would certainly kill him. If she had a team around her right now they would take time to stabilise the little guy's head and neck. But she didn't have a team—and there wasn't time.

All she had was Sebastian—the Prince from another country who was under there trying to be her right-hand man.

She could hear him talking to the little boy, coaxing him, trying to see if he could get any response. Shadows were shifting under the car; it was still difficult to see what was going on.

'Sebastian? Have you stopped the bleeding? What about his colour? Have you managed to put him in the recovery position yet?'

'Give me a minute.' The voice was firm and steady.

He doesn't have a minute. She had to bite her tongue to stop herself from saying it out loud. There was a clatter beside her. 'Sorry,' breathed a young woman. 'More help is coming.'

Sienna looked at the ground. There was a plastic tray loaded with supplies. She grabbed for the pulse oximeter. It was one of the simplest pieces of equipment they had—a simple little rubber pouch with a sensor that fitted over a finger and gave you an indication of someone's oxygen levels. She switched it on and reached as far under the car as she should, touching Sebastian's back.

'Here. Take this. Put it over his finger and tell me what the number is.'

Sebastian's position shifted. 'Come on, Gabriel,' he was saying encouragingly. He'd moved his torch. It was right at Gabriel's face, which was now facing away from her. For the briefest second she could see Sebastian's face reflected in the glass. He was focused. Concern and anxiety written all over his face.

She held her breath. His hand reached behind him to grab hold of the monitor. He'd heard her. He was just focusing on Gabriel.

She could almost swear her heart squeezed. If she were under the car right now, that was exactly how she'd be.

Focused on Gabriel. Not on any of the noise or circumstances around them.

'Watch out!' came the shout from her side.

There was a large crash and splinters of glass showered around her like an explosion of tiny hailstones. Her reaction was automatic: she ducked even lower, pulling the coat even further over her head. There were a few shrieks around her. Sebastian's head shot around. 'Sienna?'

His gaze met hers. He was worried. And he wasn't worried about himself. And for the tiniest second he wasn't thinking about Gabriel. He was thinking about her.

She didn't have time. She didn't have time to think about what that might mean. The cramped position was uncomfortable and baby wasn't hesitating to let her know it.

'His colour. How's his colour, Sebastian?'

Sebastian quickly looked back to Gabriel. 'It's better,' he said. 'He's still pale but the blueness is gone.'

Sienna breathed a sigh of relief. 'Put the monitor on his finger and tell me the reading.'

The sirens were getting much louder now; the ambulances must be almost there.

Sienna started grabbing some more of the supplies. Swabs, tape, some saline. She unwound the oxygen mask from the canister.

'Ninety-one. His reading is ninety-one. Is that good?'

She could see the anxiety on his face. His steady resolve was starting to fade a little.

If she were in a hospital she'd say no. But since they were cramped under a car with a little boy bleeding and on his side she remained optimistic. Sebastian had done a good job. She was surprised at how good he'd been. He had no background in medicine. No training. But he hadn't hesitated to assist. And the weird thing was he'd been so in tune with her. He'd done everything she'd instructed. He'd been calm and competent, and somehow she knew inside that she wouldn't have expected Sebastian to act in any other way.

She took a deep sniff. No smell of petrol. No reason to deny Gabriel oxygen. She switched on the canister and unwound the tubing, pushing the mask towards Sebastian. 'Try and hold this in front of his mouth and nose. Let's see if we can get that level up a little.'

Something green flashed to her side. The knees of a paramedic as he bumped down beside her. He lifted the edge of her coat. 'Hey, Doc, it's you.'

She jerked at the familiar voice and felt a wave of relief. Sam, an experienced paramedic she'd met on a number of occasions, gave her a worried smile. He glanced upwards. 'I'm getting you out of here. Tell me what I need to know.'

She spoke quickly. 'There's a little boy trapped under the car. He was in his buggy. He looks around three. His name is Gabriel. His mother is being cared for at the side by someone.' She almost stuck her head out from the coat to look around but Sam shook his head. She pointed under the car. 'He was blue. My friend had to move him into the recovery position and he's bleeding. His sats are ninety-one. There's oxygen under there too.'

Sam nodded solemnly. He didn't remark on the fact Gabriel had been moved. He just peered under the car. 'Who's your friend?'

She hesitated. 'Seb—Sebastian. He's just visiting.'

Sam had never been slow. 'Oh, the mystery Prince everyone's talking about. Is he a doctor?'

She pretended not to hear the first part of the conversation. 'No, he's not a doctor. He's just been doing what I told him to do.' She patted her stomach. 'I couldn't quite fit.'

Sam nodded and jerked his head. 'Right, move away and stay under that coat. Back away slowly. I'll get your friend to come out and I'll replace him.' Another siren came screaming up behind them. 'That'll be Fire and Rescue. They'll help with the car and the glass.' He gave her another look. 'Now move, pregnant lady, or I'll admit you with something or other.'

She gave a grateful smile. Sam wasn't joking. She backed away to let him do his job. She heard him give Sebastian a few instructions then, in the space of under a minute, Sebastian slid out from under the car and Sam replaced him. His colleague appeared with the Fire and Rescue crew and everything just seemed to move quickly.

Sebastian moved over to her and wrapped his arm around her shoulders. 'You okay?'

There was a tiny smudge of blood just above his eye. She felt in her pocket. No tissues. They'd used them.

She gave a nod. His jeans and jacket were muddy and dirty—as was her cream coat. Truth was, it would never recover. She shivered and pushed her arms into the damp coat. 'I'm fine. Give me a minute and I'll find something to clean your face.'

He shook his head, just as there was a shout and another shard of glass fell from the shattered shop window. Sebastian winced. But he didn't try and pull her away. He must have known she'd refuse. Instead they waited for another fifteen minutes as the Fire and Rescue crew worked alongside the paramedics and police to help all the victims of the accident.

Now she had time to take her breath she could survey

just how bad things looked. The two drivers were quickly extricated from the cars, neck collars in place, one conscious and one still unconscious.

A policewoman was standing with Gabriel's mum. The poor woman looked terrified. Once the hanging shards of glass had been safely cleared from the shop window, the fire crew surrounded the car and, on instruction, just bodily lifted it to allow Sam to slide out from underneath with Gabriel on a sliding board. The buggy was still tangled around his legs.

Sienna drew in a sharp breath as her baby kicked in sympathy. Half of her wanted to rush back over and offer to help, but she knew that Sam and his colleague were more than qualified to do emergency care. Gabriel didn't need cardiac surgery—trauma wasn't exactly her field, and part of being a good physician was knowing when to step back.

Sebastian didn't rush her. He didn't try to hurry her away from the site of the crash. As they watched all the accident victims being loaded into the ambulances he just kept his arm wrapped firmly around her shoulders.

She was glad of it. The temperature seemed to have dropped around them and the underlying shiver hadn't left her body.

A few of her colleagues who'd also helped at the scene came over and spoke to her. One of the midwives gave a wry smile. 'Can't remember the last time I treated a seventy-year-old man.' She shook her head as she headed back towards the hospital main entrance.

Sienna turned to Sebastian. 'I think it's probably time for us to go.'

He nodded and glanced down at their clothes and smiled. 'Somehow I think dinner should wait.'

She put her hand to her mouth. 'We can't go in that gorgeous car while we're so mucky.'

As they walked towards the car he let out a laugh.

'That's the beauty of a leather interior—any dirt will wipe clean. Don't worry about it.'

Her stomach gave a growl. 'Let's pick up some take-out,' she said quickly.

Sebastian gave a little frown. She almost laughed out loud. He was a prince. The last time he'd eaten take-out he'd probably been a university student. She made a note to ask Oliver about that. For all she knew, Sebastian had arrived at university with his own chef. It was time to show him how the other half lived.

He held open the door for her again. She shot him a wicked smile. 'What will we have—Chinese? Indian? Pizza? Or fish and chips?'

He made something resembling a strangled sound and gave a sort of smile. 'You choose,' he said as he closed the door and walked around to the other side of the car.

She waited until he'd climbed in. 'Pizza it is, then. There's a place just five minutes from where I live. It does the best pizzas around here.'

She settled into the comfortable seat. Even the smell in the car sent little shivers down her spine. It was gorgeous. It was luxurious. It just felt...different from anything she'd been in before.

Sebastian started the engine. It was a smooth ride; even the engine noise was soothing.

She gestured to the sleek black car following behind them. 'Do they follow you everywhere?'

He gave a little shrug. 'It's their job. They've learned to be unobtrusive. I promise, you won't even know that they're around.'

She smiled. 'Do you have to buy them dinner too?'

He laughed and shook his head. 'Don't worry. They'll make their own arrangements.'

She gave him directions, pointing him to the pizza shop.

When they pulled up outside she went to open the door

but he grabbed hold of her hand. 'No way. You stay where you are. I'll order. What would you like?'

Part of her wanted to refuse. But she'd spent so long outside in the freezing temperatures that her body was only just starting to heat up. She didn't answer straight away and he prompted again. 'What's your favourite pizza?'

'What's yours?'

Their voices almost came out in sync. 'Ham, onion and mushroom.'

Silence. Both of them stared at each other for a second and then both started laughing.

She shook her head. 'Seriously? Really?'

He nodded. 'Really.'

She held up her hand. 'Wait a minute. Deep pan or thin crust?'

He glanced outside at the thick snow that was falling around the car. 'Somehow, I think tonight has to be deep pan night.'

She gave a thoughtful nod. 'I think you could be right.'

She reached out and touched his hand, narrowing her eyes suspiciously. 'Seriously, when was the last time you ate pizza?'

He winked and climbed out of the car. 'That's for me to know and you to guess. Give me five minutes.' He slammed the door and ducked into the pizzeria.

She watched while he placed his order and talked away to the guys behind the counter. Within a few moments they were all laughing. She, in the meantime, was kind of fixated on the view from the back.

She was ignoring the grime and mud all down one side of his probably designer jeans and staring instead at the distinctive shape of his broad shoulders and muscled arms under his leather jacket. If she followed the gaze down to the jeans…

Her body gave an inadvertent shudder as baby decided

to remind her of his or her presence. It felt odd having the same urge of sensations she'd felt the last time she'd been around Sebastian. It seemed like a lifetime ago now. And yet…it felt as if it had just happened yesterday.

But it hadn't been yesterday, it had been months ago.

And months ago she hadn't been this shape. Months ago, she hadn't needed to adjust her position every few minutes in an attempt to try and get comfortable. Months ago her breasts hadn't virtually taken over her body. Months ago she hadn't spent her days considering where the nearest loo was.

Months ago she'd been happy to toss her clothes across the bedroom floor and let the sun streaming through the windows drench her skin.

She sighed and settled back into the seat.

Then sat straight back up again.

Her house. She would be taking Sebastian to her house.

Now they weren't having dinner at some random neutral venue. They were both covered in mud. She'd need to invite him in, and to clean up.

Sebastian. In her home.

The place where she'd made plans. The nursery that was almost finished. The wooden crib that had arrived and was still in its flat-pack box as she was so disappointed by it.

The drawer with tiny white socks and Babygros.

Her stomach gave another leap as she saw Sebastian give the guys a wave and pick up the large pizza box. How would it feel to have Prince Sebastian Falco in her home?

It was almost as if the atmosphere in the car had changed in his absence. Sienna seemed a little tense as he handed her the pizza box. She gave him stilted directions to her house and one-word answers on the five-minute drive.

He had to admit the smell from the pizza box wasn't too bad. The last pizza he'd eaten had been prepared by a

Michelin-starred chef. But somehow he knew that wasn't something he should share with Sienna right now.

Earlier, he'd felt the connection to her. It didn't matter he'd been completely out of his depth and—truth be told—a tiny bit terrified of doing something wrong under that car. But every ounce of his body had told him he had to help. There was no way he could leave an injured child under a car on his own, and, with Sienna's instructions, he'd felt confident to just do as she asked.

It didn't help that the whole time he'd been under there he'd been thinking about the perilous glass dangling directly above the car and Sienna's body.

They turned onto a tree-lined street. Each house was slightly different from the one next to it. Most were painted white, and most were bungalows. A few had sprawling extensions and others had clearly extended into the roof of their property.

Sienna pointed to the left and he pulled up outside a white bungalow with large bay windows and a bright red door. It was covered in a dusting of snow and there were little white lights strung around one of the trees in the front garden.

It wasn't a castle. It wasn't a mansion house. It wasn't even a chalet in the mountains. But he could sense her air of pride. He could instantly tell how much she loved this place.

He gave her a smile. 'It's lovely.'

She let out a deep breath as her eyes fixed on her home. 'Thank you. I love it.'

He walked around quickly, holding the door open for her and lifting the pizza box from her hands. She opened the garden gate and they walked up the path to the front door.

Warmth hit them as soon as she opened the front door. She gave him a smile. 'I have a wood-burning stove. Costs next to nothing. I stack it full in the morning and it burns all day. I'd hate to come home to a cold house.'

A cold house. There was just something about the way she said those words. Almost as if cold didn't only refer to the room temperature.

She walked through to the kitchen and took the pizza, sliding it into her bright red Aga stove. She bit her lip as she turned towards him. 'I don't really have anything you can change into. You can clean up in my bathroom if you want. There are fresh towels in there if you want to use the shower.'

He could tell she was a little uncomfortable. He had no problem taking a shower in Sienna's home—it might actually help warm up his bones a little—but he didn't want to make her feel any more uncomfortable than she already did. He tried not to stare at his surroundings. There was tinsel looped over the fridge. An advent calendar with doors open hanging on the wall, and an array of little Santa ornaments lining the window ledge. Sienna really did love Christmas.

'Do you want me to leave?'

He almost held his breath.

'No. No, I don't.' She slid her dirty coat from her shoulders. 'Look, I'm going to put this in the wash. Leave your dirty clothes at the bathroom door and I'll wash them too. There's a white bathrobe on a hook behind the door. You can wear that while we eat dinner.'

He gave a little nod and walked down the corridor depositing his jeans and T-shirt outside the bathroom door. By the time he'd showered—and scoped out the bathroom for any non-existent male accessories—the pizza was back out of the oven and she had some glasses on the table.

He almost laughed out loud. The dressing gown covered him. But not entirely. His bare legs were on display and, although he'd managed to tie the waist, it gaped a little across his broad chest. It was clear Sienna was trying to avoid looking too closely.

He sat down at the table opposite her and adjusted it as best he could. 'It's not like you haven't seen it all before,' he half teased.

Colour flushed her cheeks. She lifted up the diet soda and started pouring it into glasses. 'Yeah, but I haven't seen it sitting at my kitchen table. Things that happen in Montanari tend to stay in Montanari.'

He tried not to flinch. It was a throwaway comment. He pointed towards her stomach as she served the pizza onto plates. 'It seems that what we did didn't want to stay in Montanari. It wanted to get right out there.'

He was doing his best to lead up to something. He'd had four phone calls today from the royal family's publicist. The British media knew he was here. The whitewash about twinning the two hospitals had quickly came unstuck. Any investigative journalist worth their salt wouldn't take too long to find out why he was really here. He expected to be headline news tomorrow.

She set down his plate with a clatter and before she could snatch her hand away he covered it with his own. 'Sienna, are you okay?'

She shot him an angry glance and walked around to the other side of the table and sat down, staring at him, then the pizza, then him again.

He folded his arms. 'Okay, hit me with it. It's time we were honest with each other.'

She pressed her lips together for a few seconds, then blurted out, 'Why are you here, Sebastian? What is it—exactly—that you want from me?'

He sighed. 'I'm here because of you, Sienna. Even if I hadn't heard about the baby I would never have gone through with the marriage to Theresa. I'm not my parents. I can't live that life. No matter how much they want me to.' He stared at the woman across the table from him.

She had little lines around her eyes. Her hands were spotless but there was one tiny mud splash on her cheek. Her pale skin was beautiful. Her light brown eyes looked tired. Her blonde hair had half escaped from the pony-tail band at the nape of her neck. Her cheeks were a little fuller than when they'd been together last; her whole body had blossomed and it kind of suited her.

In short, he'd never seen anyone look so beautiful.

'Baby or not, I would always have come back for you, Sienna,' he said quietly. 'I thought marriage was about a union between countries. I thought I could tolerate a marriage to a friend. But as soon as it was announced I felt as if the walls were closing in around me. It wasn't enough. I'm not built that way. I just hadn't realised it. A marriage to Theresa would have made her miserable, and me miserable. It could never have lasted.'

There was silence in the room. The only sounds from the ticking clock on the wall and the rumble from the washing machine in the next-door utility room.

She licked her lips. Those luscious pink lips that he ached to taste again. 'I don't believe you,' she whispered. 'You want the heir to your kingdom. You don't want me. I was just the stranger to have sex with.'

There was hurt—hurt written all over her face. A face he wanted to cradle in his hands.

He took his time to choose his words. 'It was sex. It was great sex. With a woman who managed to crawl under my skin and stay there. A woman who has haunted my dreams—day and night—ever since. The baby is a bonus, Sienna. A wonderful, beautiful bonus that I'm still getting my head around and I get a little more ex-cited about every day.'

Part of what he'd said was true. She had got under his skin. He'd thought about her every single day. He'd just not ever considered making her his Queen.

But this baby? This baby was too important. In a way,

it would be easier if it weren't Sienna that was having his baby. Theresa had been easy to put in a little box in his head. She was a friend. She would only ever be a friend.

But Sienna? She was spreading out of any little box like a new and interesting virus. One that had started reproducing the first second that he'd met her. He couldn't squash her into some box in his head.

Because he *felt* something for her.

He just wasn't entirely sure what that was—or what it could be.

Fear flashed across her eyes and her hands went protectively to her stomach. 'This is my baby, Sebastian. Mine. I get to choose. I get to say what happens. You haven't been here. You can't just show up for the grand finale and expect to be the ringmaster at the circus. This is my life. Mine.'

He couldn't help it. Emotions were building inside him. He hated that she felt this way. 'But I want it be ours. I want it to be *our* lives. You're writing me off before we've even started. You have to give me a chance. Look at tonight. Look at how we fitted together. Do you think I could have done that with anyone else?' He shook his head. 'Not for a second, Sienna. Only with you.'

He stopped. He had to force himself. He picked up a slice of pizza even though his appetite had left him. 'Let's try and relax a little. It's been a big night. We need some down time.'

He could see a dozen things flitting behind those caramel eyes of hers.

'Stuff it,' she said as she stood up quickly. She marched to the fridge and brought out a white box that came from a bakery. She lifted out the biggest chocolate éclair he'd ever seen and put it on a plate and shrugged. 'Figure you might as well see how I deal with stress. It might give you a hint for the future.'

He sat quietly, trying not to smile as she devoured the

chocolate éclair with a fork and sipped her diet soda. The atmosphere slowly settled.

From the table he could see outside into her snow-covered back garden, framed by the now black sky. It was bigger than he'd expected with an unusual style of seat and a large tree. Next to the seat was a little bush with a string of glowing multicoloured lights that twinkled every now and then.

He smiled. 'You really do like Christmas, don't you?'

She raised her eyebrows. 'Wait until you see the front room.' She sighed as she stared at her back garden. 'I've been here less than a year. I have visions of what my back garden should look like. Our local garden centre has a whole host of light-up reindeers and a family of penguins.' She pointed at the large tree. 'And I wanted lights for that tree too, and a light-up Santa to go underneath. But if I'd bought everything I wanted to, I would have bankrupted myself. So, I've decided to just buy one new thing every year. That way, I can build myself up to what I really imagine it should look like in my head.'

He watched her as she spoke and couldn't help but smile. The more she spoke, the more of a drifting-off expression appeared in her eyes, it was almost as if she were actually picturing what she wanted her garden to look like.

'Why do you like Christmas so much?'

She gave a throwaway shrug. 'I just like what it means.' She paused and bit her lip. 'It was the one time of year my parents didn't fight—probably because my Aunt Margaret came to stay.' She smiled. 'It was almost as if she brought the Christmas spirit with her. She had so much energy. So much joy. When I was little she made every Christmas special. She was obsessed by it. And I guess I caught a little of her bug.'

It was nice seeing her like this. He stood up and lifted

his glass of diet soda. 'Okay, hit me with it. Show me the front room.'

She laughed and shook her head as she stood up. This time she didn't avert her eyes from the dressing gown that barely covered him. She waved her hand. 'Give me a second.' Then she walked along the corridor and bent down, flicking a few switches just inside the door. She smiled and stood back against the wall. 'I wanted to give you the full effect.'

He stopped walking. She was talking about her front room. He knew she was talking about her front room. But he was already getting the full effect. The full Sienna Mc-Donald effect. Every time she spoke with that lilting Scottish accent it sent blood rushing around his body. Every time their gazes connected he felt a little buzz.

She looked excited. It was obvious she was proud of whatever he was about to see.

The main lights in her room weren't on. They weren't needed, because every part of the room seemed to twinkle with something or other.

He stepped inside. The tree took pride of place at the large bay window. The red berry lights twinkled alongside the red decorations. In the corner of the room were three lit-up white and red parcels of differing sizes. A backlit wooden nativity scene was set out on a wooden cabinet. The pale cream wall above her sofa was adorned with purple and white twinkling stars.

In the other corner of the room were a variety of Christmas village ornaments. All had little lights. He smiled as he noticed the school room, the bakery, the shop and Santa's Christmas workshop.

The one thing he noticed most about this place was the warmth. Nothing like his Christmases in the palace in Montanari. Oh, the decorations had been beautiful. But anonymous people had arrived and assembled them every year. There was no real connection to the family.

Everything was impersonal. Most of the time he was told not to touch. Sienna's home had a depth that he hadn't experienced before.

He turned to face her. 'It's like a Christmas grotto in here. How long did this take you?'

She shrugged. 'Not long. Well…maybe a few days.'

He stepped a little closer. Close enough to feel her swollen stomach against his. The rest of the room was dark. He reached up and touched the smudge on her cheek. 'You didn't get a chance to clean up, did you? I wonder how little Gabriel is doing.'

She froze as soon as he touched her cheek. Maybe it was too familiar a gesture? Too forward of him. The tip of his finger tingled from where he'd come into contact with her skin. He couldn't help but touch her again. This time brushing her cheek as he tucked a wayward strand of hair behind her ear.

Her eyes looked darker in here. Or maybe it was just the fact her pupils had dilated so much, they were currently only rimmed with a tiny edge of brown.

'I'll phone the hospital later.' Her voice was husky, almost a whisper. If she objected to his closeness she hadn't said.

He took in a deep breath. A deep breath of her.

There it was. The raspberry scent of her shampoo, mixed with the light aroma of her subtle perfume and just the smell of her. For Sebastian it was intoxicating. Mesmerising. And sent back a rush of memories.

His fingers hesitated around her ear. He didn't want to pull them away. He didn't want to be out of contact with her.

This felt like something he'd never experienced before.

Something worth waiting for.

She bit her bottom lip again and he couldn't stop himself. He pulled her closer and met her lips with his. Taste.

He could taste her. The sweetness of the éclair. Now, he truly was having a rush of memories.

The memory of her kiss would be imprinted on his brain for ever. Her lips slowly parted and his fingers tangled through her hair, capturing the back of her head to keep her there for ever.

Her hands wound around his neck as she tilted her head even further to his. Somehow the fact that her swollen belly was next to his was even better than he could have imagined. Their child was in there. Their child was growing inside her. In a few weeks' time he'd be a father. And no matter what his parents might think, he couldn't wish for a better mother for his child.

His hand brushed down the side of her breast and settled on her waist.

He felt her tense. Slow their kiss. He let their lips part and she pressed her forehead against his. Her breathing was rapid.

He stayed like that for a second, letting them both catch their breath.

'Sebastian,' she breathed heavily.

'Yes?'

She lifted her heavy eyelids to meet his gaze. 'You have to give me a minute. Give me a few seconds. I need to go and change.'

He stepped back. 'Of course. No problem.'

He'd no idea what that meant. Change into what?

She disappeared into the corridor and he sank down into her comfortable red sofa for a few minutes, his heart thudding against his chest.

Maybe she wanted him to leave. Maybe she wanted him to stay.

He'd always been confident around women. He'd always felt in charge of a relationship. But things were different with Sienna.

Everything was at stake here.

Sebastian didn't do panic. But right now, if he said the wrong thing, he could mess up everything. And what was the right thing to say to a pregnant woman who'd already told you she wanted the fairy tale?

He looked around the room. The Christmas grotto. Sienna's own personal fairy tale. No castle. No prince. Just this. He tried to shift on the sofa but it was almost impossible. It was one of those sink-in-and-lose-yourself-for-ever kind of sofas.

Sienna had a good life here. She had a house that she loved. Loyal friends and the job of her dreams. The truth was, she didn't really need him. If Sebastian wanted to have a place in her life he was going to have to fight for it.

And he had to be sure what he was fighting for.

He'd meant it when he told her he'd always have come back for her. At first, it had just been words. He just hadn't said the next part—he just wasn't entirely sure what he was coming back *for*.

Someone to have a relationship with? An affair?

Or something else entirely?

It hadn't even been clear in his head until that moment. But as he'd watched her face he'd had a second of pure clarity—sitting across the table was exactly what he wanted. Tonight had given him a new perspective. If he hadn't been there he didn't doubt that Sienna would have put herself in harm's way to try and help that child. It was part of what he admired so much about her.

This might not be the way he had planned it. But Sebastian was always up for a challenge.

Sienna walked back into the room. She glanced at the gaping dressing gown and looked away. 'Your jeans are washed. I've put them in the dryer. They won't be long.'

He nodded. 'Thanks. Now, come and sit down. It's been a big day. Sit for a while.'

He could see her hesitation. See her weighing up what

to do next. She'd washed her face, pulled her hair into some kind of knot and changed into what looked like pyjamas.

She walked over and sat down next to him, curling one leg up underneath her. He wrapped his arm back around her shoulder.

Sienna wanted things to be by her rules. He wanted to keep her happy.

'Tell me what you've organised for the baby. What would you like me to do?'

She looked at him in surprise. 'Well, I've pretty much organised everything. I've turned one room into a nursery. I just need to give it a lick of paint and some of the furniture has arrived. But I haven't built it yet.'

'Let me do that.'

She blinked. 'Which one?'

'Both. All of them. Do you know what colour you want for the nursery? I could start tomorrow.'

Had he ever painted anything in his life? What did he actually know about room decoration? It didn't matter. If that was what she needed for the baby, then he would find someone to do it. Money wasn't exactly an object for Sebastian. If he paid enough, he could get it done tomorrow.

She drew back a little. It was all he could do not to focus on those lips again. He was trying his best to keep her at arm's length. Even though it was the last thing he wanted to do. If he wanted a chance with Sienna and with his baby, he would have to play by her rules.

'Well, okay,' she said after what seemed like for ever. She pushed herself up from the sofa. 'Come and I'll show you the nursery.'

He tried to follow her and fumbled around on the impossible sofa. 'How on earth did you do that? This thing just swallows you up like one of those sand traps.'

She started laughing. 'It does, doesn't it? It was one of

the first things I bought when I got my own flat. I love the colour and, even though it needs replacing, I've never found another sofa quite the colour that I love. So I keep it. The removal men just about killed themselves carrying it down three flights of stairs when I moved from my flat to here.'

He gave himself an almighty push and almost landed on top of her. 'Oh, sorry.' His hand fell automatically to her waist again. It hadn't been deliberate. Not at all. But not a single part of his body wanted to move.

This was his problem. His brain was screaming a thousand things at him. He was getting too attached. He was beginning to feel something for Sienna. Something other than the blood rushing through his body. The rational part of his brain told him she didn't really want him, she didn't want to be part of the monarchy in Montanari. She was probably the most unsuitable woman to be his wife.

But little question marks kept jumping into his thoughts. Was she really so unsuitable? She was brilliant. She had a career. She was a good person. Yes, she was probably a little unconventional. She certainly didn't hesitate to speak her mind. But, after spending his life around people who didn't say what they meant, it was actually kind of refreshing. Add that to the fact that even a glimpse of her sent his senses into overload...

She pulled back a little from him so he dropped a kiss on her forehead and stepped away. 'Blame the sofa.' He smiled.

She showed him across the hall to the nursery. So far he'd seen the bathroom, the main room, the kitchen and the utility. Two other doors in the corridor seemed to glow at him. One of them must be her bedroom.

He waved his hand casually. 'This is a nice house. What's down there?'

She looked over her shoulder. 'Just my bedroom and the third room, which is a dining room/bedroom. I hadn't quite decided what I wanted to do with it yet. There's another sitting room at the back, but the house layout is a little awkward. I think the people that built the house added it on at the last minute. It ended up being off the utility room.'

Sebastian gave a nod as she flicked the switch on the room she'd designated the nursery.

It was a good-sized room. There was a pin board on the wall covered in messages and cut-out pictures. Some were of prams, some of other nurseries, some of furniture and a few of treehouses and garden play sets.

He smiled as he looked at them all. She pointed to one of the pictures. 'That one. That's what I decided on.'

It was lovely. A pale yellow nursery, with a border with ducks and teddy bears and with pale wooden furniture.

She nodded towards the flat boxes leaning against one wall. 'It only arrived yesterday.' There was a kind of sad twang in her voice.

He walked towards it. 'What's wrong?'

She sighed. 'Nothing. It's just not quite what I'd hoped for. I'm sure it will look fine once it's all built. But there was no point in building it until I'd painted the room and put the border up.'

One of the ends of the flat-pack furniture box was open and he peered inside, reaching in with his hand to touch the contents. He got it. He got it straight away. The furniture on the picture on her pin board looked like solid oak with delicate carving and professional workmanship. Furniture bought from a store would never compare. He knew exactly what he could say right now, but he had to be careful of her feelings. She'd worked hard to make preparations for their child.

'Do you know what shade of yellow you want?'

She pointed to the corner of the room. There were around ten different little squares of varying shades of yellow. 'Yeah, I picked the one three from the end. I've bought the paint, I was planning on starting tomorrow.'

She walked over to a plastic bag. 'I have the border here, along with the matching light shade and bedding.'

He took a deep breath as he walked a little closer. 'I really want to help. I really want to be involved. Will you let me paint the room for you tomorrow? And hang the border? Once that's done I can build the furniture, and if you don't like it we can see if there's something more suitable.'

This was the point where she could step away. This was the point where he could end up flung out of the house. But she stayed silent. He could see her thinking things through. The reserve that she'd built around herself seemed to be slipping a little, revealing the Sienna that he'd connected with in Montanari.

His finger wanted to speed dial someone right now. There had to be someone around here that could help make good on his promises.

She nodded slowly then met his gaze with a gentle smile. 'Do you know what? That might actually be good… thanks.' She narrowed her gaze and wagged her finger at him. 'But you're not allowed to bring in someone else to do it. You have to do it yourself. I don't want anyone I don't know in my house.'

There was a tiny wave of unease. She could read him like a book. 'Of course. Of course, I'll do it myself. It will be my pleasure.' He looked around the room. It would be nice with the pale yellow colour on the walls.

He'd tell her things on a need-to-know basis.

He walked back to the pin board and pointed at the prams. 'Have you ordered one yet?'

The two on the board were both brightly coloured with modern designs. Nothing like the coach-built pram he'd been pictured in as a child. He gave a little smile, thinking about his room as a small child with its dark furniture and navy blue drapes.

She stepped up next to him. 'What are you smiling at?'

He gave a sigh. 'I know nothing about prams. But they both look kind of funky. I'm sure I won't have a clue how to put them together.'

Her gaze changed. It was thoughtful. Almost as if she'd finally realised that he planned on being around. Planned on being involved.

'You can buy a plain black one if you want,' she said softly. There was something sad in her voice.

His hand reached down and he intertwined his fingers with hers. 'I'll be proud to push whatever red or purple pram you choose. Why don't you let me buy you both? That's if you haven't ordered one yet.'

She paused. She hadn't pulled her hand away. He started tracing little circles in the palm of her hand with his thumb. 'Sienna, I'm here because I want to be here. I want to be here for you, and for our baby. But…' he turned to face her straight on '…this might all get a little pressured. I have to tell my parents that they're going to be grandparents.'

Her eyes widened. 'They don't know?'

'Not yet. I wanted to speak to you first. To give you a little time.' He reached and tangled his fingers through her hair. 'Once I tell them, the world will know. You won't just be Sienna McDonald, cardiothoracic neonatal surgeon any more. You'll be Sienna McDonald, mother of Prince Sebastian Falco's child. I want to protect you from that. You'll be bombarded with phone calls and emails. Everyone will want a little piece of you.' He shook his head. 'I don't want that.' He gave her a sorry smile. 'There's not enough of you to go round.'

For a moment she looked terrified. Surely, she must have expected this at some point. Surely she must have realised that the press would be interested in their baby?

Maybe his concerns about her had been right.

Her response was a little shaky. 'I don't want people interfering in my life. I'm a surgeon. I do a good job. I've made plans on how to raise this baby.'

Something twisted inside him. He wanted to say everything he shouldn't. He might only have known about this baby for a couple of weeks but every sleepless night had been full of plans for this child too.

Somehow he had to find a way to cement their plans together. There would need to be compromise on each side. How on earth would Sienna cope with his mother?

His mother's idea of compromise would be to sweep this baby from under Sienna's nose, transport the baby to the palace in Montanari and bring up the child with the same ideals she'd had for Sebastian.

For about ten seconds that had been his plan too. Had he really thought Sienna would be happy to marry him and leave her job and friends behind?

He could see himself having to spend the rest of his life having to prevent Sienna and his mother from being in the same room together.

It didn't even bear thinking about. There would be time enough for all that later. He had to start slowly.

He looked around the room. Then he glanced at Sienna's stomach. He let the wave of emotions that he'd tried to temper flood through him. That was his baby in there. *His*.

He didn't want to be a part-time parent. He wanted to see this child every day. He wanted to be involved in every decision.

And the truth was, he wanted to be around Sienna too.

He touched her cheek. 'I want to be part of those plans, Sienna. That's all I'm asking.'

She stared at him for the longest time. Her gaze unwavering.

'Let me do something to try and help. Once I've spoken to my parents, can I get one of the publicists from the palace to contact you? To try and take the pressure off any queries you might get from reporters?'

She gave the briefest of nods. At least it was something. It was a start. He hadn't even mentioned the fact that he would actually have to hire security to protect her.

'You can come tomorrow. You'll need to be up early before I go to work.'

He smiled. 'No problem. I like to be up early.' He pointed to the pin board again. 'What about the prams?'

The edges of her lips turned upwards and she gave a little shake of her head. 'You've no idea how hard this is for me.'

'What?' He couldn't keep the mock horror from his voice as he put one hand to his chest. 'You mean letting someone else help? Letting someone else be involved?'

She nodded. She waved at the photos on the board. 'I'm running out of time. I need to order the pram that I want this weekend if it's going to be here on time.' She pulled a face. 'Trouble is, I still can't choose. And the lie-down pram, buggy and car seat all go together. At this rate, if I don't choose soon, I won't even have a way to get my baby home from hospital, let alone out of the house.'

He nodded. She hadn't taken him up on the idea of getting both. 'How about we go this weekend and look again?'

She gave him the strangest look. 'Have you any idea what these places are like? The guys in the giant nursery stores always look like they've been dragged in there kicking and screaming and can't wait to get back out.'

He raised his eyebrows. 'Well, I will be different. I can't wait to spend hours of my life helping you choose between a red and a purple pram set.' He gave a hopeful smile. 'Is there coffee in these places?'

She nodded. 'Oh, yes. But you need to drink decaf in

support of me. But there's also cake. So it might not be too bad.'

Finally, he was getting somewhere. Finally he felt as if he was starting to make inroads with Sienna. They'd made a connection today that felt like it had back in Montanari.

And this wasn't just about the baby—even though that was all they'd really talked about. This was about them too.

This would always be about them.

She walked back to the door of the nursery. 'Okay, thanks. Tomorrow it is. Now let me get your clothes. The dryer will be finished by now.'

His heart sank a little. It was time for him to go. It didn't matter how much he actually wanted to stay.

He followed Sienna down the hall as she pulled his clothes from the dryer. The jeans were still warm as he stepped into them and fastened them. He put the dressing gown on top of the dryer and turned to face her.

Her tongue was running along her top lip. She was watching him. Her eyes fixated on his bare chest. He took a step towards her.

'Sienna?'

He could act. He could pull her towards him and kiss her exactly the way he wanted to. But he'd already done that tonight. This time it was important for her to take the lead.

She put one hand flat on his chest and took a deep breath as she looked down at the floor. There was a tremble in her voice. 'You need to give me some time, Seb. It would be so easy just to fall into things again. To take up where we left off. But there's so much more at stake now.'

His heart gave a little jump. Seb. She'd just called him Seb again.

She lifted her head and met his gaze. 'I didn't expect to see you again. I didn't expect you to come.'

He placed his hand over hers. 'And now?'

'You asked me to give you a chance. I want to. I do. But I need to be sure about why we're both here. I've had more time to get used to the thought of our baby than you have. And the thought of being under the gaze of the whole world is something I hadn't even contemplated.' He gave her hand a squeeze. Now he couldn't help himself. He stepped forward and put his arms around her.

'Let me help. Let me get you some advice. We could release a press statement together if you wanted.'

She pushed back and shook her head. 'Release a press statement? Those are words I never thought I'd hear. Just give me a bit of time, a bit of space. One step at a time, Seb. If you want me to give you a chance, that's the way it's got to be.'

He was disappointed. He couldn't help it. He was rushing things. But being around Sienna and not *being* with her was more difficult than he could ever have imagined.

Now he felt a sense of panic. What about the press intrusion into Sienna's life? How would she cope? He was used to it. He'd been photographed since the day he was born. But, for Sienna, life was entirely different.

She loved her job. She'd trained long and hard to be a specialist surgeon. Would she be able to continue with the job she loved if she were his wife?

At first his only thought had been about duty. His duty to the mother of his child, and to his country. His proposal of marriage had only been about those things.

Now? Things were changing. Changing in a way he hadn't even contemplated. He gave a half-smile. Was this how Oliver felt around Ella?

He pulled his T-shirt over his head and reached for his leather jacket. She handed him a damp towel. 'Try and take some of the mud off it with this.'

She was so matter-of-fact. So practical. Ten seconds ago she'd been wearing her heart on her sleeve. He wiped the jacket as best he could and slid it on.

'My shoes are next to the door.' He paused; he really didn't want to leave.

She nodded. 'Okay, then. Be here early, around seven-thirty. I'll leave you a key to lock up when you're done.'

She followed him to the door and shivered as the icy blast hit as soon as he opened it. 'Stay inside,' he said quickly. 'Keep warm. I'll see you tomorrow.'

'Seb?'

He'd already gone down the first two steps and turned at the sound of her voice. 'Yeah?'

She closed her eyes for a second. 'Thank you,' she said softly, with one hand on her stomach.

He leaned forward and kissed her cheek. 'Any time. Any time at all.' Then he headed down the path back to his car.

CHAPTER FIVE

SHE DIDN'T SLEEP a single wink—just tossed and turned all night.

Eventually, she got up and phoned to check on Gabriel. It was a relief to find out he was stable and had regained consciousness.

Seb arrived early with hot pancakes for breakfast and a hire car for her to use. He was in a good mood and only teased her a little when she gave him a list of instructions, including where he was allowed to wear his shoes.

In a lot of ways he was easy to be around. It was easy to forget he was a prince. It was easy to forget he had a whole host of other responsibilities. Ones that would ultimately keep him away from her and their baby.

The first time she knew something was off was when she arrived at work. There was a TV van in the car park and a reporter was shooting a story opposite the main entrance to the hospital.

As soon as she turned into the staff car park one of the porters gave her a nod of his head. He walked quickly to her car. 'You might want to keep your head down and go in the side door.'

She picked up her bag. 'Why? What's happening?'

'You haven't seen it?'

Her phone started ringing. She glanced at the number. Seb. She'd only just left him. Why was he ringing her already? She silenced it as Frank held out his mobile towards her.

There was a photo. A photo of her house. A photo of her and Sebastian in her doorway looking intimate.

The headline wasn't much better.

Montanari's Baby Secret

She put her hand up to her mouth. 'No. No way. Who took that photo? That was last night. Someone was outside my house?' She didn't care about her ratty hair, or the fact she was wearing pyjamas in the photo. It looked as if she'd just fallen out of bed to show Sebastian to the door—that implied a whole lot of other things. All she cared about was the fact someone had been hanging about outside her house, waiting to take a picture. Why hadn't Seb's security people seen them?

Frank glanced over at the crowd in the car park. 'What's with the different car—did you know they'd be here? Trying to throw them off the scent?' He was smiling. It was almost as if he were enjoying the fracas.

'No. My car wouldn't start last night. Sebastian gave me a lift home. This is a hire car. My car's still in the other car park.'

Frank was still watching. 'Pull your hood up and duck in the side door. I'll walk next to you.'

She glanced around the car park. It seemed to be getting busier by the second. She pulled up her hood on her cream coat and walked alongside Frank with her head down. It only took five minutes to reach her office, close the door and turn on the computer. Her phone buzzed again. Seb.

As the computer started to kick into life she sank into her chair and put the phone to her ear. 'I've seen it. Reporters are all over the hospital. I've got a job to do. I don't need this.'

'I'll deal with it. I'll speak to Oliver and see what we can do. I'll phone you later once we have a press release ready.'

She put down the phone and watched as one headline after another appeared on screen. They had her name, her age, her qualifications. There was a report about the work she'd done in Montanari. There was speculation about how exactly she and Sebastian had met.

There was even more speculation about the timing. His sudden engagement and his wedding announcement, then his even quicker plans to cancel.

There was a camera shot of the King and Queen of Montanari from earlier on this morning. Sebastian's mother looked tight-lipped and quietly furious. He hadn't mentioned them at all. She could only imagine the kind of phone call that had been.

Oliver knocked on the door. 'Sienna? Can we talk?'

She sighed and rolled her eyes. 'Are the board complaining about the *femme fatale* on their staff?'

He snorted. 'Who cares? I'm worried about you. I've called Security. They'll keep an eye out for any reporters.'

'Thank you, Oliver.'

He paused for a second, hovering around the door as only a man who was struggling to find the words could.

She rolled her eyes again. 'What is it, Oliver?'

He pulled a face. 'I've no idea what happened between you before.' Then he shook his head and smiled. 'Well, actually the evidence is there. I've known him since we were at university. He was a few years younger than me but decided to join the same rowing club. We've been friends ever since. I just wanted you to know—I've never seen him like this.'

She frowned. 'Never seen him like what?'

Oliver hesitated again. 'Never seen him act like he's in love before,' he said as he retreated out of the door.

Her head started to swim. After a few seconds she actually put it down between her knees.

Last night had been overwhelming. Having Sebastian in her home, in a state of undress and then in the middle of their baby's nursery, had felt surreal.

She just hadn't pictured it happening in her head. It had seemed so far out of reach that she hadn't allowed her head room for it.

Now, it was a reality.

Now, the man that had haunted her dreams for months was finally only a fingertip away.

But how much was he actually offering?

When he'd told her he would always have come back for her, she'd really, really wanted to believe him. But words were easy. Everyone knew that.

And the fact was he'd left her warm bed and put an engagement ring on another woman's finger.

It didn't matter what the facts or circumstances were. It had still happened.

It had still hurt.

She would love to believe that one snowy day, out of the blue, Sebastian would have turned up on a white stallion to sweep her away from all this and declare his undying love.

But the word love had never been mentioned.

Maybe she was unrealistic. Maybe she was a fool to chase the fairy tale. But after being brought up by parents who clearly didn't love each other she could never do that to her child. Would it be even worse if she loved Sebastian and he never quite loved her? How would their son or daughter feel about being brought up in an uneven relationship blighted by unrequited love?

It was too hard to even imagine.

So, what exactly had Oliver meant? He'd never seen Sebastian in love before?

Her stomach gave a little swirl. When she'd looked into those forest-green eyes last night all she'd been able to think about was how much this guy could hurt her. How much of her heart he'd already stolen despite the walls she'd tried to put up around it.

Self-protect mode seemed easiest.

He was being kind. He was being considerate. But could it really be love and not duty?

Her head wouldn't even let her go there.

There was a knock at her door and Juliet Turner, the neonatal specialist surgeon, walked in with contraband in her hands.

'Sienna? Are you okay?'

Sienna pulled her head up from between her knees and smiled. 'Yeah. Sorry, I'm fine.'

Juliet frowned. 'It seems like I'm just in time. I thought the road to your favourite coffee shop might be lined with reporters this morning, so decided to take the hit for you. Don't worry—it's caffeine-and-sugar-free.'

She set down the coffee and a mystery package in a paper bag. 'Anything I can do for you?'

Sienna shook her head and waved at the contraband. 'You've already done it. Have I told you lately that I love you?' Juliet laughed as Sienna continued, 'How are the quads?'

Juliet smiled. 'Things are looking good. They seem to get a little stronger every day.'

Juliet's pager beeped. She glanced at it and her smile broadened. 'Charlie. Better go. Wedding plans are in the air.'

She practically danced out of the door as Sienna took a deep breath. It seemed that everyone else in this hospital had managed to find love just in time for Christmas. Max and Annabelle, Oliver and Ella and now Juliet and Charlie.

There was no way she could be that lucky too.

No way at all. The Christmas fairy dust had all been used up around here.

Her phone beeped. She opened the message. There was a photo attached that made her blink twice.

'Yuck,' she said out loud. It was from Sebastian. And it was apparently the colour she'd chosen for the baby's nursery. What she'd thought was pale yellow had actually morphed into something more neon-like. She smiled at the message.

Is this what you had in mind?

She glanced at her watch. Just over an hour and he'd already painted one wall. Too bad he'd need to paint it again.

She replied quickly.

Not quite.

Then she dabbed again.

Not at all!

Sienna jerked as her pager sounded. The caffeine-free skinny latte with sugar-free caramel toppled and some of the hot liquid spilled down her pale pink trousers.

She jumped up. 'Great.' She looked around her office. Of course. There was nothing to mop it from her trousers with—and by the time she found something the brand-new trousers would be stained for life.

She glared at the coffee Juliet had bought for her. 'That'll teach me,' she murmured.

The pager sounded again and she shook her head as

she stared at the number. Labour ward. Something must be wrong.

She left the coffee and the tiny cake decorated with holly Juliet had bought to go with it lying on the table. Her appetite had abated already.

She walked quickly down the corridor to the labour ward. She could have phoned, but they usually only paged if they actually needed her.

Kirsty, one of the younger labour-ward midwives, was looking a bit frantic. 'You looking for me?' Sienna asked. This striding quickly was getting a bit more difficult.

'I need you to look at a baby. Labour went perfectly—no concerns. But since delivery the baby has been kind of flat. I called the Paeds and they told me to page you.'

Kirsty hadn't paused for breath, her words getting quicker and quicker. Sienna reached over and put her hand on her arm.

'Kirsty, tell me what I need to know.'

Her eyes widened with momentary panic, then her brain kicked into gear and she nodded. 'Caleb Reed, thirty-six plus three weeks, five pounds eleven ounces. Born two hours. He's pale, irritable and his breathing is quite raspy.'

Sienna walked to the nearest sink and washed her hands. She glanced down at her trousers. If she had a little more time she could put on some scrubs. But best not to keep the paediatrician waiting. 'Which room?'

'Number seven.'

Kirsty walked to the room and stood anxiously at the doorway while Sienna dried her hands.

Sienna gave a nod and walked inside. Lewis Connell, one of her paediatric colleagues, told her everything she needed to know with one glance.

She gave a wide smile to the two anxious parents and held out her hand towards the father, who was perched at the side of the bed. 'Hi, there. I'm Sienna McDonald.'

She left her title out of the introduction. There was time enough for that later. The man warily shook her hand. 'John,' he said, and she held it out in turn to the mother. 'Dr Connell has asked me to come and take a look at your son. Congratulations. What have you called him?'

It didn't matter that she already knew. She was trying to get a feeling about the parents and how prepared they might be for what could come next.

The mother seemed a little calmer. 'Caleb. We've called him Caleb. And I'm Lucy.' She glanced at Sienna's stomach. 'When is your baby due?'

Sienna gave a little nod. 'Pleased to meet you, Lucy and John.' She patted her stomach. 'Not until the end of January. But if I follow your example I could have him or her any day.'

The mum gave an anxious laugh. 'My waters broke when I went to collect the Christmas turkey. Can you believe that?' She looked over to her baby with affection. 'I guess he couldn't wait for his first Christmas.'

Sienna nodded. 'I guess not. Do you mind if I examine Caleb?'

'No.' It came out as a little squeak.

Sienna smiled and walked to the sink and washed her hands again. Lewis had little Caleb lying in a baby warmer. He nodded to the chart next to him and she took a quick glance. Apgar scores at birth and five minutes later weren't too unreasonable. She was more concerned with the presentation of the baby in front of her now.

She unwound her stethoscope from her neck and warmed the end.

'Definitely cardiac,' murmured Lewis. 'But I'll let you decide.'

She trusted him. She'd worked with him for a long time. Lewis was one of the best paediatricians she'd ever worked with. His knowledge base was huge over a wide range of specialities.

Caleb was struggling. It was obvious. His skin was pale. His breathing laboured. She could see his accessory muscles fighting to keep oxygen pumping around his little body. His little face was creased into a frown and his whole body moving in little irritated twitches. The thing that she noticed most was the unusual amount of sweat glistening on his little body. Instinct told her it was nothing to do with the baby warmer. She lifted the chart and looked at the temperature. It was slightly lower than expected. The pulse oximetry readings were a little lower than expected too.

'Has he fed at all?'

She looked up to Lewis and both parents as she rested her stethoscope on the little chest. Lucy shook her head. 'The midwife tried to get him to latch on, but he didn't want to. He just didn't seem ready. She said we'd try again once the doctor had reviewed him.'

She gave a nod. 'No problem. Give me a moment while I listen to his heart.'

She scribbled a note to Lewis who nodded and disappeared out of the room to get what she'd just asked for.

She held her breath while she listened. There. Exactly what she expected. The whoosh of the heart murmur confirming the disruption of the heart flow. She felt for the pulses around the little body—in the groin and in the legs, checking the temperature of the skin in Caleb's lower body.

Lewis backed into the room again, pulling the machine.

'What's that?' John stood up.

She walked towards them. 'It's called an echocardiogram. It will let me check the blood flow around and through Caleb's heart.'

'You think there's something wrong with Caleb's heart?' Lucy gasped and held her hands to her chest.

The words she chose right now were so important.

She didn't want to distress the brand-new parents, but she wasn't going to tell any lies.

'I'm not sure. I think it's something we need to check out. He seems a little unsettled.'

John and Lucy shot anxious glances at each other. John moved over and put his arm around his wife.

Lewis had positioned the echocardiogram next to the baby warmer and was talking in a low voice to baby Caleb. Sienna gave the parents a little nod. 'Are you okay with me checking Caleb a little further?'

They both nodded. She could practically see the fear emanating from their pores. This was one of the worst parts of her job. In some cases, cardiac conditions were picked up during the antenatal scans, plans could be made in advance and parents prepared for what lay ahead. But in cases like these, there were no plans.

One minute parents were preparing for the exciting birth of their child—the next they were being told their brand-new tiny baby needed major surgery. She had a good idea that was what was about to happen for John and Lucy.

Lewis gave her the nod and she switched the machine on and spread some warmed gel on Caleb's chest. He was still grizzly. His colour hadn't improved and from the twitching of his arms and legs it was as if his little body knew something wasn't quite right.

While he'd been inside his mother and attached to the umbilical cord his cardiac system had had constant support. Now—outside? His little heart seemed to be struggling with the work.

'Hey, little guy.' She spoke quietly as she placed the transducer on his little chest wall and her gaze flickered between him and the screen. Her trained eyes didn't take long to see exactly as she suspected. She could see movement of the blood flow through the heart chambers and heart valves. She pressed a button to measure the direction and speed of the blood flow and then moved to the surrounding blood vessels.

There. Exactly as she expected. She took a deep breath and took her time. She had to be absolutely sure what she was seeing. The room was silent around her. But she'd dealt with this before. She had to make sure she had the whole picture before she spoke to the parents.

Finally, she gave a little nod to Lewis. 'Would you be able to contact Max and see if he is available?'

To his credit, Lewis barely blinked. He would know if she was looking for the other cardiac surgeon that she wanted to act promptly. He gave a brief nod and disappeared out of the room.

Sienna wiped Caleb's chest clean, talking to him the whole time, then lifted him from the baby warmer, wrapped him in a blanket and took him over to his parents. Once he was settled in his mother's arms she sat down on the bed next to them.

'Caleb has something called coarctation of the aorta. The aorta is the big blood vessel that goes to the heart.' She picked up Caleb's chart and drew a little picture on some paper for them. 'Caleb's aorta is narrower than it should be—like this. That means that his heart isn't getting all the blood that it needs. His heart has to work harder than it should to try and pump blood around his body. And this is something we need to fix.'

She paused, giving the parents a few minutes to take in her words.

'How...how do you fix it?' asked John.

She licked her lips. 'I need to do some surgery on him.'

Lucy let out a little whimper as she stared at her baby. Sienna put her hand on Lucy's arm.

'Right now, Caleb is getting a very good blood supply to the top half of his body. But his pulses are weaker in the bottom half of his body—to his legs and feet. If we don't do surgery to widen his aorta then his heart will be affected by working too hard and he could suffer from heart failure.'

Lucy was shaking her head. 'Why?' Her eyes were filled with tears. 'Why has this happened to our baby?'

Sienna nodded. These were natural questions for parents to ask. She chose her words carefully. 'There are lots of ideas around why some babies have problems with their hearts, but the truth is—no one really knows. It could be a family thing. It could be in your genes. The type of condition that Caleb has is called a congenital heart defect. Have you ever known anyone in either of your families to have something like this?'

They exchanged glances and both of them shook their heads. She gave a slow nod. 'Sometimes people think congenital heart defects can be caused by things in the environment, things around us. Other theories are it could be caused by things that we eat and drink or medicines a mum might take.' She gave Lucy's arm a squeeze. She had to be honest, but didn't want Lucy to blame herself for her baby's condition. It was important that they focused on Caleb right now.

'How often does this happen?' Lucy's voice had cracked already and tears had formed in her eyes.

This was always the hardest part—breaking the news to parents that something was wrong with the little person all their hopes and dreams were invested in.

She'd always found this bit hard. But not quite as hard as she was finding it today. She blinked quickly, stopped tears forming in her own eyes. It was hard not to empathise with them. In a few weeks' time she would be beside herself if something was wrong with her baby. It didn't matter how much she knew. It didn't matter what her skills were.

For the last few months she'd practically lived her life in a bubble. She'd been so focused on the plans. The plans about maternity leave, cover, nurseries, childminders, cribs, prams and car seats.

She hadn't really focused on the actual outcome.

The actual real live moment when she'd become a mother and her life would change for ever.

Sebastian had brought all that home to her.

Maybe it was having someone around who was so excited about their baby. She'd felt so alone before. So determined to make sure everything would be in place.

She hadn't let the excitement—or the terror—actually build.

But having Sebastian around had heightened every emotion she possessed in an immediate kind of way.

He talked about it so easily. Their baby being here. Their baby being loved. Their baby's future.

A horrible part of her thought that when he hadn't known it had actually been a little easier.

Because Sebastian wanted to be involved in *everything*.

And it was clear he had plans on going nowhere.

The door opened and Max came in. He didn't speak, just raised his eyebrows and walked over towards her.

She smiled gratefully. 'You asked how often this happens. It is rare. But not quite as rare as you might think. Around four out of every ten thousand babies born will have this condition. In some babies it's mild. For some people it's not picked up until they are an adult. Some children aren't picked up until their teenage years. John and Lucy, this is Max Ainsley. He's the cardiothoracic surgeon that is taking over from me while I go on maternity leave.'

Max didn't hesitate. He held out his hand, shaking both their hands but letting Sienna continue to take the lead.

'If you know about Caleb now, does that mean he's really bad?' John looked as though he might be sick.

Sienna moved her hand over to his arm. 'It means it's something that we need to fix, John. And we need to fix it now.' She scribbled something on Caleb's chart. 'I'm going to make arrangements to move Caleb up to the paediatric intensive care unit. You'll be able to go with him, but the staff will be able to monitor him better there. I'll arrange for him a have a few more tests—a chest X-ray and an ECG.'

Lucy's eyes widened. 'My dad had one of those when they thought he was having a heart attack.'

Sienna nodded. 'It gives us an accurate tracing of the heart without causing any problems for Caleb. Once we have all the test results Max and I will review them. The type of surgery we need to do is to widen the narrow part of Caleb's aorta. It's called a balloon angioplasty. We put a thin flexible tube called a catheter into the narrow area of the aorta, then we inflate a little balloon to expand the blood vessel. Sometimes we put a little piece of mesh-covered tube called a stent in place to keep the blood vessel open.' She paused for a second. 'If we think the angioplasty won't work, or it's not the right procedure for Caleb, then we sometimes have to do surgery where we remove the narrow part of the aorta and reconstruct the vessel to allow blood to flow normally through the aorta.'

She took a deep breath. 'I know all this is scary. I know all this can be terrifying. I understand, really, I do. But both Max and I have done this kind of surgery on lots of babies. It's a really specialised field and we have a lot of expertise.'

'Do some babies die?'

Lucy's question came out of the blue and Max glanced in her direction. It was clear he was happy to step in if she was finding this too difficult. And for the first time in her life, she was.

She gave a careful nod. 'There can always be complications from surgery. Caleb is a good weight. He isn't too tiny. The echocardiogram of his heart didn't show any other heart defects. Some babies with coarctation of the aorta have other heart conditions—but I don't see any further complications for Caleb.' She stood up from the bed; her back was beginning to ache.

'I have to warn you that surgery can take some time. We could be in Theatre for more than a few hours and I don't want you to panic. I'm going to bring you some information to read then we'll arrange to transfer Caleb upstairs for his tests. Both Max and I will come back and explain everything again, and answer any questions before you sign the consent form. Is there anything you want to ask me right now?'

Both John and Lucy shook their heads. They still looked stunned. Max put a gentle hand on her back. She'd done this kind of surgery on her own on more than thirty occasions but somehow, at this stage of her pregnancy, she was relieved she'd have a second pair of hands.

She gave a final smile at the doorway. 'Don't worry, we'll take good care of Caleb. I'll just go and make the arrangements.'

She ignored the stiffness in her back as she walked down the corridor. It was going to be a long day.

Sebastian was waiting at the end of the corridor. 'Hey,' she said. 'What are you doing here?'

He shrugged. 'I came to find you to see if we might actually make it to a restaurant tonight. I booked out a whole place so we might actually get some privacy. I thought we could try and make Christmas Eve special. But I just heard you're going into surgery.'

He made it all sound so normal and everything he'd said was true. But he was also worried about how she was, following the news story about them. Sienna seemed remarkably calm, however. She was focused. Her mind was on the job. And he admired her all the more for it.

She gave a little sigh. 'Christmas Eve is normally my favourite night of the year. I love the build-up. The expectation for Christmas the next day.' She squeezed her eyes shut for a second as Sebastian reached up and brushed his fingers against her cheek. She opened her eyes again and they met his. 'But this is the life of a surgeon,' she whispered. 'This is the life that I've chosen.'

She held her breath as he nodded slowly. Her heart thudding against her chest. He had to understand. He had to understand that this was her life. If he wanted to be part of it, he had to realise there were things she wouldn't give up—things she would never change.

He touched her cheek again and leaned forward, his lips brushing against her ear as he whispered back, 'I wouldn't have it any other way.'

Her heart gave a little swell as a few of the other staff walked past. She was jerked from their little private moment. She pointed to the elbow of his leather jacket. 'You touched the nursery wall, didn't you?' Then her mouth opened. 'You changed the colour, didn't you?'

He let out a laugh at the pale yellow stain on his jacket. A funny look passed over his face. 'Yip. I did. Those nursery walls have been painted with blood, sweat and even a few tears.' He grimaced. 'There might have been a bit of a problem with the border.'

'What do you mean?'

He made another face. 'Let's just say the painting I could just about handle. Border skills seem to have escaped me. I might need to buy you another.' He gave her a big smile. 'And I might have done something you won't be happy about.'

'What's that?' Her head was currently swimming with thoughts of the surgery she was about to perform. She didn't need distractions.

'I see what you mean about the furniture. I might have ordered a few alternatives.' He held up his hand quickly. 'But don't worry. If you don't like them, they can go back.'

His phone buzzed in his pocket. He pulled it out, silenced it and pushed it away again.

'Problem?'

He shook his head. 'Nothing I can't handle.'

'What is it?'

'Let's just say it's a mother-sized problem.'

Sienna's heart sank a little. 'How many calls have you had?'

He shifted from one foot to the other. 'I spoke to her this morning just as the press release went out. Since then, there's been another twenty calls.'

'And you haven't answered them?'

He shook his head firmly. 'I've already heard her opinion once. I don't need to hear it again.'

It was a horrible sensation. Like something pressing down heavily on her shoulders. 'Please don't fall out with your mother because of me.'

'Let me worry about my mother. You just worry about your surgery. Oliver said I can go into the viewing room and watch.'

'Oh.' She wasn't quite sure what to say. It was one thing inviting Sebastian into her home, but inviting him to watch her surgery was something else entirely. It seemed he was determined to be involved in both her personal and professional life. She wasn't sure quite how she felt about that.

He bent forward and kissed her on the cheek. 'Good luck. You'll be fantastic. They're lucky to have you.'

The doors swung open behind them and Max appeared in his scrubs. 'Let's go, Sienna. This could be a long one.'

She gave a quick nod and followed him to scrub. Right now she had a baby to focus on. Little Caleb deserved every second of her attention.

And he would get it.

The viewing gallery for the surgery was almost full. Sebastian had to squeeze his way between a couple of excited students.

Sienna appeared cool. She and Max had a long discussion with the staff around them to make sure everyone was on the same page. Then, she glanced up at the gallery as the anaesthetist put Caleb to sleep, and talked some of the students through the procedure they were about to perform. Even behind her mask he could see the brightness in her eyes—the love of her job shone out loud and clear. It made him wish he'd got to meet her while she'd been at the hospital in Montanari. 'Well, guys, I guess this isn't where any of us expected to be on Christmas Eve, but this is the life of a surgeon.' She pointed to the equipment next to her. 'We are lucky at Teddy's to have the best technology around. The whole time we perform this surgery cameras will record our every move. There are viewing screens in the gallery, which you'll be able to watch. You'll find that during surgery Max and I don't talk much. We like to concentrate on the intricacies of the operation—that's why we've explained things beforehand. We will, however, be available to answer any questions you have once surgery is over and we've spoken to Caleb's parents.'

There were a few approving nods around him.

Max walked to the opposite side of the operating table from Sienna. 'Ready?' he asked.

She nodded once and they began.

Sebastian had never seen anything like it in his life. He'd known exactly what her job was when he'd first met her, but he'd never actually seen her in action. He'd never realised just how tiny and intricate the procedures were that she and Max performed. The baby's vessels were tiny.

But Sienna was confident in her expertise. She and Max only exchanged a few words. They worked in perfect synchronisation. Little Caleb truly couldn't be in better hands.

Things started to swirl around in his head. Sienna had a gift. A gift she'd perfected over years of sacrifice and training. No matter how much his mother's words had echoed in his head this morning about duty and expectations for the mother of the heir apparent, he could never expect Sienna to fulfil the role that his mother had for the last thirty years.

Sienna had a skill and talent he could never ask her to walk away from. Not if he really loved her. Not if he really wanted her to be happy.

It came over him like a tidal wave. The plans he'd spent today making. The guilt that had washed over him as the decorator he'd hired had painted the first wall that hideous colour. He'd paid the man more than promised and sent him on his way. The hours of rolling yellow paint onto the walls. The aching muscles and spoiled, crumpled border. The emergency phone calls. The special orders. All because he'd realised this was about trust. This was about him, doing something for their child. This wasn't about duty at all. This was so much more than that. So much more than he'd ever experienced before.

All because he wanted to win a place in this woman's heart.

It finally hit him. She was worth it. She was really, really worth it.

He didn't want to live a single day without this woman in his life.

And he'd be lucky if he could capture a heart like hers.

Caleb's tiny vessel was even more fragile than expected. It took absolute precision to try and widen the vessel and insert the stent to make it remain patent. Having Max next to her was an added bonus. Normally, she would have performed this procedure unassisted, but they both knew that Max was likely to do Caleb's immediate follow-up care so it made sense that they worked together.

Baby wasn't taking kindly to her being on her feet so

long. Her back ached more than usual and her bladder was being well and truly kicked by some angry little feet.

'Sienna?'

Max's voice was much louder than usual. She glanced up sharply just as one of the instruments fell from her hand to the theatre floor.

She blinked. He was out of focus. A warm flush flooded her skin.

'Sienna? Catch her!' he shouted and it was the last thing she heard.

One second she was in the middle of an operation, the next second Sienna was in a crumpled heap on the floor. Sebastian was on his feet and racing down the stairs before he even had time to think. He banged on the theatre doors, which were protected by a code. A flurry of staff rushed past the inside of the doors towards the theatre she'd been operating in. A few seconds later two male scrub nurses were carrying her out of the theatre.

Sebastian banged the door again and one of the theatre nurses turned in surprise. She gave a little nod of her head, obviously realising who he was, and opened the door from the inside. 'I'm going to phone Oliver,' she said as she disappeared off to another room.

Sebastian rushed after the two male nurses. They were gently laying Sienna down on another theatre trolley. Their reactions automatic. One applied a BP cuff, the other stood next to her, talking quietly to her and trying to get a reaction.

It was all Sebastian could do not to elbow both of them out of the way. But they were better equipped to assist her than he was, and he had enough know-how to stand back and let them get on with it.

After a few seconds she started to come around. Groggy and—by the look of it—uncomfortable.

She took a few deep breaths, her hands going automatically to her stomach. One of the theatre nurses smiled at her. 'You decided to go on maternity leave, Sienna.'

She blinked and tried to sit up, but the other male nurse put his hand on her shoulder. 'Not yet. Give it another few minutes. Your BP was low. Let me get you some water to sip.'

Sienna groaned and put her hands to her head. 'Please tell me everything is okay with Caleb. Nothing else happened, did it? I can't believe I just stoated off the floor.'

'You what?'

Sebastian couldn't help it. Her accent seemed even thicker than normal.

The male nurse glanced at him with a smile. 'I think she means she fainted.' He moved out of the way to let Sebastian closer. 'And don't worry. Max is more worried about you than finishing off the surgery. I'll let him know you're okay. He just needs to close.'

Sienna turned to her side for a second, her face a peculiar shade of grey. 'I think I'm going to be sick.'

About ten arms made a grab for the sick bowls but they were all too late. Sienna tried to get up again. 'Don't anyone touch that. I'll clean it up myself.'

'No, you won't.' Oliver strode through the doors. 'Don't you dare move.'

Sebastian leaned across and touched her stomach to stop her getting up, just at the same second a little foot connected sharply with his hand.

'Oh,' he said suddenly, pulling his hand back.

'Try having it all day,' sighed Sienna. 'And all night.'

But Sebastian couldn't stop staring at his hand. That was his baby. *His* baby that had just kicked him.

Of course, he'd come over when he'd heard the news about Sienna—and her pregnancy bump was obvious. But he'd never actually touched it. Never actually felt his little baby moving beneath her skin.

Oliver walked around to the other side. 'I'll arrange

for you to go upstairs and have a scan. We need to make sure that everything is fine—that there aren't any complications.'

Sienna sat up this time and took the plastic cup of water offered by one of the theatre nurses. 'Oliver, honestly, I'm fine. There's no need to fuss. I hadn't managed to eat before I got called into surgery. That, and my back is aching a little because I'm getting further on. I'm fine. Once I go and get something to eat, I'll be good as new.'

'You'll be on maternity leave. That's it. No more patients. No more surgeries.' Sebastian almost smiled. It was clear from the tone of Oliver's voice that there would be no arguments.

Max came through the swing doors tugging his theatre cap from his head. 'How are you? Is everything okay?'

Her voice wavered a little. 'I'm so sorry, Max. Is Caleb okay? Have you finished?'

He waved his hand easily. 'Of course, he's fine. Don't worry about Caleb. I'll look after him.' He pointed to her stomach. 'You just worry about yourself and that precious cargo in there.'

She swung her legs off the side of the trolley. 'Let me go and get changed.' She glanced at Sebastian. 'Sebastian can take me home. I'll get take-out on the way.'

She had that determined lift to her chin but Oliver had obviously seen it before. 'No way. Not until I say. Scan first.'

She opened her mouth to argue but Sebastian cut her off. 'That would be great, Oliver. Thanks for organising that. It's really important to us to make sure that everything is fine with the baby. Those operating theatre floors are harsh.' He met her simmering gaze. 'We both want to be reassured that the baby has come to no harm.'

He'd chosen his words deliberately. There was no way she could refuse. It would make her look as if she didn't care—and that would never be Sienna, no matter how argumentative and feisty she was feeling.

She turned towards him and whispered under her breath. 'Don't tell me what to do. And I can do this myself. You don't need to be there. Why don't you wait outside?'

He felt himself bristle. He pasted a smile on his face and spoke so low, only she could hear. 'How many scans have I already missed, Sienna? Let me assure you, I have no intention of missing this one.'

She met his gaze for a second, as if she wanted to argue. Then seemed to take a deep breath and gave a tiny nod of her head.

One of the other nurses appeared with something else in her hand. 'From my secret chocolate supply. You're only getting special treatment because I love you and I expect you to call the baby after me—even if it's a boy.'

Sienna let out a little laugh and held her hand out for the chocolate. 'Thanks, Mary, I know you guard this stuff with your life. I appreciate it.'

Sebastian was trying his best to be calm. Now that Sienna had woken up, the panic in the room seemed to have vanished.

A porter appeared with a wheelchair and, after another check of her blood pressure, she was wheeled down the corridor towards the scan room.

Christmas Eve. The staff in the maternity unit were buzzing. Placing bets on who would deliver the first Christmas baby. The canteen would be closed later tonight and as they walked past one of the rooms, Sebastian could see plates of food already prepared for the night-shift workers.

The scan room was dark, the sonographer waiting for them. 'Hi there, Sienna. I heard you took a tumble in Theatre. Slide up on the trolley and we'll get a quick check of baby.'

Sienna had just finished eating her chocolate bar and she moved over onto the trolley and pulled up her scrub top.

Sebastian gulped. There it was. A distinct sign of exactly how they'd spent that weekend together in Montanari. He watched the ripples on Sienna's skin. Their baby currently looked as if it were trying to fight its way out from under a blanket.

The sonographer put some gel on Sienna's stomach and lifted her scanner. She paused. 'Do you know what you're having?'

Sienna shook her head. 'Let's avoid those bits if you can. I don't really want to know.'

For the first time in a long time Sebastian felt strangely nervous. He'd never been in a scan room before. Like everyone else in the world, he'd seen it on TV shows and news clips. But this was entirely different.

This was his baby.

No, this was their baby.

He watched as the black and white picture appeared on the screen. The first thing he noticed was the flickering. The sonographer held things steady for a second as she smiled at Sienna. 'Look at that, a nice steady heart-rate.'

Ah...that was the heart.

His eyes started to adjust to what he was seeing on the screen. The sonographer chatted easily as she swept the scanner around. 'Just going to check the position of the placenta and the umbilical cord,' she said simply.

'Why are you doing that?' He couldn't help but ask.

Sienna's eyes were fixated on the screen. 'She's checking to make sure the cord isn't twisted or the placenta detached.'

Neither of those sounded good. 'What would happen if they were?'

This time when she met his gaze she looked nervous. 'Let's just say I wouldn't be getting home for Christmas.'

He moved closer, putting his hand on hers. He looked back at the sonographer. 'And is everything okay?'

The sonographer waited a few seconds before turning to nod reassuringly. 'Everything looks fine.' She pointed to a few things on the screen, 'Here's baby's head, face, spine, thigh bone and...*oops*...let's go back up. Here are the fingers. The placenta looks completely intact and the cord doesn't appear to have any knots in it.' She placed the scanner at the side of the machine again and picked up some tissues to wipe Sienna's stomach. 'Everything seems fine.'

As the picture disappeared from the screen he felt a little pang. He'd missed out on so much already. He didn't want to miss out on another thing. The baby kicked again and even though the room was quite dark he could practically pick out the little feet and fists behind the kicks.

Sienna let out a nervous laugh. 'I guess they're beginning to get impatient. There can't be much room left in there now.'

The sonographer packed away some of her equipment. 'Five weeks to go? That's when it starts to get really uncomfortable. Watch out for some sleepless nights.' She gave Sienna a wink. 'I'll go and let Oliver know that everything is fine while you two get ready.'

Sienna shook her head. 'Yeah, thanks for that, Dawn. More sleepless nights. Just what I need.'

'You haven't been sleeping?'

She'd swung her legs off the trolley and was about to pull her scrub top back down. She looked up at him. 'You might not remember, Sebastian, but I like to sleep on my stomach—' she stared down '—and the munchkin is making it a bit difficult.'

She went to pull her top down and he put his hand over hers. The baby was still kicking. *His* baby was still kicking. 'Can you wait a minute?'

He bent down, kneeling until his head was just opposite her stomach. He watched her skin closely for each tiny punch or kick. He couldn't stop the smile. 'It's totally random. You never know where the next one will be.' He looked up at her. 'What does it feel like?'

She didn't answer for a few seconds. She was watching him with a strange look in her eyes. Eventually she stretched forward and took his hand, pressing his palm to her stomach. 'Feel for yourself.'

Sienna's skin felt different than he remembered. It was stretched tight, slightly shiny. There were no visible stretch marks, nothing that made it anything but a beautiful sight.

There. A little kick beneath his hand again.

He laughed and pulled it back. The kicks kept coming so he put both hands on her stomach. He felt something else, something bigger beneath his hand, and Sienna gave a little groan. 'What was that?'

She shook her head. 'I think that might have been a somersault. It certainly felt like it.' She placed her hands next to his and leaned back a little. 'Here, I think this is one of the shoulders. The baby's head should be down by now and it looked that way in the scan. But they can still turn if they want to. It's just not that comfortable when they do.'

Her belly felt warm. And the life contained within it was just a wonder to him.

He hadn't known it would feel like this. He didn't know it *could* feel like this. And this wasn't just about the baby. He couldn't imagine ever feeling this way about Theresa if she'd carried his child. This was about Sienna too.

'Do you have a picture?'

She frowned. 'Of what?'

'Of our baby when you got the first scan. Most people get a picture, don't they?'

She looked surprised but gave a nod. 'Yes, of course I have. It's in my bag.'

'Can I see it?'

She looked around and then shook her head. 'It's in my bag. It's in the locker room. I'll get it as soon as we get the go-ahead to leave.'

He gave what looked like a resigned nod as he stood back up and lifted his hands from her stomach. It surprised her how much she wished he'd left them there. So many things were surprising her about Sebastian.

This was all about the baby. Not about her. She had to try and put her feelings and emotions in a box and keep them there. The irony of that at Christmas time almost killed her.

She could imagine the box, with all her hopes and dreams of a fairy-tale true-love romance for her, Sebastian and the baby all wrapped in glittering red paper and silver foil sitting under her beautiful Christmas tree just waiting to be opened.

Something sank deep inside her. Reality check time.

Sebastian was interested in the baby. Yes, he'd made a few gestures towards her. But no more than she would expect from a well-brought-up prince, looking after the mother-to-be of his child.

She almost laughed out loud. Exactly how many princes did she know?

She didn't even want to admit the security she felt when he was next to her. She didn't want to acknowledge the fact that, the more he hung around, the more she lost a little piece of her heart to him each day.

She couldn't admit that. She just couldn't.

She wouldn't be her mother. The woman who'd spent her whole life with a man that had never really loved her. That wasn't a life. That wasn't a relationship.

If she'd learned anything from her parents it was that sometimes it actually was better if parents didn't stay together. The tortured strain of living in that household had become unbearable.

And although she hated her father for his actions, with her adult brain she might actually understand, just a little.

Maybe if they'd separated much earlier, she might actually have enjoyed a different kind of relationship with her parents. One where they both had the life they wanted, and she fitted around it. But would that have been any fairer to a child than the life she'd had?

Sebastian pulled his phone from his pocket. 'What do you want to eat?'

She pulled her scrub top down quickly. 'Chinese. Hong-Kong-style chicken with noodles.'

He nodded towards the door. 'Give me a minute. I'll make the call and we'll pick it up on the way home.'

The room had felt claustrophobic for a few minutes there. Once he'd felt the kick from his baby, once he'd seen his baby's heartbeat on the screen, it had all become so real.

What had started from the first second he'd seen Sienna McDonald pregnant with his child, continued with her independence and snarkiness, been embodied by her vulnerability and the kiss they'd shared and culminated in feeling his baby kick after she'd collapsed, had just all built to the tornado of seeing that flickering heartbeat and touching the stomach of the woman who currently held all his dreams.

His head just couldn't sort out where he was. Oliver had hinted at signs of love. Did his friend even know what he was talking about? The guy was running around in a pink-tinged cloud.

The conversation with his mother this morning would have poured *Titanic*-icy waters over even the most embraced by love, soul and spirit.

Duty. The word sent prickles down his spine.

He hated it. But he actually agreed. It was his duty to marry Sienna and make this child the rightful heir to the kingdom of Montanari.

He'd been brought up to believe that duty was more important than anything. It was hard to shake that off.

But the feelings he was having deep inside about this baby and Sienna? Duty didn't even come near them. These feelings were entirely different.

They penetrated his heart, his soul, his very essence.

They felt more essential than breathing.

He closed his eyes as the call connected and he placed the order in the calmest voice possible. A few people strolled past him in the corridor. As he opened his eyes again it was clear they recognised him. The TV reporters outside meant that any chance of privacy he and Sienna had was gone for now.

Something else flashed into his head—the other secret arrangements he'd made today. He just had no idea if they'd actually been pulled off. He made a quick call—sighing with relief when it ended.

Sienna appeared at the doorway with a smiling Oliver. Sebastian blinked. He hadn't even noticed him appearing. 'Take her home, feed her and don't let her come back until she's ready to deliver this baby,' he said. 'Let's go for the due date—twenty-eighth of January will be fine.'

Sienna looked a little more relaxed. 'Let me get changed. I'll just be a few minutes,' she said as she disappeared into the locker room a few doors down the corridor.

Sebastian looked at Oliver. He trusted his friend. He trusted his expertise. 'Everything okay?'

Oliver nodded. 'Everything is fine. She's had a good pregnancy. Her blood pressure is fine. But the truth is, she's thirty-five weeks. She could deliver now, she could deliver two weeks after her due date. We never know these things.' He paused. 'Are you going to be around?'

He didn't hesitate. 'Count on it.'

Oliver held out his hand towards him. 'Good. I'll see you soon.'

Sebastian shook his friend's hand. 'Can you tell Sienna I'll get the car and wait for her at the side door? It might be easier than having to face the paparazzi when we cross the car park.'

Five minutes later he was waiting right at the door in his DB5. He'd always loved this car but it wasn't exactly inconspicuous. They might be at the side of the hospital right now, but as soon as he tried to pull out of the car park, they would be spotted.

Sienna came out of the door a few minutes later, her hood over her head. She climbed into the car and closed the door. 'Oh, well,' she sighed. 'That's two cars I've abandoned in the car park now. The broken-down one and the hire car from this morning.'

Sebastian shrugged. 'Leave me to deal with it. Don't worry. Let's just get you home.'

He wanted some privacy. He wanted a chance to get her away from all this and talk about the things they should be talking about.

He stopped at the Chinese restaurant—would his stomach ever recover from this take-away food?—and collected their meal, before turning ten minutes later into Sienna's street.

She let out a gasp.

If he'd known she was going to be unwell, he probably wouldn't have put all the plans in place that he had this morning. But it was too late now.

It was all done.

Her eyes widened as the car drew closer to her house. Everything was just as he'd asked for. A large Norway spruce had been transported to her garden and covered with multicoloured twinkling lights.

Icicle lights had been hung from the eaves of her house and stars around her two large bay windows.

She put her hand to her mouth as they pulled up directly outside. She still hadn't said a word but the expres-

sion on her face said it all. 'Wait until you see the back.'
He smiled.

As they walked in the entrance hall he kept one hand
around her waist, leading her straight past the nursery and
down to the back door. He unlocked it and held it open.

It couldn't have been more perfect.

It didn't exactly look like a Santa's Grotto—more like
a little Christmas paradise. He'd added lights to the rest of
the trees and bushes. A heater next to her carved wooden
seat.

The light-up reindeers and penguins from the nearby
garden centre had been transported to her back garden.
And to make it even more perfect the whole garden was
dusted with snow, which was falling in large, thick flakes.

He kept his arm around her. 'Is it what you imagined?'

Her eyes were bright as she turned towards him. 'Oh,
it's even better than I imagined. I thought it would be
twenty years before it looked like this.' Her smile lit up
her whole face.

He let out the breath he'd been holding, waiting to see
what her reaction would be. He'd wanted to do something to make her happy. She'd already told him she loved
Christmas and this was the first time they would be together at Christmas.

He was praying it wouldn't be the last.

Showering her with expensive gifts would have been
easy. But he already knew that would make little impact
on Sienna.

He had to know what was important to her. And this
was part of the little bit of herself that she'd revealed to
him.

He only hoped the rest would go down so well.

He steered her back inside. 'Let's get this Chinese food
before it gets too cold. And I've something else to show
you.'

The words were casual but obviously sparked a memory in her brain. 'Oh, the nursery. You've painted it, haven't you? Let me see what it looks like.'

She walked quickly back inside the house, striding along the corridor enthusiastically. She flicked the switch at the doorway and stepped inside.

Now, he really did hold his breath again. Had he over-stepped the mark?

She must have already had a vision in her head for how she wanted the nursery to look—he only hoped he'd captured that invisible picture.

She made a little noise—a sort of strangled sound. Was that good? Or bad?

Then she walked straight over to the new, specially carved oak cot. Ducks and bunnies were carved on both the outside ends of the cot and along the bottom bar. She ran her hand along the grain of the wood.

He heard her intake of breath. He'd taken the step of making up the cot with the bed linen she'd already bought. But along with the pale yellow walls, and the curtains that had almost been the death of him, he thought the new furniture fitted well.

She opened the new matching wardrobe and chest of drawers.

He'd replaced all the furniture she'd bought with hand-carved pale oak furniture. It was all exactly the same style, just a different quality with a price tag that most people couldn't afford. That, plus the on-the-day delivery, would have made the average man wince. But Sebastian didn't care. He wanted the best for Sienna. The best for their baby.

She let out a little laugh at the crumpled border in the corner of the room. Darn it. He'd forgotten to throw it away.

He couldn't help himself. 'What do you think? Do you like it?'

She stood for a few minutes, her eyes taking in the

contents of the room. He'd even added something extra, buying her a special cream nursing chair with a little table and lamp, and placed it in the corner of the room.

She walked back over to him, shaking her head slowly until she was just under his nose. Her eyes were glazed with tears when she looked up and his stomach constricted.

'I don't like it,' she said slowly, before opening her hands out and turning around. 'I love it! It's perfect. It just looks exactly as I'd imagined.'

'It is?'

'Yes!' She flung her arms around his neck. 'I can't believe you've done this all in one day. How did you manage?' Her hands were still around his neck but she pulled back a little. 'Did you have help?' She looked a little suspicious.

'The nursery was all me. The furniture came assembled. As for the outside decorations—I left very specific instructions.'

She raised her eyebrows. 'You can actually do some DIY?'

He laughed. 'Remember, I went to university with Oliver. The man that can barely wire a plug. So, yes, I can use a screwdriver and a paint roller.'

She was staring up at him with those light brown eyes. There was definite sparkle there.

'You did good,' she said simply.

'I did better than good,' he whispered. 'I found you.'

Her eyes widened and her lips parted a little. 'But you didn't mean to.' She glanced downwards. 'You didn't mean for this to happen.'

He shook his head. 'Neither did you. But this was always meant to happen, Sienna. I believe it. I was meant to meet you. You were meant to meet me. *We* were meant to be. This baby was meant to be. The more I see you every day, the more I can't imagine spending a single day without you.'

'But how can that be, Seb? How can that happen? I live here. You're part of a royal family in Montanari. You're the Prince, and one day you'll be the King. Somehow, I don't think I fit the job description.'

He shook his head. 'You don't get it, do you? It's up to me to think about the job description. And for me it's obvious. There's only one person I want by my side. Montanari needs to bring itself into the twenty-first century. A queen and royal mother that's a neonatal cardiothoracic surgeon? An independent, educated woman who is dedicated to her job? How can that be a bad thing? Why on earth would I ask you to give that up? I couldn't be more proud of the job that you do. I couldn't be more proud of the fact you came to Montanari to train our surgeons. I watched you in action today, Sienna. I don't think I've ever seen anything I admire more. You couldn't be more perfect if you tried.'

'I couldn't?' She looked stunned—as if it were the last thing she'd expected him to say. She looked as if she was about to say something else but he cut her off. He dropped a kiss on her perfect lips. Truth was, he'd thought about nothing else all day. She tasted sweet and as he kissed her and his fingers tangled through her blonde hair the fruity aroma from her shampoo swept around them. His hands went from her hair, to her shoulders and down her back.

He could feel their baby between them. It was stopping him getting as close as he'd like to. He intertwined his fingers with hers. 'Come here,' he whispered and pulled her through to the main lounge, sitting down on the swallow-you-up sofa and drawing her towards him.

She hesitated for the slightest second before moving forward and sitting astride him on the sofa. She looked at him for the longest time then finally lifted one hand and brushed her knuckles gently against the emerging shadow on his jawline. 'I don't know what to make of you, Seb,' she said in a throaty voice. 'I don't know what to make of any of this.'

He ran a finger down the bare skin on her arm. 'Tell me what you want.'

She shook her head. He saw the little shiver go up her spine as he ran his finger down her arm again. It was the gentlest of touches. The lightest of touches. They'd been intimate before. They'd been passionate before.

But not like this.

His hands settled on her stomach, feeling the baby lying under her skin. It seemed to be settled in one position. 'Do you think our baby is sleeping?' He smiled.

She arched her back, her stomach and breasts getting even closer. 'I hope so,' she murmured. 'But doubtless as soon as I go to bed they'll wake back up again. I think our baby is going to be a night owl and I have to warn you—' she leaned forward and whispered in his ear '—us Scots girls can get very crabbit when we have no sleep.'

He caught a strand of her hair and twisted it around one finger. 'Don't sell yourself short, Sienna. I seem to remember a couple of occasions when you managed quite well without sleep.' He released the strand of hair and let his hands brush against her full breasts then settle on her waist.

She closed her eyes and let out a little moan. Her hands pressed against his chest, her fingers coming into contact with the tiny hairs at the nape of his neck. He caught his breath. This was becoming more than he could have imagined. His body started to react.

Sienna smiled down at him. 'You like this? When I'm tired? Have an aching back? And, even though I haven't checked yet, probably puffy feet?'

'I think you're perfect just the way you are,' he said simply. He put his hands on her stomach again. 'Pregnant.

Not pregnant.' He lifted his hands higher. 'Big boobs. Small boobs. Swollen feet. Not swollen feet.'

'I'm not a queen-in-waiting, Seb.' She shook her head slowly. 'I've never wanted to be.'

'You want the fairy tale. I can give you that.'

She closed her eyes for a second. 'You can give me the palace, the lifestyle, the people.' She pressed her hand against her heart. 'But what's in here? You need someone who wants to live that life. I don't think that can ever be me.'

He put his hands on her thighs. 'But our baby will be the heir. That's written in the stars, Sienna. You can't wipe that away. I want our child to grow up loving the country that they will eventually rule. I want them to respect and appreciate the people that live there. I want the people of Montanari to love my family.'

He sucked in a deep breath. 'We should get married, Sienna. Think about it. We could make this work between us, and we could make this work as a family. Don't dismiss me out of hand like you did before. Take your time. Think about how we both want to bring our child up. Think about what's important to you.'

What was important to her? Right now her head was so muddled she couldn't think straight. Her breath had stalled somewhere in her throat. He had passion in his eyes when he spoke about Montanari. Just like the flicker she'd seen in his eyes a few moments earlier when they'd been locked in an embrace.

But when she'd pressed her hand against her heart, he just hadn't picked up what she'd meant. She wanted to know what was in *there*. In that heart that was beating in his chest.

Because no matter how hard she'd tried to fight it, she'd developed feelings for Sebastian. Feelings that she just couldn't be sure were reciprocated.

He'd focused on part of her fairy tale—but not the most important part. The part that meant she and her Prince loved each other with their whole hearts. The part that she just couldn't live without.

Sebastian lit up her heart in a way she didn't want to admit. She couldn't put herself out there to find her love dismissed. The stakes were too high.

He was talking about Montanari. Making it sound as if that should be the place they have a future together. Lots of women might love that. A prince. A castle. A new baby.

But if he really knew her, he would know that a vital component was missing.

Something gripped her. Something tight, knocking her breath temporarily from her lungs. 'Oh.' She held out one hand towards Sebastian and gripped the other around her stomach.

'Sienna? Is everything okay?' He shifted position, moving her from his knees and onto the sofa.

She was stunned. 'I don't know. I've never felt anything like that before.'

His eyes widened. 'You don't think that...' His voice tailed off. His face paled.

She was still catching her breath, wondering where the sharp pain had come from and hoping against hope it was something else entirely.

She stood up and started pacing. Sebastian was right by her side. This couldn't be happening. It was too early. She was only thirty-five weeks.

'You had that fall today—do you think it could be anything to do with that?'

Sweat started to break out on her skin. She looked from side to side. 'I'm not ready. I'm not ready for this. I should have another five weeks to think about this—to make plans.'

Tears prickled in her eyes. 'It's Christmas Eve. I was

planning on watching some TV and wrapping some final
presents.'

Sebastian glanced at the enormous pile under the tree.
'You have more?'

He slid his arm around her waist and she batted him
on the chest. 'Stop it.'

He turned her around to face him.

One tear slid down her cheek. He brushed it away with
his finger. 'Should I phone an ambulance? Oliver told me
to phone if I was worried. Should I do that now?' He was
babbling. The Prince was babbling.

It felt like an out-of-body experience. He'd always
seemed so in control. Or at least he wanted the world to
think that.

'Will our baby be okay? Will you be okay?'

Another tear slipped down her cheek. 'I'm thirty-five
weeks today. They might give me some steroids to bring
the baby's lungs on, and baby might be a little slow to
feed. But there's nothing else we should worry about.'
She slid her hands across her stomach. 'But, if I think
I'm not ready, then I know for sure that you're *definitely*
not ready.' Her heart started thudding in her chest. She'd
operated on tiny babies. She'd been doing it for years and
years. But she'd never actually *had* a baby before. And
the truth was, she was scared.

Scared of what could lie ahead.

She broke out of his hold and started pacing again. 'I
had everything planned. I knew what was happening.
Then—' she turned to face him and held up her hand
'—you come along with your kingdom and your press
team, and your let's-twin-our-hospitals, and you've just
confused me, stressed me—'

'You're saying all this is my fault?' She could see the
pain and confusion written all over his face.

Then—*whoomph*. This time it was stronger. This time
it made her bend double. *'Oohh.'*

'Sienna?'

Her hands went back to her stomach; she slid them under her loose top. This time there was no mistake. She could feel the tightening under the palms of her hands.

Sebastian strode towards her just as something else happened.

Something wet and warm. All over her living-room oak floor.

She closed her eyes.

'Is that what I think it is?'

She nodded and looked down at the darkening wet stain on her trousers. Thank goodness they were pale—otherwise she'd be panicking she couldn't tell the colour of the liquid. This liquid was clear.

'Start the car, Sebastian.'

'You don't want an ambulance?' There was an edge of desperation to his voice.

'On Christmas Eve? In the Cotswolds? We can get there much quicker on our own.'

In less than five minutes she'd changed and thrown some things into a bag; another contraction slowed her down. The front door was wide open, showing the snow-covered garden outside. Sebastian was standing with his jacket on, pacing at the front door. The car was running.

'Let's go. I'll lock up.'

She let him guide her out to the waiting car.

She groaned as he climbed in next to her. 'This wasn't what I imagined for Christmas Eve.'

He cleared his throat and shot her a nervous glance. 'Actually, I can't think of anything more perfect.'

'What?'

'We're having a baby.'

She took a deep breath and tried to clear her head. Focus. All she could focus on right now was the fact they were about to meet their child. She had to have some head space. She had to be in a good place.

'Truth is, I'm a tiny bit terrified,' she whispered, staring out at the snow-topped houses and glistening trees. Next time she came back here she'd have a baby with her.

His hand closed over hers. 'Then, let's be terrified together.'

CHAPTER SIX

'IT'S A GIRL!'

'It is?' Sienna and Sebastian spoke in unison.

Ella, the midwife in the labour suite and Oliver's new fiancée, smiled up at them as she lifted the baby up onto Sienna's chest. 'It certainly is. Congratulations, Mum and Dad, meet your beautiful new daughter.'

Sebastian couldn't speak. He was in awe. First with Sienna and her superwoman skills at pushing their baby out, and now with the first sight of his daughter.

She looked furious with her introduction to the world. Ella gave a little wipe of her face and body as she lay on her mother's chest and she let out an angry squeal. Ella laughed. 'Yip, she's here. Have you two thought of a name yet?'

A name.

His brain was a complete blank.

He still couldn't process a thought. He could have missed this. He could have missed this once-in-a-lifetime magical moment. That couldn't even compute in his brain right now.

His daughter had a few fine blonde hairs on her head the same shade as her mother. He had no idea about her eyes as her face was still screwed up.

'She just looks so…so…big,' he said in wonder.

Sienna let out an exhausted laugh. 'Imagine if I'd

reached forty weeks.' She looked in awe too as she ran her hand over her daughter's bare back. 'She's not big. She's not big at all. Ella will weigh her in a few minutes. But let's just wait.'

Sebastian shook his head as Ella busied herself around them. 'I have no idea about a name.'

He wanted to laugh out loud. For years in Montanari, the royal family were only allowed to pick from a specific list of approved names. His mother still thought that should be the case.

Sienna turned to him. 'I think we should cause a scandal. Let's call our daughter something wild—like Zebedee, or Thunder.'

Now he did laugh out loud. 'I think my mother would have a fit. It's almost worth it just to see the expression on her face.'

Sienna was still stroking their daughter's skin. 'Actually, I do have a name in mind.'

'You do?'

She nodded. 'I'd like to call my daughter after my aunt. She was fabulous with me when I was growing up and looked after me a lot when my mother and father were busy.'

She didn't say the other words that were circulating in her brain. *Or when my mother and father couldn't be bothered.*

It was an unfair thought and she knew that. But she was emotional and hormonal right now. She'd just done the single most important thing she would ever do in this life.

Her parents had never mistreated her. They just hadn't been that interested. Her aunt had been different. She'd always been good to her.

'What's your aunt called?'

Their daughter started to stir, squirming around her chest and making angry noises. 'Margaret,' she said quietly. 'My aunt was called Margaret.'

It was the last thing he'd really expected. A traditional name from an untraditional woman.

'Really?'

She looked up and met his gaze. Her hair was falling out of the clip she'd brought with her for the labour. Her pyjama top was open at the front to allow their baby on her skin.

He'd never seen anything more beautiful.

He'd never seen anything he could love more.

He blinked.

It was like a flash in the sky above him. He'd been trying to persuade Sienna to give him a chance for all the wrong reasons. He'd always liked her. The attraction had never waned.

But duty still ran through his veins. In his head he'd been trading one duty marriage for another. But Sienna had bucked against that.

She demanded more. She *deserved* more.

And it was crystal clear to him why.

He didn't want to have to persuade her to be with him. It was important to him that she wanted to be with him, as much as he wanted to be with her.

And she'd need to be prepared for the roller coaster that was his mother.

Sienna was more than a match for his mother—of that he had no doubt. But sparks could fly for a while in the palace.

His father—he was pretty sure he would love her as soon as she started talking in her Scottish accent and telling it exactly as it was.

Ella gave him a nudge. 'Do you want to hold your daughter? Sienna's work isn't quite finished yet.'

Sebastian gave an anxious nod as Ella first took their daughter from Sienna, weighed her, put a little nappy on her and supplied a pink blanket to wrap their daughter in. Two minutes later she gestured for him to sit in a comfortable seat she pulled out from the wall. 'Once she's delivered the placenta, we'll do another few checks. Oliver will arrive any minute. And I'll arrange for some food for you both. After all that hard work you'll both be exhausted. We have plenty to spare in the labour ward.'

He hardly heard a word. He was too focused on the squirming little bundle that had just been placed in his arms. The smile seemed to have permanently etched itself onto his face. It would be there for ever.

Her face was beautiful. He stroked her little cheek. The wrinkles on her forehead started to relax and her eyes blinked open a few times. He'd been told that all babies' eyes started as blue. His daughter's were dark blue; they could change to either green like his, or brown like her mother's. The blonde hair on her head was downy, it already had a fluff-like appearance and he could see the tiny little pulse throbbing at the soft centre in the top of her head.

He couldn't have imagined anything more wonderful. Less than twenty minutes ago this tiny little person had been inside Sienna, a product of their weekend of passion in Montanari. She might not have been planned but, without a doubt, it was the best thing that had ever happened to him.

They were the best thing that had ever happened to him.

Sebastian shook his head. 'Sienna did all the hard work. I was just lucky enough to be here.' He lifted one hand that had been thoroughly crushed for the last few hours. 'I might need a plaster cast, but I can take it.'

Ella smiled and went back to work.

By morning Sienna was back in a fresh bed with a few hours' sleep, showered and eating tea and toast. Margaret had finally opened her eyes and was watching him very suspiciously—as if she were still trying to work out what had happened.

Oliver came into the room to check Sienna over. 'Trust you not to hold on. You never did have any patience. I'm going to relish the fact that your daughter has obviously inherited your genes. Good luck with that, Sebastian,' he joked. He put his arm around Ella. 'Seriously, guys, congratulations. I'm delighted for you.'

He gave a nod towards the door. 'Word travels fast around here. There are a few more people who want to say hello.'

Ella looked to Sienna. 'How do you feel about that?'

Sienna glanced over at Sebastian, cradling their baby girl. 'Tell them to come in now. I want to try and give our daughter another feed. I think she'll get cranky quite soon.'

Ella gave a nod and Annabelle and Max, and Charlie and Juliet crowded into the room. Sebastian held his precious daughter while they all fawned over her, kissing Sienna and congratulating them both.

Charlie nodded at the clock on the wall. 'If you'd just held off for another few hours you could have had our first Christmas baby.'

Christmas. Of course. He'd almost forgotten this was Christmas Day now.

Sienna looked shocked for a second then threw back her head and laughed. 'Darn it! I completely forgot about that!' She looked suspicious for a second. 'Did any of you have a bet on me for the Christmas baby?'

Juliet shook her head. 'Not one of us. No one expected you to deliver this early.' She leaned over Sebastian's shoulder. 'But your girl looks a good weight for thirty-five weeks. What was she?'

'Five pounds, thirteen ounces,' answered Sebastian. Margaret's weight would be imprinted on his brain for ever.

Just as this moment would. Now he'd held his daughter, he didn't ever want to let her go.

* * *

Sienna's stomach grumbled loudly as she finished the toast. 'Sorry,' she laughed to her visitors.

She was trying to pay attention to them—she really was. But she couldn't help but be a little awed by the expression on Sebastian's face at the bottom of the bed. He was fascinated by their daughter. He could barely take his eyes off her.

She felt the same. She was sure she wouldn't sleep a wink tonight just watching the wonder of her little daughter's chest rising and falling.

'Here.' Annabelle thrust a little gift towards her. 'Something for your gorgeous girl.'

Sienna was amazed. 'Where on earth did you get a present on Christmas Day?'

Annabelle gave her a wink. 'I have friends in high places.'

Sienna felt her heart squeeze. Annabelle was the most gracious of friends. Sienna knew how hard she and Max had tried for a baby of their own; it had eventually broken down their marriage until their reconciliation a few weeks ago. And yet here they both were, celebrating with her and Sebastian over their unexpected arrival.

She opened the gift bag and pulled out the presents. A packet of pale pink vests, a tiny pink Babygro that had a pattern like a giant Christmas present wrapped with a bow, matching tiny pink socks and a pale pink knitted hat with a pom-pom bigger than Margaret's head. She laughed out loud.

She'd bought a few things for the baby's arrival but, with the rush, she'd forgotten to bring them from home. 'Oh, Annabelle, thank you, these are perfect. Now we have something to take our daughter home in.'

Sebastian looked up quickly, pulling the little bundle closer to his chest.

'We're going home?'

Oliver shook his head. 'No, sorry. Not tonight. The paediatrician wants to be sure that Margaret is feeding without any problems. I'm afraid you'll need to spend your daughter's first Christmas in hospital.' He glanced at Ella. 'Don't worry, the staff here are great. They'll make sure you're well looked after.'

Sienna sagged back against her pillows. 'I don't care. She's here, and she's healthy. That's all I care about. I might love Christmas. But it can wait.'

Max looked around the room. 'Let's say our good-byes, folks, and leave the new parents with their baby.' He rolled his eyes. 'Some of us have Christmas dinners to make.' Right on cue Margaret gave out a scream that made Sebastian jump.

Everyone laughed. They quickly gave Sienna and Se-bastian hugs and left the room. Sienna pushed the table across the bed away and held out her hands. 'I think she must be hungry. Let's see if she's ready for a feed.'

Ella came back a few minutes later and helped Sienna position their daughter to feed. The first feed had been a little difficult. She gave Sienna a cautious smile. 'Some-times babies that are born a little early take a bit longer to learn how to suck. They all get there eventually, but it can take a bit of perseverance.'

Sienna's eyes were on their daughter. 'It seems Marga-ret doesn't like to wait for anything. As a first-time mum I expected to have one of those twenty-hour labours.'

Ella shrugged. 'You might have done, if you'd reached forty weeks. You might be quite tall, but your pelvis is pretty neat.' She smiled up as Margaret latched on. 'Just remember that for baby number two.'

Almost in unison Sebastian and Sienna's heads turned to each other and their wide-eyed gazes met, followed by a burst of laughter.

Sienna waved her hand at Ella. 'Shame on you, Mid-wife O'Brien, mentioning another baby when the first one is barely out. You haven't even given me time yet to be exhausted!'

A warm feeling spread throughout Sebastian. His daughter's little jaw was moving furiously as she tried to feed. Sienna seemed calmer than he'd ever seen her, stroking her daughter's face and talking gently to her.

Ella looked up and met his contented gaze with a smile. 'I'll leave you folks alone for a while. Come and find me when you want some food, Sebastian. I take it you're staying all day?'

'Can I?' He hadn't even had a chance to discuss with Sienna what happened next.

Ella nodded. 'Of course. All new dads are welcome to stay with mum and baby. This is Teddy's. We're hardly going to throw you out on Christmas Day. This is a time for families.' She winked and left the room.

Sienna lifted her head and looked at the clock. 'I can't believe we had her on Christmas Eve. It all just seems so unreal. I thought I would spend today lying on my sofa, like a beached whale, watching TV and eating chocolates.'

A special smile spread across her face. 'I thought I wouldn't see you until next Christmas,' she whispered to their daughter. 'I'd planned to buy you one of those Christmas baubles for the tree with your name, date of birth and baby's first Christmas on it. I guess you've ruined that now, missy.'

Although she loved Christmas dearly, she'd been edgy about this year. Worried about what the future would hold for her and her baby. Sebastian showing up had brought everything to the forefront.

He was sitting in a chair at the end of the bed. Ever since her first labour pain he'd been great. After that first flicker of panic he'd been as solid as a rock. He'd rubbed her back, massaged her shoulders, and given her words of constant encouragement during the few short hours

she'd been in labour. All without a single word of preparation. They hadn't even got around to the discussion about
whether he would attend the labour or not.

He hadn't even blinked when she'd turned the air blue
on a few occasions, and chances were he'd never regain
the feeling in his right hand. She hadn't had time to think
about whether he should be there or not. And the look on
his face when he'd first set eyes on their daughter had
seared right into her soul.

She'd never seen a look of love like it. Ever.

And that burned in ways she couldn't even have imagined.

'Seb?'

'Yes?' He stood up. 'Do you need something?'

She shook her head, trying to keep her wavering emotions out of her voice. 'I wouldn't ever have kept her from
you. I would have told you about her as soon as she arrived,' she said quietly. She blinked back the tears.

She saw him swallow and press his lips together
briefly. They were both realising he could have missed
this moment. Missed the first sight of his daughter. Was
it really fair that she'd even contemplated that?

She licked her lips. 'Your mother—what has she said
about all this?'

For a few seconds he didn't meet her gaze. 'She's disappointed in me. That I didn't do things in a traditional
way. She thinks I treated Theresa badly. She hasn't quite
grasped the fact that Theresa was marrying me out of
duty—not of love.' His eyes met hers and he gave a rue-
ful smile. 'I think it's just as well I'm an only child. She
would have tried to disown me at the beginning of the
week because of the scandal I've caused.'

'But what does that mean? What does that mean for
you, for me and for Margaret?'

Something washed over her, a wave of complete protectiveness towards her daughter. She wasn't going to let

anyone treat Margaret as if she were a scandal—as if she weren't totally loved and wanted.

Sebastian sat down on the edge of the bed next to her and wrapped his arm around her shoulders. 'It means that I'll have to phone the Queen and tell her about her new granddaughter. She thought there would be a few weeks to try and manipulate the press. I guess our daughter had other ideas.'

The thought of the press almost chilled her. 'Can we keep her to ourselves for just a few more hours?' She hated the way that her voice sounded almost pleading. But this was their daughter, their special time. She wasn't ready to share it with the world just yet.

'Of course.' He smiled. His fingers threaded through the hair at the nape of her neck. It was a movement of comfort, of reassurance.

Her hormones were on fire. Her heart felt as if it had swollen in her chest, first with the love for her daughter, and next for the rush of emotions she'd felt towards Seb in the last few hours.

Everything that had happened between them had crystallised for her. His sexy grin, twinkling eyes and smart comments. The way his gaze sometimes just meshed with hers. The tingling of her skin when he touched her.

The way that at times she just felt so connected to him.

All she felt right now was love. Maybe she was a fool to expect more than he already offered. She could live in Montanari. He had no expectations of her giving up work—she could work with the staff she'd trained in their specialist hospital.

Margaret could be brought up in a country she would ultimately one day rule. And although that completely terrified Sienna, it was a destiny that couldn't be ignored.

Did it matter if Sebastian didn't love her with his whole

heart? He respected her—she knew that. And he would love their daughter.

This might be simpler if she didn't already know the truth.

She loved Sebastian. She'd probably loved him since that first weekend—she just hadn't allowed her brain to go there because of the betrayal that she'd felt. How hard would it be to live with a man, to stand by his side and know that he didn't reciprocate the love she felt for him?

Could she keep that hidden away? Would she be able to live with a neutral face in place in order to give their daughter the life she should have?

She pressed her lips together. Having just a little part of the man she loved might be enough. Having to look at those sexy smiles and twinkling eyes on a daily basis wouldn't exactly be a hardship.

And if he kept looking at her the way he did now, she could maybe hope for more. Another child might not be as far off the agenda as she'd initially thought.

She looked up at those forest-green eyes and her whole world tipped upside down. 'Your mother's name—it's Grace, isn't it?'

He nodded but looked confused.

She stared back down to her daughter's pale, smooth skin. 'I've had the name Margaret in my head for a while. But I had never even considered any middle names.' She looked up at him steadily. 'That seems a bit of a royal tradition, isn't it?'

He nodded again. She could see the calculations flying behind his eyes. 'What do you think about giving Margaret a middle name?'

The edges of his lips started to turn upwards. 'Seriously?'

She nodded, feeling surer than before. 'I chose our

daughter's first name. We never even had that discussion. How do you feel about choosing a middle name?'

She'd already planted the seed. Maybe the Queen wouldn't hate her quite as much as she imagined.

He looked serious for a second. 'Our family has a tradition of more than one middle name—how do you feel about that?'

She frowned. 'You mean you're not just Sebastian?'

He laughed. 'Oh, no. I'm Sebastian Albert Louis Falco.'

She leaned back against him. 'Okay, tell me what you're thinking. Let's try some names for size.'

He took a few seconds. 'If you agree, I'd like to call our daughter Margaret Grace Sophia Falco.' He turned to face her. 'Unless, of course, you want to call her after your mother.'

Something panged inside her. But the tiny feelings of regret about her relationship with her parents had long since depleted over time. 'No. I'm happy with Margaret. I think it's safe to say that my mother will play her grandmother role from a distance.' She glanced at the clock. 'I'll let both my parents know in a while about their granddaughter. I doubt very much that either of them will visit.' She gave a sad kind of smile. 'I might get some very nice flowers, though.'

She looked down at Margaret again, who'd stopped feeding for now and seemed to have settled back to sleep. 'Who is Sophia?'

Seb smiled. 'My great-grandmother. In public, probably the most terrifying woman in the world. In private? The woman I always had the most fun with. She taught me how to cheat at every board and card game imaginable.'

Sienna couldn't help but smile. 'You mean that the Falco family actually had some rogues?'

He whispered in her ear. 'I'll show you the family archives. We had pirates, conquerors and knights. We even had a magician.' He leaned over her shoulder and touched their daughter's nose. 'Happy Christmas, Margaret, welcome to the Falco family.'

Sienna turned to face him just as his lips met hers. 'Thank you, Sienna. Thank you for the best Christmas present in the world.'

She reached up and touched the side of his face. Her head was spinning. He was looking at her in a way she couldn't quite interpret. Her heart wanted to believe that it was a look of love, a look of hope and admiration. He hadn't stopped smiling at her—and even though she knew she must look a mess, he was making her feel as if she were the most special woman on the planet.

'Thank you,' she whispered as her fingers ran across his short hair. 'We made something beautiful. We made something special. I couldn't be happier.'

'Me either,' he agreed as he pulled her closer and kissed her again.

CHAPTER SEVEN

HE'D HARDLY SLEPT. He hadn't wanted to leave the hospital last night, but both he and Sienna had been exhausted. She only ever cat-napped when he was in the room and he'd realised—even though he hadn't wanted to be apart from them—that it would be better if he let her spend the night with their daughter alone.

Not that she would have had much time. He'd left the hospital at midnight and was up again at six, pacing the floors in her house, itching to go and see her and Margaret again.

His mother's voice had been almost strangled when he'd phoned with the news. But after a few seconds of horror, she'd regained her composure and asked if Sienna and baby were healthy after the premature delivery. He'd assured her that they were.

When he'd told her the name of her new granddaughter there had first been a sigh of relief and then a little quiver in her voice. 'I'm surprised that such a modern woman picked such a traditional name. It's a lovely gesture, Sebastian. Thank you. When will we see the baby?'

He sent his mother some pictures of Margaret and told her he'd invited both Sienna and Margaret to join him in Montanari. He hoped and prayed that they would, but placated his mother with the easy opt out about travelling so soon after delivery and making sure that Margaret's little lungs would be fit to fly.

He stood in the middle of the yellow nursery that Sienna had dreamed of for her daughter. If she agreed to join him in Montanari he would recreate this room exactly the way it was—anything to keep her happy.

Things had been good yesterday. They'd been better than good. Sienna and Margaret were his family, and that was exactly how they felt to him. He couldn't imagine spending a single day without them. He'd had a special item shipped yesterday from the royal vault at Montanari. It was still dark outside but the twinkling lights from the Christmas tree across the hall glinted off the elegant ruby and diamond engagement ring in his hand. He hadn't mentioned this to his mother yet. But with Margaret's new middle names, it was only fitting that Sienna wear the engagement ring of his great-grandmother Sophia.

The two of them would have loved each other.

He'd meant to go back to his hotel last night but Sienna had asked him to collect the baby car seat from the house so they could be discharged today. Once he'd arrived back at her house he'd decided just to stay. It had seemed easier. He should have brought some of his clothes from the hotel, because this was where they would come back to in the first instance.

He hurried outside to his car. It didn't really matter what time it was—the hospital would let him in any time. He just wanted Sienna to have had a chance to rest.

As soon as he pulled up outside the hospital alarm bells started going off in his head. Every TV station with a van was parked near the entrance. Every reporter he'd ever met was talking into a camera.

Someone spotted his car. All he could hear was shrieks followed by the trampling of feet. He got out of the car in a hurry. One of the reporters thrust a newspaper towards him. 'Prince Sebastian. Tell us about your new arrival.'

'Congratulations. What have you called your daughter?'

They surrounded him. Security. He hadn't considered security for his daughter. He stared at the news headline in front of him.

A NEW PRINCESS FOR MONTANARI!

The questions came thick and fast.

His hand reached out and grabbed the paper. He hadn't agreed to a press release. He had discussed it with his team and they'd planned an announcement for later today, once he, Sienna and baby Margaret had left Teddy's.

How on earth did the press know about Margaret already? He looked a little closer and felt his ire rise. There was a picture of his daughter. *His daughter.* Wrapped in a pink blanket, clearly lying in her hospital cot. Who on earth had taken that?

He started to push his way through the crowd of reporters. He didn't manhandle anyone but he didn't leave them in any doubt that he would reach his destination.

'Prince Sebastian, what about Sienna McDonald, the baby's mother? Are you engaged? Are you planning a royal wedding?'

Right now, he wished he could answer yes. But it seemed premature. Even though things were good between them, he hadn't asked her again yet. But the enthusiasm being shown for the birth of the new Princess was more than a little infectious. These people would hang around all day. It would be smarter just to give them a quick comment—he could find out about that photo later.

He turned around and held up his hands. 'As you know, my daughter was born a little earlier than expected on Christmas Eve. Both mother and baby are doing well and...' he paused for a second as he searched for the words '...I'm looking forward to us all being a family together very soon. Our daughter's name is Prin-

cess Margaret Grace Sophia Falco,' he finished with before turning around and walking through the main doors
of the hospital.

The noise behind him reached a crescendo.

The length of his strides increased in his hurry to reach
Sienna and his daughter. His hand slid into his pocket
and he touched the ring again. The box had been too
bulky to fit in the pocket of his jeans. But the ring was
still safely there.

A few of the midwives gave him a nod as he walked
towards Sienna's room. It was only Boxing Day so the
decorations were still all in place and Christmas carols
played in the background.

Hopefully, by the end of today, he could make things
perfect for everyone.

Sienna felt cold. She had been ignoring the TV in the corner of the room and just concentrating on her baby. The
midwives were great. Margaret had decided to have an
episode of colic at three a.m. After half an hour, one of
the midwives had told Sienna to get some sleep and she'd
walk the corridor with Margaret. Sienna hadn't wanted
to let her baby out of her sight, but she'd been exhausted.
Two hours later she'd woken with a peaceful Margaret
wrapped in her pink blanket and back in her crib.

By that time, she'd wanted to get back up. She'd had
a bath to ease her aching back and legs, and fed and
changed Margaret. Once Sebastian arrived she was hoping they would get the all-clear to take Margaret home.

Something caught her attention. A few words from
the TV. Sebastian.

She looked up as the TV reporters camped outside
the hospital all set off at a run to interview Sebastian on
live TV.

She still couldn't understand how they knew about the
baby. No one she worked with or trusted would speak to

the press. Sebastian had said he would talk to her about a press release.

She smiled as she caught sight of him on camera. His hair was a little mussed up. He obviously hadn't taken time to fix it. His tanned skin sort of hid the tiredness she could see in his eyes. His leather jacket—still complete with yellow smudge—showed off his broad chest and his snug jeans caused her smile to broaden. Sebastian Falco. Was she really going to agree to what he'd suggested last night?

Sebastian was a seasoned pro when it came to paparazzi. He wouldn't speak to them.

But actually, he stopped.

Just like Sienna's heart.

They were all firing questions to him about Margaret. Asking him to confirm the birth and her name. Someone thrust a newspaper towards him and she saw the tic in the side of his jawline. Whatever was in that newspaper had made him angry.

Another voice cut above the rest. 'Prince Sebastian, what about Sienna McDonald, the baby's mother? Are you engaged? Are you planning a royal wedding?'

A prickle ran down her spine. How could he answer that? They hadn't even finished that discussion.

Something flickered across his face, the edges of his lips turned upwards. 'As you know, my daughter was born a little earlier than expected on Christmas Eve. Both mother and baby are doing well and...' he paused for a second as a smile spread across his face '...I'm looking forward to us all being a family together very soon. Our daughter's name is Princess Margaret Grace Sophia Falco.'

Her heart plummeted.

Oh, no. Oh, no. Did he realise how that looked?

Sure enough the reporters had a field day. A woman in a bright red coat swung around and announced straight into the camera. 'We have a royal engagement *and* a royal wedding! It seems that Dr Sienna McDonald is about to become the wife of Prince Sebastian and the future of Queen of Montanari.'

The woman's bright red lips seemed to move in synchrony with the other reporters all around her, talking into their respective cameras.

A chill swept across her skin. The woman seemed to think she'd got the scoop of the century. She held her hand up to the sign of the Royal Cheltenham hospital. 'Looks like Teddy's is going to have to find another cardiac baby surgeon.' She said the words with glee. 'Once Sienna gets to Montanari she will have no time to worry about being a doctor.'

Fury swept around her. How dared they? How dared any of them assume that she would give up her job, her house, her life?

The door swung open and Sebastian strode in with a smile. 'You're up? You're awake?' He was still carrying the newspaper that had been thrust at him in his hand. 'Great. We need to talk. We need to make decisions.'

'Haven't you already just made all those for me?' She walked right up to him. 'Who on earth do you think you are?'

He pulled back and glanced towards their sleeping bundle in the corner. 'What on earth are you talking about?'

She flung her hands up in the air. 'Oh, come on, Sebastian. You're not naïve. You've been doing this all your life. You know better than to get pulled into things.' She couldn't stop the build of fury in her chest.

He'd tricked her. He'd sweet-talked her. He'd used all that princely charm. All to get exactly what he wanted.

All to get his daughter back to Montanari.

Sebastian shook his head. 'What do you mean?' He tried to step around her—to get to Margaret.

Sienna stepped sideways—stopping his path. 'You

practically just announced to the world that we were getting married.'

His tanned face blanched. 'I didn't.' It sounded sort of strangled.

She pointed to the yellow tickertape-style news headline that had now appeared along the bottom of the TV screen.

Prince Sebastian to marry Dr Sienna McDonald, mother of their daughter.

He flinched. Then something else happened. The expression on his face changed. He reached down into his pocket. 'Sienna, I didn't say we were getting married.'

'No. But with a smile on your face you just said that we were all going to be a family together soon. You practically told them we'd be moving to Montanari with you!'

He put his hands on her shoulders. 'What's wrong with you? Calm down. After last night, I thought things were good between us. I thought that maybe we were ready to take the next step.' He glanced over her shoulder. 'The right step for us—and our baby.'

She shivered. She felt as if she were in a bad movie with the villain in front of her. 'You did this,' she croaked as she looked frantically back to Margaret.

'What?' Confusion reigned over his face.

'The leak. It was you.' She pushed him away from her, forgetting for a second about Margaret as she strode forward and lifted the discarded newspaper. The picture of their baby brought tears to her eyes. 'You did this?' She couldn't actually believe it. 'To get what you wanted, you actually gave them a picture of my daughter without my permission?'

She couldn't think straight at all. She was just overwhelmed with emotions and a huge distinctive mothering urge. She'd been tricked. Manipulated. By a man she'd let steal her heart.

He'd left last night after telling her things could work. He'd introduce her to the family. Margaret could be brought up in Montanari and they could all live together as a family. He'd let her think they'd embrace a new-style queen—even though it wasn't a title she'd wanted. She could continue with the job she loved.

Sebastian looked utterly confused and shook his head again. 'What on earth are you talking about?' He took the paper from her hand. 'You think I did this? Really? Why on earth would I do that? We talked about this last night.'

'Yes. You said you'd wait. You said we'd agree to a statement. But that obviously wasn't good enough for you. You're used to getting your own way, Sebastian. You're used to being in charge. You lied to me last night. I was wrong to trust you. You made me think you would consider my feelings in all this.' She swung her hand to the side. 'Instead, you let the world know about our baby.' Tears sprang to her eyes. 'This is my time with my baby, mine. I don't want to share her with the world. I'm not ready.' She shook her head as everything started to overwhelm her. He was just standing there, standing there looking stunned.

She kept shaking her head. Now that they'd started, the tears just kept on coming. She was angry at herself for crying. Angry that she was standing here in her ratty pyjamas, hair in a ponytail and pale skin telling the Prince she wouldn't stand for this behaviour. She wouldn't be manipulated into more or less giving up her life and her daughter.

She'd thought there might just actually be some hope for them both. They could reconnect the way they had in Montanari. The memories that she had of the place would stay with her for ever.

There had been moments—fragments—when they'd

captured that spark again. But she'd been a fool. She'd been living the fairy tale in her head. Why? Why would a prince ever love her?

Things shouldn't be like this. If she were telling him to leave, she should be doing it in some magnificent building, wearing an elegant dress, perfect make-up and her hair all coiffured. She should be looking a million dollars as she told the fairy-tale Prince he couldn't manipulate her or deceive her. That she would bring their daughter up here, rather than be promised a lifetime without love.

Because that was what it really came down to.

That was what she wanted. What she'd always wanted.

For Sebastian to love her, the way her heart told her she loved him.

The clarity in her brain made her turn on him.

'You've deceived me. You've deceived me right from the start. You've spent the last few days trying to sweet-talk me. Trying to persuade me to bring our daughter to Montanari. And now? You think if you just leak the story to the press, then give them some kind of coy smile, and tell them we're about to be a family—then that's it. A fait accompli.' She flung her hands in the air again. 'Well, no, Sebastian. No. I won't have it. I won't get trapped into a life I don't want. I won't bring Margaret up in a marriage with no love in it.'

If Sebastian had looked stunned before, now his mouth fell open. He stepped forward then froze as she continued to rant.

She pressed her hand to her heart as the tears streamed freely. 'I won't do it. I just won't. I've been there. I've already spent eighteen years in a relationship like that. A relationship where I was tolerated and not really loved.' She shook her head. 'Do you know what that feels like? Really? Do you honestly think I'd bring my daughter up in a relationship like that? It's not enough. Not nearly enough. I love you. You love her. But you don't love me.

I don't want a loveless marriage. I want a husband that will love and adore me.' She looked off into the corner as she tried to catch her breath.

'A husband that will look at me as though I'm the most important person in the world. A husband that will trust me enough to always talk to me. To always be truthful with me. To support me in the job that I've trained to do since I was eighteen.' She took a step towards Sebastian. Looking into the face of the man that she'd thought would love her as much as she loved him. Being here in front of him made her stomach feel as if it were twisting inside out. It was hurting like a physical pain. That was how much she wanted this dream to come true. That was how much she wanted to be loved by him. It felt like the ultimate betrayal.

'You lied to me,' she said with a shaking voice. 'You said Montanari was ready for a new kind of queen. A queen who had a career. A queen who worked. You said that could happen. But according to the world outside, the expectation is that I give it all up. My years and years of training don't count. They don't matter. Well, they matter to me. And the environment I bring my daughter up in matters to me. I want Margaret to feel respected. To know she should work hard. To know that money doesn't grow on trees and you have to earn a living.'

She kept her voice as strong as she could. 'Your plan didn't work, Sebastian. I won't marry you. We won't be coming to Montanari.'

Sebastian felt as if he'd been pulled up in a tornado and dumped out of the funnel into a foreign land. He couldn't believe what she was saying. He couldn't believe what he was being accused of.

Worst of all were her words about being trapped inside a loveless marriage. Did she really hate him that much? She could never grow to love him even a little?

The ring felt as if it burned in his pocket. His plan had been to come in here this morning, tell her he loved her and would make this work, and propose. He'd felt almost sure she would grow to love him just as much as he loved her.

But her words of a loveless marriage were like a dagger to the heart. No matter what he promised her it seemed she couldn't ever imagine a life with him. A life with them, together as a family.

Had he really been so blind that he thought they were almost there?

Margaret gave a whimper from the crib. Twice, Sienna had stopped him walking towards her. Twice, she'd stopped him from seeing his daughter.

Sebastian felt numb.

'I'm done trying to force what isn't there. I'm done trying to be anything other than I am. You should have told me as soon as you found out you were pregnant. You should have let me know that I was going to be a father. The news blindsided me. You had months to get used to the idea. I had two weeks.'

He looked furious now.

He put his hand on his chest. 'And I wanted it, Sienna. I wanted it more than you could ever have imagined. I can't believe you're being so judgemental.' He shook his head. 'What did I say? I said I was looking forward to us all being a family together very soon. That's it. What's so wrong with that? They asked me if we were engaged and if we would get married and what did I do? I smiled. Because a tiny little part of me actually wanted that to happen.'

He started pacing.

'Do you know why? Because I was a fool. I was a fool to think we actually could have a life together. I was a fool to think you might grant me a scrap of that affection and passion you keep so tightly locked up inside you.'

He spun around towards her again.

'Well, I'm done. I'm done trying to force this. You clearly don't know how to love someone. Or if you do, it's clear that person will never be me. I won't spend my life tiptoeing around you. Margaret is my daughter, as much as yours. I'm not going to fight with you, Sienna. I will not have my daughter witnessing her parents rowing over her. If you're incapable of talking to me about her— if you're incapable of compromise—then we can talk via lawyers. You don't get the ownership on loving Margaret. She has the right to be loved by both her parents. I want to see her. I want to spend time with her. And, even though you clearly hate me, I won't let you stop me seeing her.'

He couldn't stop the words from coming out of his mouth. This woman, Sienna, who he'd hoped would make his heart sing, had just turned his world upside down. He loved her with his whole heart. He loved his daughter with his whole heart.

This morning, he'd thought he could turn this into something wonderful. He'd had the audacity to think that he and Sienna could love each other and it could last a lifetime.

Now…?

He just didn't know.

Sienna couldn't find any more words. Sebastian turned on his heel and walked outside.

She sagged on the bed out of pure exhaustion. What had happened? The tears continued to fall and her only comfort was lifting Margaret to her chest and holding the little warm body next to hers.

Her precious daughter. *Hers.* That was what she'd said to Sebastian. It didn't matter that it had been in the heat of the moment. She'd said it deliberately to exclude him. But Margaret wouldn't be here without Seb. The facts of life were simple.

The reporter in the red coat was still talking incessantly on the TV. Now, she was talking about how delighted Queen Grace was, how angry Princess Theresa was, how the people in Montanari were waiting for a formal announcement about their new heir, and how the Prince was clearly enthralled by his new daughter and fiancée since there had been no sign of him.

All she could think about was the expression on Sebastian's face. The hurt. The shock. The surprise. The words, 'I said I was looking forward to us all being a family together.'

She screwed her eyes closed for a second. When she'd challenged him on that he'd said he'd smiled because he'd hoped they could have a life together. They would get engaged. They would get married. Something tugged at her heart. The tone of his voice. The pain in his eyes. What did that mean? Did that mean he did care about her? He might actually love her?

There was a knock at the door and one of the midwives entered. She looked uncomfortable and pale-faced. She hesitated before talking. 'Seb… The Prince. He's down at the nursery. He asked if he could see Margaret before he leaves.'

'He leaves?' She felt sick. She stared down at her daughter's face. Margaret stared back and blinked. It was as if she was trying to focus. Already her eyes looked as if they would change colour. Change colour to the same as her father's forest green.

The midwife hesitated again. 'He asked if he could see her before he returns to Montanari.'

There.

She had what she wanted.

Sebastian was going to go.

It was like being rolled over by a giant tidal wave. The isolation. The devastation.

She started to shake as she gazed at Margaret. How would she feel if the shoe were on the other foot? How would she feel if someone stood between her and her daughter?

She'd chased him away. She'd said everything she probably shouldn't have said. But she couldn't think straight right now. Her heart was already wrung out by the birth of her baby.

When Sebastian had given that smile to the reporter she had instantly judged. She'd assumed he was being smug. She'd assumed he was calculating. But what if it had been none of those things? What if he'd been entirely truthful with her?

What if...what if he'd actually meant what he'd said? He'd believed they could have a life together. But did that life include love?

She started sobbing again. She didn't want him without love. She wanted everything. She couldn't let herself settle for anything less.

The midwife pulled tissues from a box that had miraculously appeared and handed her a few. She didn't say anything, just put a gentle hand on Sienna's shoulder.

She stared at her little daughter's face. He'd accused her of being incapable of love. She felt like just the opposite. As if she loved too much. She loved Margaret so much already. And right now? Her heart was breaking in two about Sebastian. She wasn't a woman incapable of love.

Far from it.

'What do you want me to tell him?' came the gentle voice of the midwife.

She nodded as a tear dripped from her face and onto Margaret's blanket. 'Yes. Tell him, yes. He can see Margaret.'

She handed her baby over with shaking hands.

She'd ruined everything and there was no way back.

* * *

The midwife took tentative steps down the corridor towards him, holding Margaret still wrapped in the pink blanket. His heart gave a little surge of relief. He turned back to the window of the nursery. The quads he'd heard everyone talking about looked tiny compared to Margaret. But he could see each of them kicking their legs and punching their tiny hands. Each fighting indignantly against their entry into the world. Their names were emblazoned over their plastic cribs. Graham, Lily, Rupert and Rose. He smiled. Traditional names, like Margaret. Maybe it was a new trend?

The midwife gestured with her head to the next room. 'Would you like to sit in here with your daughter?' He nodded and followed her inside, sitting in a large chair next to the window as she handed Margaret over. 'I'll wait outside,' she said quietly, then paused at the doorway. 'Sienna. She's very upset.' She sighed. 'I think you both need to take a deep breath.' She waved her hand. 'It's none of my business. I'd just hate you both to lose something that you love.' She turned and walked outside.

Sebastian stared at his daughter in his arms. His heart should be soaring. He should be celebrating. He should be rejoicing. But he'd never felt quite this sad.

This hadn't been the day he'd planned for.

This hadn't been the day he'd expected. In fact, it was so far away from what he'd thought would happen that he could barely even believe this was how things had turned out.

It was never meant to be like this between them. Never. Of that—he was sure.

But how on earth did they come back from this? He'd said some things he regretted. He'd said a lot of things he regretted.

He'd never been a man for emotional outbursts. He'd

spent a life of control, of restraint. But Sienna brought out a side of him he'd never thought he had.

Around her, his feelings ran stronger than he thought possible.

So, it was true.

Love could cause the greatest happiness.

And love could cause the greatest misery.

Margaret grumbled in his arms. Her little head turned from side to side, probably rooting for her mother.

Could he really go home? Could he really bear to leave them and not see them for how long—a few days, a week, a month?

He shuddered. He couldn't bear that. Not at all.

Life was precious. Life was fragile. Life wasn't supposed to be like this.

What would he do if he returned to Montanari? Probably fight with his parents. Probably take his frustrations out on those around him. All because he'd messed up the most important relationship of his life.

The relationship with the woman he loved with his whole heart.

He'd tried to forget about Sienna. He'd tried to follow his parents' wishes and get engaged to someone else.

In the end, it hadn't worked. It would *never* have worked.

His heart belonged to Sienna.

And he had to believe, he *had* to believe that part of her heart belonged to him too.

Margaret was important. Margaret would always be one of his priorities. But his other priority would be the woman he wanted as his wife.

Life ahead for him was formidable. Ruling Montanari would only be possible with a strong woman by his side. A woman whom he loved and respected. A woman who could help to lead Montanari into the modern world.

Everything about Sienna had captured his heart. Her wit. Her intelligence. Her stubbornness. Her determination. The look in her eyes when she'd first seen their daughter...

He had to win her. He had to win her back.

He'd never actually told her how he felt about her. He'd never actually put his heart on the line.

He'd been scared his feelings wouldn't be reciprocated. And that could still happen.

But he wasn't leaving her until he tried.

He stood up and walked to the door. The midwife stepped forward to take Margaret. 'No.' He shook his head. 'I'll take Margaret back to her mother.' He took a calm breath. 'I won't leave without talking to her.' He added quietly, 'I won't leave without putting up a fight for them both.'

The midwife gave a little nod of her head. 'Good luck,' she said quietly as he started down the corridor.

She'd finally managed to stop crying, wash her face and change out of the pyjamas into the clothes that Sebastian had set down in the corner for her earlier. She'd be going home soon.

Home with her daughter.

Right from when she'd started making her plans, she'd always expected to take Margaret home on her own.

But this last week, those steadfast plans had started to wobble.

Sebastian had slowly but surely started to creep his way around the edges and somehow into the middle of them all.

The night before last, when she'd seen the beautiful job he'd made of the nursery she'd been overwhelmed. It was almost as if Sebastian had climbed into her brain and seen the picture that she had stored in there.

He'd made the dream a reality.

His face when he'd looked at their daughter had taken her breath away. And when he'd then turned and met her gaze? She'd never felt so special. She'd never felt so connected or loved.

How could she go from that point to this?

She finished rubbing some make-up onto her face. Right now, she was paler than she'd ever been. She needed something—anything—to make her look a little alive again. She couldn't find her mascara, or any blusher, and there was only one colour of lipstick in her make-up bag, so she rubbed a little furiously into her cheeks and put some on her lips.

The door swung open behind her and she stepped out of the bathroom to get Margaret from the midwife. Her boobs were already starting to ache and Margaret was probably hungry again.

But it wasn't the midwife.

It was Seb.

For a second, neither of them spoke. They just stared. Finally Seb drew in a breath. 'You look…good.'

'That good, really?' It came out of nowhere. The kind of smart retort she'd got used to saying around him. Her eyes instantly started to fill with tears again—it was just as well she hadn't found mascara.

Margaret gave a little yelp and she held out her arms. 'Give me her. She needs to feed.'

He hesitated. And instead of handing Margaret over, he put her up on his shoulder. 'We need to talk.'

Sienna shook her head. 'We're done talking. We've said enough. We both need some space.'

He nodded. 'You're right. But just exactly how much space do you need?'

She frowned. 'What do you mean?'

He met her gaze. 'I mean, I don't want to leave. I don't want to go back to Montanari without the two people I love.'

She froze. Part of her wanted to believe. But part of her questioned everything.

'You just want Margaret. You don't want me. Don't panic, Seb. We'll work something out. You can see her.'

He stepped closer. Margaret seemed to be sucking at his neck. It wouldn't take her long to realise there was no milk there. He touched her arm. 'You're wrong. I do want you. I've always wanted you, Sienna—even when I didn't really know it myself. I would have come back. I would have always come back for you.'

She could hear what he was saying. He'd tried to say it before. But she just couldn't let herself believe it.

'But you didn't,' she whispered. 'You only came because of Margaret.'

He closed his eyes for a second. 'Sienna, you have to believe that even if Margaret wasn't here, *I* still would be.'

It was painful when she sucked in a breath. She shook her head. 'Words are easy. I'd like to believe you but, for all I know, you might just be saying this to persuade us both to come back to Montanari with you. This might all just be a trick to get Margaret back to your country.'

He reached over and touched her face. It was the gentlest of touches. 'Sienna, don't. Don't think like that of me. Is that really how you feel about me? I'm a liar? A manipulator?' He looked genuinely upset. His forest-green gaze held hers. 'Is that how the woman I love really feels about me?'

Her heart squeezed tightly in her chest. Her mouth was so dry she could barely speak. 'You love me?'

He stepped even closer. Margaret let out a few grumbles. His hand brushed back across Sienna's cheek and this time across her long eyelashes too.

'I love you so much I sometimes can't breathe when I think about you. I love you so much that the face I see when I close my eyes is yours. I can't let you slip through my fingers. I can't let the chance for this to become real get away because I'm emotional. You're emotional. And I'm a fool.'

She smiled. He knew how to charm a lady.

His fingers moved around her ear, tucking some stray strands of hair behind it. 'But I will, Sienna, if that's what you want. If you want me to leave—to give you space—I will. But know that I'll do it because I love you. Because you are the most important thing to me on this planet. Because I will always put what you want before what I want.'

Tears pooled in her eyes again and she took a step towards him. 'How can you do that, silly? You have a kingdom to look after. All those people. How on earth can I matter?'

He bent his head towards her. 'You matter because I say you matter. You and Margaret will always come first for me.'

This wasn't charm. This wasn't manipulation. This wasn't lies.

This was real.

'Oh, Seb,' she whispered. 'Can this really work?'

He took a deep breath. He was shaking. He was actually shaking. 'Only if you love me. Do you love me, Sienna?'

A tear dripped down her face. She reached up and touched the stubble on his jawline. Her lips trembled as she smiled. 'I do,' she whispered as she pulled his forehead towards hers.

His smile spread across his face. His eyelashes tickled her forehead. 'I think you've said that a little too early.'

She laughed as he fumbled in his pocket. 'Give me a second.'

She held her breath as he pulled out a glittering ruby and diamond ring—bigger than she could ever have imagined. He smiled at the ring. 'This is a family heirloom.

It belonged to my great-grandmother, Sophia, one of the most spirited women I've ever had the pleasure to know.' He gave her a special smile. 'She would have loved you, you know. She told me to give it to the woman that captured my heart and my soul. That's you. Will you marry me, Sienna?'

She lifted Margaret from his shoulder and tilted her lips up to his.

'A princess and a surgeon? Do you think you can cope?'

He slid his arms around her as his lips met hers. 'I can't wait to spend my life finding out.'

EPILOGUE

MONTANARI WAS COVERED in snow for the first time in twenty years. It was almost as if every weather system had aligned especially for the royal wedding.

Sienna looked at the snow-covered palace lawn, trying to hide the butterflies in her stomach. She kissed her ruby and diamond engagement ring and closed her eyes for a second.

This was it. This was when she married the man who had captured her heart, her soul and the very breath in her body. Sophia's engagement ring had been a lucky talisman for her. So much so that, when she couldn't decide on her wedding gown, late one night she'd trawled through the palace archives and found a picture of Sophia on her wedding day.

It had been perfect. A traditional gown covered in heavy lace was the last thing she would ever have contemplated. But somehow, the style reached out and grabbed her. The long-sleeve lace arms and shoulders were perfect for a winter wedding, as was the lace that covered the satin bodice and skirt. She'd taken the picture and asked the wedding designer to replicate the dress for her.

The door opened behind her and Juliet and her daughter Bea walked in. Both were wearing red gowns that matched their bouquets. Juliet gave her a smile. 'Ready, Princess?'

Sienna shook her head. 'Don't. I might just be sick all down this gown before anyone has had a chance to see it.'

Juliet walked over, her pregnancy bump clearly visible in her gown. Babies were in the air around here. She pulled at a strand of Sienna's curled hair. 'I spotted Sebastian earlier. He couldn't wipe the smile off his face. And you needn't worry about sickness. Margaret has just been sick on the Queen's outfit. I thought she was going to pass out with shock!'

Sienna threw back her head and laughed. 'Really? You mean, she'll actually have to change her outfit? Oh, I love that girl of mine. She knows exactly how to make her mother proud.'

There was a knock at the door and Oliver stuck his head inside. 'Sebastian asked me to give you a message.'

Her heart gave a little flutter. 'What is it?'

Oliver laughed. 'Hurry up and get down the aisle. He's done waiting. It's Christmas Eve tomorrow and Margaret's birthday. You have presents to wrap!'

Sienna gave a nervous nod. 'I'm ready. Tell him, I'm ready.'

Oliver walked across the room and gave her a kiss on the cheek. 'Ella and I couldn't be happier for you.'

She smiled as he left. Ella and Oliver had got married a few months before the birth of their baby, Harry. She'd never seen him happier.

Music drifted up the stairs towards them. Juliet gave her a nod and walked around, picking up the skirts of her dress.

The wedding was being held in the royal chapel, with the reception in the palace. She'd tried to memorise all the visiting dignitaries in the hope she wouldn't make some faux pas. Queen Grace had only thawed a little in the last year. She seemed a little interested in Margaret, and when she'd made a few barbed comments about the wedding plans Sienna had happily handed over the guest list and seating plan and told her to take charge, in case she seated some feuding families next to each other.

She was learning how to manage her mother-in-law and Sebastian was entirely grateful.

They reached the entrance to the chapel and Sienna sucked in her breath. The entire chapel was lit by candles, creating a beautiful ethereal glow. Juliet rearranged her skirts then set off down the aisle with Bea. Charlie watched them the whole way, his face beaming with pride. Their wedding plans had been put on temporary hold due to Juliet's pregnancy, but Sienna couldn't wait to attend the ceremony in the Cotswolds next summer.

Oliver held out his elbow. 'Two jobs for the price of one. Do I get double the salary for this?'

She bent over and kissed his cheek. 'You get my eternal thanks for being such a good friend. I couldn't have picked anyone more perfect to give me away, or to be Sebastian's best man.' She winked as the wedding march started. 'Just remember, the wedding speech will be watched the world over. I love you, but tell any Sienna-got-drunk stories and I will lace your dinner with arsenic.'

He laughed and patted her arm. 'I'll keep that in mind. Ready?'

She licked her dry lips and nodded.

As soon as they started down the aisle, Margaret started to call to her. 'Mama, Mama.' She was being held by Annabelle while Max held their daughter, Hope. Max and Annabelle had renewed their wedding vows and, after adopting Hope, were hoping to adopt two boys who were in foster care in North Africa.

Margaret was tugging at Annabelle's hair with one hand and waving at Sienna with the other. Her cream dress was rumpled—she crawled everywhere—and her headband was almost off her head. Margaret was destined to be the biggest tomboy in the world.

Sienna stopped to kiss her little hand, then carried on the last few steps to Sebastian.

He didn't hesitate. He took her hand immediately. 'You look stunning,' he said simply.

'You don't look too bad yourself.' She smiled. His athletic frame filled the royal dress uniform well, the dark green jacket making his eyes even more intense. Her heart skipped a few beats.

They fought regularly and made up even more passionately. He'd helped prepare her for the new role she'd have in Montanari and supported her in every decision she'd made. She'd started working between both hospitals but, to Oliver's disappointment, had made some plans recently to work permanently in Montanari. Sebastian didn't know that yet.

The music started to play around them for the first hymn and he leaned over and whispered in her ear. 'I didn't think it was possible, but I love you even more each day.' His thumb traced a circle in her palm. 'Ready for two to become one?'

She smiled at him with twinkling eyes. 'Actually, it's three becomes four.'

He blinked. Then his eyes widened and his smile spread from ear to ear as Sienna started to laugh.

And that was the picture that made the front page of every newspaper around the world.

* * * * *

LET'S TALK
Romance

For exclusive extracts, competitions and special offers, find us online:

f MillsandBoon

𝕏 @MillsandBoon

◉ @MillsandBoonUK

♪ @MillsandBoonUK

Get in touch on 01413 063 232

JOIN US ON SOCIAL MEDIA!

Stay up to date with our latest releases, author news and gossip, special offers and discounts, and all the behind-the-scenes action from Mills & Boon...

 @millsandboon

 @millsandboonuk

 facebook.com/millsandboon

 @millsandboonuk

It might just be true love...

GET YOUR ROMANCE FIX!

Get the latest romance news,
exclusive author interviews, story
extracts and much more!